UNDISCLOSED MATERIAL

By the same author

Given in Evidence

UNDISCLOSED MATERIAL

Jonathan Davies

Hodder & Stoughton

First published in Great Britain in 1996
by Hodder and Stoughton
A division of Hodder Headline PLC

10 9 8 7 6 5 4 3 2 1

British Library Cataloguing in Publication Data

Davies, Jonathan
Undisclosed material
1. English fiction – 20th century
I. Title
823.9'14[F]

ISBN 0 340 65396 5

Typeset by Avon Dataset Ltd, Bidford-on-Avon

Printed and bound in Great Britain by
Mackays of Chatham PLC, Chatham, Kent

Hodder and Stoughton
A division of Hodder Headline PLC
338 Euston Road
London NW1 3BH

For
Paul Evans
1945–1991

Acknowledgments

'A Prayer for My Daughter' is to be found in W B Yeats'
Collected Works, published by Macmillan.

The passage from 'The Empty Hill' is from
Memories and Praises of Paul Evans, Skylark Press 1992,
2 Ivy Place, Hove BN3 1AP. It is reproduced here with the
kind permission of Nathalie Blondel.

My thanks also to Lee Harwood and Paul Matthews.

Beginning

He dared to look down.

He was on a traverse, a ledge about four inches wide with a sheer drop below, not far by some standards, but at least a hundred feet. From the base of the cliff the scree ran sharply down another hundred feet towards the road.

At the side of the road, perhaps a quarter of a mile away, he could see sightseers standing by their cars, looking up. There was a glint of binoculars. Some tourist was watching every move he made.

The conversation he had overheard the night before in the Pen y Gwryd played itself out in his head over and over again.

'So I said to him, "How did you manage?" And he said, "Well, I just got past it somehow." Can you imagine? He's at the difficult stage of the most severe climb you can make, there was no modern technical climbing then, and all he says is, "I just got past it somehow. I just got past it somehow." '

This was supreme rock climbing country.

Scott knew he shouldn't be doing this climb. It was graded very severe and he wasn't fit enough. He didn't know enough, he'd only been climbing for the year since he had left school and he didn't think he was good enough.

'Give yourself more rope.' The man Scott was climbing with – he didn't even know his name, for heaven's sake – was shouting from the top of the pitch. Scott couldn't see him.

He pulled at the rope and more of it came down to him. It hung in a white arc beneath his feet.

He inched along the narrow ledge.

1

He had watched the French boy climb this route the day before. He had been on a split shift at the pub where he was working so he'd been able to walk up to the cliff in the afternoon to watch.

The French boy, also only about eighteen, had arrived the night before and had asked about the climbs. It was clear immediately that he knew what he was talking about.

Scott had watched him climb. He'd walked along this ledge like it was a pavement. At one point he even changed his leading foot, turning his body away from the rock and then back towards it, all the while flicking the rope out behind him.

Scott could barely inch his way along the ledge where the boy had strolled.

'When you get to Clogwyn you must lean outwards. Lean right out,' the voice called.

There was a mystical quality to this advice.

Scott heard it every time he went on the rock. 'Don't hug the rock. If you cling to it, it won't like you. Don't cling. Lean out, as though you don't need it.'

Scott tried leaning out and felt dizzy with fear. It was like a dream.

The odd thing was how unthreatening the face of the cliff looked. Every now and then there was a little outcrop in the rock where earth had gathered and there would be a piece of grass and a wild flower, neat, for all the world like a patch of someone's back garden stuck up in the sky.

His eyes would occasionally come level with just such a patch and, up there, exposed, he'd watch a buttercup nodding at him, two inches away. Then a bee would fly out past him, out into three hundred feet of nothing.

'When you reach the big rock,' the voice above said, 'you have to change feet, step through, drop your left hand, then swing out and round.'

Scott inched along a bit more.

This was where he'd seen the French boy take a nonchalant grip with his hand and hang out, looking up at the next pitch. Unlike Scott he'd been climbing alone, with no one to tell him how to do it. Scott had watched amazed when he reached the Clogwyn boulder to see him somehow dance around it, hardly breaking his rhythm.

The last he had seen of the boy was a swift vertical ascent, precise and balanced, hand over hand, taking him out of sight, going hard for the top.

Now Scott had reached Clogwyn himself. The ledge stopped,

completely blocked. There was nowhere to go but round it. It was vast and smooth. There was nothing whatever to hold on to. How was he going to do it?

'Now swing out.' Again the voice above him. God, that was frustrating. 'There's nothing to bloody well hold on to,' he shouted.

He tried to reach round it. 'Can you see my hand?' he called.

'No,' came the annoying voice. 'You can't reach for it, it's too far. You have to step through, swing out and then get the hold. All one movement.'

Scott felt angry.

'How can he expect me to do that?' He said it out loud, as though the climb would change its mind like an indulgent mother giving in to an irritable child, as though it would say, 'Well, all right, up you go, no problem.' But there was no indulgence here.

His left foot was taking his whole weight and it had begun to judder. He had to make a conscious effort to stop it. Then he realised he couldn't go back. He was getting tired. His right hand had begun to go rigid.

He shouldn't have been doing this, he wasn't fit enough or strong enough. And he was frightened.

The annoying voice above him said, 'You'll have to do it. You can't stand there any longer.'

He had already realised that himself and was preparing to make his move. Above him a great blue sky with small clouds stretched away into the distance. He could just make out the green blue of the Irish Sea far over to the west. He felt again the astonishing peace the rock gives, utter detachment.

Further up the pass he could see the road winding down. There was a car, then it disappeared behind one of the huge boulders that littered the approach to the pass.

He changed feet and stepped through so his left foot was leading. He lowered his left hand, slipping it between the rock and his body, and reached across to the boulder. It meant he was standing with his back to the cliff, his right shoulder sticking straight out into space.

'As you swing further you'll find that you get a stronger grip with your left hand. Push right out, swing round and upwards.'

'I'm doing it now,' he said. He moved his right hand till he was standing with his back completely to the rock.

He was staring out into the empty sky, about to do the Clogwyn leap.

He'd heard of it, he'd seen the French boy do it, but nothing could have prepared him for the sheer horror. He was going to have to step out into empty space.

Eventually he did what he was told.

He swung out and round, his right hand reaching for the hold. It wasn't there, he'd missed it. He was spreadeagled across the face of the boulder. His left foot lost its grip and he found he was holding on only by squeezing the massive rock between his outstretched arms. Then he began to slip. This must be a dream. 'I'm going,' he said to the man above him. 'I'm falling,' he said.

He slid off the rock like a raindrop. As he fell backwards he thought, I hope the knot will hold. From below he heard a scream. Surely the sound couldn't have reached him that quickly from the road? Where was the screaming coming from?

Chapter 1

'You haven't answered my question. I'll repeat it. Did you think it was honest?'

The witness looked at him and Scott knew that once again he was not going to answer the question. That meant it was a good one.

Instead he said, 'Well, we had been told . . .'

'No,' Scott interrupted. 'That is not an answer. Let me ask you again. Was it honest?'

'Well, we went to the house—'

'No,' said Scott. 'Was it honest?'

The policeman stopped. His head was down. The simple repetition of the question was devastating.

'I received information, and I entered the premises at six oh three.'

'Inspector. We know that. The question is, was it honest?'

The policeman looked at Scott. 'I am the inspector in charge of number six District Crime Squad.'

'I am sure you are,' said Scott. 'But that's not an answer to the question.' Finally he allowed some aggression to enter his voice. Things were beginning to get nasty.

Earlier the police officer had said, 'I am not in a job where we twist what people say.'

'He means me,' Scott had said, grinning at the jury, and he was encouraged to see them laugh. But that didn't mean he was going to win the case. You can do too well in a case. That happens just before you lose.

He waited. It was clear that the officer was not going to answer him. Often, like this, a witness would just refuse to answer. If the inspector had merely replied, 'Yes, Mr Scott, we deceived your client,' it would have been much more difficult to get anywhere. Juries don't mind much if defendants are deceived, but they don't like it if the police are not straightforward in the witness box. Now Scott was able to loosen up a bit.

'If you can't answer that, how about this, then? Honest or not, would you do it again?'

'I object to that question.'

At last prosecuting counsel stirred from where he had been sitting glumly at the end of the bench.

Scott responded, 'If Mr Cantor objects to the question, then why didn't he object when I first asked it?'

'I object to the tone in which it is being asked.'

'The tone?' Scott said. 'Tone? This isn't a social occasion.'

'Gentlemen, gentlemen,' said the judge. 'Isn't it a bit early in the day to get quite so worked up?' Before either of them could answer he went on, 'Perhaps I should rise for a moment and everyone can calm down. It may also provide an opportunity for Detective Inspector Charlton to think about his reply.'

The judge left.

After he did so the jury filed out of the courtroom. One or two of them glanced at Scott as they passed. He couldn't tell what the looks meant. They may just have reflected apprehension. Most people don't come as close to such angry confrontation, or if they do it is distanced by being on a screen. That's not so threatening. Scott turned round and spoke to his client, who had come over to the rail at the front of the dock. 'I'll come and see you in a moment.' He felt hot and there was perspiration at the back of his neck. It was very hot in the court, wasn't it?

Ramus stayed there, insistent. 'They've got to give me a "not", haven't they?'

'Who knows?' said Scott.

He was being straightforward. 'At the moment everything is up in the air. We haven't won yet. The jury may disbelieve you as well.'

The prison officers gathered round. Ramus was a category A prisoner, classified 'likely to escape', and they were not about to risk his jumping out of the dock. Scott could see two policemen waiting obtrusively at the court door. Even if Tony Ramus jumped he wouldn't get far. 'I'll come down to see you now,' he said. Then, thinking of the distance to the cells at the bottom of the building, he added, 'But I have to speak to the prosecution lawyer, so I may not be able to get there. The judge has only given us a few minutes.'

The prison officer put his hand on Ramus's shoulder and the prisoner turned away.

Catherine was standing behind Scott.

'He's gross,' she said.

'What do the jury think?' said Scott.

'They think so too,' she said.

'You sure?'

'Yup.'

A voice interrupted them just as Scott realised he didn't know whether Catherine was talking about the witness or Ramus. It was weird how one could be so involved and yet so ignorant about what was going on.

'Scott,' the voice said.

'Yes?' It was Philip Cantor speaking to him.

'Don't speak to my witnesses like that.'

Scott was astonished.

'Your witnesses? Your witnesses? They don't belong to you. You don't own them.'

The judge was right. It was a little early in the morning to get so worked up. But this trial had been like that. They had been at it for ten days now, and every evening Scott had gone home tired like a rag.

'Charlton is a senior officer. I warn you, when you speak to him like that I shall object.'

'Object ahead, object as much as you like.'

Scott turned on his heel. He left the court at speed. Catherine was almost running to keep up with him.

'Christ! What an arsehole.' Scott was furious. He couldn't remember losing his temper so badly in court before. 'I'd better calm down. I'm not normally like this, am I?'

They went to sit in the canteen.

'It's bad enough that I'm conducting this case with one hand tied behind my back, but now I have to put up with that tick telling me that his witnesses are senior police officers so I should treat them with respect.'

He thought about taking one of Catherine's cigarettes but then stopped himself.

'What does he mean? Am I meant to say, "Yes sir, no sir. Let's lock Tony Ramus up." That's going back a few years, that is.'

Catherine watched him in silence.

She enjoyed being around when he was angry. He was kidding himself if he thought he was normally calm. That was why she liked him. She looked at him tightly concentrating on the case. He didn't know what he was like, he didn't have a clue about himself, and yet, and this was unusual, he didn't make up for it by pretending to be something he wasn't.

'That's how the courts used to be,' he went on. 'They still are down in the West Country. Everything used to depend on the honesty of the police officer. They were believed as a matter of course. And everyone knows where that got us.'

Catherine was American, working in the courts for Lawson's, the solicitors acting for Tony Ramus. She had worked with Scott occasionally for two or three years now. Who she worked with depended on who Lawson's got to defend any particular case, but Scott was her favourite barrister. He wasn't the smartest and got into trouble with the courts too much, but he was certainly the most fun.

He was also honest about himself, and because of that he had an edge of danger.

'And now I have Detective Inspector Charlton telling me that there are some things he is not going to answer questions about since it would be against the public interest. And the judge rolls over and lets him get away with it.'

Catherine thought about Scott.

There had been a change recently. He didn't seem as cheerful as he used to be when she first met him. There had been all that trouble with that girl, of course, but that was a little while ago. He just didn't seem as happy as he had been. There were times when he seemed uninterested in what was going on around him. The spark was not there. She looked at him – he'd put on a bit of weight too.

'Well, I'm going to go on asking about it, whatever they say. Maybe the jury will get the point.'

He paused, and his eyes focused on Catherine sitting in front of him.

The tension suddenly left him. 'Hallo,' he said, 'I'm back. Sorry I shouted.'

'I don't mind you shouting,' she said. 'It all adds to the fun.' She sipped her coffee and smiled.

The court assembled again and Scott continued the cross-examination. 'Mr

Charlton,' he said, 'why did you not make the most basic enquiries into the offence which you say my client committed?'

'Because I caught him at it red-handed. I didn't need to.' The officer paused and then added, 'Sir.'

Scott said, 'There is no need to address me as "sir", Mr Charlton. I don't ask for it. Especially if you find it so distasteful.' The judge bridled slightly. Scott was surprised that it had taken him so long to get involved.

'It's only good manners, sir,' said Charlton.

'Well, I'm not interested in your manners, Mr Charlton,' said Scott. 'I'm only concerned with what you did as a detective.' That was a mistake. It was his anger speaking. There was no excuse for being rude. He moved on quickly.

'We have heard about a lorryload of stolen property being unloaded into a lock-up unit and yet you didn't even bother to find out who the unit belonged to.'

'I didn't need to, sir.'

'You didn't need to! You accept that when he was arrested Mr Ramus immediately explained that he was being paid to do what he was doing. And you made no effort to find that man?' He paused. 'None at all?'

'I didn't believe he existed.'

'But you can't decide that without at least enquiring.'

'I didn't need to.'

This was it again.

'Tell us why you didn't need to.'

'Because I caught your client red-handed.'

'No. Mr Charlton, we're talking about the other man. Why did you decide not to look for him? He had only left the yard a few seconds before you arrived and we know he existed because other people saw him.' Scott paused at the end of each remark as though it were a question. 'That man was at the centre of my client's explanation for being caught, as you call it, red-handed. That man had the key to the lock-up. He opened it, he was seen doing that. Mr Ramus had no key.' He paused to let it all sink in again. 'Why didn't you try to find him?'

'I didn't need to.'

'So you said. Why?'

'Because of what I had been told.'

'What had you been told?'

'I object,' said the prosecutor. 'I object to this officer being asked questions which might reveal the identity of an informer.'

'Here we go again,' said Scott.

'Withdraw that remark,' said the judge.

'It's said now, it can't be unsaid,' said Scott.

'Well, don't say it again.'

Scott turned back to the witness. 'You say you didn't do the most obvious thing in the world, trace this man. And all because of this secret information. We know that at least part of the information was wrong. You arrested Mr Ramus for handling stolen electrical goods, but when you looked inside the van it had meat in it. How do we know that the other things you were told weren't wrong as well?'

'I object to the defence asking any questions about the information that the officer received, since it may lead to the revealing of the identity of the informer.' The prosecutor repeated his formula.

The judge said, 'I have already ruled that you may not ask those questions, Mr Scott.'

'But the defence in this case is that the informer is the man who got my client arrested. He probably did it for the reward money.'

'So you've said,' said the judge. 'Now get on.'

'How can I defend Mr Ramus if I can't make the most basic enquiries?'

'Get on, Mr Scott.'

'But—'

'You'll have your time for speeches.'

Catherine watched the jury. She could see they were intrigued. This was for real.

Scott said, 'Well, as long as I don't get lost in the fog long before we get to speeches.'

He was beginning to behave badly.

Catherine thought, He'd better watch it, he's beginning to behave badly.

Scott said, 'Of course, you did make one effort to find the owner of the lock-up. You got a statement from a man. That man said he didn't know who owned it.'

'Yes.'

'We know now that the man you chose to ask about the lock-up was a crook. His partner is after him and we know he was dealing in stolen goods.'

'Well, that's what you say,' said the policeman.

10

'We did what you couldn't be bothered to. My solicitors investigated the case.'

'Mr Scott!' said the judge.

Scott carried on. 'My solicitors went to speak to the people who have the unit next door.'

'Did they?'

'Yes, and the people next door say that the man you chose as a witness and who mysteriously has failed to turn up at this trial is living where he has always lived. He's available to come and you won't call him.'

'So you say.'

'Yes, I do. The people who work in the lock-up next door are witnesses. They are outside this courtroom now.'

'Oh.'

'And we've got the landlord of the unit. He says he actually rented it out to your missing witness, the one who you say denies knowing about it. Why didn't you find that out?'

Charlton said nothing.

'So your witness, who denied knowing whose lock-up it was, is the man who actually rented it. What does that tell you, Mr Charlton?'

Charlton said nothing. There was nothing to be said. Scott could do what he liked.

'The one witness you did get turns out to be a liar, and you made no effort to find anything else out. Why not?'

Charlton could only repeat what he had said before.

'Because I had information about your client.'

'What you mean is that someone sold you some information to get a reward and you're not going to bother to make any enquiries beyond that?'

'No.'

Scott was pleased to see that Charlton had stopped calling him 'sir', and that he had stopped giving long answers.

'This was a classic set-up. It's a technique that has been used by your district crime squads for years.'

Charlton said nothing.

'A villain steals a load, takes some of it for himself, organises someone to unload the rest for him, and then tips the police off. The losers have got their lorry back, the police have got a body. Everybody's happy.'

He stopped and looked at Charlton.

Now he was going to blow the lid off it. He said in a conversational manner, 'Did you share the reward money with him?'

There was a moment's silence and then a spluttering noise.

Both prosecuting counsel and the judge intervened.

'I object—'

'Mr Scott . . . you may not . . .' said the judge.

'I may and I will. Did you share the reward with him?'

'Mr Scott. Stop it.'

'Why doesn't the officer answer?'

'He doesn't have to,' said the judge.

'I object,' said the prosecutor.

Detective Inspector Charlton looked carefully at Scott so he would remember him.

Chapter 2

'We will have the jury out.'

The judge was angry. Charlton was glowering. Scott watched him as Betty, the court usher, gathered the jury together and shepherded them to the back where they disappeared into their room.

The interruption in the trial had broken the tension.

Now Scott was going to have to spend a couple of minutes defending himself. For the jury it might not work like that. The tension might even be increased. Being gathered together they would naturally discuss what had just happened. Scott stopped trying to calculate the effect; it really was impossible to guess what went on in a jury room.

'Now, Mr Scott.' The judge turned his attention to the advocate in front of him.

Scott knew him well. Jolyon Scribner. He was known as 'Happy', a tribute both to his melancholy and his Christian name. His appointment as a judge had been the next step after a career of being a prosecution hack. Now he was really able to throw his weight around, and he did so in a low, gravelly voice accompanied by an affectation of weariness with the world. It was also clear that he thought his primary duty was to protect policemen from defence counsel, all of whom were too tricky by half.

'Now, Mr Scott. We have already been through the law.'

Scott answered, 'If Your Honour wishes me to argue the law then perhaps it would be better done in the absence of the witness?'

Now the judge was interrupted. Detective Inspector Charlton left the court grudgingly.

'Mr Scott, we have been through the law on a number of occasions. I have ruled that the officer should not be asked questions which might lead to revealing the identity of an informer, or even whether an informer existed, or whether a reward was paid to an informer.'

'You can rule that the witness need not answer the questions, but you can't stop me from asking them,' Scott replied.

'That's the ruling I have given. You may not ask questions about the reward.' The judge stopped and then, realising he had said too much, added, 'Any reward that may or may not have been offered.'

The situation was ridiculous.

If someone had made reward money out of Tony Ramus's arrest then it was important to know it. Was it the man who had disappeared at exactly the right moment, just as police arrived? That's what Scott's client had said must have happened.

'If I can't ask the questions, how can I put my defence?'

There was no answer to that.

'If I am not allowed to ask about rewards, whether one was paid in this case or whether the officer shared it with the informer, how can I put Mr Ramus's defence? That's what he says must have happened.'

'That's nonsense,' said the judge.

'How do you know?' said Scott. 'The criminal law is full of judges who didn't believe the word of innocent men – "the longer I have listened to this case the more certain I have become of the prisoner's guilt".' Scott quoted the words of the Lord Chief Justice in the Birmingham Six trial, but the irony of the massive error was lost on this judge. So much for learning from experience.

'Are you suggesting I would say such a thing?'

'No, not directly, but by not allowing me to test the evidence you are doing so.'

Perhaps he had gone too far. But no matter, that was the effect of the law as it stood. What was wrong with saying it?

The judge made a monumental effort to control himself and made sure everybody knew he was doing so. He threw down his pencil, his signal that he had come to the end of his tether. Scott's mind wandered. Throwing pencils about is a particularly petulant way of expressing yourself, but since judges can't stand up and stride about, it's the most they can do. Not all judges, though. There was one lady judge he knew who had shown her anger by suddenly shouting out, 'Where are the fucking keys, then?' Everyone in the court was trying to work out what she meant until they followed her gaze and saw her husband appearing sheepishly around the door with her car keys in his hand.

'Will you withdraw that?' said the judge. Scott hardly heard him, then came back to the present.

'Mr Scott, will you withdraw what you just said?'

Scott thought for a moment.

If he did withdraw his remark then no one lost anything, the jury didn't know what was happening. But if he didn't withdraw it then the whole trial might come to a shuddering halt. Well, it was his main job to look after Mr Ramus, not to blow the trial apart. 'Yes,' he said.

The judge looked pleased and puffed himself up. 'Well, we'll get on with it, then. Bring the jury back.'

Everybody came back into court. The trial was becoming like a French farce, people trooping in and out. DI Charlton went back into the witness box.

'Mr Charlton, tell us what you did about the man who ran off again,' said Scott. 'You arrested Mr Ramus as he unloaded the van. Mr Ramus said he had been offered the van for sale, he wanted to test-drive it and he was helping to unload it first.'

'Yes,' said DI Charlton.

'You've told us that when you approached Mr Ramus, his reaction was to say, "Don't ask me, guvner" . . .' Scott's mind wandered again, this time in the middle of a question. Do people still talk like this? he thought. Presumably they do. Tony Ramus hadn't denied saying it. 'You said that Mr Ramus pointed over his shoulder and said, "Don't ask me, guvner, ask the guy whose van it is." But instead of making any effort to find that man you did nothing.'

'They all say that.'

'What if it were true?'

'Well, they can't all be true.'

'Surely your job is to find out which are and which aren't?'

The officer didn't understand the last remark and he took the line of least resistance. He stood there saying nothing. For a moment his hand went up to his face and he looked beyond Scott at the public gallery.

I'm getting to him, thought Scott.

He said, 'Not only did you never look, but you never even asked anybody. You took eleven statements from people working in the factory units in the yard?'

'Yes.'

'All those people were there when the van was driven into the yard.'

'There or thereabouts. Yes.'

'We've had each of those witnesses here in this court.'

'Yes,' said Charlton.

That was why the trial had lasted so long. Scott had had to go through each witness asking the same questions. 'And you didn't ask any one of them whether they had seen who had driven the van into the yard or who opened the lock-up. Why not?'

'Why should I?'

'Why not? You ask why not? If a man was arrested for murder and he said, "It wasn't me, it was a man wearing a green skirt, boots and a bonnet", at least you'd ask the witnesses about it.'

'I would then,' said the policeman. The court laughed, and for a moment the tension eased. Scott regretted the question. The laughter had interrupted him. But he was able to deal with it.

'You say you would investigate then, and you laugh. But that would be an obvious untruth. In this case Mr Ramus said it was a white guy, middle-aged, balding, blue eyes but very red hair – that's an unusual description – a man called Eddie. He drove the van. And you asked nobody about such a man? None at all?'

He paused. Charlton said nothing.

'Is that because you knew perfectly well who had driven it?'

No reply.

'It was the informer, wasn't it, who set up Mr Ramus to be arrested?'

'I object.' The prosecutor, Philip Cantor, got to his feet. 'I object to that question since it may tend to show whether there was an informer in this case, or it may identify him.'

'I'll carry on.' Scott disregarded the interruption. 'Mr Charlton, you asked nobody. Clearly we are going to have to restrain ourselves from speculating why you didn't ask the witnesses this obvious question.'

He paused.

Of course, not being allowed to ask a question was almost as good as getting the right answer when it was asked. What would the jury think? With any luck they'd think something important was being withheld from them.

He continued, 'Well, Mr Charlton, you weren't in the court, but I asked the witnesses, I asked each of them the question . . . ' The prosecutor tried to interrupt but Scott disregarded him. 'I asked those witnesses the questions you didn't ask. Three of them said Tony Ramus was not the man who had driven the van into the yard. Two of them said they saw another man, and they described him. Guess what? It was a man with bright red hair. They didn't notice his eyes.'

The policeman was silent. Then he said, 'Your client was caught red-handed.'

Scott wondered whether he could do anything with red-handed/red-haired but nothing suggested itself.

'So you've said a number of times,' was the best he could manage. This was tiring.

He had been cross-examining hard for days now, and his wig was beginning to itch. What a weird affliction. Barrister's wig itch. Like tennis elbow or brewer's droop.

He looked at the clock. It was twenty to one. There was a little time to go yet before the break and he had more to ask. Then he was saved by the bell.

The judge interrupted. 'I have another matter to deal with. You'll remember I mentioned it this morning. This case will adjourn now for luncheon.' Again the court rose and everybody trooped out.

Scott stayed sitting where he was. He welcomed the respite. If he left the courtroom, Mr Ramus's family would descend on him and he would have to start trying to reassure them all over again. It was easier to sit still for a while.

After a few moments the clerk of the court got up and said, 'Juror to show cause. Call Mr Malahide.'

Only Scott, the judge and the shorthand writer remained in the court. There was a scuffling at the door and Betty, Judge Scribner's usher, appeared with a depressed-looking man in a suit. To Scott he looked vaguely familiar. It wasn't that he recognised him, more that he recognised his type.

Scribner began speaking.

He didn't address the man standing in the well of the court but the wall about thirty feet away to his left. For a moment the man didn't realise he was being spoken to.

'I have had your colleagues here before. You live protected by the law: as far as one can be protected by the law, you live protected by it. Yet when it comes to upholding that very law you say, "That's not my concern, let someone else do it. Let someone else be inconvenienced by it," What do you say, Mr Malahide?'

The man said, 'I do not feel able to make a judgment.'

Scott realised where he had seen the man before. On his doorstep, inviting him to take God into his heart. Probably a Jehovah's Witness. Certainly the suit and the name fitted. Malahide. Was that a Devon name or a Cornish name?

It was clear now. He was asking to be excused jury service since it conflicted with his religious beliefs – 'Judge not, lest ye be judged.'

Scribner continued, 'Your attitude is "Let someone else do the dirty work. I'm all right. I can get the benefit and not be put out." '

Scott reflected that he was hearing the true sound of the conscientious objectors' board bullying recruits who didn't want to fight. It was the same technique – ask a prepared question at the beginning that begged all the other questions. He could imagine Mr Malahide getting the jury summons over his breakfast table and worrying about it, conscientiously worrying, and now he had got here, there was Judge Scribner being intellectually dishonest.

It was ironic. If Mr Malahide had been a self-employed garage mechanic then it would have been easier, a matter of money, and he would have been excused. But 'conscience' – that kind of talk was a red rag to this judge. It didn't fit with his bluff English way of seeing things.

The conversation between the men became even odder. 'One of your colleagues said to me once that he couldn't do jury service if he was asked to judge the word of one person against another. But otherwise it was all right.'

Mr Malahide didn't accept that.

'I mean no disrespect to the court,' he said, 'but I will not be able to render a verdict.' His slow, persistent refusal had strength. It was the kind of strength, Scott reflected, that always wins in the end.

'You must do the best you can. We shall make certain you will not deal with cases where the issue is the word of one person against another.'

That was about as bizarre as it could get, thought Scott. All cases involve the word of one person against another. But Scribner obviously thought it was good enough and he rose for lunch looking pleased with himself. 'Two fifteen, Mr Scott. I am taking luncheon with the Mayor.'

Scott left the courtroom. He was relieved to see that the Ramus family had gone and he was able to wander uninterrupted along the passage to the lift. It took him to the top floor where the barristers had their restaurant. As he stepped out he could hear the laughter of a group going downstairs, and when he got to the restaurant he realised what had happened. The place was empty.

He picked up the menu, wondering whether to follow the others out or to eat there, when Betty came in. 'Ooh, Mr Scott, I'm glad you're here. We need you.'

'Why? What's the matter, Betty?'

'We need another person for lunch with the Lord Mayor. All the others have gone.' Now Scott realised why the place was empty. Everybody had seen what was coming and had got out while they could.

'Oh no,' he said. 'Betty. Please. Not me.'

'Ooh, Mr Scott' – every time she spoke to him she made the same sound – 'you've got to come. The judge will get really angry with me if I don't find anyone.'

'But I'm the last person he wants to have lunch with.'

She didn't even bother to pretend to deny that. 'You won't be sitting with him, you'll be sitting with the Rural Dean, and the Hon. Mrs Aitchison. Do come, Mr Scott, or Mrs Aitchison will be sitting on her own. The judge will be so upset.'

There was nothing else for it. Scott began taking his wig and gown off. 'OK, Betty, just this once . . .'

She interrupted him. 'No, don't undress, Mr Scott, you have to wear your clothes.' She turned and led him out.

The luncheon party had gathered in the large room overlooking the river.

It was the room normally used by Judge Scribner as a writing room and, to prove it was his room, he had hung a picture of his wife on the wall, painted in desperate, blistering blues and oranges. It was a picture that had disturbed Scott on his previous visits.

'Oh, there you are,' said the judge as Scott entered, in effect announcing to everyone assembled that it was Scott who had caused the delay. 'What will you take? We are sitting down now. A sherry?'

Scott looked at him. The judge was standing next to a man dressed in what Scott remembered were called Blues, a little tight waistcoat with buttons, a lace cravat bubbling at his throat, breeches that made his legs look like sticks, and, for heaven's sake, a sword. The judge was dressed in his full wig and robes. It was a staggering sight.

'Thank you, Judge, nothing to drink.' He spoke from the back of his throat in the gruff messroom voice he adopted when meeting these sort of people socially.

They sat down, and he found himself at the end of the table opposite a thin pale lady and next to a vicar. The man with the sword took it off and laid it lengthways along the centre of the table.

Both Scott's neighbours immediately started talking to the people sitting on the other side. Betty was wrong. It wouldn't have made the slightest difference had he not been there. He looked up, feeling that someone was watching him. It was the Hon. Mrs Scribner hanging on the wall. Her eyes were painted in a frantic burning blue. She was watching him like a hawk.

In front of him on the table there was a menu and a place list. He read it unobtrusively. The Hon. Mrs Aitchison was sitting opposite him as Betty had said, and the Rural Dean on his left. He was pleased to see that he himself was shortly described as 'A Barrister', which would fit whoever they got from the bar to make up the numbers.

At the other end of the table, on the opposite side, was the judge's wife. Scott had never seen her before and he inspected her for her likeness to her portrait. In life she had a faintly washed-out air. That was only to be expected – had she been found in open country looking as she did in her picture then anything might have happened.

At his elbow he heard a grunting noise, and found a prawn cocktail being slid in front of him. 'Hallo, Mr Scott.' He looked up.

It was Fred Dawson, the court keeper, normally to be found downstairs chivvying carpenters and painters. 'What you doing here, Fred?' whispered Scott from the corner of his mouth. But Fred just grunted again and moved on to the Rural Dean.

By this time those in the centre of the table were beginning to fight for domination of the conversation.

Two down from Scott sat the man in the amazing uniform. Scott examined the list. He was the under-sheriff of the county and to his left sat his wife. It was clear that they both thought conversation at the luncheon table was ill-mannered at best, and both said very little throughout the contest that followed, save to each other.

Had they tried to talk they wouldn't have got very far, for opposite them sat the judge, who was determined to be master in his luncheon room, and just down from him was the Rt Hon. Butler Jennings, QC, MP, equally determined that he should not.

* * *

'It was incredible. You have never seen a weirder sight.' Scott paused and looked at Ronnie Knox. 'Well, you might have, since you were a monk once, and I can't imagine the kind of things you got up to. But certainly I've never seen a weirder sight. Scribner in a wig, and every time he leans forward it nearly gets in the soup, like a basset hound's ears; the sheriff opposite him, sitting absolutely straight up like a pole, occasionally letting a sound out of the corner of his mouth, without moving his lips; the sheriff's wife, just as straight, not saying a word; and the bloody sword in the middle of the table glinting amongst the salt and pepper.'

Scott and Ronnie Knox were in El Vino's that same evening. Scott felt tired after spending the whole day cross-examining, all the time with the worrying feeling that he was winning too easily. They were drinking El Vino Velvin, and already Scott could feel the alcohol creeping through him. He leaned back, put his foot on the rail of the chair opposite and took a biscuit.

'They're so boring, these biscuits,' he said. 'Why can't they get some that taste of something?' The door banged open and a draught of cold air came in, heralding a group of lawyers, all identically dressed, all identically laughing at a joke.

Scott carried on with his story. 'Jennings was talking incredibly loudly, telling us how the night before he had had a drink with the King of Somewhere. Being on some sort of committee in Parliament he gets invited everywhere, or maybe invites them, I don't know. And every time he made a joke his slippery little friend Cantor laughed and Scribner got angrier.

'Then the strangest thing happened.' He sat forward to emphasise what he was saying and lowered his voice. 'Scribner just shut him up. It was obvious that Jennings was becoming the star turn at the party and Scribner was being pushed out of the centre of things. He suddenly turned on Jennings and said – it was completely irrelevant – "Shall I tell them about the Garth Boys' Home?"

'Jennings shut right up. He just shut his mouth and stopped talking. Scribner took over, banging on about the Northern Irish courts, no juries, the Diplock courts and how they should have the same here. Jennings went white as a sheet. It was astonishing. And Cantor looked like the guy who got the original curate's egg.'

'Wasn't there something about Garth in *Private Eye*?'

'Yes. It was one of their long-running scandal stories. About the British intelligence services and some buggers' muddle at a boys' home, wasn't it?'

'Well, obviously Jennings was affected by it. Was there a public inquiry? Was he a lawyer at the inquiry?'

'I don't think anyone knew anything about the inquiry or who was involved. That was the whole point of the fuss.'

They both fell silent.

Then Scott said, 'This damn case, it's going too well. I think I'm going to lose it.'

Chapter 3

Charlie Charlton's snout arrived in London in 1972.

What happened in that hot, hot summer was that Eddie Morgan turned seventeen and left the Garth Boys' Home, eventually finding himself at King's Cross Station. He had eighteen pounds in his pocket, the money with which he had been dumped at the home – so long ago now he couldn't remember it.

Eddie had nowhere to go.

He had been told that he could get a bed in Prince of Wales Crescent for thirty shillings a week, one pound fifty pence – he was still getting used to the new currency.

He reckoned food wouldn't cost him much more than that and, on the clattering train south, he had calculated that with care he would have a month, or a bit more, to find a way to get more money. At the railway station there was a map of London. Eddie worked out where he was and set off for Piccadilly Circus.

He wasn't used to such a crush of people but was pleased to notice that his first feelings weren't of fear but of freedom. Never before had he walked down a street without recognising every face he saw and, worse, being recognised. People in Garth used to know him because there he was a boy from the home, but here, here he was anonymous. People pushed past. They didn't complain, nor did they suck their breath in indignation if he was indifferent and didn't step aside for them. Here he walked down the street unnoticed.

He turned into a shop and bought some cigarettes, Silk Cut Number 3. The shopkeeper didn't even look at him. It was a transaction, not an opportunity to tell him how to behave.

He walked slowly. With nowhere to go he had no time by which to arrive. The sun shone. He felt part of the huge mass, protected, himself. He looked people in the face. He saw girls with short dresses who didn't care. There was dirt in the gutter. No one cared. He could cross the road, threading his way through cars stalled in the traffic jam. No one minded. He could sit on the steps of Eros in Piccadilly for as long as he liked. No one would move him on.

To his left there was a group speaking French – what were they, students? And to his right a boy. He was his own age, hair down his back, wearing a cotton shirt, flared trousers and playing a guitar. The player stopped, suddenly noticing the arrival who had sat down near him, turned to him and said, 'Mandrax?'

What did he mean?

'Only eight pence each. They're good. I'll give you three for twenty pence.'

He didn't want to admit ignorance, so he shrugged, got up and walked away.

'I'm always here,' said the boy, picking up his guitar.

Eddie wandered off, looking at the street names – Shaftesbury Avenue, Old Compton Street, Dean Street. He turned down Dean Street.

Halfway along a man spoke to him. 'Good show, non-stop. Come on in.' Behind him there was a dark passage from which tinny music drifted. Pinned to a curtain in the passage were some photographs. He could see a girl in one of them bending over a tall stool. A man stood near her with a cane. She didn't seem worried about what was about to happen.

Eddie broke his stride for a moment and instantly the man's bored gaze sharpened. He took the match from his mouth and gestured towards him. 'Come on in.' Eddie noticed that the man's teeth were black and rotten even though he was still young.

He nearly spoke but thought better of it and said nothing, transferring his gaze and walking on. As he moved away he expected to be shouted at for his rudeness but there was nothing. He glanced back. The man had returned to his boredom. The incident might never have occurred. Then the flat, indifferent voice came again. 'Good show, non-stop. Come on in.'

Two people who had stopped to look were doubtful. They hesitated. The doorman gestured at them. Then he called down the passage, turned and glanced up and down the street and invited the men to look inside.

From opposite Eddie could see a movement in the dark passage. For a moment a naked woman stood there, then she was gone.

The two men walked straight through the door.

'Gets 'em every time,' the doorman said to the young man watching. 'You want some?' He grinned and then shouted, 'Good show, non-stop,' to a man who walked past without a flicker.

Eddie stood on the corner of the crossing and watched. From where he was he could see down the passageway. He was intrigued. He moved slightly to the side of the parked car, and put his bag down beside it.

As he did so a voice said, 'All right, let's be having you.'

He looked up.

A police officer stood beside him. 'You're nicked for sus.'

'I'm what?'

'Sus. Come on, let's be going.'

A cracked voice shouted from a doorway behind them where a blonde woman was standing smoking a cigarette. 'He weren't doing nothing.'

'Sod off, Mary, or you'll come too,' said the police officer, and he set off, taking his arrest with him.

They walked in the warm sunlight. The policeman was inclined to be friendly. 'That were Mary. He's a Beaumont,' he said.

'A Beaumont? What on earth is that?'

'Yeah, she's a man. We regularly have to pull punters off her when they get upset.'

'A Beaumont.' He repeated the word. 'Where are we going?' he said.

'You're nicked, son.' Eddie looked at the policeman. He couldn't be very much older than he was himself.

'What for?' He wasn't surprised at the way things were turning. He was used to authority behaving quite arbitrarily. For him it was the nature of authority.

'You'll see.' The officer grinned at a man they passed. 'That's Tally. He'll see you right.' It wasn't even possible to try to work out what that meant. 'This is my sixth nick this week,' said the policeman. He didn't seem to need a reply and he carried on talking. 'Who'll you be, then?'

'I just arrived.'

'What? Here?'

'Yes.'

'In London?'

'Yes.'

25

'Just now? In London? Just arrived in London and just got nicked? You're doing well.'

The officer spoke as though the events that surprised him were nothing to do with him.

'Well, well. Where are you living?'

'Nowhere yet.'

'NFA? St John won't like that.'

Again this was meaningless. Eddie said nothing.

'Where are you going to stay?'

Without waiting for a reply, the officer suddenly disappeared into a doorway. His new prisoner stood in the street and wondered whether he should run off, but, oddly, he was finding this episode too interesting to leave. The policeman suddenly reappeared with a packet of cigarettes. ' "Trouser these",' he said. He was repeating what had just been said to him, not offering Eddie anything. He repeated it again. 'The man just said "Trouser these", that's old-fashioned talk. Right, I've trousered them.'

They walked on.

'So where shall we say you're staying?'

'Prince of Wales Crescent?'

· 'No, better not, we have trouble with squatters. How about' – the officer put his head back and thought for a moment – 'how about Tredegar Place, E3?'

'That's fine.' Eddie wasn't too sure, but he was sure he wasn't in any position to object.

'Two pound fifty a week, sharing the bathroom. No, too much. Two quid a week. Tredegar Place it is,' said the policeman, and he turned and took the steps up to the police station in two long strides. His prisoner followed him in. When he got through the sets of double doors he saw the police officer speaking to an older policeman. He recognised the stripes of rank, a sergeant behind a big oak desk. The sergeant looked down at him with disinterest. 'What is it? Sus?'

'Yeah,' said the policeman who had made the arrest.

'Name?'

'Tony Hancock.'

Eddie looked around in astonishment. It wasn't his name.

'Intent?'

'Theft.'

'From?' The sergeant was filling in a form.

'Parked car. New Vauxhall Victor Continental, KXE 260K. Dean Street.'

'Suspicion?'

'Touching a motor bike, two minutes before. EGH 984. Old Compton Street.'

'Address?'

'Tredegar Place. E3.'

'How long?'

'Two months.'

'Date of birth?'

For the first time the two policemen took some notice of him. They looked expectantly.

'Date of birth?' the sergeant repeated.

He said nothing.

The arresting officer made one up. 'Eighth of November 1955.'

'Occupation?'

'Hotel porter.'

'Criminal record?'

'None.'

After this series of questions and answers there was silence. The sergeant scratched away at the piece of paper. Then he looked up and said, 'Anthony Hancock, you are charged that on the eighth day of April in Dean Street, City of Westminster you, being a suspected person, did loiter with intent to steal, contrary to' – his voice trailed off into a recitation – 'section five of the Vagrancy Act 18 . . .' It was scarcely possible to make out what was being said. 'Do you have anything to say? I must warn you that anything you say may be . . .' Again his voice trailed off as he recited at speed, like a schoolboy with a tongue-twister in the playground.

'Do you have anything to say?'

Eddie began to speak but felt the policeman's hand on his arm. 'Steady.'

He said nothing.

The sergeant scratched away a little longer. Then, with a dramatic gesture, he tore the top copy of the pad he was writing on away and in the same movement separated it into two pieces. He handed a piece to each of them. 'Marlborough Street Magistrates Court, curtain up two p.m., the Honourable St John Harmston presiding,' he announced. 'Bail to attend.'

'Come on then,' said the constable, and he bounced out of the room. His enthusiasm was infectious and, newly christened Tony Hancock, Eddie found himself trotting down the steps in his wake. They went out on to the street again. The sun was shining and, if anything, the passers-by were moving more languorously than before in the warm afternoon. Eddie glanced up at a clock as they made they way down the road: 12.30. He had only been in London three hours and already he had made a good friend.

'What's your name?' he said to the police officer.

'Charlton. Charlie Charlton,' said the policeman.

'I'm Eddie.'

'When you're not Tony,' laughed the officer. 'Hey, come on,' he shouted, and he started running for a bus. It was a strange sight, a fully uniformed police officer chasing a bus down the street. Again for a moment he wondered whether to run off but still he did not do so. His new companion was far too pleasant to be dropped just like that.

He caught up with the bus at a crossing and jumped on to the swaying platform after him.

The policeman produced a warrant card and showed it to the bus conductor. 'He's with me. He's my prisoner,' he said, pointing at Eddie, who didn't feel in the least like a prisoner and met the conductor's gaze with a grin.

The conductor was black. Eddie had never been so close to a black man before.

'Well, mon, I'll rescue you if you want,' said the conductor.

'Lay off, Sooty,' said the policeman, and the conductor threw his head back and roared with laughter. Eddie noticed how pink the inside of his mouth was. The bus whirled them along the street in a cloud of dust and litter.

Eddie clung on. 'Here's Oxford Street,' said the policeman. 'Look, there's the Hari Hari.'

To his astonishment Eddie saw a line of saffron-robed, shaved men – and a woman – trailing in single file down the pavement. The sound of the tambourines and the slow wail of their chant reached him as the bus swept past. The wind lifted the robes of the last man, showing his green socks.

'And there's the "Eat No Protein Man". Look. It's the good weather bringing them out.'

Some distance behind the monks a tall, thin man with wire spectacles and a benevolent gaze twirled and whirled in a private dance down the pavement. Above him on a pole he carried a wooden sign. Eddie could see that the sign contained a list of foods, and the warning 'Beware of these'.

From the bottom of the sign there hung another strip of wood secured by two chains. It was an afterthought to the list above, rocking on its chains as the man twisted and danced on tiptoe. 'And sitting,' it said.

'Get ready to jump,' said the policeman. 'Do what I say. Now.'

He jumped. Eddie jumped.

They immediately found themselves in the middle of a crowd on the wide pavement. At the front of the crowd, facing it, crouched a man with a cardboard box. On the box there were three cards and a five-pound note.

The man looked up, astonished, as the uniformed officer stepped forward and picked up the note. 'Good Christ, where did you come from? I heard nothing,' said the man.

'I arrived by bus, you wally,' said the policeman. 'You should pay your lookouts better.' By the time the words were out of his mouth almost everybody had gone. The man with the box collapsed it and was crossing the road. Only a few bemused passers-by who had gathered for the display remained standing there. 'Does this fiver belong to anyone?' asked the policeman. No one said anything.

'No?' said Charlton. 'A stuffer or a shunter must have put it down and then left it there. Thank you, ladies and gentlemen, the show's over now.'

The policeman turned away, and when he and Eddie had gone ten yards he put the money in his pocket. 'I'll trouser that,' he said. He paused and then said, 'Strange expression.'

'What's a stuffer and a shunter?'

'Stuffers stuff the crowd up and shunters get people to put their money down.'

They walked off down the side street, passing the London Palladium. Eddie saw the bizarre face of Bruce Forsyth staring out of a poster. He had watched his programme once on the television when he was in the sanatorium.

Now he knew he was at the centre of things.

They turned the corner to the magistrates court.

Another police officer let them in from the public hall to the gaoler's office at the back of the building, taking Eddie's flimsy copy of the form from him. He opened a large steel gate and pushed Eddie into the cage.

It was a large square room with a scrubbed-pine bench around each of the walls. The floor was wooden and the roof opened up into a great bright skylight. It was a huge area, more like a marketplace than an enclosed room, but there was nowhere to sit, the benches were all full. The room was packed with people.

The air hummed with conversation. A juggler and a man dangling a plastic spider on a rubber string were showing each other their wares; two bogus majors wearing British Warm overcoats watched each other warily as they exchanged clipped greetings; a group of feathered prostitutes, a spiv, and a very old man talked reassuringly to a smart young man in a suit.

Two drunk Frenchmen had jammed themselves into a corner sharing cigarettes, and just near to where Eddie found himself there stood a man in a white apron arguing animatedly with a Turkish salesman who had a string of watches strapped up his arm.

A young black pickpocket was circling another young man dressed in pinstripes with a bandaged hand. The man with the bandage was clearly anxious about the time and kept looking at his watch, lifting his hand to his eyes, at the same time sadly and disbelievingly inspecting his injury.

Everybody was waiting to be called into court.

Eddie put his bag down between his feet and looked about him. Just to his right a man was whistling, a sharp, thin sound from between his teeth. He stopped and spoke to Eddie. 'What you got in the bag?' he said.

'Just my things,' said Eddie.

'Just your bag, then,' said the man, and he did a little dance, tapping his feet, finishing with a jump, half crouched, his arms open for applause. 'Yeah,' he breathed.

'Take no notice of him,' said the man in the apron, who had broken off from his dispute with the Turkish watch salesman. 'It's only Acidhead Sparky. He probably thinks you're from another planet.'

Eddie said nothing.

He had been warned that London was unfriendly but already twice today he had been spoken to in a friendly way by strangers. That didn't happen in Garth. The policeman didn't count or it would be three.

The man in the apron watched him for a reply, and when none came he said, 'Well, perhaps you are.'

Again Eddie didn't reply. He didn't see what there was to be said and he hadn't had any practice at just talking out of friendliness.

'Hey up,' said the apron man, 'don't be so depressed. Here . . .' He put his hand under his apron into a little blue bag tied round his waist and pulled out a short, stubby cigar. 'It can't be that bad – have a cigar.'

He flipped one into his own mouth and produced a Zippo lighter. He flicked it and a great yellow flame danced between their faces.

'My name's Ray,' said the man. His face, lit by the flame, seemed to dance, his expression never settling. 'Who are you? Why are you here?'

'I don't know. Something called "sus".'

'Were you?'

'Was I what?'

'Loitering with intent? Being a suspected person loitering with intent. That's what "sus" is.'

'I don't know,' said Eddie. 'I don't think so.'

'Well, you have to know, I suppose,' said Ray, 'though perhaps not. Perhaps you don't have to know you're committing an offence in order to commit it. Perhaps being careless is enough.'

He put his head back and, rubbing his neck, blew some smoke up at the glass-covered roof. 'Let's ask Harry.'

They threaded their way through the crowd of people. 'I myself,' Ray said, for a moment stopping and taking Eddie by the arm as he spoke intently, 'am here for obstructing the highway. Apparently you don't have to know you're doing that in order to do it. Indeed, I thought I was not obstructing the highway. I intended not to obstruct the highway. But St John told me. "It availeth not," he said. He said, "Mr Dash" – my name's Dash,' – the man in the apron grinned at Eddie – ' "I know you, Mr Dash, I have seen you and your ice-cream trolley. I know your excellent ice-cream. I know the standards of cleanliness upon which you pride yourself, and I know that you think you were not obstructing the highway. In fact I know you were trying not to obstruct the highway. But it availeth not, Mr Dash. You were obstructing the highway just by being there. It is an offence of strict liability." – whatever that is.'

Ray stopped and looked at Eddie, a broad, friendly grin spread across his face. 'What can you say to that? He's a fair man. St John. If you have to be screwed by the law, you might as well be screwed politely.'

'Here. Harry.' They stopped in front of the elderly man who had been deep in conversation with the young, smartly dressed man on the pine bench. 'Here, Harry, here's a problem. Jimmy here' – Eddie assumed he meant him – 'has been charged with sus. He says he doesn't know whether he committed any offence. But he would have to know, wouldn't he? To be guilty, that is.'

Harry looked up from where he was talking. 'Well, yes,' he said, 'he would have to know.' He turned to the man sitting next to him. 'That's right, isn't it? He's a lawyer,' he said, pointing his thumb at the young man.

The young lawyer looked uncomfortable and fingered a book he was carrying. 'Well, I don't know,' he said. 'I've not heard of this sus business before.'

'He's new,' said Harry. 'This is his first case. You won't find sus in there,' he said, pointing at the legal textbook. 'It's not taught at law school.'

Before Eddie could get any more advice, expert or otherwise, he was interrupted by a police officer coming to the barred door of the room. 'Hancock . . .' the voice shouted.

Eddie responded, and Ray said, 'You're on, then,' as though he were talking to an actor. Eddie joined Charlton, who appeared at that moment in the short queue next to a door marked 'Quiet!' in faded writing.

Everybody seemed remarkably cheerful, the defendants chatting with police officers, giving each other the thumbs-up as they went into court and patting those who came out on the shoulder with cheery grins.

The next offender came out, his elbow held by a police officer. 'Three months, three months, that's a bit much,' he said in a puzzled way.

'It'll pass, it'll pass,' said Ray, who had joined the queue at the back.

Charlton, properly dressed in full uniform, looked very smart. He said, 'You needn't say nothing. Just say guilty when they ask you the question.'

'Why guilty?' said Eddie.

'Because I caught you in the act, you berk,' said Charlton. 'Here we go, then.' The door had opened, and a depressed-looking man came out shepherded by a policeman in shirt-sleeves carrying a clipboard. Shirt-sleeves handed the prisoner over to another officer, shouted out 'Ten pounds or three days' and then, turning back, called out, 'Hancock.'

They all went into the court.

It was a large windowless room lit by feeble yellow lights attempting to pierce the gloom – the darkness somehow made more gloomy by the bright summer's day outside. The yellow gleam reflected off the dark panelling at the back of the court, providing barely enough light to see how far the room extended. The public benches, which did loom out of the darkness, had people scattered about on them. One man was in a deep sleep against the wall.

The officer with the clipboard swung round to the front and called out generally, 'Hancock, number twenty-eight on the list, Suspected Person.' At the same time, without even looking up, he guided Eddie up two steps towards what seemed to be a park bench set up on a wooden platform. It was fenced around with railings at just the right height for a man to lean on.

Eddie found himself in the dock, stuck up in the air – being looked at. At least, that's what it felt like, but when he looked around he saw that no one was taking the slightest notice of him. Had he floated to the top of the room and watched proceedings from there it would not have troubled anyone.

Below and to his right there were three men in dark suits, each reading a newspaper. One was tapping his teeth with a silver propelling pencil. Next to him Eddie saw the young man with the law book whom he had previously seen outside slide into the bench. One of the others moved along reluctantly to make room.

Directly in front of Eddie and below him, but facing off to one side, sat a man scribbling furiously. Suddenly he started speaking, in a loud, monotonous chant. Eddie listened for a few moments before he realised that he was speaking directly to him. ' . . . contrary to the Vagrancy Act 1897 . . .' The man broke off. 'Who prosecutes?' he called out.

'I do,' said Charlton, and Eddie saw that the policeman had gone into another box, a little higher than his, in front of him but to the left. 'PC Charlton, VS 258 Vine Street, sir.' Eddie felt better having a friend there with him.

'How do you plead, guilty or not guilty?' The scribbling man threw the question over his shoulder.

Eddie said nothing.

After a few moments the attention of the courtroom was caught by this sudden silence.

Eddie saw faces turn up towards him, like moons suddenly shining at him all around the room.

He had to say something to break the moment. He looked to his left and saw Charlton smiling at him.

'Guilty,' he said.

The court resumes its normal activity. The newspaper readers return to their reading, the silver pencil tap, tap, taps against the thin lawyer's teeth, the new young lawyer doing his first case fidgets nervously with his papers, the police sergeant in charge of the court checks and rechecks his lists so everything goes smoothly, and the man who is asleep by the door snores slightly as he returns from a tantalising moment in his dream to the open beaches of the west coast of Ireland. The policeman with the clipboard sticks his head round the door of the court out into the passage and shouts for Tom. The scribbling man beneath Eddie carries on with his litany. In the distance can be heard the sound of London's traffic.

Eddie continued to look around him. Opposite him, at about the same level, perhaps a little higher, sat a small, stout man wearing a dark suit with large lapels, a stiff collar and a small red rose in his buttonhole.

From the height at which he stood, Eddie could see what could not be seen by others in the court, that the little man's feet did not touch the ground. He was swinging his legs, engrossed in a large bound book in which he was writing slowly. He popped a sweet into his mouth.

Suddenly he spoke out loud, quite sharply. 'No, no, no. Please no, Mr Fripp.'

He was talking to the scribbling man who had clearly done something wrong. 'No, no, no. You don't say "Nothing to hope for, nothing to fear", that's the committal charge. Let me do it.

'Now, young man.' He looked up at Eddie, for even though he was sitting above him his size meant he was still below Eddie's eye level. 'You understand, do you, what you are saying?' He smiled and Eddie felt a gust of affection cross towards him. The sombre room was lit up by the man's cheery personality.

'You are admitting this offence. Please remember, what you are saying is not trivial. This offence could result in your losing your liberty for a short period. I do not say that to frighten you, but because I must say it, since it is the truth. You understand me, do you?'

Eddie hesitated. Should he say what had happened? But before he could speak Charlton broke in. 'I took the liberty, sir, since the defendant is a young man and has never been in trouble before, of explaining the situation to him at length.'

Instead of being put out by this interruption, the magistrate swung bodily round and gazed benevolently over his half-glasses at the police officer standing to attention in the witness box.

'And if I may say so, Constable,' he said, his voice soft and precise, 'if

I may say so, what you did was in the highest traditions of the police service, and the court thanks you for it.'

The friendly magistrate paused for a moment. 'You are satisfied with the correctness of his name, Constable? For I cannot fail to note that it is the name of a well-known comic artiste.'

'I am entirely satisfied, sir,' said Charlton with a straight face.

The magistrate turned back to Eddie. 'You are a young fellow who has never been in trouble before? We have nothing on the local register, Mr Gwatkin?'

The court police officer shuffled a pile of white cards. 'Nothing. Nothing, sir.'

'He has only just arrived in London, sir, this very day,' said Charlton.

'Oh really?' The magistrate looked at Eddie with new interest. 'Much as the young de Quincey arrived in London, in his case running away from school, if I am not mistaken, from the school to which I myself went. "Oh, Oxford Street, thou stony-hearted stepmother," de Quincey wrote. You must know, young man, that de Quincey left his newly found friend – a young girl whom he had met on his first day in London; they had helped each other in their mutual distress – left her in Wardour Street promising to return with money, but when he did return he was too late. She was gone. He searched for her yet she was gone. He was late. How one's heart was wrung for her, for him. You know the book, Mr Leonard?'

The lawyer doing the crossword puzzle looked up and said, 'Indeed, sir, indeed, sir,' and added, 'But sir, if we are to recall the classics, do you remember the young Samuel Butler arriving in town . . .'

The magistrate took up his words with laughter. 'Oh, very good, Mr Leonard . . . I remember. I do, I do. How he arrived in town with the benevolent magistrate sitting in the train compartment next to him? The very man before whom he later appeared just as this young man appears before me now? Oh, very good, Mr Leonard, you speak in mitigation without intending so to do. Or perhaps you do so without effort out of the very nobility of your spirit.

'We must all come to this long end, Mr Leonard, we must all come to London in the long end, must we not? That is of course if we were not born here to begin with. But on, on, we must get on.'

Eddie looked around him, but there was not the slightest attention being paid to him by anyone.

'Now, young man, you have not made a good start. But you have perhaps made a friend.' He nodded towards the police officer. I shall say no more about this regrettable event. I shall discharge you, but on condition you commit no further offences within the coming twelvemonth. Take advice, take advice. Be guided. Go now.'

Eddie stepped from the dock and as he left he could hear the magistrate still talking. ' . . . the impetuosity of youth, Mr Leonard, but if guided into proper channels . . .'

Outside, the warmth hit them. Across the road at the entrance to Carnaby Street was the juggler. A large coach puffed out exhaust smoke, a taxi driver was shouting at a man crossing the road. The hubbub replaced the dark innocence of the court.

Chapter 4

The evidence had all been called in Tony Ramus's case and all that now remained were the arguments.

Scott was listening to Cantor's closing speech. ' . . . and you may think, members of the jury, that anybody working at such an early hour in the morning, in semi-darkness, must clearly be up to no good. Yes . . .' A look of satisfaction spread over the lawyer's face and his voice rose in indignation. 'Oh yes, and these officers, who have been disgracefully attacked by the defence, stepped in on our behalf and prevented any further dishonesty.'

Scott looked at the jury. Since the prosecution always sat further from the jury than the defence, he had his back to Cantor, who was addressing the jury directly over his head. He was able to see their reactions directly. Mostly they were looking at Cantor stolidly, but one of them, a young man, casually dressed, in the back row, had allowed a look of total astonishment to creep over him. His mouth was open.

'Oh yes,' said Cantor, 'you may think that the attack that the defence made in this case on the police is designed merely to distract your attention. It is very easy to criticise police officers, ladies and gentlemen, especially easy is it to do from the safety of the court, but what do you want of the police who protect us? Our policemen are guard dogs, not lap dogs.' Cantor seemed pleased with his phrase. No doubt he had used it in case after case.

As long as he trotted out this stuff Scott did not feel particularly worried. He sounded too much like a politician, totally cut off from the jury. But occasionally he strayed, though he didn't know it, towards the point Scott was going to have difficulty in answering.

The prosecutor ploughed on, displaying his contempt for the criminal classes, and Scott began to relax as he moved away from the real point. It was nerve-racking to have to listen, showing no reaction, as Cantor moved towards his best point and then swerved away again, ignorant of what he was missing. Scott felt the urge to call out, as in a children's game, 'Warm, warmer, very warm, no, getting cool, cooler.' But he sat still and possessed, remaining silent.

Just as Cantor seemed to be winding down he suddenly came out with it. Perhaps he wasn't as stupid as he pretended to be.

'You may think this attack on the police was designed merely to distract your attention,' he repeated. 'Well, the prosecution say it was. Because consider this, members of the jury. What difference does it make if there was another man, the man the defence have taken to calling the third person? If the other man was there then maybe he was in it up to his neck too. With the defendant.'

This was breathtaking. Scott had thought Cantor might hint at the point, he was frightened he might, but he didn't think he would be as barefaced as this. The prosecution had spent the whole trial relying upon their evidence to deny the existence of the man who Ramus said had tricked him into unloading the van, but now they were saying, 'Well, if he does exist, so what? They were both guilty.'

It needed a proper judge to put that right and this one wasn't going to do it. Scott knew that the prosecution changing the basis upon which they asked for a conviction wasn't the kind of thing that worried juries. It was something you just couldn't defend against.

Cantor sat down with a flounce and stared at the ceiling of the court in astonishment at his powers of oratory. There was silence.

Scott looked at the clock. It was twenty minutes before the midday break. Unless the judge rose very early for lunch and he started his speech after the break, Scott was going to have to cut what he said in two, with an introduction before the lunch break and the rest later.

It wasn't a difficult speech to make. He had plenty of material. He had been making speeches of the same sort for fifteen years now, sometimes three a week when he was new and his cases were smaller, forty-five weeks a year. That was more than a thousand times he had stood up and said, 'Ladies and gentlemen', never, he had decided early in his career, 'members of the jury'.

He had found that there were dozens of variables that affect a speech, some more important even than the facts of the case – the look on the face of the defendant, what day of the week it was, the lighting in the court, sometimes even the weather.

No, that was wrong, the weather played a large part. He had very rarely lost a case in Lewes Crown Court when there was a bright, high sky and the wind was up. The effect of the wind off the downs seemed to make anything possible. It seemed to affect the jury's group response. He had heard that primary school teachers dread a really high wind disturbing their class – perhaps it was the same thing.

But one of the most important variables was the timing of the speech – when in the day it happens. A jury can change totally over lunch, from stony indifference before to sympathetic humour afterwards, and the other way about.

'Mr Scott.' The judge interrupted his momentary reflection. 'No doubt you will be finishing before the short break. I shall sit a little later if you wish.'

The judge was trying to hurry him. If he gave in there would be problems. There was nothing worse than getting to the parts of a speech that matter and then realising that you had only six or seven minutes before the choice came of either finishing or having to break off for an hour.

'I am sorry, Your Honour, but I can promise no such convenient timing,' he said, standing up, and turning to the jury.

The judge's remark provided him with a lead into one of his standard introductions. 'You may find, ladies and gentlemen, if you sit in these courts for any length of time, that at this stage it is customary for counsel to apologise in advance for the length of time they are going to take.'

Pause. Allow three beats.

'Well, I shall not.' Pause.

He had found that to establish the correct speed and tone at the beginning of a speech enabled him to vary both later when he wished. It was easier to move from the formal to the colloquial than the other way around.

'I may take a little time in setting out Mr Ramus's response to these charges and I shall not apologise for doing it properly.'

That was a form of litotes: the expression of a positive proposition through the denial of its negative, or in this case through the justification of the negative. To say 'I shall not apologise' was in effect an apology.

He found that the internal commentary on what he was saying had started and that he was becoming detached, watching himself working. It was a familiar feeling now, though when it had first happened to him it had been frightening. He had thought he was losing control.

He watched the jury from behind his words.

At the back the middle-aged woman – no, she was a little younger than that – wanted him to demonstrate to her why she should not convict.

The man next to her was sceptical. He could deal with that now. It fitted conveniently. 'No doubt, ladies and gentlemen, when you heard me say just now that there are problems about the accuracy of the evidence, one reaction you may have felt was scepticism.'

He changed his position and looked directly at the man.

'Well, that's not unreasonable. You probably think, "Well, the defence" – that's me – "*would* say that, wouldn't he?" It's a perfectly natural reaction. It is not surprising that you feel that way. By all means feel sceptical. You're a man of the world, you've seen a lot, no doubt people have tried it on with you.' Pause here, smile, the point is almost conceded. 'Of course, be sceptical if you wish' – conceding it gave him space so he could take as much time as he wished before he got to the point, offhand, indifferent – 'but if there are problems with the evidence then it doesn't matter who points them out, does it? It doesn't matter whether it's defence counsel, whether it's a television programme enquiring into the correctness of this verdict, or even you, afterwards, as you review the evidence in the jury room. It doesn't matter who notices it, does it, if it's correct and there are problems?'

The expression on the man's face changed for a moment and he looked up at the ceiling. It was dangerous directly to challenge a juror, but if it worked it was as good as you could get.

Scott set out his argument. It was approaching one o'clock. He slowed, repeated himself on an important point, and then paused. 'Would Your Honour find this a convenient moment?'

The court rose for lunch.

'You're doing OK,' said Catherine. 'They're all listening to you.'

Scott came back to the present.

'Yes,' he said. 'I hope they still listen after lunch.'

* * *

Upstairs in the big room overlooking the river the Bar mess was crowded. Most people were sitting at one end of the long table and Scott started walking towards them until he noticed that Butler Jennings was sitting at the end of it in charge of the conversation.

Scott heard Jennings's voice before he saw him. 'Oh yes, I dined with the King of Norway at the Commons a few nights ago. Our dining committee was entertaining him. We showed him the debating chamber and how the central gangway is the width of two sword-lengths.'

Cantor, sitting next to him, listened carefully, ready to laugh. 'And do you know what?' Jennings continued. 'I told him what Trollope said about the House of Commons. And the King said, "This Trollope, he is this writer who writes for people who don't really like books, yes?" '

Cantor looked at Jennings, trying to work out what the remark meant. There was a stray laugh, but by the time Scott had turned away Cantor had not yet decided what to do.

Going to the other end of the table, Scott slid into a seat. He looked up and found himself sitting opposite Tony Jay. 'How're you doing?' They both said it at the same time, and laughed.

'Defending a man for handling stolen property,' said Scott. 'We're shifting the stuff from a lorry six hours after it was taken. What about you?'

'I raped a girl who came home and stayed with me overnight. She slept on the other side of the bed.'

'For God's sake!' said Scott. 'When did she report it?'

'A week later.'

'I don't envy you that. Who was he?'

'He's a surveyor.'

'You don't say.'

Sally Donne sat down next to them. 'Is Tony trying to persuade you he's being hard done by?' she said.

'Are you prosecuting this, Sally?' said Scott.

'Yes,' she said. 'You should know, if you're a woman in this job you end up prosecuting sex cases . . .'

'Which are getting weaker every day,' said Scott, 'and your complainant actually slept in the same bed as the defendant, and then she cries rape?'

'Well, he ought to have kept his hands to himself,' she said, laughing as she pushed Tony Jay away from her down the bench with her hip. 'Piss off, Tony. Your client's going to get off anyway.' She said it with the pessimism of a prosecutor.

'Oh no he won't,' said Tony. 'Do you know what Sally did?' As he spoke he poked her back with his elbow. 'She asked the poor bugger whether when he screwed someone he wanted her to enjoy it. And when my chap said he did, Sally here says, "Why didn't you wake her up, then, so that she could?" '

'What did he say to that?'

'What could he say? He said he thought she was awake. So Sally asks, "Well, did she enjoy it?" I ask you, is that a decent way for a woman to earn a living? If I may be sexist for a moment.'

Sally hit out at Tony Jay again and he whooped with laughter.

Down at the other end of the table everybody stopped talking and looked at them. Butler Jennings glared.

'Ooh, it's the headmaster,' said Sally and, putting her hand up to her face, she waved at Jennings. 'He really is a pain,' she said, but she was too late. Jennings had got up and was coming down towards them.

'Hallo, Sally,' he said as he approached.

'Hallo, clammy hands,' she muttered under her breath. 'Watch out, Tony, he'll go for you too.'

'Well, if it isn't young Ms Donne,' the MP said as he leaned over her, 'and young Mr Jay. Now what are you doing? Sex cases, no doubt?'

Scott had never met the man, though he'd seen him at lunch the day before and often on the television. It was clear he thought himself the epitome of the common-sense MP reflecting the deep desires of the people. He would pop up on the grass outside Parliament in support of hanging or prison, or more of both.

Scott watched him. He had put his hand on Sally's shoulder and, to judge by the movement he was making, he was clearly enjoying it. He was fondling her. Then, to Scott's astonishment, he did the same to Tony Jay.

Jennings looked up and his eyes met Scott's. The distaste must have been clear on Scott's face. 'Why, it's Mr Scott,' he said. Scott was surprised that he knew his name. 'I was only talking to Jolly the judge about you yesterday.'

This must have been after the lunch, thought Scott. He saw that Jennings had taken his hand away from the shoulders of the two in front of him and, although he was still speaking softly, his face had now become lined with anger. 'He said you were rude to him.'

'Did he?'

'He complained to me in my position as a senior member of the Bar.'

'Did he?' said Scott again.

'I said to take no notice, since rudeness in an advocate is normally a refuge for incompetence, though I said I hadn't met you. He agreed with me.'

'Did he?' said Scott. There was little else he could say, though he knew that by the time Jennings was gone he would have thought of a retort.

The MP turned away.

'What was that about?' said Tony.

'Well,' said Sally, 'it wasn't about any conversation with some judge. More likely it was about Scott here watching him touch you up. Jennings doesn't mind what it is he's touching as long as it's relatively young.'

'That's what makes you a good prosecutor: you notice what's going on,' said Jay. He rubbed his shoulder where Jennings's hand had been and shuddered slightly.

When Scott got back to court he found that the jury had gone cold. What had happened upstairs had affected him, but it wasn't that. The break in proceedings had worked against him this time. Perhaps he had made a mistake and he should have tried to cram it all in before lunch.

The argument was difficult to get going again. It seemed to have lost its momentum. Even though he was able to demonstrate that he had the better of the argument on every point the Crown had raised, it still left the jury room to convict. And he had the growing feeling that they were going to.

He had convinced the jury of everything: that the third person had been there, that the police were either incompetent or for some reason unwilling to investigate what had really happened. He had won on every point except the one that mattered—whether Mr Ramus knew that the lorry and the stuff in it was stolen. This jury believed he did know. Scott could see it in their eyes, in the way that they moved, occasionally shifting in their seats as if to get the whole thing over more quickly. He pushed on, listening to his hopeless voice separate itself from him as he searched for a way out.

What he had said to Ronnie the night before was coming true. The case had gone too well.

In the car, driving Catherine and Sally back to London, Scott asked Sally about Jennings. 'I've never met him. I know nothing about him, though you can't miss him on the TV,' he said. 'Why should he suddenly come up with such a remark about me? He doesn't know me from Adam, and I'm hardly likely to be any sort of a threat to him.'

Sally looked ahead at a huge polystyrene statue of sumo wrestlers incongruously flexing their vast bodies on the roundabout. They were at least twelve feet tall.

'Look at that,' she said. 'What on earth is that doing here? This is Lewisham, not Osaka, for God's sake.'

He didn't answer her question. There was no answer.

'I don't know,' she said. 'Jennings is obviously hugely ambitious, and ambition comes from somewhere. Not very healthy, if you ask me. Come to that, I don't think anything about him is particularly healthy. Maybe there are some bits of himself he can't control. Most men are like that.'

Scott looked at her. She was attractive, her sober clothes making her more so. And she always made him feel slightly inferior. She knew so clearly what she wanted and was going to get it.

He said, 'But he's a politician, not the kind of person who goes around losing his temper and insulting people.'

Sally said, 'Perhaps he was telling the truth, then,' and she turned and laughed at him.

'He near as dammit said I was incompetent. My present client, Mr Ramus, would agree with him, of course,' he said.

'But your client wouldn't say it in front of everybody at lunch,' Sally said. 'He made you look rather silly. This is where I get out.' Scott stopped the car outside the tube station.

She pulled her case with her robes from the back seat and, saying goodbye to Scott and Catherine, disappeared.

There was silence.

He set off for Blackfriars Bridge.

'Why do you let her speak to you like that?' said Catherine. 'She was bloody rude.'

When he didn't reply she said, 'What's the matter? Why did you let her push you around?'

She was annoyed.

'What's so special about her?'

Chapter 5

The day after his appearance before the magistrate Eddie Morgan sat waiting for Charlton in the New Vogue Café, just opposite the Marlborough Street Magistrates Court at the top end of Carnaby Street. He had walked to the restaurant from his room at Camden Town.

He had found a place to sleep at the squat in Prince of Wales Terrace. He was told when he went there that it was the biggest squat in Europe. 'Essentially we don't believe in property,' they said. 'We want society to put all that stuff behind it.'

He had been led up some rickety stairs to a room at the top of one of the terrace houses. Inside, the curtains were drawn, the walls painted chocolate brown and the doors dark red. It was barely possible to see.

He went in and sat down on a cushion full of beans, or was it rice? It was a strange feeling, though the initial pleasure didn't last long and it soon became extremely uncomfortable. From the ceiling multi-coloured mobiles hung, twisting and turning in the smoke that drifted up from an incense burner. Eddie sat trying to adjust his eyes to the darkness.

In the half-dark a man looked at him, suspiciously eyeing his short hair, the result of the final cut from the Garth Boys' Home barber. He himself had long black hair gathered up in a ponytail. He was wearing a round tasselled hat and a long printed Indian shirt that reached his knees. Eddie couldn't see what else he had on since he was sitting with his legs crossed beneath him on a bright velvet cushion throughout their conversation. He looked very uncomfortable.

'You ought to know what we are doing here. We are not just a squat. We started out as the intellectual heirs of the Diggers and Levellers, but

47

when we came across the idea of no property at all for anyone we changed direction. But meanwhile we compromise, we compromise – we are forced to compromise.'

Eddie didn't know who either the Diggers or the Levellers were but he had seen what this man was doing before, he had done it himself. He clearly didn't have a clue what he was talking about. He was bullshitting.

But then the man said, 'The charge for your room is one pound a week plus fifty pence administration charge . . .' He paused. 'To help the administrators administrate.' He stopped talking and pulled on the large, untidy cigarette he had been rolling.

After he sucked in the smoke he held his breath and Eddie watched as the man's face got redder and redder. Why doesn't he let it out? Then he did so, with a pop. The man looked at Eddie, started giggling, and said, 'Administer, I mean, not administrate,' and he offered him the joint.

Eddie refused but saw again what he had already noticed, that drugs seemed to be common, not hidden at all if the people who used them thought you were on their side.

'Well, how did you manage?' said Charlton as he arrived in the café. He was not wearing his uniform, but there was the same cheeriness about him.

Eddie told him: £1 a week, for a room, plus fifty pence.

'An administration charge? Who gets that, I wonder?' said Charlton.

Eddie hadn't thought about it, but then he did so. 'You're right. There must be at least a hundred and fifty people living there,' he said.

Charlton changed the subject.

'What you said, you know, what you told me about Piccadilly Circus, the man on the steps by the statue, it was right.'

He paused and started fiddling with the salt and pepper as a waitress came over to them. 'I'll have some scrumbled egg,' said Charlton pointing at the menu, 'and a coffee.'

The waitress left.

'I always have scrumbled egg here. Look.' He pointed at the menu which, sure enough, said 'Scrumbled egg'.

Now they were alone he returned to what he was saying. 'What you said was right. We found packets of Mandrax, drugs, wrapped ready for sale. It was a good arrest.'

Eddie nodded at him. Charlton carried on. While he was speaking Eddie reflected on the man sitting opposite him. He talks too much, he thought. Normally one need say nothing.

Charlton said, 'I spoke to the detective sergeant and he told me to give you this.' He put an envelope on the table. It had the word Tredegar written on it.

Eddie let it lie there.

'It has two phone numbers in it. If you ring and give the name Tredegar then you'll get through all right. Sorry about the name but it's all we could think of. Better than Tony Hancock.' He laughed.

He slid a pound note across the table and said, 'There's this as well.' When Eddie looked surprised, Charlton grinned and said, 'That's only part of what we got when we sold the Mandrax on. There's always money available if you help.'

The eggs arrived with two coffees and Charlton started to eat. 'I'm applying to become a TDC, a temporary detective constable. Or an aide to CID. They were impressed by the collar and I think it'll be OK.'

Eddie didn't reply but looked interested.

'You don't say much, do you?' said Charlton.

Eddie grinned.

Charlton looked at the young man sitting opposite him. He was distinctive with his red hair and bright blue eyes. Charlton hadn't often seen that combination of colouring. He was quiet and watchful. Charlton felt he was someone he could trust.

'What are you going to do?' he said. 'Are you going to get a job?'

'Yes.'

'What do you want?'

Eddie shrugged and looked at the pound note on the table in front of him.

'Do you know what I think?' Charlton said. 'I think the way to get money is to be near people who have money.'

Eddie listened. He was hearing something useful.

'I know of a job that might suit. It's working in a club. What's called a gentleman's club.' He snorted. 'Gentlemen! It's not well paid, but the point is that the money comes from the people you deal with. Tips and things. They've got money, you get it direct from them. Hang around money and you get money.'

*   *   *

49

The Radical Club had seen better days, and in those better days the magnificence of the building had been justified by the size and wealth of its membership. The main entrance was of polished mahogany and oak, the colours reflected in the plate glass of the revolving door and the polished brass. On the walls there were great pompous portraits culminating in the huge picture on the wall at the turning of the famous staircase – a picture of the Cabinet of All the Worthies.

Not one of the ministers was looking at the painter but stood showing a profile or even, in one eccentric's case, the back of his head. The great picture hung by two massive chains and it was Eddie's precarious task to dust it.

Andrew, the head porter, held the ladder and Eddie looked down at him and the floor of the hall, thirty feet below. Andrew was telling him what was what.

'I always say to youngsters starting' – Andrew himself couldn't be more than thirty and Eddie was curious about the knowing look he had – 'I always say to youngsters starting here that it is the personal relationships that make the job worth it – and profitable. We share any tips we get. Please remember that.'

The floor and the walls of the entrance and the passage were all tiled and, as the new members stood in the entrance hall, the slightly falsetto voice of the club secretary echoed and rang as he welcomed them and took the opportunity to tell them one or two amusing stories about the club.

'F.E.Smith used to stop in at the club to use our gentlemen's facilities while walking from the Temple to the Houses of Parliament. He wasn't a member. You know some people tell this story about the Liberal Club across the way, but it was about this club, not them.'

Eddie, standing in the corner of the hall next to the entrance, ready to open the door, had heard this story before. The club secretary told it to all the new members.

He didn't listen but looked instead at the new crop. There were two of them, youngish men in their late twenties, perhaps ten years older than himself. They also looked as though they had heard the story before. The club secretary finally got to the point. 'After a while the head porter summoned up the courage to approach the famous barrister as he left the lavatory. "Excuse me, sir," he said, "this is a private club you know."

' "Oh, is it that too?" said F.E.Smith.'

The secretary's audience laughed at his gesture of explanation, pointing to the vast tiled entrance hall.

'He must have thought it was one huge cottage,' said one of the new members.

'I wish,' said the other.

Eddie overhead what was said but did not understand what was meant.

'Now I must introduce you to our staff,' said the secretary. 'Andrew is our head porter and young Edward here a relative newcomer. Andrew, Edward, Mr Davenport and Mr Jennings are new members. No doubt you'll remember them in future.'

The secretary turned back to the new members, who were looking at the slim young porter. 'Should you want anything, gentlemen, then you need only call Edward, or, if he is not here, Andrew will send for him.'

Butler Jennings smiled at Eddie and Eddie smiled back at him. 'Good evening, sir,' he said.

Eddie knew how to wear a uniform. Jennings noticed that.

'Now we must get on,' said the secretary. 'The club committee invites you to sherry. We shall take it in the committee room.'

Eddie had the opportunity to move from the squat the day after the police arrested the man with the ponytail and tasselled hat. Eddie had been arrested too, he had expected that, but was free from the police station within the hour, still in time to get to work before midday.

Now he was working a late shift and didn't expect to leave the Radical Club until at least midnight.

'Did you know we have some staff quarters here?' Andrew asked him.

Eddie did know, but didn't say so. He made Andrew go on by looking surprised.

'Oh, you didn't know?'

Again Eddie said nothing.

Andrew was getting used to the silence of his most junior member of staff and had put it down to shyness. 'Yes, we have rooms for those who want them and who are recommended to the club committee.'

Eddie wasn't going to ask to be recommended and Andrew eventually found himself offering something unasked, which he usually bestowed as a favour.

'There's a room in one of the east towers spare now. Would you like to see it?'

He and Eddie made their way through the passages at the back of the building, up a scrubbed-pine staircase twisting its way through a tower till it reached a room lit on two sides by curved windows. Despite the bright light from the windows the room appeared dingy; there was a small chest of drawers, a large brass bed, and a washstand with a mirror over it. The only concession to modernity was a telephone by the side of the bed.

'Fifteen shillings, that's seventy-five pence a week new money, straight from your wages. But the club agrees to pay you the same amount as a supplement since you're regularly on the premises at night and can be called.' He gestured to the telephone. 'You're quids in. Do you want it?' Eddie did and he didn't even go back to the squat to get his few things.

It was another beginning. Now he was saving money. With the money he had got from the police raid and what he had already put aside, he was getting to be well off. He didn't spend much on food. He had all his meals at the club.

There were even times of relaxation when he felt for a moment he was among friends: off duty, sitting late with Andrew and the club wine waiter, Prescott, tasting the wine left on the tables in the half-empty bottles.

'Things are changing in this country,' said the wine waiter. 'All this has to go.' He gestured round the magnificent dining room. 'After all, it's the seventies now, this barn of a place just can't be economic.' The room could have seated two hundred but there were rarely more than twenty or thirty a night and often many fewer.

It was empty now and to one side a waitress was moving regularly, setting out the breakfast places. The shaded lights glowed in the gold and velvet and as the tables were set the silver of the knives and forks sparkled.

'It can't survive,' said Prescott. 'Society is growing more equal. The spread of education, good housing, opportunities and all, will mean that more jobs are available to everyone. Wealth will be more widely spread – there won't be the differences we have now. People who can afford to pay a working man's wages for a week for a meal, it can't go on.'

Outside the dining room there was a crash – a glass had been broken. Prescott looked up but there was no more sound. He carried on. 'Even the Conservative government agrees with the Labour Party now about the basics: employment, housing, health. To all intents and purposes the argument is over. Consensus reigns.'

He held the crystal glass up to the light and the red colour turned in it. 'Now this is a good wine,' he said.

There was another crash and a burst of laughter. This time it was clear where it had come from – the bar next to the dining room. Andrew and Eddie got up and walked to the door.

Inside the room a young Spanish waitress was crouched on the floor, one knee bent, over a heap of broken glass which she had obviously just swept together. She was looking up. Above her stood two men. Eddie recognised them as the new members who had been recently introduced. They were both dressed in dinner jackets. One of them was holding a wine glass above the girl's face, poised to drop it.

'Excuse me, sir,' Andrew interrupted him. 'Is there a problem?'

Jennings, holding the glass, looked up. He was flushed with alcohol. His first reaction was anger and Eddie saw his face transformed by a sneer. But then the man clearly thought better of it and regained control.

'Just an accident, Andrew. No harm done. This young lady is kindly clearing it up for us.' He lowered the glass he held in his hand. 'May we trouble you for a glass of wine?'

'The bar is closed, sir,' said Andrew.

'Is there no service?'

'Are you staying the night here, sir?'

'I hadn't intended to do so. Would it make a difference?'

'Well, if you are staying, sir, then we can provide you with service in the smoking room.'

'I shall stay, then. We have something to celebrate, Andrew. We have been accepted on the official list of Conservative Party candidates. We must mark the date with a good wine. Things will be different from now on.'

'Very good, sir,' said Andrew. 'I shall send Edward here in with a bottle of . . .'

'Claret, to toast the future of the Conservative Party,' said Davenport. Andrew turned away. 'We are the future,' Jennings announced to the empty walls. His companion laughed again.

Andrew returned to the dining room and sat down. 'Drunk,' he explained to the wine waiter. 'Wait, wait.' He gestured to Eddie, who had remained standing, expecting an order. 'Let them cool down a little.'

They sat at the table amidst the lights. Prescott continued what he had been saying but the moment had passed.

*   *   *

Eddie knocked on the smoking room door then, turning, he pushed it open with his hip, all the while holding the bottle of claret steady on the silver tray. Once in the room he held the tray at shoulder height and set off through the gloom towards the fire.

Concealed in the large leather chairs before the fire the two men lounged almost on their backs, holding cigars above them. The sight exactly resembled drawings Eddie had seen in the pre-war copies of *Punch* in the library.

'Where have you been, boy?' one of them said. It was Davenport. Eddie could just make his face out in the dark.

'I had to inform the housekeeper, sir,' he said. 'Your room is being got ready, Mr Jennings, and here is your wine, sir.' He set the salver down on the low table to one side of the men, nearer to Jennings.

'How old are you, boy?' Eddie found he was angry at this form of address but his habitual silence prevented him from blurting out a remark. He paused and emptied an ashtray. 'I shall be eighteen, sir, on my next birthday. Will there be anything more?'

Jennings pushed himself up and looked at him. 'Are you on duty?' he said.

'No, I am not, sir, but I shall be here if you want anything,' he said.

'No, no,' said Jennings, 'but I shall need someone to show me my room.'

'If you call, sir, I shall show you,' said Eddie. 'You need only dial sixty on the internal system.'

Eddie had already gone to sleep when the phone woke him. He had been dreaming of his time at the boys' home. It was as though his dream were reminding him that he was master of himself and that now he could do what he wanted. Eventually the bell penetrated the dream and he slipped from the bed to the floor, pulling on his dressing gown. He picked his way in the darkness down the familiar passage to the hall desk, where he found Jennings waiting. It was late, about half past one.

'This way, sir,' he said, and they set off to the back of the building.

'Is there anyone else staying?' said Jennings.

'No, you are the only guest tonight, sir,' said Eddie.

'Very quiet, then?'

'Yes, sir.'

'Where are the staff quarters?'

'At the end of this passage.'

'Can they be disturbed?'

'No,' said Eddie, puzzled, turning round as he opened the door for him.

He found Jennings standing with a five-pound note in his hand.

Chapter 6

'So you lost the case? So what? He was obviously guilty anyway.' Catherine laughed. 'Well, I mean, unloading a truck in the middle of the night and, surprise, surprise, it turns out to have been stolen. Of course he knew.'

'That's not the point.'

'What is, then?' said Catherine.

'The point is I blew it. Going into the lunch break we were ahead, coming out we were behind.' Scott grinned. 'It was like one of those cartoons where the cat goes into the drainpipe after the mouse but then comes out in front. What the hell happened?'

He was packing his bag the day after his speech. The judge had summed up and the jury had convicted Mr Ramus.

He folded his barrister's gown and put it in the bag, then he put his stiff collar and white bands on top.

'Something happened at lunch yesterday, didn't it?' she said. She was sitting on the robing-room table, indifferent to the looks of other members of the Bar. She wasn't meant to be there but no one was going to say so. They were too well mannered.

'At the jury's lunch or at mine?' Scott started to unpack his bag. He had had a wig stolen at Bournemouth Crown Court once and had been nervous about losing this next one ever since; it was old and he had had it for years. He checked underneath the robe. Yes, it was there.

'At your lunch,' she said.

'No,' he said. 'Nothing.'

'Well, what was Miss Hoity-Toity saying in the car yesterday, then?'

Scott thought, Why does Sally upset her so much? That was the second time she had mentioned her.

He said, 'Oh, there was just a bit of an argument over lunch.' That was putting it a big strongly. It hadn't quite been an argument, just an insult, but he wasn't going to go into details. Or so he thought. Catherine was extremely persistent.

They walked down to his car. 'What was the argument about?'

'Nothing, really.'

'You can't have an argument about "nothing really". It's not possible. Even in this country.'

Scott looked at her as he opened the car door; her hair was very red and she carried herself like a dancer. She was certainly a change from the clerks that were normally sent to court with him.

He thought he'd tease her. 'I don't fancy Sally Donne, you know.'

She gave herself away. 'You'd be mad if you did,' she said, getting into the car. 'She's about as interesting as – what do you call them? You have them here – a lacrosse stick.'

Scott decided it was about time he paid some attention to this lady. 'Why do you wear lace mittens?'

'You're changing the subject,' she said. 'What was the argument about?'

He nearly said 'Oh, nothing' again, when he realised that there was absolutely no reason not to tell her what had happened. Why not tell her? Why be buttoned up all your life? It was a phrase she might have used.

'It's a bit complicated,' he said.

'Try me.'

'We were having lunch.'

'That figures.'

'I'll tell you the story if you'll let me.'

'No problem,' she said, waving a mittened hand. She turned and faced him, resting her chin on her knuckles like Betty Boop. 'Do you want me to sit still too?'

'I got into an argument with that man Jennings. Do you know him?'

'Know him!' she said. 'He's gross. He makes most politicians look clean-living and honest.'

'He was on the radio this morning,' he said, 'suggesting that travellers should be moved on. He's an absolute shit.'

'I can imagine,' she said. 'What happened.'

'Well, he suddenly went for me at lunch.'

'Isn't that allowed in your English lunching rooms?'

'Of course not. We behave properly at luncheon.'

'Oh,' she said.

He stared ahead of him at the traffic lights and then pulled over to his right.

'Why're you stopping?' she said.

'I need a drink.'

'What about me?'

'You too,' he said.

'They went into the Perkin Warbeck and Firkin. A sign in the window said 'Perkin's Firkin' Great'.

'What does that mean?'

'It's far too complicated to explain,' he said. 'What do you want to drink?'

They sat in a large wooden settle at a table that smelt of beer.

'Is it true your mother was a beauty queen?'

She said, 'I'll tell you after you tell me what happened at lunch.'

'OK, then. Jennings was in the Bar mess and he came over to where we were sitting. He put his hands on Sally Donne's shoulders and then he touched a friend of mine, Tony Jay. He was rubbing them both at the same time. I looked at him and he saw me. So he insulted me.'

'You mean you looked at him,' she said, giving the word 'looked' a twist. 'Haven't you ever seen a bit of honest sexual harassment before? And you sneered at him. No wonder he disliked you.'

'Well, we thought it was that. Sally said that.' He watched her sniff when he said the name. 'But I've been thinking about it. I think it was something else. I mean, what he did to Sally wouldn't have looked odd if she hadn't said, "Here comes clammy hands." To anyone else watching it would have just seemed friendly. I mean, he's much older than them.'

'Pree – cisely,' she said.

'Well, it wouldn't have looked odd to me. I think something else upset him, something that happened the day before at the judge's lunch. Something he didn't like other people seeing.'

'Lunch seems to be an exciting time for you English.'

'Yes, well,' he said. 'I saw him being put down by Scribner.'

'What?'

'I saw him being snubbed by Judge Scribner. At lunch. He was talking too much so Scribner introduced something into the conversation that shut him up.'

'What was that?'

'It was a reference to the Garth Boys' Home scandal.'

'What was that?'

'It was one of those scandals that the English upper classes get up to pass the time. Something to do with young boys, sex, politicians, that sort of thing. I never understood it. It ran in the back pages of *Private Eye* for years.'

'Do Englishmen ever like ordinary sex?'

'I suppose they must or we wouldn't keep the show on the road,' he said. 'Now, it's your turn. I have a friend at the Bar called Tozer. Well, "friend" is putting it a bit strongly. He's someone who bugs me. He tells me that your mother was a beauty queen. Is this true?'

'Yes, it's true.'

'Where?'

'Does that matter?'

'Yes.'

'Alexandria.'

'Where's that?'

'Virginia.'

'What did she do to deserve that, then?'

'What sort of a dumb question is that?'

Scott looked at her without saying anything. He was enjoying playing up to her idea that all English guys were stuffed shirts, like John Cleese in that film about fish.

'You're like that guy in the fish film,' she said.

'Why do you say that?' he asked.

'Because you ask dumb questions,' she said.

'Did your mum have a can like yours?' he said.

'What?'

'A high can. As in "I like your can".'

'Where d'you get that?'

'In Elmore Leonard. It's what he calls a bum. You'd say butt. All the girls in his books have nice high cans. He's always remarking on it.'

He drank some beer.

He was beginning to feel very relaxed, forgetting about Mr Ramus. It was the pressure of the case lifting from him. Life starts up again when a case ends. You lift your head, find you've been preoccupied and say, 'What's been going on, then?'

He looked at her. Was she thinking about his opinion of her can?

But she wasn't. She surprised him. She said, 'I'm going to a poetry reading this evening. Do you want to come?'

'You can generally find a parking space around Hanover Square,' he said, as they edged past a bus filling up with Japanese tourists. 'It's the shape of the place. It never fills up properly.' Sure enough there was a parking space just a little up the road from the church with the stone dogs outside.

'Why are there dogs outside?' she asked.

'I don't know,' he said. 'I'm full of guff about London, but I don't know about those dogs at all.' They walked back along Princes Street. 'For example, I know that up there is Tom Brown's the tailors. If you go in there you can sit on a saddle to have your riding breeches measured.'

They looked up at the first-floor windows. 'I used to pay so much for my suits there that it spoiled reading the newspapers. You'd read of some American Mafia man who had fabulous suits and they cost nothing compared with Tom Brown. So for me this Mafia don becomes a cheapskate wearing tacky suits. Now I go to a chap in Craven Street. A lady barrister who has her waistcoats made there recommended them.'

They went into Oxford Street and turned right, going down away from Marlborough Street. There's a court there. That's where everyone starts off.'

'Let's forget about courts,' she said. 'We're going to listen to some poetry.'

They reached the pub where the meeting was being held. Downstairs it was normal – gilt, velvet, tassels on the lampshades – but she took him to the corner of the bar. 'Hi, Beamish,' she said, and a large fat man turned round from where he was pressing a glass against an optic containing whisky.

'Hallo, miss,' he said. 'They're all upstairs.'

They went into the passage that opened up from the door in the corner.

The passage was completely bare, save for a phone on the wall which had some taxi cab numbers stuck to it. There was a faint whiff of lavatory. At the end there were some linoleum-covered stairs that disappeared upstairs and out of sight. Scott thought of the hundreds of different meetings held in rooms over pubs. Marxism would probably not have got off the ground at all if publicans hadn't been so broad-minded.

The upstairs room was crowded.

Immediately Scott felt out of place in his suit. Most people there were casually dressed. Catherine was obviously well known and she left him almost immediately. 'Get me a drink,' she said as she pushed her way through the crowd.

Scott looked around. By the wall was a man standing with a tray, counting out change. Scott made his way over towards him. 'Can I have a beer,' he said and, turning hopelessly to where Catherine had gone, 'and another something,' straining to see her.

'Catherine drinks Campari, God help her,' said a voice next to him.

'OK,' said Scott, 'pint of beer and a Campari.' He gave the man with the tray some money and was given change.

'Are you a friend of Paul's?' said the man who had spoken.

'No,' said Scott, 'I don't think so.' That seemed rather flippant so he tried to make up for it. 'Who's Paul?'

'He's why we're here. Paul Evans was a poet, a friend of Catherine. Everybody here was a friend of his.'

Scott looked around the crowded room and for a moment wondered what it must be like to have so many friends.

'I'm sorry. What do you mean, was a friend,' he said.

'He died. Paul died in a mountaineering accident. He was walking in North Wales and he fell off a mountain.' The man stuck out his hand. 'My name is Lee Harwood.'

Scott nearly said 'I'm sorry' again, but managed to stop himself. 'Good to meet you.' He looked around. 'This Paul must have been a special guy.'

Before the man could answer there was a tapping noise and the room fell silent. At the same moment the barman with the tray appeared, carrying Scott's drinks. He scooped them up and set off across the room towards Catherine. 'You didn't tell me this was a memorial,' he said to her.

'Sshh,' she said, 'it'll do you good.' She turned and faced him. 'It'll do you some good to know there are other people in the world apart from you and your incisive colleagues.'

The man who had spoken to Scott stood up near an old piano and addressed the room.

'Paul died while climbing the Clogwyn y Person Arête on Crib-y-ddysgl.' Scott was surprised to hear Welsh spoken and he felt the language stirring within him. It was a long time since he had been home.

'If one is to reason with death – a desperate though possibly comforting measure –one could say it was the best way he would have wanted to die. In a way Paul lives on in us still.'

Scott remembered Auden, 'the poet became his admirers', and suddenly the atmosphere in the room began to sweep him out of himself, his argumentative, tense self.

He thought of Mr Ramus. By now he would be in reception at Wormwood Scrubs. He was newly convicted, so the prison staff would be moving him to a different block and, even though he had been there for the last three months awaiting trial, the prison would receive him as if they had never known of his existence. Stripped, checked for disease. Showered. Banged up.

Lee Harwood's voice continued. 'I sent Paul the story of St Philip Evans who was arrested as a Popish priest in 1678 and imprisoned in Cardiff Castle while the country was scoured for witnesses. Eventually, the story goes, a poor woman and a dwarf testified, whereupon the jury were instructed to find him guilty.'

Scott returned sharply to the present from the jury that had that afternoon put Mr Ramus down.

'While the saint was playing tennis he was told that his execution would take place the next day. This did not deter him from finishing the game.

'Our Paul would have liked that. Our Paul Evans was a great tennis player in St Anne's Well Gardens in Brighton and in Liverpool.'

Scott noticed the untouched beer in his hand. He had been whirled away to three different places in as many minutes. He took a gulp and looked around him.

The room was deathly silent and he saw that some of the people listening had tears in their eyes. Who was this Paul Evans?

Another speaker stood up. 'Trust you to die on a mountain, Paul. You never cared for ropes called "God" or "politics" or even "career" to hold you, but lived fully, somehow always on the edge of falling.'

Scott listened. It was refreshing to hear people making speeches about what they meant, not repeating instructions contained in some brief, what someone else told them to say. He noticed he was still holding the Campari he had bought Catherine. He looked around for her.

It was odd how he found himself diving into the event and then emerging from it, now part of it, now an outsider, looking at what was going on as though it were on a screen in front of him, then becoming an actor.

The speaker stopped and sat down to ragged applause. There was a pause and Scott saw Lee Harwood speaking to Catherine. She stood up on the platform by the piano.

'I've not been in this country long. But when I decided to come here one of the people I looked forward to meeting was Paul Evans. Carlyle Reedy had told me about him and I had seen some of his poems.'

She stopped and looked around her. Scott could see she was a good public speaker.

'Before I was even here I had got to know his family – Rhiannon, Catrin, Lucy – sweet Lucy – and the people around him. I had begun to see Taldir, the place he seemed to return to for growth but eventually from which' – she looked down and read from a page – 'his "follies banished him to exile that was permanent."

'I met him when I got here. But of course, I didn't know him as well as those of you who grew up with him.

But now the poet has become his admirers,
His words are modified in the guts of the living . . .

and I suppose my guts are entitled to modify Paul's words as much as anyone's.'

Scott was startled to hear the very poem he himself had brought to mind being repeated as though his own thoughts were being broadcast.

'I won't read anything that I've written. It would be presumptuous,' she said. 'Rather I want to read from *The Empty Hill*, an elegy Paul wrote for a hill farmer. For many of us the hill is even emptier than before.'

She picked up a thin yellow book and read. There was no ceremony; the words just came out.

' "Mourn you buzzards . . ." ' Scott felt the hairs on his neck rise as she started to speak.

'You'll hear his tractor rattle past no more
Nor watch him from the zenith, as you pour
Intensity of seeing on the hill . . .'

She read the whole poem. It became difficult to listen to it as a whole, but phrases went straight into him.

'You've left the mountain top.
The child's a woman. The world spins without stop.'

How would it be, Scott wondered, to work surrounded by beauty, or beautiful things? Or at the very least not surrounded by tension and anger and shabbiness, where every observation was a confrontation.

There were other places to be as well as a criminal court.

Chapter 7

What happened was this.

'Lawson's have got another case for you, sir. They want a conference as soon as they can.' Scott's clerk pointed at a set of papers he had put on Scott's desk. 'It's at the Elephant and Castle and it's going to start at the end of the month.'

Scott examined the pile gloomily. Even the prospect of a good case didn't cheer him up. He had been feeling low lately. All the fun had gone out of his work. He was finding he had to make an effort to do all the things that before had been easy, all the things that before he had wanted to do. Reading case papers was one of them, and getting ready for an argument was another. If your whole life is having arguments, then it doesn't do to want a bit of peace and quiet.

'You're doing well there, sir, their work's pourin' in.'

Again the thought didn't cheer Scott as it should have done. He had never in the past been hugely busy or even very successful so he should have been pleased.

Still, he thought, it's all money.

'I spoke to Tim Lawson. Apparently the client is a bit upset. He knows a bit about the system and he wants a good job done. His name is Hector.'

Scott sat down and started paying attention. 'Philip Cantor is prosecuting it. He left a message that he wants to speak to you about the case. Here's the number.'

Cantor again. Scott was still angry about the result of the last trial. That was some weeks ago but time still hadn't improved the way he felt.

As his clerk left the room Scott picked up the phone and dialled

Cantor's number. He had never directly disliked Philip Cantor, which was odd since there were plenty of people who did. And they had good reason. For a start he was the most arrogant man Scott knew and his way of speaking, a languid voice drawled out while examining his listener for any sign of stupidity, didn't help. Scott tried not to become one of his victims by saying as little to him out of court as possible.

'Cantor?' he said when he heard the phone answered. He could imagine him leaning back at his desk, casting his eyes to heaven as another annoyance surfaced. The man had a way of arching his fingers and his eyebrows at the same time.

'You wanted to speak to me about Hector. I think we are against each other.'

'Oh, it's you again, is it?' Cantor said. His sing-song voice echoed his name. Scott felt something stirring in him.

Cantor said, 'I have to tell you two things.' It wasn't his style to wait around and say hallo. 'First of all, we have got some material which we are going to ask the judge not to disclose to you.'

'Not again.'

'Yes, again.'

Scott could feel the edge in the man's voice.

'And secondly this . . . the first defendant . . .' Cantor broke off. 'Have you read the papers yet?'

'No,' said Scott. 'I was only given the brief a moment ago.'

'Oh.' Cantor managed to make even that sound like intellectual laziness. 'Well, there are four defendants and one of them . . .' Scott could hear the impatience in his voice. Cantor didn't like conveying mere information; it was too banal. 'One of them won't be at the trial. The court knows all about it. He can't be got there.'

'Why not?'

'When he got bail he went to Spain. Extradition will take at least nine months. So we'll go on with the trial without him.'

'Will we?'

'Yes.'

'We'll see,' said Scott, 'when I read the case papers.'

'We will anyway,' said Cantor, closing the conversation.

The conference with the client and the solicitor happened about a week later.

John Hector turned out to be a heavily built, friendly man. He had a large, jolly wife who let her husband get on with whatever he was doing, putting up with the occasional intrusion from the police. They had six children, one of whom had been arrested as well.

Hector was indignant.

'The police are trying to make me seem like some sort of pooftah, Mr Scott. What will my kids think of me?'

Scott said, 'Mr Hector, the man who has gone missing—'

He was interrupted. 'Mr Scott, that's obvious. He's working with the police. He's a bloody grass. Now these photographs . . .'

Hector wanted to talk about photographs that had been found at the flat where he was arrested. They were certainly pretty odd, made up mainly of young, fair-haired boys doing strenuous exercises. They reminded Scott of Leni Riefenstahl, except for the people with canes.

'Pervert,' said Hector, being rather more direct.

'Mr Hector,' said Scott, trying to get the conference on the right track, 'your defence is this: you say the flat wasn't yours. The police say it was. You say you had only gone there to see the man who was living there, to buy a car from him. You say none of this incriminating material in the flat was yours, none of the pills, none of the drugs, and especially not the photos.'

Scott added the last bit to calm him down. Hector wasn't a homosexual sadist – at least Scott thought it very unlikely. It was much more likely that Hector was the one who beat up the nonces in prison than it was that he was one himself.

Hector nodded. 'That's right. I'd never set eyes on the place before that morning. Nor had Tom.'

Tom was his son.

'Who's defending Tom?' Scott asked.

Tim Lawson checked through his file. 'Phil King is for Tom and John Plumstead is for the other man caught with them. Hallinans are doing it.' Hallinans were another firm of solicitors.

'We don't know who was acting for the chap who ran off. They let him escape if you ask me, Mr Scott.'

Tim Lawson was a sensible solicitor, not given to fantasy. If he thought it had happened then it could well be so.

Scott said, 'Now let's get down to the main points, Mr Hector. First. How do we prove that it wasn't your flat?'

It seemed an odd question to ask. Most people would think that proving that you lived in one place and not in another was a pretty easy thing to do. Certainly Hector thought so. 'But that's bloody nonsense, Mr Scott,' he said. 'They can't say that. I've lived in Braintree since I was a kid. My wife has lived there with me for twenty-four years. Our neighbours all know us.'

Scott knew different, and that it wouldn't be so easy.

He said, 'But Mr Hector, if you get up and say that, then the prosecutor will reply "of course" ' – he emphasised the 'of course' in the particularly annoying way in which he knew Cantor would do it – ' "of course you live in Braintree, Mr Hector, everybody agrees that. But you also have a flat in Highgate that no one knew about." '

He nearly added, 'Where you committed these vile offences,' but he decided to leave that till later. 'Once the prosecutor has said that, then you can prove you have a house in Braintree 'till you're blue in the face. It won't make the slightest difference. The jury will think you have two houses. All very suspicious.'

Hector stopped short. Scott saw a shadow pass over his face, as though for a moment he sensed the unreal world that lay ahead of him.

'But I've never even been to Highgate before, Mr Scott.'

'You know that, Mr Hector. Your wife may know that. But if the jury were willing to accept it directly from you, then they might as well take the short cut and accept your word that you didn't commit this offence.'

Again Hector was brought up short.

Scott both enjoyed and didn't enjoy this part of the job. He enjoyed it because he was working properly, using his experience, showing his client the difficulties. But he didn't enjoy it because it was a little like a bullfight. His knowledge of how a case was prosecuted made it easy for him to puzzle the client, who, after a while, would stand amazed, defeated by the tantalising cape, astonished that reality seemed to go out of the door when he stepped into Scott's room. This was often much more demoralising to a defendant than the allegation of the offence itself.

'Well, they've got to prove I do live in that flat,' he said.

'Yes,' said Scott, 'that's right. They have to prove it. The prosecution must prove everything. But sometimes it's enough for the Crown merely to assert something to have the jury turning and looking at the defendant and saying, "Well, that fits."'

'Part of the problem we always face, Mr Hector, is that everything you say is suspect. Juries are inclined to say, "Well, he *would* say that, wouldn't he?" The very act of denying something, even a true denial, looks suspicious.'

The classic example, though in a slightly different way, was the Yorkshire Ripper case. Everybody knew perfectly well that the man was loony, which was what the trial was about, and indeed right after the trial he was packed off to an asylum. But all the prosecution had to say was 'He's pretending' and they convicted him.

Scott continued out loud.

'The more you say you live in Braintree the more the prosecution will say, "It's all part of the plan. We found him in the flat with all this stuff. Of course" ' – he used the same tone of voice as before – ' "the very fact he's pretending he doesn't live there shows just how dishonest he is. He's wriggling." '

'But none of my clothes are there.'

' "All the cleverer the deception," they'll say. "He wouldn't leave any telltale signs, would he?" '

'They haven't found my fingerprints all over the place.'

'They don't dust for fingerprints to prove someone wasn't somewhere, only to prove that someone was.'

'But no one around there would have seen me.'

'You were careful not to be seen.'

'I didn't rent it.'

'You sent an accomplice.'

'In a different name from mine?'

'Of course.'

'Well, it's hopeless, then, isn't it?'

'No, Mr Hector, it isn't hopeless. It's only important to appreciate what we are up against. Now we know what not to say, we can begin to deal with it in the proper way. Now tell me this . . .'

Scott opened his notebook, picked up something to write with, and they started in earnest.

They were sitting in the conference rooms of Scott's chambers. It was a large room, a bit difficult for the observer to judge its age, until he was told it was built by Christopher Wren. It was so old that it predated all the usual styles.

Two large windows opened on to balconies that overlooked Fleet Street. On a summer's day it was possible to stand there and watch open-top tourist buses go past. Occasionally someone went out in a wig and gown, which provoked a frenzy of cameras on the top deck.

Tim Lawson had come along himself, which gave some indication of the gravity of the case. 'I've asked Catherine to come too,' he said, as she came into the room. 'She'll be with you throughout the trial and I want her to see it from the start.' As he looked at Scott his glasses flashed. He was one of the most conscientious solicitors Scott knew.

'I've already told Mr Hector that the evidence in the case is, I am afraid, very compelling.' He turned and smiled at Hector to make his remark less painful. 'Though Mr Hector doesn't agree with me.'

Hector took his cue: 'No, I do not, Mr Scott. The whole thing is rubbish. I was at this house to buy a car and suddenly half the district crime squad are coming out of the wall. Two of them came through the bloody window and we were two storeys up, for God's sake.'

Scott took Hector through the events of his arrest in detail. The story was that he had stopped to pick up his son Tom, and they had driven to Highgate.

Scott and Hector worked out the route he had taken. 'We had breakfast on the way,' he said. Scott looked at Tim Lawson, who immediately said, 'No, we've checked. A busy café, fifty or sixty customers between eight and ten in the morning, although if we had known what was alleged against Mr Hector on the day they were arrested we could have got there. As it was, we had to wait two months and no one at the café could remember a thing.'

The defence had had to wait nearly eight weeks before the prosecution told them enough of the allegation against Mr Hector to alert them to the importance of their movements in the morning. After that sort of delay no one was likely to remember whether Hector had been in the café on that day. By then even the flat where the offence was meant to have been committed had been relet and was occupied by new people.

It was a regular problem with defending.

As Scott went over the journey with him, Hector's portable phone rang. Everybody jumped. Hector pulled it out and started talking. It was clear that he was being sold something.

After the conversation had finished he said, 'Sorry about that, Mr Scott, I had to talk to him. I can't say where I am, can I? It reduces confidence.'

Scott said, 'Did you have that phone with you that morning, Mr Hector?'

'Yes,' he said, 'always do.'

'Did you phone anybody?'

Hector thought for a moment. 'Well, I rang the flat to say I was on my way and I think I rang Eric, my mate, for the same reason.'

It always amazed Scott how often evidence that helps a defendant lies, unnoticed, in the one place where you'd think it would always be noticed – in the defendant's head.

'Who did you speak to at the flat?'

'Whatsisname. The guy I was doing the deal with. The grass.'

'We're halfway there, Mr Hector. The call will be recorded on your bill. We need it, Tim.'

It had taken the criminal world, lawyers and defendants a little time to realise that mobile phones were as good as spy cameras. But now people were beginning to catch on. The police had been way ahead on that.

The conference wound on. It was very tiring, oddly, more tiring than court work. It was like a lengthy argument demanding huge amounts of energy.

After an hour and a half Tim Lawson had to go. 'Before you go, Tim, tell me more about the missing defendant.'

The solicitor sat down again. 'Well, they haven't given us all the details yet, but I heard his circumstances read out when he got bail. There didn't seem much known about him – he seemed to live rather a shadowy existence.

'My guess is that he's a confidence trickster. He looks like a doctor or a lawyer or something, but he had no contacts, no one who could help him make bail. I don't know how he eventually got out. I've written to the Crown asking for full details about him and for copies of all the documentation they have on him. He won't turn up, you can be sure of that. I have my doubts about how he got bail.'

Lawson left amidst lots of handshaking and Scott turned to the last matter he wanted to ask about.

'When you were interviewed, Mr Hector, you and your co-defendants each gave a different reason for being at the flat. Why was that?'

Hector looked sheepish. 'Well, Mr Scott, it was a dirty deal, wasn't it? I was going to buy his motor and it wasn't straight. Me and Eric were each putting up two grand and it was worth near sixteen if it was straight. Naturally I wasn't going to tell the police that, was I?'

Big lies have little lies upon their backs to bite 'em, Scott thought. He said, 'Can you prove that?'

'How can I, Mr Scott? No one is going to agree they were interested in buying a bent motor. But the car was there, it was downstairs. We saw it.'

There was nothing more to be said and Scott was starting to wind up when Hector said suddenly, 'Do you believe me?'

It was a surprising question from someone who knew the rules as well as Hector.

Scott tried to get his usual answer out. 'I try not to think about it, Mr Hector. I'm more use to you if I'm sceptical about everything.' But it sounded somehow lame and didn't work.

Catherine, who had sat saying nothing for the whole time, suddenly spoke.

'What Mr Scott is saying is not that he doesn't believe you, Mr Hector, but that it doesn't matter to him whether you are telling the truth or not. If he were prosecuting you, he would do just the same as he is doing now, only he would be doing it against you.'

Although it was precisely what he meant, Scott thought it sounded rather nasty when someone else said it.

But Hector didn't seem to mind. 'Thank you, Mr Scott,' he said, 'I'm well satisfied.'

Chapter 8

Catherine laughed at him. She could see that her interruption had annoyed him. 'Am I just meant to sit there and say nothing?' she said. 'Knowing you barristers, I probably am. At least he understood what I meant.'

Hector had gone, groping his way down the dark staircase towards Fleet Street where his wife was waiting.

Scott said, 'You put it a bit brutally, didn't you?'

'It is a bit brutal. Think how you enjoyed showing him how difficult it was to prove where he lived or didn't live. It was a sort of authorised bullying.'

If anyone else had said it Scott would have been upset.

He suddenly understood part of what had been happening to him. In the past few weeks he had missed Catherine's attitude to what he was doing. She didn't think it was important, or clever, or useful, or any of the things they assumed it was in the Temple. Perhaps it wasn't. Perhaps she was right and he was stuck in some sort of second-hand world, feeding off other people's lives. He had a horrible feeling she was right. He had enjoyed the way she saw everything as though it were new and needed to be justified. Years of good education had taught him to accept things too easily. He had missed her challenge.

He had been thinking of ringing Lawson's to get her number and had kept a vague lookout around the courts to see if he could see her.

He hadn't acknowledged to himself that he had been doing this, but when she came in with Lawson he began to realise what had been happening. Normally he tried to take no notice of his feelings – that way difficulties lie – but now he found it was good to be with her.

He said, 'What have you been doing since we last met?'

He looked at her critically. She was dressed in a long flowing black dress that showed her tanned shoulders; she was carrying a briefcase like a pianist's satchel and affecting – at least he assumed she was affecting them; he had never seen her wear glasses before – a pair of granny glasses.

The overall look was French, someone who might be in a photograph advertising up-market perfume. Quite out of place in the Temple.

'Oh, nothing.'

'I've not seen you wear glasses before,' he said.

'No.' She put her hand up to touch them, the action of someone not grown used to glasses yet. 'They're new. My eyes are slowing up. I'm getting older.' She sounded resentful.

He was astonished. 'Why, how old are you?'

'I'm thirty-two,' she said.

This time Scott's astonishment showed. 'You're not.'

'Why so surprised?' she said. 'I suppose in your world order I'm meant to be a little chit of a thing?'

This was such an accurate remark that he didn't even try to deny it.

'If I had a baby I would be what is called an elderly prima gravida.'

Again, she had anticipated precisely what he was thinking. She wasn't so much younger than he was. He had thought at least ten years separated them.

'Have you any immediate intention of becoming gravid?' he asked.

'It's always on the cards,' she said.

'Well, we'd better go and have a drink now before you have to give up alcohol for your child's sake.'

'Put it that way,' she said, 'and how can I refuse?'

It was nearly seven o'clock by now and the rooms were almost empty, though there was another conference going on next door. As they left his room Scott could see light under the door and they could hear a voice. 'Well, yes, you've been wrongly arrested, but in English law that doesn't make a bean of difference. Now in America we'd have had a helluva run, all the evidence thrown out.' It was John Plumstead.

'In America he'd have been shot while trying to escape,' Catherine said as they let themselves out on to the wooden staircase.

'What an amazing place,' she said in the dark. The ancient staircase wound around a central pillar, down past great black doors on each floor. Even the ironwork was hundreds of years old. It was pleasing to see something so old being used, not being prettified into an imitation of itself.

'Imagine living here,' he said. 'There was a time when the whole place had a village atmosphere, and it's still a little bit like that on Sundays. If you come here then you can see hugely old judges tottering about. Someone whose job included sentencing people to death.'

They reached the bottom of the staircase and paused under the windows jutting out over Middle Temple Lane. 'I once came down here and bumped into the Lord Chief Justice scurrying down from the Law Courts carrying a huge bunch of flowers. It was rather pleasing. There wasn't a policeman in sight.'

They stepped out into Fleet Street and joined the remains of the rush hour. He said, 'Where shall we go? Let's go somewhere different for a change, not El Vino's.'

For a moment they walked in silence. 'You left the reading without saying goodbye,' she said.

'No. It was you. You disappeared.'

'I didn't.'

'Well, you got lost in the crowd, then. I couldn't find you so I went.'

More silence.

'Did you enjoy it?'

'Yes, it was astonishing. The trouble is I wouldn't know how to find something like it again. Where do they happen?'

'Easy,' she said. 'Read the noticeboard in the Poetry Society.'

They went past the Printer's Pie pub and turned right into the lane that led past St Bride's, the printers' church. 'It won't be long before people ask why this is called the printers' church?' he said.

'Why is it called the printers' church?'

'Because of Fleet Street. It used to be full of newspapers. They're all gone now, though the *Beano* is still published across the road.'

'What's the *Beano*? You're forgetting I'm a foreigner.'

The moment they had turned off Fleet Street he sensed again the detachment from the city that he felt when turning into the Temple. An alleyway led down the side of the church past an old pub where the drinkers spilled out on to the path. There wasn't much space to squeeze past and the men with their pints of beer were not going to move for her so he went first, turning slightly and putting his hand on her back to help her through the gap.

'You're meant to ask permission before you touch me,' she said. Her back was strong and he could feel her moving beneath her clothes. 'Where

I come from permission is required for each of the seven stages of physical contact. "Y'all just ask now," ' she said in a Southern accent.

She was laughing at him.

He saw the men with the drinks in their hands swivel round to watch her progress down the lane. It seemed to him that she was walking with a little more sway in her hips. She knew she was being watched. They went down some steps and into the lane ten feet beneath them, turning one way and then the other into a covered arcade.

For a moment they stopped outside the Clarke-Hall bookshop. 'This is where all the review copies end up,' he said. 'You can buy second hand here before you can buy new in other places. Apparently this whole area was full of bookshops years ago and now this is all that's left of it – along with the market stalls up the Farringdon Road.'

They stared at a biography of Conrad.

'How do I formulate this request for permission?' he said to her reflection in the window.

'Ah, that's for you to decide. It's a man's world,' she said.

They turned away and he led her immediately into a narrow staircase that opened straight off the arcade. There was no sign or notice saying where they were going. The walls of the stairs were lined with the front pages of elderly newspapers.

Catherine stopped before one that reported 'Bishop's attack upon the King'. She saw the name Mrs Simpson under a dark, almost black photograph. It wasn't possible to say whether the photograph was of the King, the bishop or Mrs Simpson.

'This place was started for the sub-editors of *The Times*. Their offices were just across the road then. They were too brainy to sit in the pubs with ordinary journalists.' He pushed at a door. 'And it's just tottered on ever since.'

The door opened on to another short flight of stairs.

'John Buchan used to come here. Do you know who he was? Look, there's a photograph of him.' He added, 'I don't suppose John Buchan figures very large in America.'

She stopped and looked at him. 'Thirty-nine steps. Did I guess right? We just went up thirty-nine steps?'

'Good God,' he said, 'you're amazing. Permission to push you upstairs?' This time he felt her body respond to his touch.

They went up into a large room, clearly taking up the whole of the top floor of the building. Catherine heard a low buzz of conversation.

To one side there were two old oak refectory tables, lit along their length by lamps whose light was reflected in patterns from the polished wood. On the other side of the room, divided by a strip of red carpet and set underneath a high studio window, there were round-backed chairs at small tables, each, again, with its own dark green reading lamp.

Above the tables, the façade of St Bride's Church rose, vertiginous, into the evening sky. Catherine paused. From where she stood she couldn't tell whether it was the real thing or a painting.

At the back of the room was a mahogany bar. To the side there was a wall covered in brass pegs. Each peg had a number beneath it engraved on an ivory disc.

Catherine stood at the top of the stairs and looked. On the walls there were more newspaper front pages, blue-crayoned cartoons, and above, at the top of the stairs, there were bookshelves. As her eyes became more accustomed to the darkness she could see that the upper parts of the rooms were all lined with bookshelves.

'What is this place?' she said.

'It's a club,' he said. 'It hasn't got a name. It's just called the Club, or Mary's.'

They moved over to the bar. Behind it sat a large woman on a tall stool, occasionally knitting, but more often just looking out into the room. She greeted Scott by name, and welcomed Catherine. Then she said, 'What will you have?'

Scott turned to Catherine and said, 'Bloody Mary is the best bet at this time. If we eat perhaps we can have some wine later.'

The woman behind the bar put her head back and shouted, 'Kenneth, another bucket.'

They sat down under the large window. Catherine could see that the view outside had tricked her. It was a painting, but a painting on the wall opposite the window fifteen feet away.

'It's a mural,' said Scott. 'There's a similar thing outside John Betjeman's old house in Smithfield. His upstairs window looked out on to a blank wall and years ago someone painted a picture there to give a view. A sailor returning home to his widowed mother, I think it was.'

'It's amazing,' said Catherine. She could see the detail now, down to the pigeons roosting in the belfry.

'The facing wall, the one we're sitting behind, is covered with white glazed tiles which reflect the light on to the picture so that even the shadows seem to change. Once I was sitting here and a sunset was reflected on to it. The whole thing became rose red.'

Kenneth was coming over to them.

'Rex Whistler painted it. He was a member here.'

The bucket containing crushed ice arrived. A glass jug was buried in it.

'Rex Whistler,' she said. 'What a great name.'

'It's a hands-in-your-pockets sort of name. It's a leaning-on-a-balcony-viewing-the-promenade sort of name,' he said. 'I thought your speech at the poetry meeting was great.'

She was silent for a moment, thinking. Then she said, 'Paul Evans was a lovely man, a free man. He had no use for places like this. Then again he would have liked the books.'

'What do you think of Mr Hector?' he asked.

'It's just like that Ramus case. Same police officers, same situation.'

For a moment Scott couldn't remember the names. It had been two months ago and he had no long-term memory for cases.

'Ramus, Ramus.' He repeated the name, trying to get a hook on the memory.

'Come on, Mr Wonderful,' she said. 'Ramus – he was caught in the yard receiving stolen goods. You managed to get him convicted. The point is that Charlton was the police officer in that case too.'

'Oh yes.' It all came back to him in a heap. 'I knew I'd been against Cantor recently but I didn't remember the other names. Not Charlton? Was he in it?'

'Cantor prosecuted it, and he's prosecuting this one too. Isn't that odd?'

'No, not so odd.'

'I've compared the papers. A lot of the police officers are the same. And it happens to be the same prosecuting barrister doing it.'

'It's just a coincidence,' he said. 'The Crown Prosecution Service go to the same sort of chambers all the time. Some barristers they own completely, since they do exactly what they are told to do. Cantor is one of those.'

They drank the Bloody Mary.

'He'd die before admitting it, though,' said Scott.

The drink was extremely strong. Scott said, 'Kenneth puts celery in, which is why it's so special.'

They looked at each other. She gazed back at him and he began to realise again just how beautiful she was.

'Why is it called hitting on someone?' he asked her. 'In that film about the psychopath who eats people and has to wear a mask to stop him, this girl, this woman actress who is the FBI agent, meets two guys in a basement somewhere and one asks her out to dinner. And she says, "Are you hitting on me?" Why's it called hitting on someone?'

'Because that's what it feels like.'

'Why should it feel so bad?'

'It doesn't if you want to be hit on. But then of course the guy's not hitting on you.'

'If he manages to avoid doing the hitting-on thing, does he still have to go through the seven stages of permission?'

'Oh yes. That's mandatory,' she said. 'If he thinks he can get that far.'

'We need Margaret Mead in to work all this out.'

'Was she a member here too?'

The Bloody Mary was beginning to work on them and the tension of the conference was disappearing.

Scott watched Catherine and wondered about her. For a moment she refused to meet his eye, and then she looked at him directly. They said nothing, then he realised that all the time they had been talking together they had in fact been talking about something else. Every word was electric.

'It's the same defence,' Catherine said. 'Hector is running the same defence as Ramus. He says he was set up as well. The routine is too similar to be a coincidence.'

'I thought you said Ramus was obviously guilty.' He remembered the case now.

'Of course he was,' she said. 'He specialises in receiving stolen property. That's why he was set up. That's the whole point. What's the point in setting up an innocent person? It's guilty people who are wrongly convicted. For a start no one's going to believe Mr Ramus when he denies it, are they?'

'You didn't.'

'No, no more did you.'

'That's the bit you explained to Mr Hector so gently. I don't have to believe my clients. I don't think about it.'

'That really is a bunch of bull,' she said. 'You can't not think about it. Of course somebody has to defend people knowing that they are probably guilty. But in the end it's bad for you, spending energy and emotion on something that only has an intellectual justification. It's misusing a part of you that matters. In the end it'll wither you, it'll dry you up.'

She challenged him. This was the question he would not face.

'Just imagine doing something you could be wholehearted about, no need for any half-arsed intellectual justification – writing a book or painting. Painting that picture, for instance.'

They looked at the picture above them.

'It wouldn't be so bad if you were wildly ambitious, like that Sally woman. People like her get their satisfaction from some received idea of what success is. That's why she's like she is, a sort of professional doll. But you're not.'

The picture had gone grey-green in the early evening London light. Scott could see where the painter had reproduced the detail and texture of the stonework.

He didn't reply.

'What you do is an expense of spirit in a waste of shame.'

Silence.

'Speaking frankly,' she said.

Chapter 9

Nineteen seventy-two. Summer. A young man had been sitting on the steps of Eros in Piccadilly playing a guitar and selling Mandrax.

Paul Gregory imagined the scene as he read about it; he would have had long hair, one of those cheesecloth shirts, sandals? – did hippies wear sandals? – and those bell-bottomed trousers. Loon pants, they were called. It was all curiously innocent. He read the whole report and then flicked through the papers pinned to the file.

The young man had been arrested for possessing a controlled drug with intent to supply, and the trial had ended with a sentence of imprisonment at the Inner London Crown Court, Judge McLeay presiding, six months but suspended, as all first convictions had to be then. Gregory remembered his criminology. It was those suspended sentences which, instead of reducing the prison population, set it off on its explosive rise. The law of unintended consequences operating.

How old would the young man be now? Nineteen then, over twenty years ago, middle-aged now. Mandrax. Whatever happened to that?

Well, there was nothing unusual about the case. It was quite small, insignificant really. A police officer, off duty, PC Charlton, spoke to a man sitting on the steps in Piccadilly, then arrested him, searched him round the back of Boots the Chemist and found some individually wrapped tablets of Mandrax hidden in a bag. It was just a drugs bust. The officer found the guy by chance.

Gregory noted the dates and the names, jotted down the main facts of the story and stood up to get the next file. If there was a pattern here he was going to have to read all the files before he found it.

* * *

He looked out of the window at some cows chewing. He hadn't even been told what this investigation was all about. He chose another file at random. It involved a police raid on a squat. At the back of the file there were a number of press clippings, unusual for an official file. 'Police go commuting in dawn raid on hippy drugs den', *News of the World*, January 1973.

Forty policemen, 'commuter coppers' the newspaper called them, using a train to get close to a squat in Camden Town unnoticed, had burst their way into the backs of a group of houses built beside the track. There was a photograph of policemen streaming down a railway embankment. Someone had made some money telling the press, so that wasn't new.

He turned to the front of the file and read the reports. Thirty people arrested, sixteen prosecuted for possession of drugs, six prosecuted as a group for supplying drugs, eight released without charge. It wasn't serious. The drugs were cannabis and the amounts were very small, though the six suppliers had been charged together as conspirators.

Again there seemed to be nothing unusual about the case. He was beginning to wonder whether he would ever work out what he was looking for, let alone whether he would find it.

The court papers had witness statements from various police officers, and as he read them a remark clicked in his mind. Two policemen arresting a man heard him say, 'Nice one, boys. Who gave you the phone call?' Wasn't that the same as the remark made by the hippy on the steps of Eros in Piccadilly? He checked with the first file. Yes it was, or very nearly.

Who were the officers in charge? Gregory checked: DS Croke in the drug raid, PC Charlton in the first. Charlton was a witness in the second case so here was a connection already. There was a long interview with the man singled out as a ringleader about money found in his room, stuffed in a large velvet cushion. The man was saying it was the 'rent' he had taken from the squatters. The police suggested it was the profits of drug dealing.

He stood at the window. This was different from his normal investigations – they started after a crime was discovered. But in all these cases the police knew in advance what was going on. The defendants in the Piccadilly trial and in the squatter case had each said something like 'Who told you?'. He checked through the notes of all the cases he had – he had read about fifteen now. He was right.

There were at least three stolen-goods cases where the police were waiting in the yard, two drugs raids, a robbery in a post office and a number of others. The police had been ready and waiting, or when they busted the place knew exactly what to look for and where to look. In the raid on the Radical Club they had gone straight to the correct bedrooms.

Arranged in advance. What was happening here?

Two days later he had read everything and he was sure. He phoned Arlot. 'I need some more documents,' he said. 'Who do I ask?'

Arlot didn't answer directly but replied with a question. 'What documents particularly.'

The career records of an Inspector Charlton.'

'Anything else?'

'Access to police standing regulations, not the up-to-date regulations, though I'd like to see them for comparison. The regulations for the seventies and eighties – regulations dealing with the use of informers.'

Arlot was silent. Gregory immediately felt he had scored a hit.

'Anything else?'

'Yes. A transcript of one of the trials, and also' – here he was being very hopeful –'what Charlton is working on now.'

'We'll have to talk about that. You can have the Charlton records now, also the old informer rules – that's easy as there were only about three. The rest you'll have to wait for.'

Gregory was pleased. If the documents he wanted were ready for him and didn't have to be dug out of some cellar, then he must be on the right track.

The police raid at the Radical Club in late 1973 didn't stay in the newspaper headlines very long. This wasn't surprising. Even to the press the club no longer provided a specific and easily presentable idea of England, as did the Athenaeum, White's or the Jockey Club. It had become second rate.

The only real interest for the press was that a Conservative Party parliamentary candidate named Davenport pleaded guilty to an offence involving a young man. But he was only a candidate and was soon forgotten.

The police had arrived at the club in the early hours of the morning and had found Davenport in one of the guest bedrooms. He was with a young rent-boy who, three hours earlier, had been leaning on the meat rack at

Piccadilly in a line of young male prostitutes, contemplating another hungry, lonely night.

The boy, Peter Snaith, said that he had been brought to the club in a taxi after he had received a note summoning him. He had made three pounds out of Davenport, more than he normally charged, mainly, he said, because of the smartness of the surroundings.

He was quite clear that he hadn't been hurt. This was harmless fun compared with what he would normally be asked to do for that money. 'But then,' he remarked in an echo of Victorian times when clubs were clubs, 'Mr Davenport was a gentleman.'

The doctor confirmed Snaith's story. He found a flaccid rectal passage, signifying regular anal intercourse, and he confirmed that the boy's explanation that he was a male prostitute was likely to be true.

Charlton had some trouble taking the boy's statement about what had happened, and he ended up with three versions.

In the first he got the short account, the one that destroyed Basil Davenport's political career, the one that was used in court. The other two were much more complicated and extensive. This was not the only time Snaith had been to the club.

There was another member who organised everything and the boy gave a list of names and titles of those involved. Charlton chose which statement he wanted to use. The others he left sealed in the file.

They had worked out how to manage the whole investigation when he and Eddie had originally planned it, sitting over scrumbled eggs in the New Vogue Café. This one was going to be different from their usual set-ups – small drug dealers or friends who had bought whatever Eddie could steal. This was altogether more important.

'Look,' said Eddie, 'Jennings's other friend, not Davenport, the one with odd tastes, he's political too, he's actually an MP or a judge or something. If he's arrested or even mentioned then the whole thing will be out of your hands.'

Eddie had, in the time he had spent in London, begun to see the whole structure of power. 'They won't let you handle it. You just won't be senior enough.

'But if we keep it limited then not only will it be your arrest to deal with but you'll have another option: you'll be deciding who is kept in and who is kept out. You'll get Jennings on your side. He'll be grateful.

'Let him know that you could have hurt him but didn't, and you'll have a friend, a friend in the Home Office . . . well, it's obvious. Who's your ultimate boss? The Home Secretary. What could be more valuable?'

Eddie stopped for a second, then he said, 'Scratching backs is a better way of getting on than licking arses. Jennings is a château-bottled shit. He'll do anything to get out of it.'

Charlton looked startled. 'What?' he said. 'A château-bottled shit? What a great expression.'

Eddie knew he had him.

'I'm delivering him to you on a silver salver, nicely warmed to room temperature, if you want him.'

'A château-bottled shit,' repeated Charlton. 'That's nice.'

The Radical Club raid intrigued Gregory and he kept returning to the file. It was the case that made Charlton, got him away from the small cases he was doing as a new detective.

It was fully reported in Charlton's career file. His interviewing technique was recommended. Getting the young male prostitute to co-operate had not been easy and his supervising officer used the case as the basis for advising that Charlton should receive a formal commendation.

But what interested Gregory was the outside influence that subsequently became involved in Charlton's advance. Attached to his yearly service summary there was a reference to an internal memo from the Home Office commending his 'mature discretion and intelligence' in dealing with the matter of the Crown v. Davenport. Amazingly the document was still in the file. Gregory marvelled at the total efficiency of police personnel. The care with which they watched their men spoke of great anxiety.

When he returned to the original case papers with the information from Charlton's career, Gregory went through it again in detail.

Davenport had not been harshly dealt with, quite the opposite. The judge had noted the fact that there was no element of corruption involved in the case. The young boy had as good as admitted (Gregory smiled – he had admitted it, for heaven's sake) being experienced in these matters, and there did not seem to the judge to be any element of 'beastliness' in the offence beyond what was specifically charged.

He conditionally discharged Davenport. That wouldn't happen nowadays, Gregory thought.

The file also contained an envelope attached to the inner sleeve with a treasury tag. On its outside there were a series of attendance notes signed by the police solicitors. He examined the envelope. It was sealed and dated over the sealed flap with the same date as the initial prosecution report form. Despite the solicitors' notes it did not ever appear to have been opened. It seemed quite likely that nobody else had ever looked at it since Charlton had finished putting the whole file together. No one else had needed to.

Gregory slit the envelope open before worrying about whether he should or not. He had been asked to investigate this series of cases and he was going to do so.

It contained two dockets. One marked 'Informant file: Tredegar'. The other marked 'Undisclosed material'.

Gregory turned to the informant file. It contained little more than a note that valuable and, as it turned out, completely reliable information had been given. There was also an order for payment, and Gregory was astonished at the amount of money.

The other docket contained two long statements from the rent-boy, setting out in detail what had gone on in the club.

Gregory had been at Customs long enough to see some of the magazines people brought into the country, but the inventiveness of the members of the Radical Club – particularly on the snooker table – surprised even him. It was also clear that it wasn't just the one boy who had been providing services to club members and friends.

Throughout the second statement the boy had talked about the room next door to the one where he was found. How he had been hearing screams. How Davenport had taken no notice and how the screams had not long stopped before the police came. Gregory couldn't remember any of this. He checked the original witness statements. He was right. There had been no mention of it at all.

He checked the general statements. It was clear that there were at least two other guest rooms in this part of the club and both had been entered by the police, but there was no mention of what was found there. Obviously there were others involved, perhaps even arrested that night. Who were they? What had they been doing?

He kept checking. At that time there was no duty to keep lists of people arrested in a particular case as there was now. Then the officer in charge could do almost what he wanted, he need keep no records at all. It was extraordinary that such a lack of control could have continued so long. The judges were right when they used to say that they weren't there to discipline the police; one thing was certain, they didn't.

Gregory searched the file to see if there was any clue. Property – perhaps it would be in the property records. Gregory looked for the property sheets. The return of property to men who had been arrested was one thing that was always recorded.

Eventually he found it, clipped to another sheet.

Yes, there were five other names, but Gregory could hardly make the signatures out. Andrew Smith was one – that would be the head porter. He had been in the two long statements Snaith made. Then Jennings, and another two that looked like Walters and Morgan.

There was another signature he couldn't read at all. The name looked deliberately obscured to him. But the property collected for that name was rather special. Yellow metal watch and chain – that meant gold – white metal propelling pencil and – this was rather unusual – a gold daffodil lapel badge and a silver-topped cane. And some money, a lot of money, four hundred pounds.

There was no clue as to who it was. But he must have been a customer. Gregory leafed through the papers and found a record from a police surgeon. Someone had been taken to hospital. He wondered what the surgeon's report would have shown. Homosexual sadism? It seemed very likely.

He had just discovered the 'mature discretion' that the Home Office had so readily commended in the young police officer.

Arlot stepped into Paul Gregory's office and said, 'Look, it's about time you met some of the other people who work here.'

That was entirely true. Gregory hadn't met any of the others in the house since his first day. He'd met Arlot the morning he came and that was a total surprise. He hadn't known why he had been sent for; all he was told was that there had been a request that he should work outside Customs on a specific assignment.

When he saw Arlot, even bigger than when he had met him before, he realised who had sent for him, but even then Arlot didn't tell him why. He only showed him a bundle of files and asked him to form an opinion.

'Let's walk to the pub across the fields and have a drink.'

They set out across the wet grass. It was warm for February but still wet and a little depressing. Arlot said, 'This is Tristan, but we don't tease him about his name. He organises travel if you need it. Tony is researching and here's Sally, Sally Donne. She gets them down, you might say. Advising us on prosecutions.'

Gregory acknowledged the others and waited, quite interested to hear how he would be introduced. Perhaps that would tell him what he was doing there.

But Arlot didn't say who he was. Perhaps they knew already.

Then Arlot confirmed what Gregory thought was happening. He said, 'You know, part of what we do is important, and part of it is not. Part of it is helpful, part of it is not. If you demonstrate, by prosecuting policemen, that police investigations are unreliable, then you reduce the confidence of the public in the courts and the police. That's unhelpful.'

They walked on. Gregory stepped on a piece of turf that was more than usually squishy. He followed the damp line with his eyes and realised that where he had stepped was the beginning of the stream that flowed out of the field at the other end.

Arlot carried on talking. 'Innocent people are not usually wrongly convicted; it's guilty people as are wrongly convicted. There's no need to convict innocent people. And as for guilty people, it's only ever a question of what they're guilty of.'

They walked on past the placid cows, through the meadow.

'I don't see anything wrong with that,' said Arlot. 'The public are like these cows, they don't want too much excitement. The only excitement most people enjoy is righteous indignation. That's the simplest feeling there is. The crappy newspapers exist on it, it's a kind of wanking. You're just exciting yourself.'

On the other side of the hedge a pub squatted complacently behind its neat lawn. There was a cartwheel with out-of-season geraniums hanging from it near the door.

'On the other hand the helpful part is that this work employs happy bands of people like us,' said Arlot. They stepped into the cool bar. 'Three pints please, gin for Sally, and a shandy for Tristan. In separate glasses, please.' He leaned on the bar, his huge forehead only inches from a Toby mug hanging on a rafter. They were the only customers.

'I'll tell you this for free,' Arlot said. 'Justice is a seamless robe.' They moved to one of the tables by the window. 'By which I mean you can't unpick it. What works first time is what it is.'

He looked round at them.

'And that means,' he explained, 'a system which brings together in the same trial' – he counted on his fingers – 'an honest policeman, a competent lawyer and a jury that listens – all in the same trial, mind you – is about as much as you can ever hope for. And most of the time you won't get that.

'Well, what do you say, Mr Gregory?' He became formal.

This was the first time they had met since Gregory asked about the police records and Gregory decided he wasn't about to answer Arlot's question. Instead he said, 'I have to go to France to see someone.'

He wanted to see Davenport.

'Well, Tristan will fix that.'

Other than that Arlot showed no interest in Gregory's request.

He said, 'Talking of travelling, when I started in the Metropolitan Police we used to be able to travel anywhere on London Transport by showing a warrant card. Don't know if you still can.

'We got it on condition we kept a watch out while on the tube. Well, one day I saw Nick the Hook on the Northern Line. He was standing right by me. This was in the days before the South Americans arrived and men still carried their wallets in their back pockets. Funny business. Still, there you are.

'I saw the Hook put his hand out through the slit in his working coat. He wasn't more than six inches from me.

'I had some of the old-fashioned handcuffs with me and when he stuck his hand out . . .' Arlot interrupted himself. 'Now to understand this story you have to know that in order to pick pockets properly the dipper has to have a distraction, a cigarette burn in the evening paper, for instance, or one chap I knew used to pull people's toupees sideways. Nick the Hook stuck his hand out and he's purposely not watching his hand but distracting the mark with the other one. I put the handcuffs on it, and cuffed the other end to one of the grab-rails.

'Then I got off and he had to carry on to Arnos Grove or somewhere. Maybe he's still there.'

He paused. 'I don't like people who are pickpocketed. It shows a lack of awareness. They are not aware of what is going on around them. Like those people who stand in front of you, and you know, you just know, they're going to step back on your foot. And you're right, they do. Makes me sick.'

* * *

91

Finding where Davenport lived hadn't been easy at first, though in the end, when Gregory found out how to do it, it was simple enough. The difficulty had been working out how. He had tried every way he could think of until he remembered that in the case papers there was a document setting out Davenport's occupation, his school and his college at Cambridge.

It was the college which knew where he was. Their fundraisers knew all the addresses. Davenport's was near Grasse.

Gregory flew to Nice, then he took a taxi to Grasse.

They had spoken on the phone and Davenport had agreed to see him, oddly without asking why.

It was the first time Gregory had been that far south. He immediately understood the pictures on the wall in his room at the top of his house – they were so full of light that distance seemed destroyed. And here it was before him. The landscape seemed to rise up, flat as though painted on a backdrop. The cypress trees writhed with colour.

He and Davenport sat on a terrace looking down at the hills above the Mediterranean and, as he listened, Gregory understood why Davenport had agreed to see him so easily. He was lonely.

'You know,' Davenport said, 'when I was a managing director I used to hear the unions telling their members not to sell their jobs, and I used to think, What the fuck are they on about? Look at the money we're offering. In the end friends of mine were buying back jobs from the workforce for thirty-five thousand pounds a time. That was more money than some of those buggers – even skilled machinists, mind you – had seen in their lifetime.

'Of course, now I know the unions were right.' He poured Gregory more of the red drink – 'Istra Bitter, rather special' – and carried on talking. Gregory had no need to say anything.

'I sold my job for twelve and a half million, and then I had to come and live here in order to keep it from the taxman. So now I'm bored sodding stiff. So's she.'

He gestured to a woman whom Gregory had assumed was his wife, tanned to a leathery copper colour, sitting at the other side of the pool. She had paid not the slightest attention to Gregory.

'It's amazing how right the unions turned out to be. While everyone else was talking about a soft landing at the end of the eighties, these Labour chappies were saying that the whole economic miracle was like a hysterical pregnancy, just blown up by a need to believe.

'And they were right. Unbelievable. They were all right. I made a huge pile of money out of that bloody woman Thatcher – talk about hysterical pregnancies, she was the midwife and I know it. The whole thing was a con trick. I met her once. She was as mad at a hatter.

'I mean, she was the kind of person, if she'd come into your drawing room, you'd start edging her out, giving her a drink and talking about the weather to keep her calm.

'And the bunch that's taken over from her now. I knew a lot of them. I was at Cambridge with them. I ran with them for a while. You really had to see what they were like then to appreciate just what wankers they are.'

He looked at Gregory. 'What do you want to see me about?'

He was a large, fat man who wheezed as he spoke. He continually wiped sweat from his forehead, and his eyes, set deep in the folds of flesh on his face, danced with laughter. He was clearly no fool. Gregory saw no point in pretending, or leading up the matter slowly. 'It's about the Radical Club,' he said.

'I thought so,' said Davenport. 'I knew one day someone would come to see me. But why you? You're Customs. Why are you interested?'

'Customs do more than you'd think. We've got an interest.'

'Well, what do you want to know? I'm not embarrassed. One of the advantages of a good education is you're prepared to take whatever sex is offered you.'

'I want to know who the other people were. And why you? Why did they only pursue you?'

'Because I wasn't prepared to buy my way out of it. I was offered, but I didn't want it. Oddly enough it was one of the best things that ever happened to me. I got away from the bunch and I made a million.

'You know, eighteen months after all that business I was the first person to send a television camera down a sewer, or at least the first person to do it properly. We revolutionised sewer work. And to think I might have been stuck with that bunch. Dining clubs. Lord North Street. The 1974 intake. Desperately looking for a job in the City. Bloody hell.'

Gregory was not following him, and his look showed it.

'We were all politicos. You didn't know? Well, the whole thing was in the papers.'

It hadn't occurred to Gregory to look at the newspapers.

'Was it?' he said lamely.

'Yes. Not everything, of course, only my name, no one else's. But if you read it carefully you could see there must have been others – politics, of course. You get all sorts of strange people in politics.'

'Who was Jennings?'

'He was someone I ran with then. For heaven's sake, you must know him, Sir Butler Jennings, famous backbench rentaquote – he wants to hang everybody. Nasty little runt. He's the chairman of some committee. He bought the police off because otherwise his political career was ruined.'

'I don't know all the names.'

'Jennings was a member of the Radical Club. There was the head porter, Andrew something, a porter boy – he used to hire himself out – called Edward. They all got nicked. Someone told the police, and when everyone stopped twisting only I got done.

'Buying the police off was perfectly common then. A detective sergeant was about the most powerful man in London at that time. Look at that Croke character. He got away with it for years. He used to share the reward money. The only people who didn't know what was going on were the judges. But then they are always the last to know things.'

'Is this what you meant when you said you thought someone would come to see you eventually?'

'Yes,' said Davenport. He got up to fetch another drink. Gregory was already feeling tired from the heat and the travel, and the alcohol was beginning to slow him down.

'Look,' Davenport said, 'where are you staying tonight? My wife is going out to dinner with some woman down the road and I'm heading for La Tourette. Want to come? Damn good food, better than what you can get in London. I can tell you the whole story.'

Chapter 10

Elephant and Castle Crown Court

R v. Hector and Others

Coram: H H J Scribner

Philip Cantor, Prosecuting
Jeremy Scott, Defending
Philip King, Defending
John Plumstead, Defending

Pleas: Not guilty (All to everything)

Day 1

Cantor was talking to defence counsel.

'I have to tell you that I have already been to see the judge and he has agreed to the prosecution's application to deny you certain relevant information we have . . .' He paused, searching for the right word.

'He's letting you keep it secret,' said Scott.

'Yes,' said Cantor.

'What kind of information?'

'I am not at liberty to tell you.'

'Did he read everything that you want to keep from us?'

'I can't tell you that.'

'How do we know that he has seen everything you want to keep secret?'

Cantor looked at Scott. He was beginning to get annoyed. Scott was suggesting that he himself had kept something back from the judge.

He was about to lose his temper when John Plumstead intervened, soothing the atmosphere. 'Come on, Philip, we know that Scribner sometimes doesn't even look at what is shown him.'

'I can't say anything about what happened when I saw him,' said Cantor.

'That means he didn't,' said Scott. 'You know Scribner. He probably didn't look at a thing.'

Cantor said, 'I've told you everything I'm bound to tell you and I'm not taking this.' He turned away.

'What was that all about?' asked Catherine.

'Undisclosed material,' said Scott. 'The prosecution are bound to show us all the material they have that is relevant to the case, even if it helps to acquit the defendant. But some things they can keep secret. The identity of an informer, for instance, or the information an informer has given to the police.'

'Who decides what the police have to reveal?'

'That's the point. The prosecution used to make the decision and, naturally, that led to abuse. Now it's the judge. But that means he has to see all the material. Some judges just ask prosecuting counsel's opinion and then follow it without bothering to read the papers – so we're back to where we started.'

Catherine thought for a moment and then she said, 'You mean the prosecutor gets to go in and see the judge without anyone else present? Without the defence being there? That can't be right.'

'That's the problem, but in this country there's a tradition of trusting authority. We're waking up, though.'

'Who's to say what the prosecutor's telling the judge?'

'Exactly. You can't know.'

'He could say anything.'

'Knowing Cantor he probably did. And knowing Scribner he probably believed it.'

Catherine changed the subject.

'You told me that the mixture of Cantor and Charlton in this case was just a coincidence. Now we end up with the same judge as last time. He's not even a judge from London. Don't tell me that's a coincidence too.'

'It has to be,' said Scott. 'It wouldn't be possible to manipulate the court lists.'

'Why not?'

'It would be just too complicated.'

'Saying it's too complicated is another way of saying you trust them. Who says it's too complicated? Someone has to choose a judge to hear a case.'

'Look . . .' Scott stood up as he heard the tannoy announcing that their court was ready. 'We've got enough problems defending this case without getting involved in conspiracy theories as well.' He lifted his hands. 'Enough already.'

'That's not right. You don't say it like that. You didn't grow up with it. It's like this . . . Enough, already,' she said.

'All parties in the case of Hector and others please go to Court Two.' The public address system repeated the summons as Scott and Catherine went down in the lift.

'No hurry, no hurry,' said Scott. 'They've kept us waiting till nearly lunchtime and now they want us to rush.'

The lift arrived at the ground floor with a bump and the doors opened on to the main entrance hall of the court. It was full and the atmosphere was steaming slightly as people shook the rain off their clothing. Scott pushed his way through the crowd near the door to court number two. As he did so he put his finger to his lips. 'Don't say anything,' he whispered. 'This lot's probably our jury panel.'

They reached the entrance and, opening the first door, found themselves in a small passage leading to the door of the court itself. An usher stood by the court door holding it slightly open, peering inside. She turned and signalled them to stop. 'He's sitting. Don't go in for a moment.'

It was Betty.

'Hallo, Mr Scott,' she said. She pushed the court door open slightly. 'He'll be a time yet. They've given him a bail application to do before he starts on you.'

'Well, why on earth were we called down here?'

'You know what he's like,' she said. 'He doesn't like waiting.' She turned and picked up the cigarette that was burning in the ashtray on a small shelf on the wall.

In the silence she said, 'He's not so bad. He's a bit lonely, but he's a lovely man really.'

Scott didn't respond, which made her continue. 'He always asks after the family and he gave my Diane a really nice gift for her wedding. A pheasanty sort of silverish thing. She's got it on the window sill.'

'Come on, Betty,' Scott said. 'Stop making excuses for him. He's a lazy old bully. He enjoys pushing people around – if he thinks he can get away with it.'

Betty tapped ash from her cigarette and smiled. She was determined to be loyal and stick up for her judge. 'No, no,' she said. 'It's just he never gets the chance to see anybody, stuck in that room back there.'

She turned to the door and, holding the cigarette behind her, peered through the crack. 'Mind you, he had a real party this morning. He opened a bottle.'

'Really?' said Scott. 'Who'd want to come and drink with Scribner at that hour?'

'Well, there was your Mr Cantor.'

'He's not mine,' said Scott.

'Your case then,' she said. 'And that policeman, Inspector Charlton. The one you argued with last time. And that Butler Jennings, the MP.' She said this over her shoulder as she watched the court.

'What? They had a party?'

'Yes,' she said. 'I had to go along to Court Three to get some glasses.'

'But they were meant to be discussing our case.'

'Well, they weren't,' she said. 'That Jennings and the judge were laughing. I haven't seen the old man so happy for some time. And the policeman, he was drinking with them too.' Betty's tone stiffened as she spoke. Scott grinned at Catherine.

'I'm surprised Scribner let the policeman in. He's normally a stickler for that.'

'Well, he didn't worry this time.' Betty turned and put her cigarette down in the ashtray. 'And he called him by his first name. They all did.'

She turned away from them and pushed the door open. Scott could see into court. The judge was just getting up. 'Court rise!' Betty called and she climbed the steps to pull back the curtain over the judge's door. Scribner disappeared.

Scott and Catherine walked in. 'What's happening? You tannoyed us.'

'He's risen for lunch,' said the clerk.

'But you just called us.'

'Not me,' said the clerk. The court emptied as Scott and Catherine stood there.

'How many times do I have to repeat it?' said Catherine. 'There's something going on. Why would the policeman be in there with the judge? And that Jennings character. He was at court the other time. And they were meant to be looking at this undisclosed material stuff, not drinking together.'

'What can we do?' said Scott. 'I can hardly call Betty as a witness to show there's a conspiracy between the policeman and the judge, can I?'

'Why not? If something has happened, why shouldn't it be mentioned? Or are there some facts that don't count?'

Of course she was right. Great chunks of Scott's life were involved in playing the game and not mentioning things that he knew perfectly well had happened. 'Look,' he said, 'it's just Scribner. He often gives people a drink. If he's not an alcoholic it's only because people like him have pickled themselves for so long that no one knows what normal is like any more.'

'The trouble with you,' she said, 'is that though you're happy enough to make allegations against people in the witness box when it's all intellectual fun, you can't see what's in front of your nose in real life. This whole trial is dishonest.'

He looked at her.

'You can't see it because you're part of it,' she said.

The case began at two o'clock.

By then the day had darkened and it was raining steadily on to the domed roof of the court. The lights high above shone feebly in the gathering gloom. Scott felt at home. After all, he had been sitting on wooden benches in large draughty rooms for as long as he could remember, and it wasn't just the wooden benches and the gloom – even the people were the same as they had been at school.

The magistrates used to wear overcoats in court when Scott started out as a lawyer, just as his classics master used to wear an overcoat in the cold classroom.

The ushers and the staff at court were the same as the staff in the offices, dormitories and kitchen at school, and he had the same relationship with them, Betty, Fred and Bill, as he had had at school – friendly but not real.

Even his client was a kind of raw material, someone to talk about, just as he had used the characters in novels at school and university. You could talk about them endlessly but you couldn't get to know them. Reality seemed always to be at one remove.

'You have an application, Mr Scott?' said Scribner. 'Now? Even before we start the case?'

'Yes,' said Scott. 'I have discussed it with Mr Cantor. He agrees that the application would be better made now. Mr King and Mr Plumstead agree, and although they would be much better at putting the matter than I, since I am first on the indictment I must start.'

'All right, then. But let's not keep the jury waiting,' Scribner said grudgingly. Immediately the judge had set the tone for the case, which was to be uniformly bad tempered.

'The application concerns material that the Crown have in their hands, which affects the case, but which they are not prepared to show the defence.'

'I know. I know all about it,' said Scribner. 'Get on.'

'The defence application is that we should be shown the material.'

'You mean I should tell the police to give you the name of an informer so that your clients know who has grassed on them?'

'Your Honour, no.'

Of course the judge was right. The information probably did include the name of the informer. Of course it was the man who had not turned up at the trial, the man the defence would say had been allowed to run off. But the application was much more important than that. 'The defence say that this case is a set-up. My client has been deliberately engineered into a position where he could be arrested, enticed into a honeytrap.'

'Never heard the phrase,' said the judge.

He would have had to have been living abroad to have missed it. The papers had been full of just such a case in the previous weeks.

'Your Honour has seen certain material, I understand?'

The judge said nothing. Scott began to tire of the elaborate dance that convention demanded of him. 'Have you seen the material?' he said.

The directness of the question took even Scott himself by surprise and the judge reacted angrily. 'I am not going to answer that, Mr Scott. You may not interrogate me. Your application is refused.'

Scott stood still for a moment. He hadn't even set out the reasons for the application yet. How could the judge refuse it? But he wasn't going to argue now. What he knew about the judge's behaviour that morning was something he couldn't use – but at least it meant he knew he wasn't completely in the wrong.

The rain thundered on the roof as he sat down and the jury panel filed in to be selected. The trial had begun.

John Hector sat in the dock at the back of the court looking down at the people surrounding him.

He was raised up from the floor of the court as though sitting in a box at the theatre. He was being held up to show; he felt everyone watching him all the time. After all, he was the reason that they were all there.

It was almost impossible in the circumstances to behave normally. He found that if he took too great an interest in what was going on he forgot he was being watched, then he'd look up to find some guy looking at him directly and inspecting him. But when he acted as though he didn't care he could hear their voices saying, 'Look at him, he doesn't care.'

He couldn't lean over to his son and say anything. It looked conspiratorial.

Once he tried laughing at one of the jokes the lawyer made, but when he looked up he saw the judge glaring at him – as though he had no right to take part.

That's what he really felt. He felt he wasn't taking part in the event, and yet all the time, sitting there in the midst of these people who were being asked to decide what had happened, there it was, dinning in his mind, the knowledge of what had actually happened.

It had all started at the Potato Patch in Rainham. The whole crowd was there, the pub was full. It was Sunday morning, there were little bowls of cheese on the bar and everyone felt better for the roast that was cooking at home. He pushed his way towards them and as he did so his phone rang.

He was greeted with a cheer.

'Hey, hey, Hector,' – they all called him that – 'what are you dealing in now?'

He looked up and grinned. 'Carrots, I got carrots,' and then carried on with the conversation on the portable phone.

He had forty pallets of carrots that were not going to be carrots much longer, but horses don't mind that and he was going to triple his money selling the stuff to the local stables.

As he spoke on the phone the crowd at the bar gathered around him. Wherever he went, his grin, his energy, his friendliness made people feel better. Their own lives became less ordinary.

He came off the phone in a rush. There was a pint of beer in his hand and his smile swept the people standing around him. 'Now . . . I got no more carrots,' he said, putting the phone away and opening his arms. 'I got dosh instead. I'm in the market. What have you got?'

'Well, there's a guy here trying to sell a car,' said Tom Hopkins, the barman, 'a big Range Rover.'

'Is he now?' said Hector. 'Well, what are we waiting for? Introduce me. What's his name?'

'Eddie Morgan,' said the barman.

John Hector would buy or sell anything. He didn't give receipts and he didn't expect them in others. He didn't ask where things came from and didn't want to know. Mostly this meant he was buying stock that was being sold off to clear, or to make room for a new line, or stock that other people who didn't have his energy or resourcefulness couldn't sell. But sometimes it meant the goods had been stolen, and a new Range Rover at less than half price meant just that.

Hector watched prosecuting counsel speaking to the jury, saw how his mouth opened and closed in a self-satisfied way. He despised him. This man was so sure of himself, sure of the way things were, the way things should be. The words just came out unconnected with experience.

'The defendant Hector' – he seemed to think he could call him Hector, just like that, no Mister, as though he was talking about a servant. It was different from the way his friends did it, it was demeaning – 'the defendant Hector made contact in a public house in Rainham. The Crown will call the barman.' Cantor shuffled his notes to find the man's name, couldn't, and then carried on. 'The barman will tell you, ladies and gentlemen, of the occasion when he introduced them, Hector to Morgan.'

'He, ladies and gentlemen of the jury, could not then have known what they were going to do. The Crown say that after this meeting Hector and Morgan agreed to manufacture, sell and distribute a million tablets of what the doctors described as, quite literally, a lethal mixture of heroin, amphetamine and Ecstasy.'

Cantor enjoyed saying that. It might catch a headline.

He continued, 'A tablet that came to be known in the clubs of Brentwood, Rainham and south London as the "Pink Primer". A tablet that could have killed.'

Hector looked at the jury as they watched the lawyer, opening the case, saying what he would prove. Were they just accepting what he said? It all sounded so plausible.

He had been found in the flat with the bloody man Morgan. In the very room where he was sitting there were packets of powder, bowls on the floor, all the equipment for mixing and weighing, and in the back room down the hall there was a small, efficient machine for filling capsules with the powder. And a million empty capsules in the cupboard.

But he had only gone there to look at the car.

All right, the moment he walked into the flat he knew the guy was obviously up to something else, and it didn't take much guessing what it was, but then, that wasn't his problem – he just wanted to buy the car.

Hector heard the prosecuting barrister carry on. 'The police arrived at the flat and found Hector, his son and an associate sitting in the' – for a moment Cantor hesitated over the word. Drawing room? Front room? Neither was quite right but could he bring himself to say it? Yes, lounge . . . he had to say it – 'in the lounge of the flat, surrounded by drug-making equipment.

'The Crown say, ladies and gentlemen, that it is clear that the defendants were caught in the act of preparing drugs for sale.'

Hector remembered the moment. He had been sitting on the big settee, he was about to make a phone call, when the windows had seemed to open up like a mouth and figures had burst into the room.

Scott sat listening to Cantor opening the case. He looked at the jury sitting damply, squashed up in the wooden box on the side of the court, and was reminded of the illustration in *Alice in Wonderland*. He wouldn't have been surprised if they had all suddenly taken off, flapping and squawking around the court in response to the droning speech Cantor was making.

Earlier, when he started his speech, Cantor had introduced Scott to the jury and he had bobbed up and down in response to the introduction. Even then he thought he noticed scepticism in the eyes of some of them. Of course, it was far too early, they hadn't heard anything, and all he was really seeing was a projection of his own feelings. Perhaps it was scepticism about the whole proceedings, the silly uniforms, the funny language. Anyway, it was a start.

Cantor was getting to the bit in the evidence about the pub now. Scott had thought when he read the case papers that Cantor wouldn't be able to resist it, and he couldn't. 'The defendant Hector first met Morgan in the Potato Patch public house. Later Hector claimed he had been there selling some carrots, and was hoping only to buy a car. Members of the jury, selling carrots . . .' Cantor's face creased up and Scott realised that he was smiling. 'Ladies and gentlemen, selling carrots,' he repeated in exactly the tone of voice Scott had imitated when he had seen Hector in his rooms. 'You may think that public houses are not places where you carry on trade, rather they are places of amusement and relaxation.'

The jury looked stolidly back.

Scott realised that Cantor was beginning to lose them. This was the Elephant and Castle Crown Court. A lot of its work came from East Street market. Cantor didn't realise he was talking about something that was the daily experience of the jury, and they weren't about to be lectured on it by someone who had looked and sounded as though he had never been in a public house in his life.

'Not places where you carry on trade' – Hector could hardly believe his ears. He couldn't remember a time when going to the pub had not been business. Almost everyone he knew was connected with the group from the Potato Patch.

He had arranged to meet this Morgan later and had given him his phone number. But before they met again Morgan had rung him back. Did he know of anyone who could shift some boxes? Of course he did. His son could fix it.

Hector knew everybody and had somebody for every job. Shift them and store them? He could fix that and he did, and got paid good money. Of course, now it turned out that the boxes had the empty capsules in. How was he to know? And now his son's fingerprints were all over them.

If he had been involved, did they really think he would have let that happen? No way. But that wasn't an argument they could use. Or so Scott said. You can't tell a jury that you're normally such a good villain that you don't make silly mistakes.

The prosecution barrister was still talking.

'The man Morgan is not in the country. He did not surrender to his bail, so, members of the jury, you will not see him at this trial. What the Crown says is that the defendants who remain to be tried conspired with the absent Morgan to commit this offence.'

It's obvious, isn't it? Hector repeated it to himself for the hundredth time. It jumps out at you. He looked at the jury. Morgan set me up and then disappeared. How much did they pay him? It's common now. Nowadays you can't get involved in anything in case it's a set-up, everyone in the trade knows it.

Then he reminded himself. This was different. It wasn't just a little bit of handling, moody wine or perfume, this was the real thing. Class A drugs. Fifteen years at least.

Morgan sat in the public gallery above the court, watching them talking about him. Charlton had told him not to be there but he couldn't resist it. It wasn't the first time he had been in at the kill. The man Hector had met now looked completely different. Anyway, they'd only been face to face about three times: there wasn't a chance of his being recognised.

Cantor had opened the case to the jury in the afternoon and Scott began to worry that he might have to start cross-examining right at the end of the day, just as the heat and the damp were beginning to affect everyone in the court. But he had forgotten the judge's need to get back home.

'That's enough for the day,' Scribner said, the moment Cantor turned to call his first witness, and he gave the standard warning to the jury. 'Don't speak to anyone about the case,' and he was out of the door.

The tension of the court dissipated and Scott felt himself beginning to relax.

It was this wonderful moment of relaxation which prevented him from working effectively after a day's trial work had finished. As the tension left him there was no way in which he was going to load up more tension. Some people seemed able to stay in gear and switch to another case. Look at the man Lawson, for heaven's sake.

Scott couldn't; if he had lots of work on he had to do it in the early morning before the court sat. He remained in counsel's benches for a moment.

The jury were being told how to organise their papers. Betty was giving each one a folder and he was interested to see that at least half of them had made notes which needed putting away.

They weren't quite the usual mix. They were a bit younger and there were three black guys in their twenties. You don't usually get more than one young black man –Scott supposed it was because they were generally less settled so they weren't on the electoral roll.

He had been defending young blacks for fifteen years and liked them a lot – they never whined. But the odd thing was that because the guys he met were a particular selection – they'd all been charged, otherwise he wouldn't have met them – they reinforced what was in reality only a prejudice: that young black men tend to be criminals. He didn't meet any others.

He supposed it would be the same with many of his friends at the Bar. After all, people like him were becoming judges now. However hard they tried, their only experience of young blacks was in the courts as defendants.

That would change.

As he watched, it did just that. One of the three young men stepped out of the jury box and Scott could see the book he was carrying: *The Essentials of Post-Graduate Psychiatry*, Grune and Milavic.

Cripes, the guy was a medical student or a doctor. Why was he doing jury service? He didn't have to. And then Scott realised why he would want to do it. Any intelligent young man in his position would. You only had to watch the crowd in the hall in the morning, mainly black, to know why.

'Come on.' Catherine poked him in the back. 'Do you just want to sit here?'

The odd thing about education was that it took you out of the present. If you weren't careful it took you away from seeing how things were now. You saw *why* things were what they were, you saw *how* they became like that, you saw everything except how they were now.

'Are we going or what?' said Catherine. 'Everybody else has.'

'Let's go,' said Scott.

Betty bustled back into the court carrying glasses that she had just emptied and cleaned. She was beginning to close the court up.

'Good to see you, Mr Scott. It's just like the old days. Do you remember the fun we had? There was a bet . . .' She turned to Catherine to tell her the story. ' . . . that Mr Scott couldn't get from the dock at the back there up to the Lord Lieutenant's chair without touching the ground. And Mr Scott arranged for me to put a pile of Criminal Appeal reports just here by the old Chief Constable's chair so he could swing across.

'You did it, didn't you?' she said to Scott. 'I'd told the judge about it and he was watching from the cubbyhole.' She pointed to a small door that was set into the woodwork of the court furniture by the witness box. 'And the next day in his summing up the Perfect English Gentleman – that's what we called the judge, miss – told the jury this long story about a man doing an initiative test that involved swinging around just like Mr Scott did.'

She added reflectively, 'He's gone now.'

'What?' Scott spun round. 'He's not died, has he?'

'Oh no,' said Betty. 'I meant he's gone from here. He's gone to Belmarsh. Sad, really. But you haven't, Mr Scott. You're still here. Still climbing in the windows, are you?'

'What's with this maudlin crap? This relationship you have with court staff and doorkeepers?' Catherine said. 'What's wrong with proper relationships? Your life is like a bloody novel.'

She was saying exactly what he had been thinking. Where did she get this ability. Where did she get this . . . there was no other word for it . . . wisdom?

When he didn't reply, Catherine went on.

'I suppose that's what's meant by being institutionalised. It's easier to make a relationship with a porter, or the ground staff, than with Mum and Dad.'

She began to enjoy herself as she connected ideas.

'No wonder you like trials. It's a way of dealing with human relationships without the responsibility of having them yourself. And if barristers are successful they send the kids away to boarding school, and that starts the whole thing over again. God, think of all those unsatisfied wives.'

They had reached the crossing outside the court and Scott was looking for a taxi.

'No, let's walk. This way,' said Catherine.

They set off down towards Borough High Street where the war memorial was marooned by the traffic rushing round it.

'I like this area,' she said. 'It's been forgotten a bit.' On the left was a row of cottages that Scott guessed were originally alms houses, or were meant to look like them. On the chapel opposite the end of the row there was a home-made sign painted on a piece of board. It read 'School of the Performing Arts. Television a speciality'.

'Let's go in,' she said.

She pushed at the door, it swung open, and they found themselves in a small entrance hall. There was a notice on the wall in front of them:

'This is St Barnabas Parish Hall. Please behave appropriately.'

Scott drank in the smell of dusty floor, old books and macintoshes. The Church of England engulfed him.

'What *is* appropriate for St Barnabas?' said Catherine. 'Who is he the patron saint of? Perhaps performing arts.'

She opened the arched door facing them and it creaked in a satisfying way. The noise was much louder inside. They were in a large hall, unfurnished save for a few chapel chairs, each with a ledge for prayer books on its back. The whole place vibrated to every footfall. At the far end great windows rose up to the roof, opaque, green, covered with wire mesh.

On their left the wall was filled with noticeboards. The first was mounted with a gilded fleur-de-lis, and underneath it read 'St Barnabas 42nd Cub Pack'. There were pictures of small boys in green shorts and shirts. One of them was standing demonstrating the cub salute, another was crouching down touching the ground before him with outstretched fingers.

They examined it. 'I never understood what "Dib dib dib" meant,' said Scott.

'What's Akela?'

'I think she's a she-wolf, in charge of all the little wolf cubs.'

'Another mother substitute?'

'Yes. I suppose so.'

They left the hall and Scott said, 'Let's try to get into the church itself, to have a look.'

They went round towards Pepper Street, through a small garden neatly cut and kept. At the end, at the top of a flight of stairs, a Christ hung in the wet.

The side of the building had been boarded up and the entrance was locked. Scott thought of Larkin with his bicycle clips. Wandering into churches was not going to be possible much longer.

A car drew up and parked in a muddy space cordoned off by the entrance and a man got out.

'We were trying to get into the church,' Scott said.

'It's not a church any longer. It's a recording studio. The church was bombed in the war.' The man started unlocking the door. He was perfectly friendly and willing to talk.

'Who looks after the garden?

'We do. And a group of the local residents. They're pleased we keep it tidy and free from vagrants.'

'Is there nothing left?'

'No, all gone.' The man beckoned them in. 'All you see now is lots of hessian.'

They went into the long hall which had been broken up into large studios. 'We get all the groups here. We had Arctic Nightgowns yesterday.'

Scott looked at some photographs.

'When they get their photographs took, they hang their guitars on the Christ outside. That was the altar.' The man busied himself turning on the lights. 'I don't suppose He minds. See that brick wall there? We put that there. We had to do that – part of the agreement. There's a fresco there painted by a German airman in the war. He was in the church. He painted it. He was living here.'

'What? He was sheltered here?'

'Yes. He was here for two years.'

'Given sanctuary?'

'So they say. You can't see it now, it's all bricked up. We covered it with plastic first.'

'On the run in central London during the war? Every man's hand against you. And you get sanctuary at St Barnabas? Amazing,' Scott said.

'What are you going to do about Hector?' she said when they got outside again. 'It's obvious he's been set up.'

'What can we do? We can only fight the case. There isn't anything else. Juries' verdicts are horribly final.'

They stood back to look at the church again.

'You can see where it was. The garden must be where the nave was.' He went on, 'That's why the whole system depends on most allegations in the criminal courts being true, because there's no real way of testing them properly – at least not in the way that a doctor or a research scientist would categorise as being efficient. It's hugely hit and miss.'

'You mean Charlton can get away with it?'

'Getting away with it doesn't mean anything. The law specifically allows people to be trapped into committing crime. The offence is falling into the trap. You don't have to.'

'This is different. The offence Hector was going to commit was not the offence he is charged with.'

'But that's the danger of committing any offence. It puts you at risk.'

He turned. 'There's no performing arts school here, only scouts. And probably ballet. Come on, let's go and get some tea.' They moved away from the hall and down the back streets towards the Thames.

'Things aren't always fair,' he said. 'Here's a good example. I'll break it down for you. You get in a fight, something that can happen on the spur of the moment and – listen carefully – you foresee that it's a reasonable possibility that someone will get badly hurt, even though you don't intend it to happen at all. Someone does and that person dies, then you're guilty of murder. Even if you never wanted it.'

'What, even if you don't want anybody to be badly hurt?'

'Yes, so long as you realise they might be. And it gets better. You can be found guilty of murder even if the chap who did the actual killing is acquitted. There's a Hong Kong case that exemplifies that last bit.'

'Is that right?'

'Yes. All perfectly logical. At least it seemed so to the judges who decided it at the time.'

They walked past the gleaming front of the new *Daily Express* building and up the slope on to Blackfriars Bridge.

'Of course, the judges in that case were probably dealing with someone who was clearly guilty and deserved everything he got. Which may have affected their decision a bit.'

The wind blowing off the Thames caught their breath as they stood above the river, watching a man picking about amongst the pottery shards on the shore below.

'It's what accountants call a results-led system,' he said. 'Mr Hector took a chance dealing with this guy Morgan, and now he's trapped. Juries don't have any sympathy for people who say, "But I wasn't committing that offence, I was committing another." Nor do judges.'

Chapter 11

Outside, the next day, it was bright and sunny. There was a fresh wind and the court felt cheerful in the changed atmosphere. It was a good day for jury work; people felt positive. Ideas and images would be easy to convey and there was none of that lowering gloominess that leads to convictions.

Old Tom Hopkins, the Crown's first witness, was worried. He had been the barman at the Potato Patch for years and here he was, being asked to give evidence against one of its most popular customers. He answered the questions from the Crown prosecutor mechanically, telling how he had introduced Hector to Morgan. But he didn't go into detail.

Now it was Scott's chance. He guessed that the barman was going to be helpful and he was right. He couldn't imagine why the prosecution were calling him at all. He stood up and leaned back, quite relaxed, and looked puzzled.

There was no point in attacking this witness. Let him tell his own story. 'You said that you introduced Mr Hector to this man. But you didn't say why. Had you seen the man in the pub before?'

'No, it was the first time he'd come in.'

'He came in . . . ?'

'Yes, he came in, he was stood there for a while. Drank whisky.'

'Stood there . . . ?'

'Yes, just stood there, looking around.'

'Looking . . . ?'

'Yes, looking for somebody, I'd say.'

'He knew who . . . ?'

'No, he had to ask.'

'Doing . . . ?'

'Well, doing nothing, save looking for someone, I suppose.'

Scott could just have easily have asked straight out, 'Was the man looking for somebody?', but the answer wouldn't have sounded so transparently honest. As it was the way he was putting the questions made it seem as though the answers were nothing to do with Scott at all, and certainly not exactly what he was hoping for.

'Eventually he . . . ?' Scott was going to finish the question with 'he spoke to you' if he had to, but there was no need. The witness had become used to finishing his questions for him.

'He asked me who bought and sold in the pub. Well, that made me a little leery. I'm a little careful, because being where we are, you just don't know what's going on nowadays. Not nowadays, anyway.'

Scott had to be careful not to make Tom Hopkins look as though he was on Hector's side, so he didn't enquire what that meant. He just said, 'You're near a market. Do any traders . . . ?'

'Oh yes, we have lots.'

'Buying and selling . . . ?'

'Oh yes.'

'Anything . . . ?'

'Anything you name.'

'Potatoes?' There was laughter.

'No, not potatoes, but that morning Hector had done a deal in carrots. I remember now. That's right. That's why he was so cheerful.'

'The pub. Not just a place for amusement and relaxation, then . . . ?'

Scott used the words Cantor had used in his opening speech, but, with a small pause, he turned the phrase from being merely a little pompous into being absurd.

The barman looked at him. Expecting something more. After all, he hadn't heard the prosecutor's opening speech and hadn't heard the phrase. After a pause he just said, 'What . . . what was that?'

'Exactly,' said Scott.

He could go back to his first question now. 'You didn't say why you introduced this man to Mr Hector.'

'Well, he wanted to sell a car, and I knew that John Hector sometimes bought cars. A Range Rover he had. The man, that is.'

'Mr Hector told you . . . ?' Scott did not make his question clear.

'No, this man told me he wanted to sell a car. I said, I know a man who buys cars.'

'No, I meant did Mr Hector tell you that he sometimes buys cars?'

'No, no. Hector didn't tell me. I knew. He buys and sells for a business, everyone knows that.'

Scott had got what he wanted without ever putting a leading question, save the idea of buying and selling. He had never needed to suggest an answer. To the jury the witness seemed completely independent.

Since it had gone so well he went for broke.

'Did you ever see this stranger again?'

'No, never.'

'But Inspector Charlton. You saw him?'

'Oh yes.'

'He interviewed you to find out what you knew?'

'Yes.'

'Though I guess somehow he already knew what you've told us, didn't he?'

'Yes.'

'I don't suppose you know where he got that information, do you?'

'No.' The barman looked puzzled. He hadn't even thought about it.

'Did you ever see Inspector Charlton together with this man Morgan?'

'No.'

'Together with him. Talking to him?'

'No.'

Scott sat down.

When he had begun as a lawyer he would have made the mistake of saying something in reply to the last answer, something like, 'No, I suppose you wouldn't have seen them together, would you?' But now he had learned there was no need. He had associated Morgan and the inspector in the jury's mind.

That was enough for now.

Re-examining, Cantor tried to repair a little of the damage. 'It's right, isn't it, that you had no idea where the inspector had got his knowledge of your introduction from?'

It was a mad question. What could Cantor be thinking of? John Plumstead snorted. His snort was famous.

Scott got to his feet. He said, 'Mr Cantor called this witness. He mustn't make suggestions to him. He can only ask questions. The question should be, "Did you know where the inspector got his information from?" '

Cantor couldn't refuse to ask the question properly now, though he tried to.

'I will leave it,' he said.

Scott prevented him.

'He has put the question. He must wait for an answer. Ask it properly.'

The jury grinned at Cantor's discomfort. They had begun to realise there was a battle going to take place in front of them.

Cantor was forced to repeat the question in Scott's words.

'Do you know where the inspector got his information from?'

'Well, it must have been from the man himself. Hector didn't know the fella had been asking for someone to buy a car off him, did he?'

The answer meant little, save that it was just the answer Cantor did not want. The policeman and the man in the pub were becoming entwined in the jury's mind.

'But, Mr Scott, it's bloody obvious I've been set up.'

The court had risen for ten minutes so the judge could have a cigarette. 'We'll take a quick break now, ladies and gentlemen,' was how he had put it, and Scott and Hector were standing outside the courtroom at the window, watching the trees waving in the London wind.

'One moment I'm happy buying and selling carrots and the next moment they suggest I'm running a drugs factory with some character in London.'

Hector still thought of himself as a countryman. His house stood at the end of the row of houses built off the London–Southend road, and every autumn during the stubble-burning they had rat problems.

'What would I want with drugs?'

'Money, Mr Hector. You'd be hoping for lots of money,' said Scott. 'That's what they'll say.'

Hector looked distressed at his directness.

A tramp walked past on the pavement below the window and paused to examine a rubbish bin.

'Look,' Scott said, in explanation, 'I'm no use to you if I don't tell you the strength of the case against you. One of the easy things in the prosecution of cases of this kind is that the defendant always has a motive: the crime itself.'

The tramp pulled out a broken umbrella and struggled to open it.

'If you hadn't been caught you would have been making a pound profit on every pill – or so the Crown will say,' he had to add quickly as he saw Hector catch his breath. 'Now that comes out at a million. So the question isn't "What would I want with drugs?", the question is "Who wants a million pounds?" '

Hector was quiet for a moment and Scott's mind went back to the conference they had had together. He had to bully him, or at least that was his excuse. It was to let Hector know what they were up against.

In the background the tannoy announced, 'Would Jonathan Taylor of counsel *please* go to Court Six. The court is waiting for you.' Jonno was late again.

'The problem is, Mr Hector, that not only have you got a motive for committing this offence – a million pounds – you've also got a motive for saying you didn't do it. To avoid being locked up.' Scott nearly added 'for ever' but thought it wasn't necessary.

'If I was prosecuting and I had those two points in the bag I'd have no difficulty in getting you convicted.'

Hector didn't catch the last remark. He was still working out how merely being accused of an offence was enough to give him a motive for having committed it.

Scott was talking about something different, something Mr Hector couldn't appreciate. What Scott had to concentrate upon wasn't just the evidence, but Cantor. Already Cantor had screwed up his opening address, and now he'd made that little mistake. Paint your opponent out of the case and you're halfway to an acquittal.

Hector persisted with his point. 'But, Mr Scott, I know that this man Morgan set me up.' In his frustration he hit the window with the side of his fist and it made a hollow noise. 'How do I know? I just know. He has to be an informer. If the judge knows that he was the informer then he ought to tell us, shouldn't he?'

'He's not going to tell us without a struggle,' said Scott. 'We're going to have to realise that.'

'Are you going to ask again?'

'Of course, but I need more. The more we're able to show that Morgan came looking for you, the more it becomes dishonest for the judge not to let us know if he was the informer.'

The tramp outside gave up trying to get the umbrella to work and dropped it. It fell to the ground and then, blown by the wind, skittered across the road. A large lorry coming off the Elephant and Castle roundabout trapped it beneath its tyres and crushed it, like an insect in a lizard's mouth.

The trial began to draw out as the witnesses each dealt with various aspects of the case.

Cantor called a forensic scientist, Dr S. John – he always insisted on the initial – from the Metropolitan Police Laboratory. The doctor opened his briefcase and pulled out notes that showed how the tablets that had already been prepared must have been made from the chemicals found in the bowls in the room where Hector had been found sitting.

Scott watched him.

The man was perfectly pleased with himself. He made a little show of giving evidence, listening with exaggerated care to the question and then meticulously and obviously referring to his notes for the answer.

Scott got up and said, 'But the odd thing about your evidence, Dr John, is what you've left out, isn't it?'

It immediately set the witness back.

It provided him with an impossible choice. If he showed that he knew what Scott was talking about and he agreed with it, then half of Scott's work was done, but if he looked puzzled and said, as he did, 'I don't understand,' then there was going to be trouble.

'It's not so much what you do prove, as what you can't prove that's interesting, isn't it?'

Again the witness was unable to say anything in reply.

Either way he was caught. He was beginning to lose his bearings. 'What do you mean?' he said.

Scott changed tack. He wouldn't be allowed to do that again.

'You are an expert scientist, a witness, independent of the prosecution, aren't you?'

'Yes, of course.'

'The whole ethos of the Metropolitan Police forensic laboratory is that the people who work there are independent of the people who own and fund them. The people who pay your salaries. That's right, isn't it?'

Dr John said yes.

'But oddly enough you don't give evidence for the defence, do you?'

'No. But we could do.'

'Have you?'

'No.'

'Ever?'

'No.'

'Never?'

'Just where is this leading?' Cantor interrupted.

The judge, whose look of distaste had been growing, joined in. Scott had been aware of it and was waiting for the interruption.

'Mr Scott, this is all very clever, but do you have a question for the witness? Preferably one that is about the evidence he has given.'

The judge was trying to be cutting, but he could hardly have said anything more convenient.

'Certainly, Your Honour,' Scott said, 'but I'm not going to ask about the evidence the witness has given. It's the evidence he hasn't given that is interesting.'

Scott had calculated, and immediately he realised he was right, that the judge had not bothered to read the witness's statement in advance. The judge subsided.

The next question was difficult. Not the answer – Scott knew perfectly well what that would be. The challenge was to present the point as dramatically as possible. He chose the high route.

'You can prove my client never touched the drugs in that room, can't you?'

'They must have had gloves on,' said Dr John immediately.

So the story was going to start in the middle. Now he was into the real thing, not arguing with the judge, not just teasing Cantor. The atmosphere in the court changed. Suddenly it was serious.

Though the jury didn't understand what followed they could see that it was important. They watched intently.

'That's the only explanation, isn't it?'

Dr John had committed himself.

'Yes,' he said.

'Because of the tests you did?'

'Yes.'

'Because the tests you did could detect even molecular deposits of the chemicals involved? That is infinitesimally' – Scott acted it out with his fingers squeezed together – 'infinitesimally small traces of it.'

'Unless the swabs weren't accurate.'

'You wouldn't say that if the tests were positive.'

'There'd be no need.'

'But the defence would ask you that question?'

'Yes, of course.'

'And you'd reply, Well, they're always accurate?'

'Yes. Most of the time.'

'So why are you raising the doubt now?' That was a risky question, leaving it open for the witness to choose his reply from anywhere.

Scott could feel the pressure of his wig on his forehead. Even the texture of the cloth of his suit against his knee where he stood, apparently relaxed with his foot resting on the end of the bench, was livid to the touch. When he breathed in he could feel the cool air going into his throat. Here was the chase.

Dr John had no answer to it, though. 'Well, there are occasions,' he said weakly.

'Why mention them, then?'

No answer.

'You threw doubt on the tests. In this case. Normally you wouldn't.'

No answer.

'You wouldn't have done it if the tests had supported a conviction.'

No answer. Dr John nearly said something, then stopped himself.

'Here the tests don't support the Crown case, so you cast doubt on their validity. On what basis do you do that?'

'I didn't cast doubts. I merely said "If they were accurate." '

'That's not casting a doubt?'

'Well . . .'

'Would you have volunteered that remark if the tests had proved that Mr Hector had been up to his elbows in the stuff?'

Again Dr John could not, or would not, answer.

It was time to explain to the jury what this was all about.

'Let's go over it again so we're clear. The police took swabs from Mr Hector's hands?'

'Yes.'

'And from the hands of the other two people in the room?'

'Yes.'

'Those enable you to test for heroin or cocaine?'

'Yes.'

'What is their accuracy?'

'One part in a million.'

'You mean that if the slightest trace of these drugs had been on their hands the swabs would have revealed it?'

'Yes. We're talking about a very small amount.'

Scott wanted to be absolutely sure the jury got this. 'Not the amount that a cook would see floating in the air after pouring flour into a bowl?'

'No.'

'That would be incomparably larger?'

'Yes.'

'Or a handyman emptying Polyfilla into a bowl, ready to mix?'

'No.'

'Incomparably larger?'

'Yes.'

'In fact the test might well pick up dust on the hand of a man who had merely been in the room while someone else was handling the powder?'

'Yes. If he had been there a little time.'

'How little?'

'Ten minutes would do it.'

'Is that because you and I, we all are surrounded by an atmosphere containing many millions of particles of various substances?'

'Yes.'

'And if this amount of chemical were lying in a wide bowl then the whole place would become contaminated?'

'Yes.'

'So in daily life you only have to be with someone whose clothes smell of tobacco to pick up that smell?'

Dr John had by now forgotten the difficult moments, and was becoming pleased about the accuracy of his tests.

'Yes,' he said, 'these tests are astonishing. The faintest contact with the substance we are seeking will give a positive result.' He remembered what he had said earlier. 'That's why I said "If the tests have been conducted accurately." '

'But by that token a negative test is all the more surprising – it's when you have a positive result that you have to fear contamination.'

The scientist became lost in his expertise again, forgetting why he was there.

'Yes, that's right. A negative test can't be the result of contamination, can it?' He thought the point amusing and tried to share the joke. The jury only saw that the doctor was now accepting anything that Scott put to him.

'Let's be clear. Three men are sitting in a room. They are interrupted' –

he paused and lifted his notebook so that he could ostentatiously quote the exact words Cantor had used in opening the case – 'they are interrupted, "caught in the act of preparing the mixture of drugs".'

Cantor would be regretting those words now.

'It's not a big room. Look at the photograph. You can see the mixing bowls. You can see the powder. If mixing of drugs was going on then the men in the room would have had traces on their hands.'

'Unless they had gloves.'

'That's what you said at the beginning. The only explanation for the lack of the drug on their hands, if they were involved in the mixing, is if they had had gloves on.'

'Yes.'

'You mean if they were not wearing gloves they must have had traces on their hands. They would have traces of the chemical on their faces – no gloves could prevent that – in their hair, on their clothes.'

'Yes.'

'No gloves were found.'

Dr John did not answer immediately. There was no reply to be made. It wasn't a question.

Scott behaved badly.

'Why did you not tell us that at the start?'

Silence.

'Whose side are you on, Dr John?'

There was a sound from the judge. Scott could feel it rising.

'Answer me. If Mr Hector had been sitting at the bowl mixing drugs then traces would certainly have been found on his hands?'

'Without doubt.'

'And there were none?'

'No.'

'Whose side are you on, Dr John?'

Paul Gregory sat watching Judge Scribner from the front row of the public gallery fifteen feet above the court.

He wasn't alone. A nondescript, sandy-haired man sat on the benches behind him. A safe distance away a tramp slept gently. Next to Gregory was an American and his wife who were also leaning on the edge of the gallery. They were gazing at the scene below in frank astonishment.

'I'm a judge myself,' the American had said to Gregory during a moment when the court was doing nothing. 'My wife is a lawyer too. Probate.'

Gregory had politely enquired what he thought of what he was watching. 'Remarkable. Remarkable,' the judge said.

An argument was developing in the court below. Save for the judge and the witness, who were facing Gregory, it was difficult to see who was talking at any one time.

Suddenly Gregory saw prosecuting counsel get up and start to complain that what was being said was irrelevant.

Gregory hadn't caught the name of the witness at the start of his evidence – he had been talking to the judge – though it was clear he was a police officer of high rank. He had spoken of arriving at a premises – he called it the suspected premises – and arresting a man.

It was only when counsel for the Crown said, 'I object to Inspector Charlton being asked that question' that Gregory realised whom he had been watching.

So this was Charlton.

Annoyingly the American judge interrupted. Clearly he thought that Gregory understood what was going on.

'Why can't he ask him that? Seems reasonable to me.'

Down below in the court Scott took no notice of Cantor's interruption and repeated the question. 'Why did you come to the flat at that time?'

'I'm not going to answer that,' said Charlton.

'I object to the question,' said Cantor.

'Why not? Why won't you answer?' said Scott to Charlton.

'Because it may lead to the identification of an informer.' Cantor answered the question Scott had just asked.

'He can answer it,' the American judge said to Gregory. 'No problem. He can say, I went because that's when I was told to go.'

'Why should the answer lead to the identification of the informer?' said Scott. 'You could just say, "I went because that's when the informer told me it was the best time to go." '

'I'm not going to answer it,' said Charlton.

'That's right, though, isn't it?' said Scott. 'You went at a prearranged time. A time arranged with the informer.'

'I'm not going to answer,' said Charlton.

Cantor said, 'He is not bound to answer since it may identify an informer.'

'It may identify what the informer knew, not who he is,' said Scott.

'That's right,' whispered the American. 'We have the same problem Stateside. Information doesn't necessarily identify the giver. Of course, it may do. It would do so if there was only one person who could have known the accused was going to be in the flat at that time.'

Cantor said, 'Your Honour, I want to raise a point in the absence of the jury. I object.'

'That's what you don't want to admit, Mr Charlton, isn't it?' said Scott, disregarding Cantor again.

'Stop it, Mr Scott,' said the judge.

'This is exactly what happened last time,' said Catherine, pulling at Scott's gown.

'That's because the whole of this case is a set-up, isn't it? Isn't it, Inspector Charlton?' said Scott.

'Say nothing,' said the judge to the witness. 'Be quiet, Mr Scott. Leave us, please,' he said to the jury.

'This is a joke,' shouted Hector from the back of the court.

'Prison officer. Take him down,' said the judge.

The jury looked to see Hector being hustled through the door to the cells.

'Does this often happen?' said the American judge to Gregory.

'Mr Scott. I seem to remember that when we last met there was a problem between us.'

'I will not discuss this in the absence of my client,' said Scott.

'This does not affect your client, it concerns your behaviour in my court.'

'This case is continuing and anything you say may affect it,' said Scott. 'I will not discuss the matter in the absence of my client. He is entitled to hear what is being said.'

'Mr Scott, your manners towards me are of no concern to your client.'

'They are if they reflect my conduct of this case.'

'Mr Scott. You will behave . . .'

'I shall take no further part if my client does not return immediately.'

Scott heard the door to the court creak and he saw some barristers pushing their way in. It was amazing how quickly the word of a row got around.

'Well, if you wish your client to hear my rebuke, then I shall have him brought up. Officer . . .' The judge signalled to the door.

The court sat in silence for what seemed a long time.

Scott felt a movement at his elbow. It was Tozer. He groaned, thinking, That's all I need.

'What's up? Why's Scrib so angry?'

Cantor looked over and nodded at Tozer, who grinned back at him.

The trouble with this, it seemed to Scott, was that, unless you were really clever, you could never be sure you were behaving properly. Oh yes, the client liked it, so did his family, but that didn't mean to say you were right. After all, Scribner, however much of a shit he was, wasn't a beginner. Perhaps Scribner was right, perhaps he was behaving badly.

They waited for the defendant to be brought back. It was a long way to the cells from this court and Hector had been taken all the way down only to get the message that he had to be brought back again.

'Scribner won't let me cross-examine,' said Scott.

'What's new?' said Tozer.

Even that wasn't much support since Scribner was perfectly right to stop him, thought Scott. He knew he was taking liberties, but on the other hand how else could you defend in a case like this?

It was all very well being the brave barrister, standing up for your client, as on TV, but that was too simple. Perhaps he was pushing it too far.

'Is that Catherine behind you?' said Tozer.

Oh Christ, here we go again, thought Scott.

He looked at Tozer, who grinned back.

'Shove off, Tozer,' Scott said.

He thought, Obviously I'm not allowed to ask Charlton who gave the information about the flat, but I must be able to suggest to him that this was all set up, mustn't I? Of course I bloody must. He realised that his temper was rising. He heard the door to the cells clatter and the whole thing started up again.

'Mr Scott, I have ruled that you may not ask whether there was an informer, or who it was. You are persisting in doing so.'

'No I am not,' said Scott.

'Mr Scott, I am the judge of what happens here. You asked who was the informer.'

'No I did not,' said Scott. It was lucky the judge had taken this tack. If he had just accused Scott of plain bad manners, Scott knew he would have had much more difficulty in replying. 'If you remember, I only asked why he had arrived at that time.'

'That is the same thing.'

'We're not to know that. Only someone who knows who provided the information will know whether it is the same thing. It may not even be true. The timing may have been a pure accident, though I notice that Mr Charlton hasn't said so.'

Again he had been lucky. The judge was in effect confirming the point.

'I say you may not ask the question.'

'Do you mean that the whole question of whether the police were tipped off to arrive at the flat at exactly the same time as my client was there has no bearing in the case? That my client can't allege it?'

'No, I do not,' said Scribner.

'If he can allege it, then I must be allowed to ask about it.'

'You shall not. And that's an end to the matter,' said Scribner. 'We will recommence this afternoon.' And he pushed back his chair and left the court.

To Scott it felt like a small victory. Perhaps he was worrying too much. Worrying was no way to win cases.

Scott saw Gregory come through the court doors. What the hell is he doing here? he thought.

Even with the American jostling him up in the gallery, Gregory had been able to follow what was happening. Scott was suggesting that the whole thing was a set-up, and the judge was stopping him from doing so. If this wasn't what he'd been looking for in all those papers, what was?

The visiting American judge gave him the opportunity to find out what was going on. He turned to him and said, 'Would you like to meet the lawyers? I'm sure they'd be happy to speak to you.'

'Why sure,' said the judge. 'That would be interesting. Thank you. Do you hear that, Jane?' he said to his wife. 'Let's go meet the lawyers.'

'This gentleman is a judge from . . .' Gregory paused and turned to the judge.

'From the Frank Harris courts in Detroit.'

'And he said he'd be pleased to meet the lawyers. This is Mr Scott, Judge. He is counsel for the defence.'

The judge said, 'Jerry Kennedy, my name's Jerry Kennedy. Pleased to meet you, Mr Scott. You're doing a good job, Counsellor.'

Catherine looked at Scott. How was he going to like that? She nearly laughed out loud.

Scott was on his best behaviour. He liked Americans. 'Why thank you, Judge.'

'Call me Jerry, and here's my wife, Jane,' he said. 'I liked your argument and, more, I liked your tone. I like a man who stands up for what he thinks.'

Scott coughed.

'And so does Jane. My wife Jane is in probate, but I work in the criminal courts.'

Gregory said, 'Your case is that the raid was set up in advance as part of a plan . . .'

Scott looked at Gregory. What was he doing here asking questions? But the American took it up. 'You're right. How can you put it to the witness if you can't ask the question?'

He suddenly noticed Catherine. 'That's the point, isn't it, ma'am?' When Catherine replied, the judge swallowed her accent like a hook.

'Why, you're from America. Where, now? Do you hear that, Jane? I should say Virginia by your voice.'

Catherine admitted it. 'I'm not a lawyer, though,' she said.

'You're not? What are you doing here?' said the judge's wife.

'She's being modest. She's a much better person than a lawyer. She's a poet,' said Scott.

'A poet.'

There was a moment of silence broken by the judge's wife. 'I don't like these courts, never did. We all need a bit of poetry after the arguing. Can you give us some poetry?'

'Why, yes,' said Catherine. She opened her mouth and words came out as she looked at Scott:

'In courtesy I'd have her chiefly learned;
Hearts are not had as a gift but hearts are earned
. . . And many a poor man that has roved
Loved and thought himself beloved
From a glad kindness cannot take his eyes.'

Silence.

The silence was broken.

'I must interrupt,' said Cantor. 'I have to ask you whether you mind me speaking to Inspector Charlton, even though he's in the witness box. I have

127

to arrange for some papers to be brought.'

'No problem,' said Scott.

'Yeats,' said the judge's wife. 'You quoted Yeats.'

Chapter 12

His Honour Judge Scribner's lunch was spoilt. The case was beginning to worry him and, worse than that, Scott was getting on his nerves.

He didn't feel at home. He wasn't in his own court centre where, being the senior judge, things were done as he wanted them. He wished now he hadn't given in to the pressure to come to London to try this damn case. He looked around him. He had risen early and had arrived at the dining room before anyone else. It was a large, gloomy room, with a long table at one end, the other end filled with heavy brown chairs grouped around an old carved fireplace. The chairs were covered with the kind of old shiny leather that succeeds in looking like plastic. What was it? Wash cloth? In one corner there was an umbrella stand with an old umbrella sagging in it. He looked at the window sill where there was a set of old Law Lists from before the First War. They weren't there for show. They just weren't used any more.

He opened one at High Court judges. Each judge was listed with his home address and phone number. As far as he could make out, most of them seemed to live in Phillimore Gardens, or failing that, some other part of Kensington.

He remembered the old story of the High Court judge who had died and whose life had been so private that they didn't know where to pay his wife's pension. He ran his eye down the list. No, all of them listed their addresses here, and yet, paradoxically, they lived much more private lives then than now.

These days the whole damn thing was public. You were public property, what you said was public property, what you thought was public property. He had to watch what that young slip of a journalist girl was writing more than anything else in his court. Opinions. You weren't allowed to have them any more, in case they upset the bloody newspapers.

He took a drink.

Years ago he had joined the judges' luncheon club at this court, £1 for life membership, organised that way to deal with the licensing laws. Why on earth they had to create some fiction to deal with the licensing laws he could never understand. After all, who enforced the damn law?

Well, at least he could serve himself his own drink.

He subsided into one of the low chairs. There wasn't even a newspaper. He sat with his back almost horizontal, his feet stretched out in front of him, looking at the ancient fireplace.

They'd all be coming in soon.

In this court the judges never sat at the luncheon table in a fixed order. At his own court he worked out the order of sitting every morning, but here there was the awful moment when he found himself walking towards the table not knowing who he was going to be next to.

It could be anybody – a full-time magistrate doing his month a year in the crown court or even, as had happened yesterday, some temporary judge, a new assistant recorder, yapping on about probation hostels and intensive therapy courses.

He'd been taken around one of those courses once. It was full of people – no, full of yobs – sitting around in groups discussing why they were stealing and mugging people.

Why, for God's sake! Pretty damn obvious why. They were plain dishonest.

He had tried to be civil to the fellow sitting next to him throughout the meal, but really, it was a bit much. He had last seen this particular assistant recorder at his own court when he'd turned up to do an application for bail, stuttering and yelping like a beginner. Yet there he was now sitting next to him at the judge's table, large as life.

No, he wouldn't come back to this court, however much they asked. He heaved himself up – there was that pain in his shoulder again – to look at the table behind him. Wasn't there even a book to look at here?

A voice said, 'Morning, Scribner,' and he looked round. It was Harborough, one of the few he had some time for, though not much. He stood up as Harborough began to pour a large vodka.

'What are you doing skulking here, then?'

'Came up early,' said Scribner. The two old men looked at each other.

After all these years they had nothing much to say.

'Had a good morning?' said Harborough.

'Same as usual.'

'Me too.'

'They don't know when to stop, most of them.'

'No.'

'On and on. Do they think I'm a fool?'

Scribner's hand came out like a claw and raked across the bowl of peanuts set on the drinks table. He dragged a handful of nuts up and started to feed himself.

'What've you got on?'

'Drug factory.' Scribner's head was tilted back as he sucked in the nuts. Salt and brittle flaked on to his sleeve and shirt front.

Harborough watched in distaste.

'Who's doing it?'

'Scott and Cantor. That Cantor man.'

'Oh. I know Cantor. Any good?'

'Bloody fool.'

'Oh.'

Pause.

'How long's it going to go for?'

'Three weeks. Three more weeks in this damn place.'

The door opened and two men came in. One was medium height, round, an Asian face, the other, slightly behind him, carefully closing the door in case it swung open again, was smaller, silver-haired, wearing rimless glasses.

'Oh God,' said Scribner, 'the salt and pepper brigade.' His hand went out to the peanuts again.

'Thank you so much,' said His Honour Judge Teflin as Harborough handed him a glass of water.

'No charge this time,' said Harborough.

His Honour Judge Saddiq on the other side of the table started energetically mixing tomato juice with Worcester sauce. The three of them stood in silence while behind them there was a grunting noise as Saddiq, massively overweight, manipulated the bottles.

The silence was about to stretch into embarrassment when Teflin spoke. 'I'm having a little trouble with my indictment.'

'Oh God,' said Scribner.

Teflin blinked at him. 'No, really,' he said. His glasses flashed. His voice, soft with a plaintive northern accent, was quiet, but determined. 'No, really,' he said. 'Counsel has discovered it was not signed.'

'Sign the bloody thing yourself,' said Scribner.

'Oh no, I couldn't do that,' said Teflin. 'I checked. It must be signed by an authorised officer. I don't think I am one of those, am I?' He smiled at such an idea.

Saddiq, who because of his size, had to come round the table sideways, ended up panting by their side. 'Katkhuda on indictments,' he said. 'Damn good book. Even I can understand it. Look it up, it's all in there. Invaluable work.'

'It's the fault of your bloody stupid court clerk,' said Harborough to Teflin. 'He was probably sent over from the Ministry of Ag and Fish and doesn't know an indictment from a milk churn. Nothin' for it. You'll have to start again.'

He nearly poked Teflin in the ribs with his elbow but thought better of it. 'Never mind, though, it'll give you a chance to get your schedules in order.'

'There is that,' said Teflin, and he took a delicate sip of water.

'Oh God,' said Scribner.

The group was interrupted by the arrival of Butler Jennings.

'Hallo, Jennings. What are you doing here?' said Harborough.

'Come back to pass sentence in that case I was doing here the other day.'

'Good to see you. What will you have?'

Scribner and Jennings stood opposite each other.

'Gerald here' – Scribner jerked a hand full of peanuts at Teflin – 'Gerald here's in a frightful tizz about his indictment.'

'Oh, I wouldn't say that,' said Teflin. 'Just an ordinary matter.'

'Damn worrying to a chap though,' Scribner said. Teflin decided that he was being teased and took a firm hold on his glass. His spectacles became slightly misted.

At that moment Betty appeared. 'Sorry to bother you, sir,' she said to Scribner. 'You're needed on the telephone.'

Scribner's departure lifted the tension from the group.

'Well, I've got that girl Clarke in front of me,' said Harborough. 'Damned attractive I say.'

'What's your case all about?'

'Dirty films. Mainly animals. The thing is with this girl Clarke, it's nice to have a pretty woman to look at occasionally – especially when all there is to watch for hours on end is bums with pimples on.' He snorted. 'Odd, those pimples. They're always there. Start up a dirty film, count to ten and there's a pimple on someone's bum. I suppose you can't powder people's bottoms in the same way as you can their faces.'

Harborough grinned as he got into his stride. He enjoyed telling stories.

Teflin took two crispbreads, a tomato, and an apple and went to the other end of the table from where Harborough sat. He liked Harborough enough, but felt he did go on a bit sometimes. He reached for the bottle of sparkling water – he tried to drink two and a half pints of water every day – and as he did so Jennings sat down next to him.

'I thought I saw you earlier in the judges' corridor,' said Teflin.

'I had to go in to see Scribner about the case he's doing.'

'Is it difficult?'

'I believe there are problems.'

Jennings changed the subject. 'Look,' he said. 'I've got four black kids up for sentence. Three of them have never been in trouble before and one is a regular offender – detention centre, youth prison, the lot. The four of them go into a shop, steaming in, and take some sweets. It's clear that the experienced one organised it. But what do I do with the others? Organised theft – what's the prison tariff here for that?'

'Age?'

'All under twenty-one.'

'They're black, you say?'

'As it happens,' said Jennings.

Teflin's plodding approach began to annoy him. He wished he hadn't asked for advice now.

'I just wondered why you told me they were black?'

'It's not important that they were black, just a description. I could have said four tall kids.'

'Now that would have been odd,' Teflin said, 'if you'd said "Four tall boys went into a shop." ' He reached for the water. 'Do they all have to go into custody?'

'Yes.'

'For stealing some sweets?'

''Course they bloody do – terrified the shopkeeper,' said Jennings. 'They have to be taught a lesson.'

'What do the probation reports say?'

'Give 'em a holiday, probably,' said Scribner as he took the chair opposite.

Teflin looked up and said, 'That's probably because they've never had one. All they've ever known is wandering about the streets.'

'Oh God,' said Scribner.

Teflin decided he wasn't going to put up with this any more. He was finding that he was really quite put out by the behaviour at lunch today. But he was interrupted.

'We're going to stop all that.' Jennings's mouth opened and the words started to come out. 'We're going to stop all that tommy rot. I was speaking to the leader of the Home Affairs Committee the other day. There's going to be less money on mollycoddling and more on prevention. A sense of personal responsibility . . .' He had made this speech a number of times before and it was always well appreciated. 'And by prevention I mean more prisons. If a man is in prison he's not out stealing, is he? As the Home Secretary said, prison works.'

He looked around at his audience.

Teflin stood up, said, 'I'll get some coffee,' and left. Jennings found himself talking to Scribner alone.

At the other end of the table His Honour Judge Harborough said to His Honour Judge Saddiq, 'Walker the Talker, that's what we called Charlie Walker. I was co-defending with Walker the Talker, and he decided he was going to laugh this case out of court.' Harborough paused, enjoying the memory of the fun he used to have at the Bar. Time was, he thought, when the whole thing was run for our pleasure.

At the other end of the table Jennings said, 'How do you put up with that stuff every day?' looking over at Harborough.

'I don't,' said Scribner. 'You know damn well I've only come down for this one trial.'

'Of course,' said Jennings. 'Sorry. I was thinking of the old days when you were here all the time.'

'I'm not staying much longer either,' said Scribner. 'Once I've sorted this mess out I'm going back.'

He stopped and looked at him. 'Your mess, Jennings.'

* * *

'I think we had better have the documentation here.'

'Should we be seen talking to each other? I'm still giving evidence. I'm not supposed to speak to anyone.'

'It's OK. I told Scott I was going to speak to you. He's agreed.'

Cantor and Charlton were in the passage opposite the court. The door to the passage was open and they were standing where it opened out at the bottom of a narrow staircase. From where they were they could see, but could not be seen by, people leaving the court.

At that moment Scott came out with the American judge and Gregory.

'Who are they?' said Charlton.

'Just some American lawyer touring around the courts.'

'Come to watch the great Jeremy Scott, has he?' Charlton was still angry.

'No. He just happened to be here. Look, I think we had better have all the documentation here. Up till now the judge has just taken our word for it, but if Scott gets any further he may want to see it.'

'Why?'

'So when he says he has looked at it, and he decides the defence are not entitled to see it, then it's true – he has looked at it.'

Charlton objected. 'If he has already made the decision, then what's he worrying about?'

Cantor was continually amazed at the rigid way in which policemen thought. 'Of course he has agreed, but that's not the point. He has to go through the motions to show he has made his decision properly. What decision he makes is up to him. All the appeal courts are interested in is whether he went through the right procedure.'

Lawyers always astonished Charlton. If the judge had already made the decision, why did he have to pretend? That didn't make what he'd done any better or worse. It was still the same decision he had already made. If you are going to break the rules at least be honest about what you're doing. Don't pretend you haven't done it when you're with people who know you have.

If the judge was worried about how what he was doing looked, then, as far as Charlton was concerned, he wasn't to be trusted.

'Hang on a moment,' said Cantor, and disappeared round the corner.

Charlton waited. He had dealt with lawyers for a long time. He wondered what would happen if he said, 'Well, it's all been agreed, why should I bother? Who cares about appearances?'

Cantor came back and said, 'Look, I just arranged to ring Scribner. I'm going to tell him the documents are coming. Can you get them here this afternoon?'

Charlton hesitated.

'He's not going to read them, is he? Do you really think he'll spend his afternoon trawling through all that stuff? He just wants to be able to say he's seen it. Don't worry.'

Jerry Kennedy thought Catherine was neat. He was sitting in the public canteen downstairs. In front of him there was some hot water in a styrofoam cup and he was prodding at the tea bag floating in it, encouraging it to turn the mixture a darker brown. Catherine was sitting opposite him, next to his wife.

'This Scott,' he said, 'he's a member of a law firm?'

'No,' Catherine said, 'he works on his own.'

'On his own?'

Judge Kennedy thought of his namesake in the Kennedy novels. 'He's got an office and a secretary, then?'

'No,' said Catherine, 'he works completely on his own, although he's a member of a group. They are all freelancers but they get together in a group called chambers. They work from the Temple, just below Fleet Street.'

The judge knew about the Temple and was going to visit it. 'We gave them a law library,' he said. 'Now you tell me what all the fuss in this case is about.'

Catherine found herself trying to explain what was happening.

'We think that the whole allegation against Mr Hector is a set-up. The guy who owned the flat enticed Mr Hector into it, and then let the police know he was coming so he could be arrested for the drugs that were there. If that's the case then there must be records, but the judge won't let us see what records there are.'

'Why not? If it's true he was set up then, OK, the guy's innocent, and if it's not true then there's no harm in showing the records. Why should the court worry?'

'Don't ask me,' said Catherine. 'I haven't heard such concentrated rubbish talked for years. Ask him.'

Scott and Gregory were approaching the table carrying coffee.

'What's this all about, then?' said Judge Kennedy to Scott.

'We say it's a set-up,' said Scott. 'But there's no easy way of fighting the case since the whole point of a set-up is to make it look as though the guy you're setting up actually committed the offence.'

'But who'd want to set him up?'

Scott made a gesture. 'It's a natural extension of police work, I suppose. All policemen think they know who the criminals are and if you can't catch them at crime then you might as well find a crime to catch them at. You have sting operations in the US, don't you?'

'Yeah, but we have strict rules against entrapment. You don't have them, Catherine says.'

'No. But we have this. You'll be impressed.'

Scott fished around in his bag and pulled out a printed document. It was headed *Instructions to Undercover Officer*. He gave it to the judge, smiling. 'That's what we've got.'

The judge looked at it and burst out laughing. ' "*In such a case,*" ' he read out loud, ' "*when a police officer has infiltrated a group of people . . . officers are entitled to show interest in and enthusiasm for proposals but the officer must try to tread the difficult line between showing interest and enthusiasm sufficient to keep his cover and actually becoming an agent provocateur.*" Whose instructions are these?'

'The Home Office.'

'Who are they?'

'In effect they're the police authority.'

'You mean they employ the policemen?'

'Yes.'

'Whose side are they on, then?'

Scott shrugged. He didn't have to explain anything. The judge was way ahead of him.

'What do the courts say?' said Kennedy.

'Nothing. To entrap someone is perfectly legal here. No defence.'

'Nothing? They say nothing?'

'Well, that's not quite fair. If they ever come across a clear case where they can attach no blame to the defendant they'll probably throw it out. But most defendants are a little bit to blame and there's never such a thing as a clear case.'

'Can you do nothing?'

'Not without the papers proving entrapment. The prosecution have all the papers and can refuse to show them to the defence.'

'Where do they get the papers from?'

'The police.'

'You mean the police are meant to hand over documents which might prove they've been misbehaving? They're meant to destroy their own case? Where do your judges live – fairyland?'

'Yes.'

'They expect the police to bring a case to court and then tell everybody that the case should not be brought?'

'Exactly. Any policeman with any sense will hand over nothing. The most recent phrase that's used to justify the refusal is the need to protect "matters of operational sensitivity".' I had a case the other day where that meant they tried concealing that a helicopter was hovering over the main road.'

'What are you asking to see in this case?'

'How the raid began. That would answer most of the questions. Why did the raid happen exactly at that time? Have they any record of contact with the man Morgan?'

Gregory leaned forward. 'Who?' he said. He hadn't heard the name properly. 'Was that Morgan?'

Scott looked at him. 'Morgan,' he said. As he did so he was puzzled. He hadn't yet worked out why Paul Gregory was here at all. He'd assumed he was just showing the judge around the courts. Why, then, should he show interest in this case?

'But of course, they won't let us look at the papers. You should ask him about it,' Scott said. 'Customs officers are just as secretive.'

'Who do you mean?' asked the judge.

'Customs,' Scott repeated. 'Mr Gregory is a Customs officer—'

'I'm a Customs officer,' Gregory interrupted before explanations started being called for. 'I met Mr Scott in a Customs case.'

'Oh,' said the judge. He picked up the tension between them, and didn't push the matter any further.

He looked at his wife. Thirty years of living together worked. She understood immediately and changed the subject. 'But you, Catherine,' she said. 'Tell us about yourself. What are you doing here?'

They went back into court. Scott could see that the lunch break had not improved Scribner's temper.

'Mr Scott, I tell your client through you,' the judge said, 'that another outburst of the sort we heard before the break will mean that he will lose his liberty for the duration of the trial.'

Scott looked at the jury. They were not impressed. The days when judges had the monopoly of wisdom and natural authority had long been frittered away by their behaviour in the eighties, and it showed more and more on the faces of juries.

'Now, have you any more questions for Detective Inspector Charlton?'

'Indeed I have,' said Scott. He felt the familiar tension coming over him. He took his time. It was the balance between tension and calm that he needed to get right.

'I have this letter here, Mr Charlton. It's from the South-East District Crime Squad. It has your name on it.' He waved a sheet of paper at Charlton. '819 2281. Is that the number?'

Charlton paused for a moment and looked surprised. Scott looked at the paper again. 'Sorry. I read the wrong number. 819 7615. Is that the number?'

'Yes,' said Charlton.

As he launched into the questioning, Scott felt the separate dialogue starting up in his head. He asked himself, What is Gregory doing here?

'Before the break I asked you why you went to the address where Mr Hector was arrested just at the time you did, Mr Charlton.' He paused. 'I'll leave that,' he said, before the judge interrupted him, 'for the moment.'

Instantly the tension in the court had returned to where it was before the break. It was as though he had thrown a switch. Tension was what made the whole thing work.

'You went on this raid? But you're a detective inspector. Why?'

'Why not?'

'Because officers of your rank don't normally go on raids, do they?'

'Yes, they do.'

'But it has to be special, doesn't it?'

Both Scott and Charlton knew the answer was yes, but they also knew that Charlton could give any answer he wanted. The jury knew nothing about police procedure and Charlton wasn't about to tell them.

'Depends what you mean by special, Mr Scott.'

'Unusual, then.'

'Same answer.'

'Were you in charge of the briefing beforehand?'

'Yes.'

'That's when you gather the police officers together and say what will be happening?'

'Yes.'

'And, if you are able to do so, among other things you try to decide who will make the actual arrest?'

'That can happen. It doesn't always.'

'Did it happen this time?'

'I can't remember.'

'So you can't remember whether it was decided in advance that, for instance, you would be the one to arrest Morgan?'

'No, I can't.'

'But you did arrest him? I mean you, yourself?'

'Yes.'

'Had you met him before?'

'I knew what he looked like.'

Scott didn't pause for a moment. It was important not to let Charlton know that he had heard the answer. Really heard the answer. Heard what Charlton hadn't said.

'He was handcuffed. Was he wearing gloves?'

'No.'

'Why weren't his hands swabbed?'

'They weren't.'

'I know. Why not?'

'We didn't think it necessary.'

'Why not?'

'We took advice.'

'From whom?'

'Forensic.'

'What did they say?'

'Don't bother.'

'Why not?'

'Because if he was in the flat then he could say that he got drug traces on his hands through contamination.'

'Why did you swab the others' hands, then?'

'Because they were sitting at the table where the drugs were.'

'Where was Morgan?'

'Morgan was in the kitchen.'

140

'Doing what?'

'Getting some coffee.'

'What was he wearing on his feet?'

'Socks.'

'Whose flat do you say it was?'

'Your client's, Mr Scott.'

'What was Mr Hector wearing on his feet?'

'I dunno.'

'Boots, Mr Charlton.'

'If you say so.'

'No, Mr Charlton, not if I say so. A list of his clothes was made.' Scott waved part of the custody record.

'If you say so.'

Scott felt something. He turned around and looked up at the gallery. Gregory was still there.

'Were Customs involved in this case?' he asked.

For the first time Charlton looked puzzled. 'No,' he said.

All the questions Scott had asked up till now had been to the point.

Scott had had an old friend at the Bar, called Roland, an old-fashioned lawyer. He had died recently. He always used to say there were questions 'anent the subject' – and questions that weren't. What did that mean? 'Anent the subject' – strange phrase.

Charlton looked more relaxed. Now was the time to go for him.

'I asked you a moment ago, had you met Morgan before?'

'And I answered you.'

'No you didn't.'

Charlton looked at him. 'I think you'll find I did.'

'No you didn't. You said "I knew what he looked like." '

'That's my answer.'

'Well, here's my question. Had you ever met him before?'

'I don't have to meet someone to know what he looks like.'

'That's no answer.'

'That's for the jury to decide.' Scribner's voice, pitched at a level to demonstrate strained patience, interrupted.

'The question is had you met him before?'

'I've already answered that.'

'Mr Charlton, do you remember that you gave the defence a pile of unused material, boxes of documents?'

Charlton waited to see where the sudden change of subject would go. 'Yes,' he said carefully.

'First this, though. Here is a printout of Mr Hector's portable phone bill.' Scott handed it up. 'This will be properly proved, Your Honour,' he said to the judge.

Charlton looked at it.

'You'll see that about an hour before the raid Mr Hector phoned the flat.' He directed Charlton to the number. 'Odd for someone who lives there, yes?'

'We don't say he lived there all the time,' said Charlton.

'Well, let's look at what happened. Here's a printout for the use of the phone at the flat. We found it in one of those boxes you gave us.'

Lawson had done the job well.

'Moments after the phone is put down on Mr Hector's call, someone in the flat picks up the phone and dials 819 2281. That's your number, isn't it?'

'No. You read out our number. It's 819 7615.'

'I'll say it again, Mr Charlton. The number I read out to you was the squad room main phone. This number, 819 2281, is your private extension, isn't it?'

There was complete silence.

'Please answer me.'

Charlton looked at him.

'Mr Charlton. I can ask my solicitor to go outside and telephone that number now. It's your number, isn't it?'

Again Charlton said nothing.

It was difficult to lie direct.

'I'll repeat what the documents show, in case you didn't understand. Moments after Mr Hector rang the flat, a call is made from the flat to your phone.'

Charlton said nothing.

'What was being discussed, Mr Charlton?'

No reply.

'The weather?'

There was silence so heavy that it pressed in on everyone.

Scott changed the subject.

'At the time of the raid, had you ever spoken to Morgan before?'

Charlton opened his mouth and made a sound.

Scott heard it, and knew he had got him. Charlton was going to have to tell the truth.

When policemen get a confession they say a man has 'coughed'. It had taken Scott ten years of court work to understand that the expression was the literal truth. When you lie, you lie with your lips. And when the truth comes it's because your lips have run out of lies. The truth comes coughing from your throat.

That sounds like Yeats, he thought, comes coughing from the throat. From 'The Lake Isle of Innisfree': 'for peace comes dropping slow'.

He had heard the cough from Charlton, though he guessed he was the only person in court who had done so. Where he was now was a place he had been before – the only one listening, the only one really listening. It was a lonely place.

'So you had met him before?'

'If you call it meeting.'

'Why didn't you say so?'

'Well, it wasn't what you'd call a meeting.'

'Why?'

'I arrested him.'

'When?'

'Oh, a long time ago.'

'How long ago?'

'Fifteen years ago, maybe more.'

'And fifteen years later you immediately recognised him?'

'Did I?'

The questioning had been so sustained that Charlton had forgotten his witness statement.

'Yes, you did. As you walked in the door you said, "Eddie Morgan, I'm arresting you for conspiracy to manufacture drugs." You recognised him?'

'I must have done.'

'After fifteen years?'

'Not necessarily.'

'Had you met him in between times, then?'

'I may have had a photograph.'

'Did you?'

'I can't say.'

'Why not? If he'd been arrested before, then there would be a photograph available. You'd have got it from the files for the briefing. Unless of course you knew he was there already and there was no need for one. Why can't you remember?'

Silence.

'Which is it?'

'I'm not prepared to say.'

'Why not?'

Cantor took the cue. He stood up, affecting weariness. 'I don't want to sound like the Prime Minister repeating the same thing over and over at Question Time, but my learned friend is asking questions designed to get evidence out of this officer that he knows the officer cannot give; he is trying to get details of the information the officer had been given.'

Scott said, 'Oh, so there was information given, then?'

The judge said, 'Mr Scott, be careful.'

Scott said, 'You arrested the man fifteen years before and you walked in and had his name immediately on your lips?'

Charlton made no reply.

Scott went on, 'It looks as though you already knew he was going to be there. How could you have known that . . . ?' He paused, and then said, 'Of course, as I have been reminded, it's for the jury to draw the conclusions.'

He changed tack.

'Why did you arrest him for manufacturing drugs?'

'Because that's what was being done.'

'But how did you know? You had only been in the flat for two seconds, and the first thing you said was, "I arrest you for being concerned in the manufacture . . ." '

Silence.

'You had not even been into the main room.'

Silence.

'How could you have known?'

Silence.

'You were telephoned by the man in the flat?'

'I am not going to answer that,' said Charlton.

'That's plain from the printout of the telephone bill.'

The tension in the court had grown more and more intense as the questioning continued. Scott had been watching Cantor to see how he would react. Save for the interruption a moment ago there had been nothing. He guessed that Cantor had at last realised that interruptions only hurt him. He was right.

'Let's repeat it, Mr Charlton. Here was a man padding around in socks, in – you claim – someone else's flat, making them coffee. You walk in the door. You hadn't seen him for years, though he's just rung your number. You immediately remember his name and arrest him for an offence that you don't know he's committing.'

Charlton looked at Scott. There was a long silence.

'That's a normal day at the office for you, is it, Mr Charlton?'

Both Philip King and John Plumstead laughed on cue. It was reassuring to work with people who could see what was happening.

'Mr Scott, when you are in my court you will behave yourself,' said the judge.

'I didn't think I wasn't,' said Scott.

He realised he was starting something it might be difficult to stop. He tried to change the subject. 'I was repeating the evidence the officer had given.'

He found only that he had made it worse.

Scott looked at Scribner. He wasn't just upset, he was furious.

He started his next question. 'You knew perfectly well Eddie Morgan was in that flat, didn't you?' – but was interrupted by a shout of rage from the judge.

'What do you think you are doing?'

Scott looked at the judge, shocked. He had been annoying the judge by keeping on at the witness, but he hadn't been behaving particularly badly, had he?

Scribner picked up the exercise book in front of him and slammed it on the desk.

'What do you think you are doing?' he repeated in a rising shout. 'I have ruled that you may not . . .' He picked up the book – as it was lifted Scott could see the notation on its corner, Judge's Notebook E 542 – and slammed it on the desk again. Four or five pencils went skittering along the length of the bench and clattered to the floor, '. . . ask questions like that!'

'Like what?' said Scott.

At this point whatever he said was going to make it worse. Scribner had clearly lost control.

Scott watched as the judge drew breath.

'What do you mean "like what"?' he said at last. 'You know perfectly well that I ruled you should not ask questions that might reveal the informant.'

'No you didn't. You said the witnesses needn't answer them.'

'It's the same thing.'

'No it's not. How else can I put my case to the officer?'

Scott watched the jury. He decided he had better go the whole way. The judge had said what he had in front of the jury, so why shouldn't he?

'My case is that Mr Hector was enticed into the flat with the sole intention that he should be arrested.'

Scribner made a mistake. He said, 'What is your evidence for that?'

Now Scott was also angry. 'The phone call. Anyway, I don't need evidence. My client doesn't have to prove anything. The real evidence is that Mr Hector knows it's true, and he's going to say so. He was going there to buy a car, not drugs. He certainly doesn't live there.'

'I'll thank you not to make speeches in front of the jury.'

'You asked the question. I answered it.'

Scribner stood up.

The effect was extraordinary.

'Mr Scott, you have totally disregarded my rulings.'

Scott was tired of being bullied. He was tired of being sniped at and continually interrupted as though he were some ill-mannered intruder, the same, as far as the judge was concerned, as the man he was defending. It was like walking through deep mud.

'No I have not. I have done what I have a duty to do. And all the while you and Cantor there are yapping round my ankles, trying to make it difficult.'

In the shattering silence he heard himself say out loud, 'Old clothes upon old sticks to scare a bird.'

His memory surprised him. It was Yeats again.

The judge was so astonished that he stood in complete silence. Scott looked at him and the words continued in his head:

O body swayed to music, O brightening glance,
How can we know the dancer from the dance?

Scribner said, 'Mr Scott. Those words. By them do you mean me?'

There was a moment when Scott could still get out of it. He could

146

withdraw it all. He could say, 'No, of course not, Your Honour.' But why should he? It was the truth.

'Yes,' he said.

Scribner left the court.

As the judge slammed his way out of the room Scott thought to himself, Bloody poetry, what's it got to do with anything?

'You're in trouble now,' said Catherine.

Chapter 13

A message came out from the judge's rooms discharging the jury, stopping the case. Cantor got his papers together and looked at Scott. 'That was stupid,' he said.

'Yes, I suppose it was,' said Scott.

'I don't suppose you'll be doing this next time.'

'No, I don't suppose I will.'

'Maybe that'll save a lot of the fuss.'

Scott was left alone in the court thinking about what he'd just done. It wasn't the kind of behaviour to be expected in an English courtroom. He felt as though he had clumsily broken something delicate. It was just a waste. He didn't even have the excuse of having done something brave or worthwhile, standing up for someone maybe. It was just the end product of being sniped at for years, for years not replying, putting up with decisions that offended common sense. At last his patience had run out.

He remembered talking to one of the lawyers who had defended one of the major terrorist appeals, one that succeeded. He had said that the only pleasure left to him before that victory was to see just how intellectually dishonest he could force the court to be. A dry sort of pleasure, and one that eventually saps your resilience.

There was a scuffling noise at his elbow and he looked round to see a messenger holding a brown paper envelope.

'Are you the lawyer in Hector?'

'Yes,' Scott said.

'I've got these for you.'

'Thanks. Just shove them down there.'

The interruption broke the moment and Scott got up and left the court.

* * *

In the central hall Hector stood, obviously waiting for him. Scott was going to have to apologise. He went over to him, but before he could speak Hector said, 'It's not your fault, Mr Scott. You were doing good. It was that judge. He was looking to stop you.'

Hector's wife put her hand on his arm. 'Don't you worry, Mr Scott. It was all for the best. That judge was unfair all the way through.'

Scott was amazed by their generosity. They were going to have to go through another trial entirely because of him, and the only thing they were concerned about was his feelings.

'Look, Mr Hector, I'm very sorry . . .'

'Now, don't you worry, dear,' said Mrs Hector. She would clearly have offered him a cup of tea if she had had the opportunity. 'It'll all be for the best. You'll see.'

Scott wasn't so sure. 'I don't know what's going to happen now,' he said. 'It'll be at least a couple of weeks before it can start again.'

Still, Mr and Mrs Hector were more concerned about him than about their own plight. It was amazing. Scott compared their decency with what he had to do to earn a living. In what he did there was absolutely no place for saying what you really thought, of course there wasn't. What he thought was completely irrelevant and, if it intruded, it was worse, it was dangerous – he'd just proved that.

In his disillusion – and how everybody would laugh at this if he ever said it out loud; how Tozer would laugh! – it seemed to him that it was the Hectors who were the honest ones.

'I don't know what will happen.' Scott realised he was talking about what the judge was going to do to him, but the Hectors didn't think that.

'Never say die, me,' said Mr Hector. He sounded like someone out of an Ealing comedy. There are worse things to be, Scott thought. 'The truth will out. I may be a bit of a villain . . . I may have been a bit of a villain,' he corrected himself, 'but I didn't do this one, I don't do things like that. My Annie knows that, don't you, Annie? And she'll tell anybody.'

'I do. I do,' his wife said, looking at her husband with admiration.

It's a shame that what's blindingly obvious isn't admissible as evidence, Scott thought as they walked away.

Where no one could see them talking together Charlton had said to Eddie Morgan, 'Why did you risk coming here?'

'Because it's half the fun. I wouldn't want to miss seeing them struggle.'

'Is that why you do this?'

'I rather think it is,' said Morgan. 'I was made to struggle once and I don't owe anyone anything.'

Charlton turned to move away. He had never enquired into Morgan's life before. They had been doing this together for so long now that motives weren't relevant.

Morgan said, 'You tell me something. Why did the judge stop it?'

'I think he was nervous.'

'Of what?'

'Because of the phone call you made. Because you used the phone to let me know they were coming.'

'So what?'

'I think the judge realised that they were going to be able to prove you set the whole thing up and that he was going to be forced to give them some of the papers. What else could he do? He took the opportunity when it came and stopped the trial.'

'But you said the judge wasn't going to see those papers.'

'He saw Jennings over lunch and Cantor was told to get them down to him.'

'Jennings told me he would never let any judge see them.'

'Well, he changed his mind. Cantor made me send for them.'

'Where are they now?'

'The trial blew up before they arrived. The judge took his chance to stop the case when that defence counsel was rude to him. The papers will have gone back to the squad office by now.'

'What did you say?'

Scott repeated it.

'To Scribner?'

'Yes.'

'Oh God.'

'I don't think he understood it.'

'It sounds pretty clear to me.'

'Well, yes, the obvious meaning may be clear.'

'What you're saying is that he didn't recognise the quotation?'

'No. I don't think he did.'

'Frankly I don't think that matters very much. What are you going to

151

do? Run a defence in front of the Bar disciplinary committee that the judge should have understood the line as Yeats meant it?'

'Well, that's how I meant it.'

'How's that, then?'

'Well, I think Yeats meant that all the life and spirit had gone out of him. He was talking about himself.'

'That's great. Perhaps you should tell the tribunal that you wanted Scribner to give his opinion on what Yeats meant.'

Scott looked at Ronnie Knox glumly. He had returned to chambers and found his friend with his feet up in front of the fire.

'That's not what Scribner will understand, he will think – sorry, correction – he *did* think you called him a scarecrow. And that's not generally allowed in legal argument nowadays.'

'What will happen now?' said Catherine. Both of them paused.

'Oh God,' said Scott.

'Well, that's a very interesting question.' Ronnie leaned back thoughtfully in his chair. 'These things are by no means as simple as they seem. The fact that it was Scribner he insulted will go in Scott's favour to begin with, but that'll cause only a tiny fraction of hesitation before the full finagle hits the fan.'

'Oh, thanks,' said Scott.

'Mr Hector said he wasn't angry. He said he thought it was the only thing Jeremy could do,' said Catherine.

'Who's Mr Hector?' said Ronnie.

'He's the client.'

'No, no,' said Ronnie. 'We mustn't mention the client. That would only complicate matters. This is no longer anything to do with the client, save perhaps as an aggravating factor right at the end.'

He rehearsed what might be said in a grave voice. ' "And what's more, Mr Scott, you let your client down." No, no, what we have here is a clear example of the establishment about to deal with one of its own. The rules of engagement are infinitely complex.'

Ronnie was beginning to enjoy himself. He pulled some whisky out from behind a book on the cy-près doctrine.

'The first movement of the dance is that Jeremy here apologises to everyone. The *apologia brevis*, followed immediately by the *apologia repetitiva* – a complicated slow dance involving repeated bowing gestures to all parts of the auditorium.

'He has to apologise even to those who weren't there. In fact, especially to those who weren't there. That sets the tone of the dance. You see, the offence is not against Scribner so much as the notion of Scribnerishness. He's insulted the Platonic ideal of being a judge. Insult one and you've insulted the lot.'

'Plato thought nature but a spume that plays upon a ghostly paradigm of things,' Scott said.

More Yeats. Scott was beginning to unwind. What he had done began to seem more funny now than anything.

'Once he has apologised to everybody – his head of chambers, the leader of the circuit, the leaderene, the presiding judge of the circuit, you, me; once he has done that, then he can start taking advantage of his new position. He has to become the walking embodiment of the person who has offended but now sees the error of his ways. All in all, what has happened is that the people who matter are now one up on Scott.'

He poured whisky out for all of them.

'One-upness is what it's all about. At this point, enter stage left the spirit of gentlemanly behaviour, dressed as an Etonian, escorted by an old crone representing "the way things have always been done on this circuit." '

'Why can't they just hold him in contempt or something?' Catherine wasn't impressed by all this. 'It would be a damn sight more straightforward.'

'Not possible. Our society assigns everybody a role. All societies do probably. You can't be rude about the system and then just carry on as though nothing had happened. Scott now has to be "the man who was rude to a judge, and of course now realises that what he said was quite improper, regrets it, and is unlikely to do it again. Your Honour. If you please." He has to play this part for forty days and forty nights.' Ronnie drank his whisky. 'You can't just apologise to Nanny, you have to abase yourself.'

'I don't see it,' said Catherine. 'The judge was being incredibly rude, interrupting, making it impossible for Jeremy to do what he was there for. What was he meant to do?'

Scott looked at her. He was prepared to believe that he had behaved rather badly, and was surprised to find that Catherine saw it differently, much in the way the Hectors had seen it.

She saw his look. 'Well, of course I'm right. You were just behaving normally. You may have screwed up as far as your silly closed world is concerned, but to an outsider you looked perfectly real for a moment.

Here's an elderly, nasty man, trying to bully you, and after endless provocation you're eventually rude back to him. It happens all the time in the real world.'

'There you are, Ronnie,' said Scott, 'you defend me before the disciplinary committee and we'll run that defence.'

'If we do that it will be like one of those games illustrating geometric progressions of increase. We meet in front of the committee, run that defence and there's suddenly two of us up on a charge. We then get Reggie Bott in to defend us, he repeats it, and then there's three of us up. We could suck the whole Bar in.'

'I think it's more important than that,' said Catherine, angry with them. 'What you don't realise is that because you're not prepared to say out loud what you can see is happening in front of you, your clients think you're not on their side. And perhaps you're not.'

She started to get up to leave.

'Hey, hang on,' said Scott. 'You're about to storm off, but remember we're here because I did say what I thought.'

'Yes, and now you're ashamed of it,' she said. 'Instead of saying "Well, I told the truth for once" you're working on an apology.'

Scott realised that she was serious, and more, that she was right.

'Look,' he said. She was leaving. 'I'm coming,' he said.

She walked away.

'Thanks for the drink, Ronnie.'

'I'll draft the standard form apology for you when you change your mind,' Ronnie said.

'I've got two things to do, drop these papers off and see the chap who fixes my car, then I'm free. We can go out.'

She turned to look at him, and he quickly changed what he had said.

'Perhaps we can go out together this evening?'

'All right,' she said. 'That's better.'

Scott thought that despite her need for equality she was quite happy to muck him about a bit.

'I'll just give the case papers to the clerk.'

He took the bag from her, and started sorting the papers. 'I think I put them all together. Have we put in the extra stuff the office sent down?'

'What extra stuff?'

'You'd gone when it arrived,' he said. 'I haven't even looked at it yet.'

They walked into the clerk's room and the junior clerk said, 'Mr Scott, the chap who repairs your car is on the phone. He needs you to meet him at the gate in two minutes or they won't let him in.' He grinned at Catherine and added, 'Hallo, miss.'

Scott hurried from the room, but not before he saw Catherine grinning back at the junior. Clearly this modern woman thing could be turned on and off pretty much as you liked.

'Don't forget the weekend seminar starts tomorrow for you, Mr Scott,' his clerk shouted after him.

At the gate Scott found Richard Pisarski arguing with the security guard.

'We can't let you in here. No. Oh no,' the man said, shaking his head. By now there was a queue of cars behind them.

'At least look at the letter.' Richard was waving a fax at the man. Scott could see it was the one he had sent that morning.

'No. I'll have to ask you to leave.'

'It's OK,' said Scott, interrupting. 'He's come for me. He's come to fix my car. He does my car for me.' He was beginning to repeat himself in his haste.

'Well, excuse me, sir,' said the security guard. 'We can't go just breaking the rules for our own convenience. I may know you, but who's to say—'

'Oh, for Christ's sake!' Scott had had just about enough of this crap today and he stepped forward and pressed the button. The barrier began to rise and Scott saw the guard tilt his head back in amazement, watching it go up.

'Come on,' Scott said, 'we're over there.'

'I thought we'd swap cars,' said Richard. 'I may not be able to finish yours for a couple of days. You keep this. I'll drive yours around.'

'OK,' said Scott, becoming aware for the first time of the car Richard was driving. It was an old-fashioned Mercedes coupé, with bits of what seemed like corrugated iron on it.

'What a great car. Does it go all right?'

'Everything works, even the compressed-air central locking system.' Richard pressed the button on the door and the locks closed with a soft wheezing sound. 'I'll swap the stuff over from the boot.'

Scott could see that there was a fuss over by the gate. The barrier was up and people were driving through unnoticed. The security guard was pointing in their direction, talking to another uniformed man.

'Look, we had better do this quickly,' Scott said as Richard's head appeared from behind his car. 'Here's my keys. You leave in the other direction. When shall I ring you?'

'Give it four or five days. A week if you want.'

As they changed cars Scott could see a determined little group set off from the gate towards them. 'Hop in,' he said to Catherine, who had appeared from chambers looking pleased with herself. 'We'd better go before they get here.' They drove off. 'What do you think of the car, then?' he said as they left the little group of officials in the distance.

He drove back to his flat. It was like driving a boat.

Chapter 14

'Where do you live?' asked Scott.

'Forest Hill,' said Catherine.

'Where's that?'

'Near Penge,' she said.

'Now you're only trying to annoy me.'

'It is. It's near Penge, and Catford and Hither Green and Bellingham and Honor Oak. All those places.'

'How do you get there?'

'By train.'

'How long does it take?'

'Hours,' she said. 'I try not to go there.'

'But you have to go home, don't you?'

'A lot of nights I crash in London.' Scott hadn't heard that expression for years.

'How do you manage for clothes and things?'

'I carry them around with me. Anyway, tomorrow I'm going away for the weekend. I'll be able to stay away longer now this trial has collapsed.' She pointed at the bag she had put behind the front door of his flat.

'Where shall we go?' he said.

'It's your invitation. Don't you have to go somewhere, though? Your clerk said something.'

'The seminar? No, that's tomorrow. I can go tonight or arrive there tomorrow morning.'

'Well, then. You decide.'

'I can't offer anything as good as the pub you took me to.'

'I liked your club place.'

'We don't want to go there, do we?'

'No.'

'How about the Royal Court? It's only up the road. It's *Oleanna* or something, about people being superior to each other. David Hare.'

'OK,' she said. 'Do we have to hurry?'

'No. There's plenty of time. I'll phone.'

'I'll change. Where's the bathroom?'

He pointed and she took her bag and went in. 'Can I have a shower?' she shouted.

'No problem.'

Before he phoned the theatre he started to clear things away.

The doorbell rang.

Scott turned the kitchen tap off, put the glasses to one side and dried his hands. It seemed a very domestic activity. He went to the door and opened it, still holding the towel.

At first he could not make the figure out because the light was behind the shape in the doorway. It was a man, a large man, but Scott couldn't see his features.

'I want to speak to you,' the shape said, and in the same moment Scott realised it was Charlton.

Charlton, the policeman. What did he want?

'What about?'

'You'll see,' Charlton said, and he pushed Scott back into the room.

Later, when he looked back on it, Scott was amused that the only words he could find were so obvious.

'You can't do this,' he said.

'Can't I?' said Charlton. 'Who's going to stop me?'

He pushed Scott again, making him fall now.

'It's not so easy for you when you're on your own, is it . . . sir? And you haven't got your silly costume on to protect you.'

He kicked Scott hard on the thigh.

Scott heard himself shout out, 'Hey!'

'I don't suppose you'll answer back so easily either? Will you . . . sir?'

He pulled Scott to his feet and hit him in the face.

Again Scott heard himself shout out.

His head felt as though the top had been lifted off. He watched Charlton as the policeman prepared to hit him again. For a moment he was able to speak.

'Is this for what happened in court?'

'Partly,' said Charlton, and he hit Scott in the stomach.

Now there was real pain, making everything else seem irrelevant. He felt as though there was a cupboard on top of him. Then he realised it wasn't a cupboard but a huge weight of water. The only problem was how to get another breath. He knew there was something that you should do in this situation, but he couldn't remember what it was. If he could remember he might do it.

He lay on the ground expecting to be hit again.

It wasn't at all like in films. It wasn't so simple. For a start, time didn't seem to exist. He couldn't work out whether he had been lying on the seabed for only a moment or for longer. And the films left out the indignity of it.

There it was again. Charlton kicked him in the leg. It was odd how painful that was. Legs are indifferent items. He wouldn't have thought they'd get mixed up in this sort of thing.

Then, quite clearly, he remembered. That's wrong. If you're Irish you're quite likely to get your leg busted or shot – by some jerk who comes crashing in through the door.

Charlton had said something. It had sounded like a question. 'What do you want?' he said, trying to reply.

He looked up. Charlton was sitting in the armchair, talking to him. What he was saying was quite clear, but Scott couldn't understand it. His head was ringing, then it started buzzing. Obviously the eggs were done.

'I'm sorry. I don't know what you're talking about.'

'You're lying.'

'I'm not,' said Scott. 'I've only just climbed aboard.'

Charlton looked at him. He was puzzled. 'What?' he said.

It seemed perfectly obvious to Scott. He had been in the water looking up, the heavy weight had been removed, there had been a buzzing noise, that was the eggs, everything was ready now, so he climbed aboard. 'I've only just climbed aboard,' he repeated.

'Stop pissing me about, you cunt,' said Charlton. 'Where are the papers?' And he kicked Scott in the head.

Scott fell back into the water, and the buzzing noise began again. It wasn't an egg timer, that was a mistake, it was a depth pressure device telling him he mustn't dive too far down.

When he looked up, Charlton was pulling some books off a shelf.

Slowly Scott got to his feet. He looked at himself in a mirror opposite and was surprised to see he looked quite normal. That was odd since he felt like an alien. He tried to move to a chair but when he leaned on a table it didn't support him. He fell over.

'Are you alone?' said Charlton.

'Yes,' he said.

He tried to get up again, this time moving across the room on his hands and knees to get to a stronger table on which to pull himself up.

'What do you want?'

'You know damn well what I want.'

'No I don't,' said Scott. He wanted to say it in a friendly, convincing sort of way, so that this man believed him. But the atmosphere was all wrong.

'Don't piss me about.' Charlton turned towards him again.

Scott suddenly remembered what it was he was meant to do in this situation. You hit the guy back.

'No I don't,' he said, 'unless you mean that.' He pointed to a shelf.

Charlton turned away to look and Scott hit him with a marble table lamp.

How hard do you hit someone? Scott didn't know. Once he had a client who had killed a man in a kebab house. His client had picked up a chair and hit a customer over the head with it. Of course, it cracked his skull and killed him almost immediately.

Scott's client had said, 'I didn't know that was going to happen. I thought that if you hit someone over the head with a chair, the chair broke. I've seen it on the telly dozens of times.'

Scott understood what he meant. On the television the guy who is hit either shakes his head and then carries on, or he disappears out of the film. No one ever got killed being hit by a chair – except in real life. The jury hadn't been impressed with this explanation and they convicted Scott's client of murder.

Scott hit Charlton as hard as he could just above the elbow.

Charlton stood there. At first he looked as though he was going to fall over, but he didn't. His eyes opened wide and he tried to say something. Scott didn't want to talk to him any more so he hit him on the side of the head and Charlton went straight to the ground.

'I need to cut his trouser leg off,' Scott said, and he began to look for a pair of scissors.

'What the hell is going on?' Catherine appeared, wearing a towel.

'Didn't you hear this guy hitting me? He just walked in the door and attacked me.' Scott knew it sounded improbable so he didn't go into it at length. 'I have to cut his trouser leg off.'

'Why?'

'Because that'll prevent him going anywhere.'

'What on earth are you doing?' she said.

'I'm looking for the bloody scissors,' he said. He felt like crying. He had never felt so much pain. Since . . . He couldn't remember. He didn't think he had ever felt pain before.

'Sit down,' she said.

She smelt amazing. Why was she having a shower in his flat? It seemed almost as odd as this man walking in and hitting him. Of course, if this were real life then he would be able to cope. His hand found a pair of scissors and he bent down to start cutting.

'Oh God,' said Catherine, watching him. 'What shall I do?'

'Get dressed,' said Scott.

As she went past he pulled at the towel and it fell down, revealing her naked back. He saw a direct connection between violence and desire. 'If you don't I'm likely to move to stage seven all in one go without asking permission,' he said. But his mouth wasn't working properly and he wasn't sure it came out right.

He was going to have to do something about that.

'It's the police officer in the case. Charlton.'

'Is he all right?'

'I don't know. I knocked him out. Knocking people out is much more dangerous than people credit. You watch a boxing match, if the guy is knocked out the doctor goes wild. Anyway, I've cut his trouser leg off.'

'Why did you do that?'

'I've no idea.'

'Come on.'

'I've no idea. It seemed to be the right thing to do at the time. Like hitting him was. I wasn't myself.'

'What did he want?'

'I don't know. Though I don't think he likes me. I can't say I blame him for that.'

'He's waking up.'

Charlton lifted his head from the floor.

'He's not dead, then.'

'Not completely.'

'Are we all right?'

'I don't know. I've never been in this position before. Pour some water on him.'

'Is that right?'

'All I've got to go on is what happens in films. Although I once went to a first aid competition that my father was judging in Aberdare. They poured water on people. My father was the judge.'

Scott remembered being at a rugby match in Cardiff when a man fainted and lay on the ground next to his father while his father watched the game. Scott had been disappointed, thinking that since his father was a doctor he would do something spectacular. In his experience medicine seemed to be lots of doing nothing.

Catherine poured water on Charlton's face. He opened his eyes and said, 'You hit me.'

'Yes,' said Scott. 'I'll hit you again if you don't go.'

Charlton heaved himself up and staggered to the door.

'I didn't think it would be so easy,' said Scott.

'I'll come back,' Charlton said as he went.

'If you do, I'll call the police.'

'Don't be so silly,' said Charlton. 'I am the police and I'll bring more. What happened to my trouser leg?'

'It got torn off in the struggle,' Scott said.

'I'm going to have you too,' said Charlton to Catherine. 'You're both in this and you're both in trouble.'

'What do we do?'

'I don't know.'

'Do we report this to the police?'

'What do we say to them?'

'If we don't, then what do we do?'

'I think we make a record of what happened.'

'How?'

'Photographs and doctor. And we write a statement out. And then we go off somewhere for a while. The only question we have to answer then is why we didn't go to the police. If it's ever asked. Unfortunately if it is asked, it's a rather good question. But I'm not going to risk the good intentions of any policeman on this one.' He got up. Moving was becoming more difficult, not less, and his face ached.

'I'll get a bag. I've got a camera. We take the bit of trouser leg with us.'

Across the road there was a doctor who knew Scott's uncle. That was the way things were. They knocked and told the doctor's wife the problem: Scott had been attacked and he needed a record of the injuries. Could Sir Noël help for a moment?

'You're JD's nephew, aren't you?' she said.

'Yes, and I'm one of Sir Noël's patients,' said Scott.

'I'll fetch him now,' she said. 'You just wait here.'

They sat in the waiting room furnished with copies of *Country Life*. On the mantelshelf there were invitations, including one that reported that 'I am commanded and requested to invite you to a reception . . .' It had a royal coat of arms on it.

'What a smart doctor you have,' said Catherine. 'I didn't know private doctors like this existed any more in this country.'

The doctor examined his bruises and made a note of them.

'This is in case I sue,' said Scott, and within the hour they were on their way back to the flat.

As they came to the corner directly across from his block of flats they saw a white Sherpa police van.

'We'd better leave immediately,' Scott said. 'It looks as though Charlton's come back in force.' He had parked the Mercedes a little way down the road. They got in and drove away.

'What are we going to do?'

'You keep asking that.'

'Are you all right driving?'

'Yes. I think I'm doing it rather well. I'm feeling better now.'

The car slid along almost of its own accord.

'What . . . ?'

'Are you asking what we're going to do again?'

'Yes.'

'Get some money.'

'Good idea.'

'Right.' He stopped the car outside Hallinans' office in Victoria. 'You'll be safe here. They're a good firm of solicitors. If you're in trouble they'll probably run out to protect you. I'm going over there.'

He crossed the road to the cashpoint.

In books people who are running away don't need money, so he got a lot out just to be sure. She was watching from the car and, as he got in, she reached across and touched his face.

'Does it hurt a lot?' she asked.

'It hurts so much it makes me angry,' he said.

'What did he want?'

'Search me.'

'No. Come on. He must have wanted something. We have to try to work it out. It must be to do with the case.'

'Perhaps they want me arrested for contempt.' He thought about it. 'It's possible. It's happened before. There was a guy who said something or did something, I don't know what it was, to a judge in the old crown court that used to sit in St James's Square.'

He turned off over Lambeth Bridge, heading for the New Cross Road. 'That barrister had actually left the court when the judge sent a policeman after him to arrest him. Funny thing was, as I remember, at first the policeman refused and said he had no power to do it. He was probably right. Anyway, the barrister sued the judge. Got nowhere. You can't sue a judge, or at least it isn't easy.'

'Perhaps they were arresting you for contempt then?'

'But why should he hit me?'

'That's what he's like.'

Scott thought for a moment. 'Maybe it's the car park thing.'

'What's that?'

'I had an argument with the car park attendant at the Temple.'

'Don't be silly.'

'Oh, you can't be so sure. I had a friend who had an argument with one of the car park people and he was called up to be told off by a Lord Justice of Appeal. These are major matters of status.'

They were beginning to get clear of central London and were feeling less tense.

'Status, my God. I once asked one of the circuit committee why it was that only the circuit committee get to vote on the election of the circuit leader, why not the whole membership? And I got about as friendly a reaction as if I had said that, on balance, I was in favour of child abuse. The whole merry-go-round is self-electing, self-justifying. I could easily imagine being arrested for rudeness to the Inner Temple car park man.'

They were moving faster now through the scrubby outskirts of London.

'Where are we going?'

'Let's go to Forest Hill, where you live.'

'We can't.'

'Why not?'

'Because the person I live with wouldn't approve.'

The person I live with. Scott realised he felt jealous.

'You live with someone?'

'Yes.'

'Who's that, then?'

'Winifred.'

'Winifred?'

'Yes.'

'What sort of a name is that, then?'

'It's a perfectly ordinary name. A bit old-fashioned. But then she's a bit old-fashioned. She's a librarian.'

'A woman.'

'Yes.'

'You live with her?'

'Yes,' she said. Then she turned towards him and said, 'What you mean is do I live with her as in do I sleep with her. No, I don't. I sleep on my own, at least I have done recently, since there don't seem to be any men around for me to get into bed with.'

That was pretty clear.

'Where are we going?' she said again.

'We'll be going north in a moment, or at least we will after we've gone through the Blackwall Tunnel.'

'And then?'

'And then, and then . . .' He thought about it. He said, 'Perhaps we can go to the seminar.'

'What seminar?'

'The judges' seminar.'

'What's that?'

'The Lord Chancellor holds seminars for all judges to discuss sentencing.'

'You? A judge?'

'Sometimes.'

'You're not.'

'Yes I am, I'm a recorder. I've been appointed by the Queen. I've got a piece of paper with her name and mine on it. That's a part-time judge.'

'Is this true?'

'Yes. I sit as a judge for a month a year.'

'Do you enjoy it?'

'Yes, I do, rather.'

'Why?'

'It's no strain. Because the result of the case doesn't matter to me.'

'But you send people to prison.'

'Not often.'

'Who was the last person you sent to prison?'

'A man who hit a woman with a brick. He said she had cut him up when he wanted to overtake her. I had no choice really.'

'No, I suppose you didn't,' she said.

Chapter 15

'I think things are getting pretty dramatic,' said Gregory on the phone to Arlot.

'Go on.'

'Well, I went to the trial in London. You remember I told you I was going to watch a trial?'

'Yes.'

'And . . . It sounds silly, but a lot of things fell into place.'

'How close to action are we?'

Gregory found the question quite surprising, especially given the indifference with which Arlot had treated his work so far.

'Well, I should say pretty close. In fact I think the other side are moving already.'

'The other side?'

Gregory was getting some reaction out of him at last.

'I think there is another side now. It's got that clear.'

'We'd better talk.'

'When?'

'Now.'

'Where?'

'I'll come to you.'

'Where?'

'The fish bar at Victoria. Overton's. A bit along from where the number eleven stops outside the sex shop. I'll be there in half an hour.'

Gregory found that Arlot had got there before him. As he gave his coat to the waiter he could see him hunched on one of the stools at the end of the bar. He looked totally out of place, yet, come to think of it, there was a scaly look about him, as though he were covered in gaberdine. Like Mr Fisher on the lily-pad.

'Um, hallo,' Arlot said as Gregory sat down. 'I ordered some food and some wine. And things.' He waved a piece of bread vaguely at the food in front of him. 'And I'm expecting some more in a while.'

He didn't seem inclined to talk about much else.

'What we used to do. We used to have lunch here, then we'd go to Brighton on the Brighton Belle which left at three o'clock. Camp coffee and Lord Olivier, as they say. Walk on the beach. Throw some stones at the pier. To English's for supper. And you didn't feel you'd moved at all. You'll eat?'

Gregory was hungry suddenly, and sitting on the bar stools gave the whole thing a curious intensity, like being at a trough.

'What's happened?' said Arlot.

'Well, it's come together a bit.'

'Uh huh?' Arlot was mopping cheese sauce up.

'How much do I need to tell you?'

'Not much I suppose.'

'Why didn't you tell me what you knew at the start, then?'

'It was better you found out. Then you'd know what was the truth and what was guesswork.'

Gregory considered asking about security, but then decided he'd better not. The barman put two seashells down in front of him. They were covered in potato and were steaming.

'Watch it,' said Arlot. 'They'll be bloody hot.'

'I went to this trial.'

'Who was in it?'

'Well, the names you'll know: Charlton, Morgan and Cantor.'

'Was Jennings involved?'

'No.'

'What about Scribner?'

'Yes, he was the judge. Is he connected?'

'Yes. He ran the inquiry into the Garth Boys' Home.'

'What's that?'

'Well, you'd better look it up, hadn't you?'

Clearly Arlot wasn't going to unbend just because they were eating fish together.

Gregory said, 'The trial was like all the others you gave me to look at.

168

The police arrived out of the blue just at the right moment. The defendant, Hector, immediately claimed he'd been set up by an informer. The whole trial then began to revolve upon whether or not the defence should be told who the informer was and what information he gave.'

'When we ran informers it was the police who decided who was told what. And that was that.'

'But this one went wrong because defence counsel managed to show that the police raid must have been the result of a tip-off. The next thing he was going to do was to ask the judge for the background papers again, but the judge stopped the trial.'

At last the scallops had cooled enough to be eaten, though he still found it difficult since the shells skittered around the plate when he tried to get at the fish.

'And there's more,' he said. 'I knew the defence counsel, Scott . . .' Then he remembered. 'Of course, you know him too. Obviously he owed me one so I decided to go to speak to him and I followed him to the Temple where his offices are. When I got there he'd gone, but while I was waiting in the main room – nothing's private there, you know – Charlton and Cantor walked in.

'They interrupted everything and were shouting about some papers Scott was meant to have taken away from the court. The clerk said he couldn't do anything, but then Charlton pulled out his warrant card and Cantor said Scribner had sent them.

' "If we get the papers back now, there's no harm done," they said.

'So Scott's clerk searched the brief but there was nothing. It was amazing. All this was happening under my nose. I got out of the room and at the bottom of the steps there was Jennings waiting. That was about five o'clock.

'I thought I'd find Scott. He was in the phone book, so I got his address. It took me a while to get there but when I did Charlton had arrived already with a vanload of police. Searching his flat, I guess. Scott had gone.'

He sat back, exhausted by the urgency of the tale. 'Now, what's happened? You tell me. You're the policeman.'

'I know what happened. Scott has got the informer file.'

'How do you know?'

'Because all informer file movement requests generated by that squad are notified to me. The file was called to court just after lunch. Someone must have given it to Scott by mistake – or he stole it.'

'Well, Charlton will say he stole it, won't he? Not that it matters. Anyone with that information is in real trouble.'

Arlot gave Gregory some wine.

'I wonder where he is now?'

'Wherever he is, he's about to be squashed,' said Arlot.

Chapter 16

'I can't go to a seminar for judges,' Catherine said.

'I think it would be the perfect place to hide. Who'd think of looking for us there? You can't get much more lawful than a gaggle of judges on a weekend out.'

'I still can't go.'

'Why not?'

'Well, for a start, I'm not a judge.'

'You can mingle.'

'I can't pretend to be a judge. Don't be a dope.'

'You can be a guest, a researcher. You're already an American – that gives you a head start. As far as I can make out most young Americans are researchers.'

He had switched from the motorway to the old main road to Cambridge. He didn't fancy driving past large orange police cars sitting up on their little motorway mounds. It was a warm evening and there was little other traffic about. He said, 'I remember driving along this road once in an old sports car and it was so dark that when I looked up I couldn't say whether the roof was up or not.'

'How long does it last?'

'The seminar? The whole weekend.'

'What, you sleep there?'

'Oh yes, it'll be a conference centre sort of place, if it's like the others.'

They were approaching Cambridge, just where the Pink Geranium restaurant used to be.

'We all have breakfast together,' he said. 'Sixty judges. That's a strange experience. The first time I went, one of them came down to breakfast in a rugger shirt and was warned off. Not the correct dress code for a judge's breakfast, apparently.'

There was silence. The car was extraordinary. Occasionally it made a whooshing noise, but other than a faint humming and the noise of the tyres on the road the outside world slid past them as though on a cinema screen. He thought about it. Of course Charlton wouldn't have the number of this car.

'Judges. Funny word. In the plural it doesn't seem to work properly. Like trouser in the singular. Of course you can use it as a verb, you can judge something, you can trouser something.'

'Why did you cut his trouser leg off?'

'So he couldn't get about.'

'But why should that stop him?'

'Well, it would me.'

'What did he want?'

'I really don't know. I just can't imagine. He seemed pretty angry, though, and he was searching the bookcase, so it must be a book or papers or something like that.'

There was silence as they began to become aware of each other's company.

'What an extraordinary thing to happen,' he said. 'No one ever hit me before. Except Willington at school.'

He thought about it. Why had Charlton come?

He said, 'Once I took a prosecution exhibit home by mistake. I remember thinking then that they might come after me. Can you remember, did we take anything out of the court?'

'No, I don't think so. We didn't handle any original exhibits. Everything we had was a copy wasn't it?' she said.

The road swung in a big curve northwards.

ı here used to be a warning sign here, Dangerous Bend in French,' he said. 'I suppose they thought that anybody who had a driving licence had a degree. Either that or it didn't matter if non-French speakers were killed.'

He thought about Charlton again.

'He said he'd come back and he did. Let's ring Bill to see if they told him anything. He's the porter at the flats.' There was a telephone box up ahead. 'Look, we can do it from here. I've got a telephone credit card.'

Bill had never seen anything like it. One moment he had been leaning on the counter rolling a cigarette and staring out through the door, and the next he was surrounded by policemen. 'Though they didn't look like police, Mr Scott. Right yobs, some of them.

'They went upstairs to your flat and they were about to kick the door in. So I said, "I'll get the spare key." They insisted I remain to see what they did, but it made no difference, me being there. They threw everything all over the place. I said there was no need for that and one of them called me Granddad. I told him he had asked me to be there and so I was, but if they were going to behave like that I was going. And the top one asked me to stay. He asked where you were. I said I didn't know. He asked me about your car, and I told them a green Volvo, an old one.

'I said, What's wrong? And he said you was interfering with the court of justice. I said, Well, he's in courts all the time. And he said, I know.

'Then they left. It's all locked up now. He said there's a warrant out for you. And for me to tell you if I saw you.'

Scott was staggered. 'A warrant for your arrest.' He said it out loud, to see if it felt the same when he did. Interfering with the court. That must be obstructing the course of justice. Well, it wasn't assault, it was worse. Charlton hadn't come back because of the assault, he had come back to get what he was searching for.

Scott stepped out of the old-fashioned phone box and the silence of the fields seeped into him. To their right a slow hill rose up in a great sweep. Darkness was creeping down towards the road. He was wanted and on the run. It seemed ridiculous. Then for a moment he felt a twinge in his back, as though he were waking from a long sleep.

'Well, they'll have to find me first.'

'What?' said Catherine.

'I said, They'll have to find me first.'

Later it became pitch dark. The lights of the car picked out the road as it stretched straight ahead.

'The place should be somewhere here on the right,' he said. A dark shadow loomed up, the shape of a roof just visible as an even darker patch in the dark sky, then a large hedge that ran alongside the road, and suddenly light spilled out on to the tarmac, making the cold, flat road seem even more desolate.

'Yes, this is it,' he said. A sign announced the grand name: Madely Hall.

They pulled into the drive and the car's tyres made a crunching noise on the gravel. It reminded Scott of the opening sequence of a 1950s movie. 'We're like the scientist and his attractive assistant arriving to investigate strange goings-on at the Grange,' he said.

She turned towards him, her face lit up by the lights from the door. He realised that looking at her was becoming a very easy thing to do.

'That's reckless stereotyping if I ever heard it,' she said. 'A flat contradiction of the equal access process.'

'What?' he said. 'Equal access to what?'

'To me.'

Scott remembered. 'Remind me, what level am I on now?'

'Level four,' she said, 'but calling me an attractive assistant throws the whole process into doubt.' He kept looking at her. Her whole face was mobile and when she smiled she seemed to glow. He said, 'Well, the handsome scientist and his attractive assistant. What happens is it becomes a race to see who can get to level seven first, the hero or the deranged foreign professor whom they've come to investigate.'

He pulled out the bags and pushed the hydraulic locks down. They hissed sadly.

'Most times, you'll be pleased to know, it's the handsome young scientist who gets there first.'

They scrunched across the gravel towards the main entrance. 'But often it's a damn close-run thing.'

The tension of their arrival was getting to him. If there was a warrant out then they'd have found out where he was going by now. He noticed that he had already started worrying what 'they' would be doing. Charlton had already been replaced by a nameless force, all-seeing, all-powerful.

The main doors opened on to a large pillared hall. The floor was stone-flagged with faded carpets spread across it. To their right was a vast grate with a flaming log, the size of a barrel, crackling into the chimney.

They both stood and stared.

'The Lord Chancellor has really pushed the boat out this time,' he said.

To the left there was a counter let into the wall and behind it stood a smiling receptionist. 'Can I help?'

Scott had hoped to drift in less conspicuously. After all, it wasn't the best place to get arrested, but then what was?

He went to the counter and gave his name. The woman checked a list. 'Ah yes,' she said. 'Recorder Scott. One moment, please.' She went through a door to the back of the office. Catherine came over to him. 'Is everything all right?' she said.

'I don't know. She's gone off to check something. That could mean anything.'

In the office they heard a telephone making the sound of a connection. 'Is she ringing?'

There were voices. The words were indistinct. They heard a man say, 'Yes, he is, I heard this evening.'

Scott covered his anxiety by talking. 'I get enough tension in real life.'

'We're in real life now,' said Catherine.

'Hardly,' he said. 'How many times have you been on the run with a wanted man? Doesn't happen, does it?'

The woman came back. She had something in her hand. The voice talking on the phone said, 'Well, if he's leaving, who's going to take over on *Question Time*, then?'

'Here's your name-tag, Mr Scott.' She handed him a tag that said 'Jeremy Scott, Recorder'. 'We would prefer that you wear it at all times.'

Scott pinned it on and as he did so he saw that the receptionist was holding another badge saying 'Guest'. She was looking at him, wanting him to speak. He took the plunge. 'Ah, should my guest Cath . . .' Catastrophically, he realised he didn't know Catherine's surname. That said something about the way they worked. He only knew her by her first name, like a servant.

The lady at the desk rescued him. 'Yes, of course you have a guest with you. Madam, here you are. We're pleased to welcome you on Mr Recorder Scott's introduction. Perhaps you would care to sign?'

He and Catherine looked at each other.

'Well, that's all right. I can book you both in: Mr Recorder Scott and guest.'

The receptionist scribbled in a book, and started punching numbers on a computer keyboard. 'I shall just . . .' she said, hitting the Return button on the word 'just', ' . . . rearrange the rooms, since you'll be wanting a little more space than we had originally assigned.' The small office sprang into life as the computer began printing. The receptionist looked around with pleasure at the noise as the machines chuckled away. 'Like chickens, aren't they?' she said. 'You'll be in the central building, then, up the main stairs over there. Here is your key, a timetable, and a local guide for Ms . . .' She stumbled over the sound so successfully that she seemed to have said a name. ' . . . should she wish to go out sightseeing in the daytime. Supper will be served late tonight, breakfast from seven. The bar is through that door.' They walked towards the stairs, conscious of the receptionist's eyes.

'Recorder. She called you "Recorder",' hissed Catherine.

'Yes. That was odd,' said Scott. 'No one else ever has before. It's wrong actually.'

'And she assumed I'm your tootsie.'

'My what?'

'Your doxie, floxie, little Miss Whatsit. You've got all those words in English. In America we'd say main squeeze, bitch . . .'

'Oh. You mean my mistress?' He was almost laughing out loud.

'Yes,' Catherine screeched. 'I've never been so humiliated—'

'Hang on,' said Scott. 'You're beginning to sound like someone's mother.'

As they turned at the bend of the grand staircase they both looked down and the receptionist smiled up at them.

'Go on,' said Scott, 'wave.'

'I will not,' Catherine said, but then the receptionist transferred her attention to the phone which started ringing.

Both of them stiffened. As they turned out of sight the receptionist looked up at them.

It was Catherine's turn to talk nervously. 'So this is what it's like, all you judges and recorders.' She managed to make it sound like a term of abuse. 'You go off together and you bring guests with you . . .'

'Well, I don't actually think that's right,' said Scott. 'These events are usually very ordinary and everybody behaves impeccably. Save for the occasional rugby shirt. Even the luxury is completely wrong. You shouldn't get the idea that this is what it's like normally.' He laughed. 'Do I sound like a politician?'

'You sound insufferable,' she said.

'Insufferable or not, I've got us a bed for the night,' he said as he opened the big door to their room. 'Look.'

The room was stunning. A huge bed hung with drapes at the head and foot faced into a bay window that looked out into the night. Facing the windows and the fireplace were two wing chairs, and, in front of them, miraculously, a blazing wood fire.

He walked over to it. 'It's gas-effect,' he said, 'but what a room. Do you think they've kicked out the senior judge to accommodate us? Mr Justice Sir Bernard Bumbleberry is probably having to sleep in my small bachelor bed down next to the paddock.'

He bounced on the huge feather bed. 'This isn't what you'd call a bachelor bed, is it?'

Catherine made a humphing noise and went into the bathroom, slamming the door. Scott looked around at the amazing room and then lay down on the bed.

He felt he was sinking down and down. Then he realised he was hurting all over. 'I'm not surprised,' he said. 'I don't get beaten up much nowadays.'

When he awoke he couldn't move. His head ached and his legs and back were stiffening. His right arm had been underneath him as he had turned over on the bed and now it was numb.

'Come on,' a voice said, 'you can't just lie there like that. Either go to bed or get up.'

He knew her voice but he couldn't remember what he was doing. He set his memory to work at it. Eventually he grasped an image that was recent: he was leaving London, ringing Bill. Talking about the police. The large house. He looked around the big room. What had seemed absurd hardened and resolved into reality.

'What do you want to do?' said the voice.

'I think I should like a drink. Let's go and get a drink. But first my teeth. I have to wash. Then let's go downstairs.'

They found the bar, a large room – it must have been the morning room of the old house – with a scattering of men sitting around it.

'I'm the only woman,' said Catherine, in a whisper, as they crossed the huge carpet.

'No you're not. There's Louise over there.' Scott waved across the room. 'And there by the big window, there's Isobel. There's lots of women nowadays.'

'Two,' said Catherine.

The men at the bar were uniformly dressed in tweed jackets and well-pressed trousers, with the occasional yellow sweater. They leaned negligently on the bar, clubbable, chatting.

He ordered drinks and they stood at one end of the room, surveying the people.

'Observe the shoes,' said Scott. 'Well polished, creased. Never new. Of course, you can tell the occasional shit. He'll have a gold buckle affair and no laces.'

There was a low hum of conversation.

'That's one, he's a Bunty Sporling sort of bloke. Only ever wears his father's clothes. He was photographed in some newspaper wearing them once.'

'Who's Bunty Sporling?'

'There's a photo of him in the Old Bailey Bar mess, "From Bunty Sporling to his chums at the mess, 1914". Presumably he sent it to his chums just before he went out to get shot at the front.

'See him over there?' They looked at a man talking animatedly to his companion. 'That one. He's known as the Detective Sergeant. He's talking to the Perfect English Gentleman, who's a lovely man. The Perfect English Gentleman is the judge who's been sent to run the court out near Tilbury. He had an argument with his senior judge over some message he threw in the wastepaper basket.'

'Do you know them all?'

'Most of them. Look, there's Buffy. He's the wittiest man I know. Except for my friend Guy whose brother collects lawnmowers.'

'Are you going to go on like this all the time?' she said.

'Why not?'

'Because it's, it's . . .' She was puzzled as to what to say. 'Not boring . . .'

'Thank God for that . . .'

' . . . just irrelevant.'

'Why irrelevant? Not relevant to what?'

'To what's happening.'

Scott was beginning to feel light-headed. Perhaps it wasn't such a good idea to have a drink given the state he was in.

'Oh God,' he said, 'I suppose I ought to do something, give myself up or whatever one does. On the other hand, what for? I don't even know what I've done. Why should I kowtow to Charlton. He won't even tell me why he came to my flat.'

'Perhaps you didn't give him a chance.'

They sat down at a table near the fire. It was extraordinarily restful. 'Of course I gave him the chance. It's he who didn't give me the chance. He was just a bully.'

'Where have we heard that before?' she said, and before he could reply, 'Whoops, look who's here.'

As she spoke, Butler Jennings walked into the room, crossed to the bar and ordered a drink.

'They're all round us,' said Catherine.

'If he comes near me I'm going to tell him what a shit he is.' Scott laughed. 'It'll be like that Thurber cartoon where the guy walks up to someone and says, "I'll fight you any time, you and your rabbit." '

Catherine looked at him blankly.

'Of course, there's no rabbit,' he explained. 'The man offering to fight is drunk. But in the cartoon there's a great big badly drawn rabbit. Jennings and his rabbit, Cantor.'

Again he felt the twitch in his back that he'd noticed earlier when he had been told that Charlton was after him. When he felt it before it had meant Charlton didn't matter. Now it was saying that there really wasn't a very great need to behave properly any more. Things don't matter that much. If things stop mattering then you have a kind of freedom.

'Have your done your homework?' a voice behind them said.

Scott turned and laughed.

'Hey, Stephen, are you here?' he said. 'Catherine, this is Stephen. He's an old friend of mine. We used to be at the Bar together before they promoted him. We call him Stephen K – after the chap in the book.' He told Stephen, 'Catherine's here as an observer.' It didn't seem to cause any surprise, so he pushed on. 'She's come to watch us.'

'Another observer? Well, we spend our whole time being observed nowadays, to see if we're racist or sexist or just plain out of touch. Which point of view are you going to be observing us from?'

'Nothing particular. It's just to keep you on your toes,' said Scott.

'That's normal, then,' said Stephen. 'Have you done your homework?'

'What homework is this?' said Catherine.

'We get a set of cases that we have to read before we come. It's that yellow book I had. I've done some of them,' Scott said, 'but then something came up.'

A roar of laughter from just down the bar interrupted them. A group had gathered around Jennings, and Scott could hear him say, 'Well, the King of Norway was meant to be sitting next to me—'

A voice stopped him in his flow – 'Wasn't he called Hakon or something?' – and Scott watched with amusement as a flash of annoyance appeared on Jennings's face at the interruption.

'What about the window-ledge case? Number four in the book,' Stephen said.

'What's all this about?' said Catherine.

'It's one of the test cases we're going to have to do.'

Another voice interrupted. 'It's about conditional intent. The man was standing on the ladder at the bedroom window, naked in his socks, with his penis on the window sill . . .' Scott turned and saw it was Jennings. 'The court said he was a burglar since he had entered – even if only a very little bit of him – since he had entered the room.'

Jennings was grinning at Catherine and Scott found himself particularly disliking the grin. There was nothing soft about it; it was all teeth and skull.

'Trust Jennings to start talking dirty,' said Stephen. 'Do you know our Mr Butler Jennings? The most influential MP at the Bar – especially now we've got a Home Secretary whose legal knowledge is limited to being briefed in planning cases by female Tory councillors. May I introduce Catherine? She's an observer . . .'

'I think we've met, haven't we?' said Jennings.

'I don't think so,' said Catherine. 'I would have remembered.'

At first Jennings seemed not to notice what she had said, then Scott realised he had taken it as a compliment.

'You watch out for Jennings,' said Stephen. 'He'd bring back hanging for burglary if he had the chance. It would be a form of short, sharp shock, the "crack-down" school of criminology.'

There was a flash in Jennings's eyes, as though he had just remembered something, then Scott saw what he had seen so often on the television. Jennings's mouth opened and words came out.

As he spoke Scott watched his eyes. He had the faraway look of someone discreetly checking his wristwatch during a party. ' . . . here are the figures – since hanging was abolished . . .' His eyes flicked to one side and Scott followed his gaze. Over at the door the senior judge had come in, immediately identifiable by his glossy nondescriptness. ' . . . we have seen a sharp rise not just in murders . . .' Jennings's voice carried on quite separately from the rest of him.

The senior judge started to greet people and began to circle the room. ' . . . naturally the people least affected by crime, especially violent crime, make the biggest noise against hanging; what we need is some good old-fashioned common sense . . .' He became even more detached from his opinions. ' . . . one has the spectacle of the House of Commons completely disregarding . . .' The senior judge stopped, ending up in their group standing at the end of the bar. ' . . . completely indifferent to the views of their constituents who, after all . . . Good evening, Sir Anthony.' Jennings's voice did not vary a note; only the subject-matter changed. 'It is good to see you.'

Here was a meeting between two grandees of the system. Scott watched with interest.

'Why, hallo, Jennings,' the judge said. Was there a trace of condescension in the remark? After all, the respective status of these two was paradoxical. Becoming a High Court judge was all to do with huge intellectual success and, just as important, being acceptable to a tight group. Jennings was a populist. It didn't matter what rubbish he talked, he didn't have to pay any entrance fee. But he had the power.

Sir Anthony Tippett introduced himself to the group with the ease of a host. This was, after all, his conference. 'I'm a little late,' he said. 'There was some confusion over the allocation of rooms.'

He smiled in a confidential way at the group. 'I haven't missed anything, I hope?'

'Only Jennings here on his high horse about law and order,' said Stephen. 'And you'll be happy to know that he feels he represents the *Sun* reader.'

There was a moment of coolness. 'Yes,' said the judge. 'Well, we've all had our difficulties with the *Sun* newspaper.'

It was the usual complaint. The newspaper was continually on the lookout for examples of sex offenders being given probation. The sentencing system was being taken over by judges' fears of appearing in half-moon glasses on the front page, labelled 'old git'.

'That's because you don't represent *Sun* readers,' said Jennings. 'Look at this North Country case . . .' Two child killers had recently had the length of their sentences effectively increased by the Home Secretary. ' . . . the Home Secretary was quite properly influenced by a poll run by the *Sun*.'

'He'd twist in the wind,' said another voice, 'at the slightest breath of public opinion.'

Scott watched Jennings. How would he react to the populist charge? Was it right to run the law on the whim of a tabloid newspaper, famous

181

mainly for its headlines? Or would he choose patrician detachment as his role?

Catherine solved the problem by interrupting. 'You should elect judges, like we do where I come from.'

They all turned on her.

'But the decision would be so uninformed,' was the first remark. It was the standard response, but Stephen K defended her. 'What's informed about it now? I wouldn't have got this job if I hadn't gone to Eton and been in the right set of chambers.'

'You mustn't say things like that out loud,' said Sir Anthony, 'even if it is true.' They laughed.

Scott could see that Jennings didn't know which side suited his view of himself better. Clearly he had not decided which image to project yet.

'But if they're elected,' Scott said, 'the whole thing would be decided by the political parties, and we'd end up with yet another layer of people beholden to the party line.'

This was a little close to the bone, and Jennings swung round to look at him.

'You don't mean me, I hope?'

'You'll do,' said Scott.

He wondered whether to laugh and take the edge off it. But he didn't.

The silence following this remark was broken by a call from the door, 'Dinner is served, ladies and gentlemen,' and the group broke up.

'You've done quite well today. You've been rude to a judge, nearly killed a police officer, and now you've insulted a Member of Parliament,' said Catherine. 'You deserve to be arrested.'

Chapter 17

'How are informers organised?'

'It's a very tight system.'

'Do they always deal with one officer?'

'Yes, they have a handler assigned to them. He's the contact.'

'How much contact do they have with their handlers?'

'As much as they like. After all, without informers most crime squads would be lost. You don't stop crime by plodding up and down the street, even in a big Sherpa van. Not proper crime. It's like most things, you have to buy your way in.'

'How does it work?'

'There's proper structure now, though it used to work on an *ad hoc* basis. Eventually it became difficult to work out what people were up to. Any time a detective was goofing off somewhere he wrote up the time unaccounted for in his police diary as "meeting informant" – anything a detective didn't want to talk about came out under that heading.'

Arlot poured out more wine; the bottle seemed tiny in his hands, the glass more like a sherry glass. Gregory found himself thinking about Arlot's size. 'Acromegalic' – the word suited the man; he looked rugged, vast. He had read that the illness could be treated now, it was all something to do with hormones. If he touched him would he catch it? Strange idea. Of course he wouldn't.

'It got so the whole informer business became uncheckable, and it also became a very good excuse for sitting in public houses. Now informers have proper handlers and detailed records of contact.'

'Contact names?'

'Obviously. Contact names and contact numbers.'

'Can we get access to an informer file?'

'No.'

Gregory couldn't tell if Arlot was pleased at that or not.

'Even if our investigation is into the activities of an informer?'

'No,' said Arlot. 'They're not going to let anyone see it. If it got about that a name or some information had got loose from an informer file then the whole system would begin to fold up. People have been killed for less.'

Gregory looked at him. He waited to see if Arlot would say anything else. He didn't.

'Who is Morgan, then. Where does he come from?'

'I don't know.'

'Who's Tredegar?'

'I don't know.'

'There are references to Tredegar in one of the files that Charlton dealt with.'

'Could be anyone.'

Gregory wanted to say, 'Why don't you tell me.' He knew Arlot knew, but it would be no good. So instead he asked, 'Where do you suggest I start?'

It was the kind of question Arlot liked and he gave a clear answer. 'Well, I suppose you'd better go out and meet some people.'

Gregory arranged to meet at the Greyhound in Dulwich. It seemed a good place, neutral, not too far from Brixton, yet not the West End. Suburban and neutral. He arrived early. It was still quiet. The pub was large, with well-upholstered chairs set in great windows looking out over the main street.

It was a weird place, Dulwich, obviously wealthy but curiously provincial. In any other Western capital a place like this would have a row of exquisite shops, but here . . . Gregory could see a second-hand clothes shop across the road and he had walked past another one when he parked the car. Not that you'd notice that it was a second-hand shop at first glance, but when you looked twice you saw it was the real thing; what on earth were the landlords doing letting the place decay like this?

He bought a beer and took it over to one of the windows. He stood and watched as a jogger approached. The man was perfectly dressed in dark blue nylon from head to foot, with huge white jogging shoes. He bounced past, not even working up a sweat. Gregory watched his shoes disappearing into the distance.

The road emptied and he watched for a few moments, then he saw a face approaching. Perhaps this was the man he was meeting. 'He'll be wearing two thousand pounds' worth of clothes,' Arlot had said.

Gregory wasn't sure what two thousands pounds of clothes would look like. He had told his wife what Arlot said, that he had to meet someone and the only way he could identify him would be how he was dressed, and he'd told her, 'I don't know that I'll spot him.'

'You will,' his wife said.

It was odd. There were certain things his wife knew about and about those things she was completely confident. She hadn't even bothered to ask whether he would be safe, which was her usual worry. 'It'll be something about the way the clothes hang on him. Not flashy or anything, in fact quite ordinary. They'll be simple colours – but rich, the texture will be rich. The sort of cloth you can keep looking at.'

She was right. When the man came into the bar, at first Gregory decided it wasn't him, but when he looked again his eye caught the curl of his leather jacket and he realised what his wife meant.

He thought he himself was hidden in the window, but the man turned from the bar and came straight over to him. He must have been spotted the second he came in through the door – there had been no other time to look around. Even then there had only been a moment.

'Mr Gregory? I was told you'd be here.' The whole thing seemed very matter of fact.

'Me? What have I done? Since coming to London?

'What happened was I started just after I arrived in London. I met the Hook. It was something to do and it was exciting. What more could you want? The money? Well, there weren't much money to begin with since the Hook took it. I just carried and blocked and I never got to see what was taken.

'But then one day McGregor stopped me and said, "You know how much the Hook got off that South African? Seven hundred dollars, that's how much." I was pretty shocked, I can tell you. I didn't know McGregor and I didn't know he knew me, but I asked the Hook and he lied. I knew he lied by the way he lied. It isn't easy to lie properly and he'd had no practice. I wasn't going to have him lie to me.

'I was young then so I did something about it and the Hook didn't work again, but I also found out there was a lot of money to be made and that the Hook had been hanging on to most of it for a long time. Then I discovered that he was working for Charlton, so it was no wonder he didn't share it.

'On the other hand he taught me well and I suppose that since the whole thing was dishonest there was no reason for him to be honest to me. So I never held it against him.

'You don't know what it's like. You can't. You hold on to the bar so tight you think you're going to faint. Or you stand rigid, you make some muscle work under the skin. Or you press your leg to the floor – anything to shut out the roaring sound and the voice. You can hear the voice.

'Your lawyer has told you what the sentence is gonna be, but he can't know. The small part of a word makes all the difference, eight or eighteen. And then it's finished, it's not going to be changed. Sentences don't get changed. Or if it gets changed it's for some arbitrary reason, some senseless reason no one understands.

'You'd think there'd be some connection between what we think about someone going up for an appeal and the result. After all, we're human. We're in prison. We know as much about crime as some lord sitting there, damn sight more me, but no, there's no connection.

'The ones that seem like they should get a result get a knock-back and the ones that shouldn't, as often as not they're the ones that don't come back to the nick. They've gone. They get immediate release. Never have understood it.

'There's a tariff. It's called a tariff. A tariff for crime. Now that's bloody odd. I looked it up. For sale, it means. Everything's for sale. Even crime.

'Listen. I was down Charing Cross tube station and I looked up and there was McGregor. Our eyes met and I took off. Up the stairs, I went round a couple of places and headed for the ticket barrier and there he was, he'd got there before me. I said, "What do you want?" And he said, "You're at it, aren't you?" And I said, "You *know* you saw me do nothing." And he said, "I don't care," and he took me into the room they have there.

'Well, there's a couple of police in uniform there, having a rest or something, and I said, the moment we went in the room, "You listen to what he's going to say and watch if he says he saw me take something from persons unknown, because I've taken nothing and I've tried nothin'," and he looked at me, and the uniform police looked at him and they watched to see what he was going to say and he said nothing.

'The blokes he was with down on the platform, they'd got lost, and I said, "Are they coming?" You see, if he was going to say I had stolen something from some girl in a red macintosh, for instance, we'd see what they had to say about that when they arrived.

'After a while they never turned up. And we were looking at each other, McGregor and me. And he said to me, "You know, I could have you, even though these two are here." He was talking to me and I wasn't watching what they were doing or even if they were looking. It was just like it was me and him in the room. Just the two of us. Strange. And then he said, "Get out, but I want to see you, make it Wednesday at twelve. You come up to Stoke House, that's the headquarters. But alone, you come up alone."

'So I arranged for my solicitor to be there with me. We went up at about twelve. And we went in to see him. He took one look at me and he said, "You bastard. I said you were to come up alone." And then he said, "Look, I want to speak to you alone," and the solicitor said, "That's OK."

'And we went into the room and that's when it started. He said to me, "Look, you know me and I know you. You're a fully paid-up mechanic. You've done your time." That's what he said, those are the words he used, "You're a fully paid-up mechanic."

'And then he made an offer. He said that I was to carry on working. He said, "We can't stop you, you'll carry on. But what you can do is you can help us reduce the competition. If you're out working and you see someone at it then you let us know and we'll come over and nick him. You don't need to ring us every day, just maybe once or twice a week, we'll give you the number and you ring. And then you scarper off to King's Cross or something. And we won't bother you. We'll leave you in peace."

'I nearly said, "You don't bother me anyway," but of course that would be just asking for it and I saw that this was different. I'd been in the job for a long time, that's what he meant by the expression fully paid-up mechanic, and I'd heard of this before.

'So I said, "You'd better give me a week to think about it," and he said, "Look, if we do this we'll be doing our job. We'll leave you alone but we'll be getting a few bodies." '

Gregory looked at the man and the man smiled, rather shyly, Gregory thought. It was a curiously uncertain action in the circumstances. The glasses on the table between them were empty and the man said, 'I'll get another couple in.' He got up and went to the bar.

'I said a week, so I could get out. I would have had to pay them eventually. Or share the money I got for the information. That's always been shared with the officer. So I didn't agree to do it.'

It seemed obvious to Gregory that he had agreed, but he wasn't about to tell him what he thought. 'Tell me more about the sharing,' he said. 'Who shares?'

'Well, you pay them for the freedom to work uninterrupted and you share the informer rewards. I don't know. If the officer has five or six informants all working, then he's making good money.'

The man had obviously forgotten his denial of becoming involved. 'You pay, but it's safer, no chance of arrest. The only thing you've got to worry about is the others, if they find out what you're doing.'

'Is it a lot? Does it cost a lot?'

The young man looked at Gregory and spread his hands. 'What's a lot? How can I go and get a job now? You want me to earn a hundred and fifty a week pissing about on a building site?'

'What did you mean by working for Charlton? You said the Hook was working for Charlton.'

'Well, he decides, doesn't he? He says who can work and who can't. And it's not just my work. He runs the whole business.'

'Do you know him?'

'Charlton I'm not talking about.'

'Why not?'

'Because I know who's in charge. I'll not tell you about Charlton. Best talk to Eddie Morgan about him.'

Gregory remembered the name in the case, Morgan, Eddie Morgan. 'How do I find him?' he said casually.

The man looked at him. 'I wouldn't know,' he said.

'You said you came to London. You didn't grow up here, then?'

'No, I came. They wanted me to go on the meat rack, but I wasn't having that. No, too fucking dangerous. I wasn't getting into that. You saw that boy who was killed. He was picked up on the meat rack. You go off with some guy. Nobody knows where you're going or who you're with. Or what he's gonna do to you.

'No, I wasn't going to do that. I done it before. I've never talked about that to anyone but I saved up money and came to London to get away from it and now I'm OK. Look, I'm having a drink in here, it's a smart place here and no one pays me any attention. They don't know what's inside me.'

'You said "they" wanted you to do something. Who are "they"?' said Gregory.

The young man looked surprised. 'I thought you knew. I thought that was why you were talking to me. The Garth Boys' Home. That's where I was. I suppose I assume everybody knows, that it shows, even through these.' He pulled at his clothes contemptuously. His soft leather jacket fell back into place.

'Another thing. Who was the Hook?' said Gregory.

'The Hook? He was a genius pickpocket. He could pick your pocket while you were walking towards him. He was the best, Nick the Hook was.'

Gregory went to the Colindale Newspaper Library. It was an old-fashioned building set in the middle of a grey, characterless area of North London. Of course it wasn't characterless. Gregory knew better than that. The moment you go to live in any part of London it becomes interesting, instantly losing its anonymity. Then you can see the lines of the old village high street beneath the bloated new shop windows. And the old lane too, but it's clogged now with traffic trying to cope with its winding curves.

He manoeuvred his car into a parking space, locked it, checked there was nothing showing on the back seat, and went inside.

The library was quiet like a library should be. Readers glanced up at him resentfully as he walked by. Gregory recognised the look from his own days at college. He had done it himself. When you settled down to work every ripple of activity was a reminder that you were not going to be able to make your concentration last, that, sooner than you hoped, you'd drift away into thinking about something else. The resentful looks were an attempt to shift the blame.

He puzzled out how the library system operated. He had to fill in a slip, show on it where he was sitting and what he wanted. The bound copies of the newspapers were so bulky that they had to be brought out on trollies.

He chose the *Telegraph* and asked for the volumes on either side of the time he was looking for. Not looking for – the time he was guessing at. The *Telegraph* was the place to find it. They reported everything. He turned the pages.

A place he remembered living in rose up from the pages like a dream – the advertisements for pensions, the five stages of pleasure for chocolate, an advertisement for a bank: 'I know a bank where the wild thyme grows.' He must have seen them a thousand times; they had slipped out of everyday experience and were gone as stealthily as they had slipped in.

He leafed through the pages, reading the triviality that makes up day-to-day newspaper coverage, then, remembering why he was there, he turned to the parliamentary pages.

Eventually he found it. An inquiry was being held into allegations of impropriety and improper behaviour at the Garth Boys' Home in North Wales. The inquiry had been set up by the local council, and a barrister had been appointed to chair it. Gregory read on but he didn't have to read the name. He knew what it would be: Jolyon Scribner, QC.

There had been questions in the House. That was a phrase that used to mean something – fat men at dinner would splutter out that they would ask a question in the House. Now you could buy one.

He turned to the 'Yesterday in Parliament' section. There were two whole pages, much of it verbatim reporting of speeches. Not like now, he reflected, now it's all parliamentary sketch writers cracking jokes. No one in their right mind would read these columns of newsprint if they were served up.

He found another entry: Mr Butler Jennings asking the minister about the Garth Boys' Home inquiry, objecting to the results of a private hearing being published at all, saying it would be unfair since the evidence given at the inquiry was not to be available for examination. Mr Jennings said there should be no publication at all in those circumstances.

Replying, the minister said it was not his responsibility, the inquiry was being held by a local council and was nothing to do with him. He had no control over the matter. He did however note the Honourable Member's concern. The Speaker at this point intervened to rule any further questions out of order. The minister had no responsibility, he repeated, and he could not be questioned about the matter.

It was easy to guess what side Jennings was on, and it wasn't the side that wanted the whole story to come out. Jennings, Morgan, Charlton, Scribner. Things were falling into place.

Chapter 18

'I've had a terrible time waking you up. It's way past breakfast and your conference starts any minute.'

Scott was trying to sit up in bed.

'You've slept nearly ten hours. You collapsed. I almost couldn't get you on to the bed. Don't you remember? You wouldn't help at all.'

Despite trying, Scott could remember nothing of the night before. He could barely remember where he was.

'Did I behave badly?' he said.

'Well, you started off by being rude to Jennings – you were about to be difficult with everybody else, but then you stopped and decided you wanted to go to sleep. We didn't get as far as eating anything.'

'You mean I went straight upstairs?'

He was sitting on the edge of the bed now, trying to focus on where he was. His ribs, where he had been kicked, were so stiff he could hardly bend over to get his shoes on.

'Just about,' she said, 'and then you fell over in here.'

'Ten hours,' said Scott. 'I don't feel as though I've slept at all.'

'There's a quarter of an hour before your meeting starts. I've got some coffee for you.' She turned and started clinking china. 'You're covered in terrible bruises.'

He pulled on his trousers.

'You fell asleep. I did your homework for you and then I watched TV.'

Scott tried to tie his shoelaces but found that he couldn't bend any more. She handed him the coffee and kneeled at his feet to tie them up for him.

'You're a ruin, aren't you. Are you normally like this or was it all the policeman's fault? You'd better drink the coffee and go now.'

He felt as though he was being sent off for a day's work by his wife. He looked at her head from above as he sat on the bed. He didn't touch her.

He went downstairs to the reception hall and studied the blackboards that had been set up, keeping a wary eye on the reception desk. He got nothing from there save an enquiry as to whether he had slept well. Was being here crazy or was it the safest place of all? He couldn't work it out.

He was due in a group discussing specimen cases for sentencing, and arriving on time he was able to sit and watch other members of the group come in.

Sarson was there. He was a London magistrate known for his bad manners. There was a judge from the West Country, Watters from the Old Bailey – he was in charge of this group – another barrister Scott didn't know, a solicitor, and Isobel from Tom Handley's set.

The others were chatting.

Scott positioned himself so he could see out of the windows over to the lawn. Behind it was the car park and the entrance. If anyone arrived he would see. He felt unable to join in the conversation. What was he doing here? Why didn't he just leave?

The group was finally complete when a whiskered man joined them. Scott checked his list. He was a judge advocate-general's appointment – an army judge.

'Here we are, then,' the man said, clapping his hands. 'I'm ready, I'm ready. Ready when you are.' His enthusiasm was pleasing; perhaps it would mean Scott wouldn't have to say very much. His head ached rhythmically. It resolved the dilemma about whether or not to leave. He didn't suppose he could if he tried.

'Are we all here?' said Watters. 'Then perhaps we should be getting on. We don't have much time. First you could give me your work sheets so we can compare results.'

Sarson spoke first. 'I haven't done them all, I'm afraid. No time.' He dared Watters to object.

'Nor have I,' said the army man. 'Had to travel too far to get here. No time.'

'Well, I don't expect everyone's done all of them,' said Watters in a conciliatory manner. 'It doesn't matter too much. Let's get on.'

He opened a loose-leaf file. 'Case one. An estate worker. He and his brother run a little business hiring themselves out to estate owners and

192

farmers, so he's not a complete ninny. He was found at home with two ounces of cannabis and pleaded guilty to possession with intent to supply. The defendant's twenty-five years old, no previous convictions, or at least nothing relevant – a bit of trouble with a car. Married with one small child. The supply of the drug, he told the police, would be to his friends.'

Watters looked up.

'Now what would we sentence him to? The drugs were worth quite a lot, but not a huge amount. Supplying drugs. The Court of Appeal has said that it's always serious. Now what have we? Sarson, what do you say?'

'Three years.'

Scott had thought Sarson was going to say that. He looked at him. He was a heavy man with a pasty face which was, at the same time, inflamed. Scott assumed that the colour was the result of drink, but who knew? Maybe he was ill. People weren't always as obvious as they seemed to be. For a moment he was going to give the magistrate the benefit of the doubt, but then Sarson said, 'It's a scourge. The streets are full of it.'

Scott's momentary sympathy evaporated. There was no benefit of the doubt to be given. The man was just stupid and, what was worse, used his stupidity to hurt people.

'Steady on,' said Watters. 'It's a class B drug, you know, not the worse drug offence.'

'Nevertheless. He's supplying . . .'

'Yes,' the army judge interrupted, 'he's corrupting young people. Three years, spot on.'

'He'll be out in eighteen months anyway,' Sarson added triumphantly.

Scott looked around him. He felt he was in a foreign country. Had any of these people ever met anyone who smoked cannabis?

A car was arriving in the car park. He couldn't see who it was.

The barrister joined in. 'In the case papers it says that two ounces is enough to make four hundred and eighty-three cigarettes. Now that's enough to, to . . .' He paused and the army judge cut in, 'Enough to debauch a regiment.'

The barrister went on, 'Look how much money these people have. I once had a case involving money in a bank – thousands and thousands. It had come from Colombia.'

'No,' said the solicitor, 'that would be cocaine. If it was cannabis it would probably come from North Africa. Do the papers say whether it was resin or grass?'

This conversation seemed as detached from reality as was possible, made even worse by his devoting only half his attention to it. The car outside moved out of sight, and then backed partly into view again.

Cannabis. Scott thought of the time he had worked for the Forestry Commission. The sun had pricked his eyes through the whole long, dry summer. After a day stooping in the earth, he had felt weary. A lovely word. Not just tired, but weary. As he walked home he remembered how the movements he had made repeatedly during the day – bending, lifting, twisting – still rippled in his body. He had used his body properly and as he walked he could feel it recovering, restoring itself. It was a feeling he had not had for – how long? Years and years. After a day in court he could not rest in the same way. He would give a lot to feel weary like that now and again, not just fagged out as he did nowadays on his way home.

Lenny, one of the foresters, had kept a small patch of cannabis at the end of one of the lines of saplings. It had been harvested weeks before and left to dry in the heat. He remembered the smell of it as they approached the hedge where it hung.

Afterwards they would walk slowly, hardly speaking. A grunt or a word was enough to convey all that needed to be said. There was a walk of four miles home in the evening light and as they tramped Lenny would crush and roll the grass, twist it with some tobacco and hand him a joint.

Of course, that was a supply of drugs. The memory had lain quiet for years now – it was a time Scott hardly ever thought about. Lenny a supplier, and a cultivator of cannabis. No doubt there had been enough in that small patch to debauch the whole of Hadlow Down. How the magistrates would have enjoyed saying that. It was odd how distant it was from the evil these judges thought they were preventing.

'Nevertheless the guidelines say prison for supplying,' said the solicitor.

Scott hadn't wanted to remember Hadlow Down but a part of him seemed to be waking up, a part that had been gone for a long time. There was a figure who had clearly come from the car passing behind the hedge. He couldn't see him clearly.

'Anybody disagree?' said Watters. 'Prison, you say, obviously, but for how long?'

Another car pulled into the car park. A woman got out.

'Yes, I disagree,' said Scott.

Sarson looked at him with surprise.

194

Scott said, 'This isn't an offence you smash up a man's life for. What's he done? In fact, if you think about the charge, nothing yet. He's got some cannabis with intent to supply. The evidence that he was a supplier probably amounted to nothing more than his agreeing with the police when they asked him whether he'd give it to friends. The policeman says, "Well, you'd give it to your friends if they asked, wouldn't you?" and he says, "Yes." There it is, enough evidence to convict of possession with intent to supply. He's no more a dangerous criminal than I am.'

Maybe that was a remark inviting trouble, he thought. A grey, official-looking car with two aerials drove into the car park. But nobody got out. The woman got in and it drove away.

The barrister looked at Scott with astonishment. He practised banking law and had never defended a criminal case.

'That wouldn't be enough evidence, would it?' he said.

'Plenty. Ask Sarson here,' said Scott. 'I've seen it a dozen times. The conversation doesn't even have to happen in the presence of a lawyer. The question could be asked during a search of the house – it's so short and simple that lots of judges wouldn't even say it amounted to an interview. If it's not an interview it doesn't have to be written down. Then when it comes to a trial, it's the word of the officer against the defendant.'

He was beginning to lose control, he could feel it. 'And we sit here talking about debauching regiments. Two ounces of cannabis resin wouldn't make anything like four hundred and eighty-three cigarettes.'

He turned over the papers in silence, aware that he was in effect singing the praises of fox-hunting at an animal rights meeting. 'Four hundred and eighty-three cigarettes. Really! Whoever heard such nonsense?'

There was silence. The army judge looked at him, more shocked than in disagreement, Scott thought. No one said anything.

He ploughed on. 'The man is married. He's working, he has a small business, he has a house. He has a child to support. What kind of person do you think he is? Someone who creeps round school gates putting LSD stickers on the back of children's hands? He's just a chap who has friends around and they share a joint. There's no scales, no plastic bags, no great piles of money, and he's honest enough to admit what he does. Some criminal.'

'We can't be sure about that,' said the banking lawyer.

'It's good enough for me,' said Scott. 'If I didn't lock him up I wouldn't feel I was letting a maniac loose. And there's one thing I certainly would not be doing if I only fined him. I wouldn't be alienating him and all his friends from the law.'

Watters surprised them all. 'I agree,' he said. 'Scott here has said what I was going to, though perhaps with a little more emphasis.' He smiled, instantly defusing the tension Scott had created.

The rebuke reminded Scott why he was never going to be made a full-time judge. The job was all about balance and at the moment he wasn't showing much of that.

'Well, there you are, a difference of opinion. I suppose it's the luck of the draw who this chap came up in front of.'

'Probably Dowden, if it happened in Wiltshire. Look, it's Devizes Crown Court,' said a voice. 'He'd have locked him up for ever, just for the pleasure of listening to himself saying it.'

'Move on, let's move on,' said Watters.

Scott reflected.

It was a perfect example of Old Bailey sentencing. Watters was a full-time Old Bailey judge. The judges there were so used to trying people charged with cutting people's heads off, or raping whole dormitories of women, that a little bit of cannabis hardly troubled the surface.

'Next case, next case.' Watters was getting into his stride. 'Bit of an odd one, this. It gives rise to a spread of opinions. Here it is. Lady in a lift. Going to the tenth floor. Chap gets in. They are in there alone and he puts a hand on her breast and says something.' He ruffled the pages. 'Here we are. "Nice pair you got, love, do they weigh you down?" Pretty odd remark if you ask me. He's a perfectly respectable sort of chap. Thirties. No convictions for anything. Well, what do we do? Indecent assault. The woman in the lift was rather upset.'

It was the solicitor's turn to give the first opinion. 'A little over-upset, I should say.'

Scott watched Isobel. This would get her annoyed.

The solicitor went on, 'It's a small indecent assault. I think it's been put in to remind us that the maximum penalty for indecent assault has been increased and that nowadays a small fine is not enough – we should mark it with a big fine.'

Charlton pulled into the car park. Scott did not notice him. He was watching Isobel. She caught his eye. She was beginning to react. Oh, well, she would – but it was only an indecent assault, not very serious, for heaven's sake.

Watters turned to Scott and looked enquiringly at him. At that moment Sir Anthony Tippett slid into the room. He was carrying a clipboard and a slim gold pencil. 'Carry on, carry on,' he said. Scott could hear a faint echo of national service in this curious repetition of commands. The army judge had done it too, and Watters. Well, at least Tippett hadn't come in to ask Scott to step outside for a moment. He supposed that was how such a tricky situation would be handled.

'I agree,' he said. 'It's been put in to remind us of the increase in maximum sentence, and that you can now order compensation for shock and distress . . .'

Isobel interrupted him. 'But look at the reports. This is a serious case. The woman was off work for nearly a month and finds it difficult to go into lifts any more . . .'

'No great loss that, I should say,' said the army judge. 'I never do myself actually . . . always take the stairs.' He laughed and then stopped when he saw Isobel's stony look.

'The point is that what seems like a small silly matter to you isn't to her. This is a very nasty assault. She probably thought she was going to be raped,' Isobel said.

Scott smiled at her anger and Sarson said, 'Well, in my court this sort of thing is always dealt with by a small fine and a bind-over, always has been, always will. Maybe a little money nowadays for hurt pride. Buy herself a new hat.'

Isobel had seen Scott's smile and was angry, but this last remark nearly made her take off. 'You can't just deal with this by compensation. Buy herself a new hat indeed!'

'I should say not,' said Watters, 'and Scott certainly didn't. He gave him three years in prison.' He held up the written sheets they had all handed in.

'Three years?' the solicitor said.

They all looked at Scott astonished.

'Did I?' said Scott.

He had been about to say that stiff compensation and a bind-over would be about right. Then he realised what had happened. That's what Catherine had meant by 'I did your homework'. He hadn't thought anything of it at the time.

'Yes, well, three years.' Scott tried to sound judicial. 'Perhaps that's a little over the top.'

'A little!' Sarson said. 'Even I wouldn't give him that. What would you give someone who puts his hand up a woman's skirt then? Life?'

'Why not?' said Isobel, who was losing all grasp of reality, surrounded by these men. 'That's the maximum. Not life, of course, but why not? Which is more serious – selling a bit of dope or assaulting women in the lift and scaring the life out of them? Scott here has given him the same sentence that you did for the dope. Just right, I say.'

Charlton was downstairs talking to reception.

Watters said gently, 'But Miss Quigley, in the written submissions you only gave him three months.'

'Well, I didn't have Scott's courage. Three years is what he deserves.'

Sir Anthony Tippett cleared his throat in a well-bred, emphatic fashion. 'I think it might help if I told you what actually happened in this case. The man pleaded not guilty before Her Honour Judge Southwood. He was, naturally, convicted' – there was some laughter around the room – 'and he was sentenced to three months' imprisonment. That was upheld by the Court of Appeal.'

There was silence.

'What did the drug-seller get, the man who had the cannabis?' someone asked.

'The Court of Appeal, I think, said . . .' Sir Anthony leafed through the papers on his clipboard. ' . . . that three years was unappealable. Yes, here it is. "Well within the range of sentence that the judge was entitled to pass," they said. So, three years it is.

'Gentlemen, we had better adjourn for coffee now, hadn't we?'

'Well, the right man got three years, didn't he?' said Sarson, laughing.

Scott turned on him.

'You did well,' said Isobel. 'First you show that you're soft on cannabis, then you go crazy and lock someone up for ever, and finish by losing your temper with Sarson. That's the way to endear yourself to those that matter.'

They were trailing down the stairs towards coffee.

'And all of this in front of Sir Anthony Tippett, the chief honcho. He's bound to recommend you for judge, isn't he?'

Scott again felt a lightening of mood.

'Luckily I don't think it matters very much,' he said. 'I'm in enough trouble already.'

He looked around to see who was close to them and dropped his voice. He had always liked Isobel and he felt inclined to confide in her.

She leaned towards him and said, 'Oh, what have you been up to? Do tell me.'

'I was in front of Scribner and it all went rather wrong.'

'No problem then,' she said. She repeated the old joke: 'This is an appeal from a decision of His Honour Judge Scribner. You can move on to your second ground of appeal, Mr Scott.'

Scott grinned.

'Well, yes, partly that, but I insulted him and he stopped the trial. It's at least a wasted costs order against me.'

'Insulting Scribner, that might even cancel out one of your mistakes this morning –losing your temper with Sarson.'

'But then it got worse. Something happened, and the bloody police were round at my flat last night, and I ran off . . .'

Isobel became serious. 'The police came round to your flat? You ran off? What on earth for?'

'They were on about something going missing. It must have been from the trial I was doing. As far as I know they are still after me.'

Isobel didn't take the point up immediately. Then she said, 'You say they are still after you? Tell me . . .' She paused. 'Look, I overheard that poisonous Jennings on the phone this morning. Was he involved in this in any way?'

Scott was astonished. 'Yes. How did you know?'

'Because I was at the counter where we collect the newspapers. He was on the phone. I heard him ask for an inspector, and then he said, "Tell him he's here. Yes, here, now." He seemed absurdly excited and it was all a bit odd.

'That was about an hour and a half ago, nearly two hours ago. If they're coming up from London they could be here soon.'

Scott looked around him as though the door was about to burst open.

'Tell me, Jeremy, what have you done? What do they say you've done?'

He said, 'I don't know, honestly, I don't know. Look, I'll have to go.'

Scott slipped out of the room. The passages of the large house had the deserted air of school corridors during lessons. In the distance he could hear the comforting noise of a vacuum cleaner. He sniffed. The very air seemed sharper. He began to run.

He made his way through the old house towards his room. Along the gallery dust hung in shafts of sunlight pouring through the tall windows. Below him he could see the moss-covered lawn reaching down to a great cedar tree.

According to the short history of the house left in their room, the local hunt would meet on the lawn each year and the huntsmen would call up to the son of the house to come down to ride. Just like Newbolt. The boy wouldn't respond. He couldn't. He had died in the trenches and would never respond again, but each year they called, watched by the boy's father from the gallery. The image of the old man stopped Scott in his tracks. He tasted the momentary stillness of the hunt, the regret of death. And then started running again, down the short gallery stairs to the hallway. There was no one there. He crossed the flagged hall and started up the main staircase. He turned where Catherine and he had turned the night before. The same receptionist was looking up at him.

She spoke to someone inside the door behind her and Scott knew that she was speaking about him. She might as well have sent him a message.

He quickly made his way to the large room where they had slept. The door was open. He stopped. Through the crack where the huge hinges held the door away from the jamb he could see a man's back bent over the dressing table. There was a scratching noise as drawers were opened and closed.

He could see where he had left his jacket on the bed that morning. His keys were in it, and his wallet. Where was Catherine?

The figure straightened up and walked over to the desk. The phone rang. It was picked up. Scott could hear the man say, 'Is he?' He turned from the phone to look towards the door. It was Charlton. Scott anticipated the movement and slid away from the crack. He wasn't seen. He half expected Charlton to come towards him but he did not. The door to the bathroom opened. Charlton was going to wait for him, out of sight.

Scott needed only to reach into the room. One, two steps and he had his jacket. As he left he saw the key to the door, large and old-fashioned. He shut the door softly behind him and locked it.

He took the staircase two steps at a time and was at the desk when the receptionist stepped out of the office. It probably didn't even look as though he had been in his room, he had been so quick. To her it would appear as though he had changed his mind.

She looked behind him up the stairs but otherwise showed no reaction.

Charlton was probably still in the bathroom, waiting silently.

'Miss Wade,' Scott said, inventing a name. 'Catherine, my guest. Did she go out?'

The receptionist looked worried. Scott looked at her and she dropped her eyes.

'Has she gone?' Scott said.

'Yes, only a few minutes ago. I told her where you were. She said she'd try to find you but if she could not I should give you this note.'

Scott put the note in his pocket and thanked her. 'Well, I'd better get back to my session.'

He turned and walked slowly down the passage. He strained his ears but could hear nothing. Perhaps Charlton was still in the bathroom. Soon he would be banging on the door, or using the phone. He turned the corner. The phone rang. He started running.

The car park was at the bottom of the lawn behind the cedar tree. He took the quickest way. He climbed through the window out on to the lawn. The grass gave way gently beneath his feet and he ran easily from the house.

At the windows of the coffee room to the left a line of judges watched in astonishment, their cups half lifted to their mouths as they looked out over the lawn. When Scott reached the corner to turn into the car park he looked back up at the great window of the room where he had slept. He could see Charlton staring out at him.

He had two hundred pounds in his pocket, his car keys and an address in Catherine's handwriting. The Upper House. Nr the Water Board Farm. Clwyd. North Wales.

Chapter 19

The day was bright and clear. A wind blew across the fields and Scott wound both the windows down to let the breeze waft straight through the car. He put one of Richard's tapes in the stereo and drove west.

He had only a rough idea where he was. He had arrived the night before following written directions, not using a map, knowing only that he had turned west from the main road north of Cambridge.

He must be in the Midlands somewhere, he guessed, near Leicester or Peterborough. A mile further on he saw a sign, 'Leicester 25 miles', and then another sign to a village, 'Cottesmore 4 miles'.

That was a hunting name, wasn't it? This was certainly hunting country. He could see the fields stretching out flat on either side of him, hedge after hedge running parallel into the distance.

There was a flurry and the car pulled a little to the left. A great gust of wind had come over the flat fields from his right. He felt cold, but it wasn't real cold affecting him, only the realisation that he was no longer in a centrally heated room. The sun cheered the surroundings, the trees and hedges shone with light. A sense of freedom settled on him.

The road ahead widened and off to the right there was a gravelled parking area. He pulled the car over and climbed out. He hadn't taken a straight route away from the conference centre and had driven at least twenty miles, so the chances of Charlton finding him weren't great. On the other hand he didn't think he minded very much if he did.

He leaned on the car, watching the distant landscape, and then he remembered the note that had been left for him at the receptionist's desk.

He took it out and read it in the cool morning air, leaning on the bonnet of the borrowed car. It was short. Catherine had seen Charlton checking the cars in the car park and was going to look for Scott. If they got separated she would be at this address. There was a small map and some directions. She had obviously realised what Charlton's appearance had meant and like Scott wasn't going to wait around to argue about it. Well, that gave him somewhere to go.

Was there a map? He searched the car, under the seat, in the boot. It was all very tidy. There was some technical stuff about the car, a big manila envelope, a map of London and Essex, and nothing more.

Well, North Wales was north-west of here, the other side of Leicester. He could head in that direction.

He drove away. He could feel the spring weather sweeping the countryside. The surface of the road was becoming dry and dusty in the bright sun and all around him the trees and bushes were sprouting with life. The way ahead turned and started dropping slightly to his left. The car glided down the road.

In the distance he could see a petrol station, new, clean, full of things unconnected with petrol. He pulled in, filled the car and paid for it with a credit card. Oil, water, the lot. He bought a map, *A to Z: Midlands and West*. It covered Peterborough to Anglesey.

The garage wasn't busy, and returning to the car he spread the map on the bonnet, leaning over it, holding the edges down like an officer out on a field day. The wind picked at it as he began to trace the route.

There was a movement behind him and he looked up. His stomach turned over. It was a large police car, covered in screaming yellow and pink stickers. The door was open and he could see the gadgets arrayed around the front passenger seat. On the seat itself was a half-eaten apple.

'Excuse me, sir,' a voice behind him said. Scott turned. A vast policeman dressed in what seemed like sailcloth was looking down at him. 'Can I help?' He was wearing a badge where a breast pocket would be. It was in luminous blue: 'POLICE' it said.

On the other side of the car another officer stood watching them.

'Can I help?' The officer repeated his question. He was clearly used to having this effect on people. He indicated the map.

'Yes,' said Scott. 'I'm trying to get to Wales.' It seemed ridiculous.

'North or south?' said the policeman.

'In the middle, I think.' Almost at random Scott put his finger on a lake, bent down and read the name. 'Lake Vyrnwy.'

'You don't want to go on the motorway? That's why you're here?' The officer was indifferent. He didn't seem to be asking for any purpose.

'No. No,' Scott said. 'I'm on holiday. I'm just ambling along.'

'Ambling,' said the policeman, 'that's good,' and he stuck a large stubby finger on the map. 'Well, the difficult bit's here, sir. You don't want to get caught up in what up here we call the urban conurbations.' For the first time Scott noticed the man's accent. The policeman had clearly marked him out as a being from down south.

The finger traced a road that weaved away from Leicester towards Lichfield. Where Samuel Johnson came from.

'Well, thank you, Officer, that was very kind.' Scott began to fold the map. The other policeman had got into the car and was on the phone. But the first officer wasn't finished. 'Now, to get to that road,' he said, 'you go down there and take the second turning to the right.'

Scott listened mechanically. He knew he could never hope to retain all this. He was wondering whether to hurry the thing up or whether to wait until the police themselves had finished at the garage, to see if they would leave before him.

He decided to wait, and took the battle to them. 'Can I look in your car?' he said. He walked over. It looked like a spaceship inside. The apple on the seat had added its smell to the leathery, washroom atmosphere. There was a magazine stuffed down between the seats under a fire extinguisher. It looked lived in, which Scott supposed it was, twenty-four hours a day probably.

The other policeman finished his call and turned a blank face to Scott. He obviously didn't appreciate his colleague's friendliness.

'Amazing,' said Scott, adopting a saloon bar tone, the kind of voice he used to admire Tozer's latest Maserati. He straightened up. The other policeman didn't want him intruding into his car and he made it obvious. There was a faint whiff of socks.

'Well, thanks a lot,' said Scott. 'I appreciate your help.' He walked back to the garage shop. He opened the door and stepped inside, looking up at a row of magazines. They mainly featured bottoms.

The police Jaguar pulled away from the petrol pumps and disappeared in a roar. So they weren't looking for him, or if they were, they were being particularly clever about it.

He hung around the shop, the man behind the counter watching him carefully. He bought a newspaper and left. He followed the route the policeman had pointed out. There was nothing. They weren't there. They weren't looking for him.

Of course they weren't. Charlton was acting on his own. He remembered before, when Isobel had said it wouldn't take them long to come up from London, how odd it had sounded. Of course it was odd. If there was a warrant out the local police would have been round immediately. Charlton wouldn't have come on his own. There was no warrant. Charlton had some private grudge. He was acting freelance.

'He's just gone out to his car,' Charlton said when the receptionist came up and opened the door. 'He didn't see me. I came in to leave the message. I stepped into the loo and he came into his room and locked the door on the way out. I didn't realise till I came out again.'

He walked towards the large window and pointed. 'I saw him going over the lawn when I was telephoning down.'

'You had me really worried. I told you not to go into his room.'

'No problem, no problem,' said Charlton. 'He'll be pleased when he sees me. It'll be a surprise. If he went over the lawn he must have gone to the car park. Is that right?'

The receptionist nodded.

'I'll follow him out,' Charlton said.

She stood back from the door to let him out. She knew she shouldn't have let him upstairs and she was tempted to go and check the room. His story sounded odd. But it seemed rude to check up on him. That was what Charlton was counting on. She let him leave.

Moments later he was running across the lawn in the direction Scott had taken. This time only the maids clearing up the coffee cups saw anything. The judges were reluctantly returning to the hall after the break. They were to be lectured on the dangers of racist and sexist stereotyping and Scribner wasn't looking forward to it.

Charlton turned his car left towards London. If Scott had gone any other way then he would be impossible to find. If he had gone to London then perhaps he could be overtaken, but Charlton wasn't hopeful.

He eventually reached the main road south. No sign yet of an old grey Mercedes.

He had got the description of the car from a man sweeping in the car park who had seen Scott running out, but he had no number. He had thought Scott was in a green Volvo but he must have switched cars. That showed he knew he was being followed. Why change cars, and why leave this place in such a hurry?

It was clear he had the documents and if he was running that meant he had read them. If he'd read them then he couldn't really be allowed to wander around, could he? It was all very well for the others with their dinners and drinks parties, but when it came to doing something he was the only one who could do it.

Charlton had got the information about the green Volvo from the old porter at Scott's flat and he'd got other information as well. He'd been able to do what he wanted in Scott's room while the old man had been in the hallway.

He'd got Scott's bank account and credit card numbers. He had his phone number, a printout of his pre-programmed telephone dialling settings, and best of all he had the number of his telephone credit card.

He could get the address of any cashcard machine Scott used within half an hour of its use, and any telephone he used immediately. He only had to ask.

He asked. He dialled one of the pre-loaded numbers on his car phone. 'Can I speak to Ted?' he said. In response there was first silence, then a tinny tune began to wind out of the loudspeaker as he was put on hold. After a while another voice said, 'Yes?' Charlton didn't say anything and then, when the voice repeated its request, he said, 'I was hoping to speak to Ted.'

'Who are you?'

'Someone who wants to speak to Ted,' he said.

He pulled out past a Norbert Dentressangle lorry, and thought to himself, Norbert the Nark. He always thought the same thing when he saw one of the Dentressangle lorries. Perhaps there was a Monsieur Norbert Dentressangle, a large man, living a well-padded life just outside Brussels. Norbert the Nark was a Robert Shelton character, out of the *Fabulous Furry Freak Brothers*. If you didn't know it then you didn't. Probably not in Brussels.

The voice at the other end didn't persist in its enquiry and the music started playing again.

After about a mile, when Charlton was doing eighty again, another voice answered, 'Yes?'

'Is that you, Ted?' he said. He pulled over to allow a big BMW to sweep past.

'Yes. Is that you, Charlie?' said Ted.

'I need the numbers dialled on a telephone credit card, and the places from where the calls were made.'

'No probs. Give me the details.'

Charlton rummaged about amongst the papers on the seat next to him. He remembered hearing an American businessman describing how he had bought a car because it had a good coffee-cup holder. When was someone ever going to put a bookshelf on the passenger seat? As if to prove his point some of the papers slid off the seat and fell to the floor.

'When do you need them?'

'Immediately you get them, if not sooner.' Charlton had Scott's card number ready now and read it out.

'It belongs to a Jeremy Scott living in Chelsea,' said Ted immediately. 'When do we get the authorisation?'

'You already have it. It's one of the standard batch, only we left it off by mistake. We'll amend the application if you send it back. I want a running commentary on this one.'

More silence. Charlton passed a coach full of tired schoolchildren. HH registration. They came from Hamburg. One of the faces leaning against the window was fast asleep. Services five miles.

'Ted?' he said enquiringly into the emptiness of the car interior.

'Yes?' said the voice.

'I'm going to pull into a service station. If I cut this connection try me on the other phone.'

'How far?'

'Five, no, four miles.'

'I'll have it by then unless you're driving faster than you ought to be.' More silence. 'Yes, here it is. He used the phone last night. He rang . . . hang on. He rang a number in London. Here it is.'

'That's his flat.'

'No. Nearly right. Same exchange but it's the porter's number.'

'Nothing else?'

'No. Nothing else. Wait a moment. There's a call in progress now. He's actually making a call now. He's ringing London. Here's the number.' Charlton could hear him punching buttons. 'It's a garage. Danson Lane.'

'That's where the other car is, then,' said Charlton.

'What?'

'Nothing. Can you hear what he's saying?'

'The impossible takes half an hour's notice,' said Ted. 'No. All I can work on at the moment is the computer billing responses.'

'Where is he, then?'

'Hang on. Here's the search. He's ringing from a call box in Lichfield.'

'Where?'

'In a pub.'

'Which?'

'The Samuel Johnson.'

'A bit predictable,' said Charlton. He pulled off the motorway into the service station, looking to see if there was any way he could turn back north.

'Look, I felt I had to tell you I've left London for a holiday,' Scott said down the phone. 'I've gone in your car. I'm going to drive it around a bit.'

Richard was as helpful as he always was. 'That's OK. I'll use yours, then.'

Scott wondered about how he was able to get on with people like Richard and yet was able to make no close friends. His father had been the same. He'd always had a chap he knew at the back of some small garage or shop. As with him, they had been his father's only real friends. It was what Catherine said – there was no danger in it. On the other hand he liked Richard rather more than the people he had to work with, so perhaps Catherine was wrong after all.

'I'll be in touch, then.'

'You do that.'

He stepped out of the phone booth into the pub. It was all pretend eighteenth century, with bookcases above the settles, but the books were a little too high to reach.

He had only stopped since a pub called the Samuel Johnson in Lichfield seemed so obvious. He thought about having a drink then decided he'd better not. He'd get sleepy and he had three or four hours' driving to do yet.

His car was in the car park beside the pub, right next to a bank. He checked his cash. He could do with more. He stopped and thought. Perhaps it was better not to use the card. His bank card could be traced and using it would leave a trail anyone could read, so he'd better not. He'd disappeared now and it was better to stay disappeared.

Chapter 20

Gregory met Butler Jennings when the MP was standing in the House of Commons surrounded by a delegation from the Surrey branch of CrackDown.

It was an easy delegation to deal with. Jennings had seen them first in a committee room and then, since Parliament wasn't sitting, he was able to guide them around the half-deserted buildings and show them the Chamber.

The Surrey branch were impressed by the grandeur of it all, although, and they kept this to themselves, they were disappointed by the homeliness of the leather benches and carved seats.

'You see this gangway in the middle . . .' Jennings gestured up and down the area separating the two rows of opposing benches. 'The distance between these two lines is the length of two swords. I needn't explain why.' He was rewarded by a ripple of laughter from the members.

CrackDown was a group dedicated to the reinvigoration of the criminal law. They campaigned for the rights of the victim who had been, as they saw it, long neglected in favour of a quite unnecessary, indeed absurd, emphasis on the rights of the criminal.

They had recently – because there was no one else to choose, was there? – appointed Jennings their honorary president. Jennings told them about the silk top hat, sometimes called for, and the cry of 'I spy strangers', which he commented must have inspired the *I Spy* books.

He spoke with pride of the duties and the service that a Member of Parliament must offer, although he was bound to agree, when asked, that unfortunately there were those who did not serve with the selflessness that was rightly expected of them.

For a few moments he spoke reflectively of the falling standards that beset both Parliament and the nation. 'There is something that I feel should be said. If necessary, it should be said from the rooftops, so that those who seek to diminish the rule of law hear it loud and clear. It is this: one of the greatest forces for good in this society of ours is indignation, and even better than that righteous indignation – the indignation of the righteous.

'Too long have people like you, ladies and gentlemen, failed to speak out, perhaps from a sense of propriety, perhaps because you did not want to push yourselves forward, but now, with the formation of your organisation, you are doing so. It is right that you do so, for the defence of what is right is no vanity. You demonstrate no pride by defending decency; there is no fault in self-righteousness.'

As Gregory watched, he noticed with surprise that Jennings was a small man, dwarfed by some of the group that surrounded him. But, by his sheer energy, he dominated them.

His hands were everywhere, expressively smoothing or clutching at the air; calming, then angry, showing frustration then finally resolve.

His skin had the curious sheen that attaches itself to faces more normally seen on television, blessed now as though by the addition of the miracle ingredient, real life. His voice was continuously modulated, wheedling and persuading, full of inflexions that, had they been used in ordinary circumstances, would have astonished the listener with their obviousness. But oddly, in this place they were just right.

By now Gregory could understand why, when some people heard him on the television or the radio, they were forced to turn the set off, for to give the voice a moment's freedom was to find yourself entranced by it – or revolted by its wheedling sound.

He watched Jennings's mouth open and close, the lips speaking, and, as he watched, he realised something was wrong.

He saw Jennings's eyes. Despite the animation of his face, the ready smile and the expressiveness of his mouth, his eyes were dead. Or at least they were detached, the eyes of a trader, ordering and directing the rest of him in the unfolding, the praising and the presentation of the goods he was selling – but all the while watching his customers with contempt.

'We should harness righteous indignation, ladies and gentlemen. We all know the people who are the evil in our society. You only have to drive along the streets near this House' – he gestured vaguely in the direction of Stockwell – 'and you will see that people, law-abiding, decent people,

people whose families for generations have safely walked their home pavement, have now fled those pavements, driven into their houses.

'The streets are not safe. I suggest that such a situation is quite alien to our society.'

The members of CrackDown nodded. There were soft, urgent noises of agreement, breathed out amongst the group surrounding the small figure in the centre. It even sounded as though one or two were saying 'Hear hear', again characteristic of the place in which they were gathered. It was the sound of assent, by-passing the brain completely, acclamation by the belly.

The members of CrackDown felt that the 'enemy' had been identified. 'The rule of law, ladies and gentlemen, is not negotiable. It is not something that can be picked up or discarded like a, a . . .' Jennings stumbled over his words for a moment as though puzzled in his recall of the very hatefulness of the vocabulary that the enemy used. ' . . . like a faddish multi-cultural value judgment, to be chosen or disregarded at will. No, it is a sword, not unlike the swords I told you about, which were stretched out from behind each of these lines' – he gestured down the line on the floor of the Chamber, forcing the crowd around him back a bit, allowing him to raise his voice slightly – 'a sword of truth, as well as a weapon of defence.'

He began to get his metaphor slightly tangled but his listeners did not notice. They were caught up in the moment, seized by the energy that can be created from the repetition of simple shared truths.

He tried again: 'The sword of truth which sets those whose indignation is righteous apart from other people . . . people who would have been called unrighteous by those who first sat in this Chamber. It is a distinction that deserves to be remembered.'

His teeth smiled.

He allowed the last, rather convoluted remark to settle, then his whole body shed the strutting intensity that he had built up and he began to exude the friendliness of the man putting a tankard of beer in your hand and his arm around your shoulder. He had changed back into a saloon bar companion.

'Well, ladies and gentlemen. Unfortunately I cannot stay, I have another appointment, but it has been my privilege to meet you. I hope we shall do so again soon.'

They moved as a mass towards the central lobby, just beyond the entrance to the Chamber.

There Gregory waited.

Jennings shook the hands of the group and then turned, as though waiting for someone. He had obviously remembered the appointment Gregory had made.

Gregory approached him, put his hand out and said, 'My name is Paul Gregory.' He said it with a gushing friendliness quite alien to him. It was remarkable how the display he had just seen enabled him to do so. He said, 'Basil Davenport has written to you, I believe.'

Jennings turned and looked at him.

His eyes flickered over his face and clothes. There was a pause before he reacted, and then he smiled, put his hand out and said, 'Well, hallo.'

For a moment Gregory doubted whether he was going to be able to do what he had come to do. He had never met anybody like this man before.

'It's an honour to meet you,' he said.

Jennings watched as though Gregory had merely moved a pawn forward, opening the game, but Gregory said nothing more, forcing Jennings to speak. He had decided he would say as little as possible. Talk at random and eventually you end a sentence saying something you don't need to say.

'Well, thank you for that,' said Jennings. 'It is always a pleasure to meet someone from what Americans call law enforcement agencies. Now, you must forgive me, what was it Basil said? Was it tax?'

'Near enough.' Gregory laughed to show he wasn't offended by the mistake. 'I'm from Customs.'

There was silence.

In the end it was Gregory who spoke. He was right, this wasn't going to be easy. 'I'm not here officially,' he said.

Jennings seemed to relent, or perhaps he was rehearsing a speech for something else. He said, 'No bother, no bother, we are lucky here in the House. Here things are neither official nor unofficial. They just happen. Perhaps dividing events into those sorts of categories – official, unofficial – isn't even sensible. For if we want to make something official it becomes so.' It was a remark about power.

He put an arm on Gregory's shoulder. 'But let me buy you a drink,' he said. 'You must know that if Basil Davenport sent you, that's as good as an offer of a glass of whisky.'

They walked down a long corridor.

Everywhere around them the heaviness of decoration pressed in.

Gregory felt they were in a building designed for another sort of people, people who were certain of themselves. It was clear that Jennings was fulfilling a real need. How much better to be governed by a Gladstone than the present crew. He could almost feel the members of CrackDown aching for the certainty of funny old-style hats and coats.

'Celia's Bar,' Jennings said. 'Here we are. We're allowed in here.'

They pushed a door leading into a large room with high windows overlooking the Thames. Jennings led Gregory to a table and then went over to the bar.

'There are complicated rules,' he said when he came back. 'That sounds a bit rude, but there are elaborate regulations about who is allowed into which bar and who isn't, who's allowed to pay and who isn't.'

He had bought two whiskies. 'Not so unreasonable, since meetings like ours are the staple diet of this place, and where to meet is almost as important as what is said.'

He sat down and smiled at Gregory. Again the teeth. They were sitting by one of the windows. In the distance, upriver, Gregory could see the new MI5 headquarters, curiously Babylonian in their look. Behind them was Stockwell, and behind that Brixton.

'I haven't seen Basil for years,' said Jennings. 'Last time I heard of him he was marketing himself as "the man who can see down sewers", or "I have looked and seen the sewer" or something. Struck me at the time as rather a risky way of going about things. Still, there are you.'

He took a pull at his whisky. He dipped his head towards the glass as he raised it. Gregory realised that he was a drinker. Wasn't there a saying about a lonely bachelor living on whisky? Or was that someone different? If he was drinking then perhaps he would not be so difficult to cope with.

'He's a great success, though,' said Gregory. 'He sold up and moved to France.'

'Did he take that woman with him?' asked Jennings.

'Well, he wasn't alone when I met him.' Gregory didn't want to affect a familiarity with Davenport that he couldn't sustain.

'Is she a bit scrawny?' asked Jennings.

'A bit,' said Gregory.

'Dissatisfied?'

'Yes.'

'In fact an old ratbag?' Jennings seemed angry. He got up as he spoke.

'I can't speak for her being a ratbag,' said Gregory, 'but from what I could see I wouldn't be surprised.' While Jennings stalked off to the bar, Gregory pictured the woman sitting on the other side of the pool. When he and Davenport had gone off to the restaurant he was astonished to see her sitting on the other side of the room. He never got closer to her than that. Despite sharing the same house, she and Davenport obviously led quite separate lives.

Jennings reappeared, carrying more whisky. Gregory's glass had been topped up but he himself had a new drink.

'I never liked her,' said Jennings. He stopped and took another drink. 'I would speak more strongly but I don't really know you.'

There was a shift. Gregory had miscalculated the situation. Jennings was on home territory and Gregory realised that having too much to drink in this place was just something you had to be able to do; it was like changing personalities.

He checked himself and noticed that it was he who was dropping his defences, he was the one who thought he could relax. But of course it was he who was the stranger.

'I spy strangers,' he said.

'You heard my little talk.' Jennings laughed.

'Do you have to give it often?' It was better to fall into the role of the admiring visitor.

'Too often,' said Jennings. 'Did you listen?'

'Yes.'

'I'll ask you a question you're probably too sophisticated to answer. Did you agree with me?'

'No,' said Gregory. He had to take a line and this was the best one available. Then, as though he had decided to admit something, he said, 'No, these people don't count. I think we're talking about something too serious for people like these. We're meant to be protecting them, not enlisting them.'

Jennings looked at him. He hadn't expected that.

'I mean, I'll tell you this.' Gregory leaned towards him a little too confidentially. 'The problem is not that crime is abnormal, it's that it is normal. It's normal. Completely normal. Do you know what a doctor told me once? The difficulty with cancer is not that it is death but that it is a form of life. Strong life. Too strong. In a way it's the same with crime.

That's what I feel sometimes when I interview people I arrest. I feel respect for the energy. For their energy.'

He drained his glass and sat back with the slightly self-satisfied look of someone who has said what needed saying.

The declaration of faith rather threw Jennings. He had been expecting the normal flattery that seemed to come with what he was doing. Either that or the dismissive look of the liberal who wouldn't listen to the figures he could marshal – the number of agencies there were to look after criminals as compared with victims, or the exact number of people killed by released life prisoners, fifty seven at the last count.

Gregory took advantage of the moment.

'This isn't a game any longer.' Then he was silent. He didn't want to carry on for fear of overdoing it.

'What do you mean by that?'

'Well, with no disrespect, you're a barrister, you know how courts work. I know what I could prove in a court, and I know what I'm allowed to prove. Very rarely are they the same thing.'

Jennings seemed suddenly to make up his mind. 'Look,' he said, 'I should like to go on talking but I can't. What are your arrangements now?' He looked at his watch. It was getting on for eight o'clock. 'I'm invited to a meeting. I know you would be interested. Perhaps we can take this whole subject a bit further.'

'It isn't a meeting so much as a dinner thing. I'm sure we'll be able to manage with another voice.'

There had been a cab waiting for them as they reached the gates into Parliament Square and now it was bucketing along. Jennings was pulling on the grab-handle so hard that when the cab cornered he swung in the air momentarily, his feet splayed out on the cab floor, almost as though he were water skiing.

'We're a group. We meet every so often, in the way groups do. When we meet we talk about things. You must be prepared to be shocked.'

The cab dived for a gap behind a lorry. Jennings swung out towards Gregory and then back, hitting the side panel with a thump.

'We eat at the main Happy Eater, or is it a Little Chef? Who knows? I can never remember. All I do know is that the waiters are all called Rocco and they love to give us those Devils on Horseback things. It's their idea of elegance.'

217

The Cab dashed across Piccadilly Circus and, pushing between a bus and a car, circled in front of the Café Royal.

'But first I want you to meet Sally.' They crossed the entrance and made for a lift. 'She's a kind of unofficial membership secretary, though I suppose she trusts my judgment.'

The lift took them to the top. There was a passage being patrolled by a waiter, who, on seeing Jennings, hastened – it was the only word for it – to open the door for him. 'We're a branch of the Radical Club,' said Jennings as he burst into the room.

There were about six people in the room, gathered at the far end where a waiter was serving drinks from behind a table. In the centre of the room there was a dining table with a white tablecloth laid for a formal meal. As far as Gregory could see there were far more places laid than there were people already there.

They advanced across the room and one or two of the faces turned in welcome –indeterminate, suited men and a woman dressed in a smart, slim skirt with an embroidered waistcoat.

Gregory noticed the waistcoat first, then her face. It was Sally, the woman with whom he had crossed the field on the way to the pub. Arlot had made the joke, 'She gets them down.'

'Hallo,' she said. 'You're Paul Gregory.'

'You know each other?'

'Yes,' she said. 'Mr Gregory was an officer in a case I prosecuted. Do you remember me? I'm Sally Donne.'

It was such an easy lie that Gregory had no difficulty in responding. 'Yes. I remember.'

'Then you'll have things to talk about,' said Jennings.

By now one or two of the others had gathered round to welcome him. They shook hands. Gregory thought he recognised them as lawyers, then one of them said, 'My name's David. I'm in property. You're from Customs. Well, it's a pleasure to meet you.'

Jennings hadn't mentioned his job. These people had been told about who he was in advance.

'But you're not just a taxes person? You're involved in the war on drugs?' The phrase set the tone for the evening.

'It's a disgrace,' he was told. 'The whole system is calculated to defend the indefensible. I really despair when I see the lack of standards in the social services. A child of fourteen, he was totally uncontrollable.

218

Where were the parents? That's what I ask.'

Then Gregory saw Philip Cantor. That was surprising, he thought. From what he'd seen of him this sort of conversation wasn't his style. Neither was it Sally Donne's, come to that. He watched her. She hardly joined the conversation at all.

He heard the word CrackDown. The property developer was talking about cost. 'It became self-supporting early this year and I have no contact with it now. In fact I may even get my money back.'

'David pays for us,' said Sally, who was standing next to Gregory. She lifted her glass to the property developer and smiled. 'At least, he pays for this side of it. He doesn't get any more involved than that.'

Cantor came over to them and said, 'You're from CrackDown?' It was clear what he thought and he didn't conceal it in his tone of voice.

'No, no,' Sally said. 'Paul here is one of Butler's introductions. Paul Gregory, Philip Cantor.'

Cantor smiled at him. 'We've met,' said Gregory. 'At least, that's putting it a bit strongly. I was with the American judge watching the case you were prosecuting – Hector, at Elephant and Castle.'

Cantor watched suspiciously, so Gregory decided to disarm him. 'He was very impressed by the standard of prosecuting.'

Now Cantor beamed. This was only as it should be. Gregory's next comment was not so easy. 'What we couldn't work out was why the case stopped so suddenly.'

'Because defence counsel was bloody rude to Scribner.'

'No, no. The argument. I was trying to explain the argument of law to the judge and why it was that the defence couldn't ask questions they wanted to ask.'

Cantor glanced at Sally. 'Oh, that was nothing. The judge ruled that he couldn't ask about some material which we refused to disclose. Scott should have accepted his ruling.'

He cut across Gregory's questions and spoke to Sally Donne. 'Hector's going to start again this week despite what was said earlier.'

'Where's Scott?' said Sally.

'We don't know. Jennings saw him at Madely Hall on Saturday morning, then he disappeared. Charlton went looking for him.'

'Who'll be the judge?'

'Scribner's going to do it again.'

'Will Scott be there?'

219

'No. Scribner's spoken to Hazel. If Scott comes back she's going to tell him that the circuit committee thinks it would be better since it's the same judge that he does not do the case again. It's all been arranged. If he says he's going to then he'll be told there will be a complaint against him about his behaviour last time. That'll stop him.'

'But will it? You know what he's like. He's an idiot.'

'I don't think we need worry because Charlton said he wouldn't be back at all.'

Cantor paused and handed some peanuts around.

'Scott was always heading for a fall,' he said.

As though she suddenly remembered that he was present, Sally turned to Gregory and said, 'I'm sorry, Paul. You won't know anything about this. Just arrangements.'

There was a knock and a voice invited them to sit down. By now there were eight present and at least one more was expected, since the place on Jennings's left, the place at the head of the table, was empty.

They started to eat – pastry, things with fish – when there was a general welcome. Gregory looked up. A short, elderly man came into the room. Gregory felt that his face was familiar.

He walked gravely over to the table, where the men stood while he took the main seat. As he acknowledged his welcome he stood for a moment with his hand in his waistcoat pocket, drawing back his jacket. Gregory could see a gold chain. It looked a little too decorative, out of place, rather dandyish.

The newcomer's eyes met his for a moment then moved on.

The chain wasn't the only gold he was wearing. For a man clearly dressed as a member of the establishment it was surprising. On his right hand he had a wide gold ring and in his lapel – Gregory suddenly paid attention – he had a little gold daffodil.

'That's His Honour Judge Scribner,' said Sally. 'You probably don't recognise him without his wig.'

Chapter 21

Scott stayed that night in a room above a café. Music played below until about three in the morning when everything ended with the old-fashioned noise of scooters and motor bikes, but it didn't disturb him. He had fallen asleep at eight and woken just as the little town was getting moving.

He had slept so well he could taste it. The aches of the fight with Charlton were receding. He felt better.

No one was up yet downstairs and he let himself out into the mountain air. It felt thin and clean against his face. He crossed the road. As in all Welsh hill towns there didn't seem to be any real distinction between the town itself and the hillside around it. He stepped out of the café and was immediately on short, springy grass, marked everywhere with sheep droppings. He looked up at the high peaks. That must be Snowdon. It had its strangely ordinary shape.

Two sheep came up the road, past the café, and decided to jump up on to the path he had taken, to the bank where he was standing. One was following the other, but it would have been stretching a point to say one was leading. They were moving in the strange detached way mountain sheep have. One of them bleated at him, so he moved. They jumped down and wound off down a sheep path towards a stone hut with a corrugated-iron roof.

When he turned he could see that there was now some activity in the café. The lady who had welcomed him yesterday, Mrs Hannay, was letting steam out of a huge urn. Breakfast was ready.

Scott ate hungrily and then she brought him tea. There was no point in asking for coffee – this was the heart of tea country. He was in North Wales, just west of the big lake. He had worked out that the farm must be only a short distance from where he was, but he could not find it on his map, the scale was too small. He had come to this town since the postal address was the same. Nor could he work out which of the roads that were marked would take him in the right direction. It was not even clear which were roads and which tracks. He needed a better map.

He drank the tea. He wondered if the coffee he normally drank in the morning hurt him. Things like that do. You only find out the damage being done when you stop – if you stop.

Right now he felt much the same about his work. Here there was no work tension, no tightening of the stomach when he surveyed the day ahead, and only now it was not there did he realise how much it had always been part of his life.

He read Mrs Hannay's paper.

But of course, there was Charlton, and now he was tense again. His theory that Charlton was working on his own wasn't much use since he couldn't prove it, and every time he passed a police car he still thought they were watching for him.

If Charlton was on his own then the chances of his being found here were nil, but if there was a warrant out they only had to spot the car registration.

Again he tried to work out what had made all this happen, but causes were the most difficult thing to guess at. Who could tell what motivated someone? He had once defended a man who had killed someone for sitting in his seat in a pub. It was a senseless thing to do since it effectively meant the killer would never sit there again. Perhaps Charlton was bored, perhaps he was tired of being attacked in court. Small human emotions are much more likely to set things going than great conspiracies.

He realised he was reading the newspaper without taking anything in at all. He looked at it again. It was the *Express*. No wonder.

Mrs Hannay stood beside him. 'You've slept well, then?'

Scott said yes.

'Not disturbed by the music?'

'No. What music?'

Mrs Hannay started cleaning the table. 'Not many people are disturbed. Those who arrive are too tired, specially the walkers.' She cleaned the ketchup bottle with care. 'But you'll not be a walker? You came in a car.'

Scott could not remember much of what had happened when he had arrived. He wasn't entirely sure where he had put the car, then he remembered parking it in the car park behind the house.

'You've come a long way, then?'

'Yes,' said Scott. 'I knew I was tired but not how much.'

'Will you be staying?'

'No, I'd better leave later on this morning.' He was working out what he had to do. 'Do you have a phone?' he said.

Mrs Hannay had hoped for a longer conversation but there you were. 'Yes,' she said, pointing at the door to the stairs.

Scott entered his credit card number. He waited to see if the lady who welcomed him on behalf of the telephone company spoke in a Welsh accent. She didn't, so Scott cut her off and punched in his code number. Cutting her off felt rude even though she was a recording.

He got his clerk at home. Clerks are always being rung at odd hours and his did not seem to mind. Or at least he didn't show it. There were no messages and he was lucky, no cases had been fixed for the Monday. He said he was going to be away for a short while, and he would ring.

Then his clerk mentioned Hector. 'The case won't be relisted again for at least a week. When it comes on again will you still be doing it? The solicitors and the client still want you.'

Scott realised that he didn't want the strain again, but knew of course he would have to do it. 'I'll have to, won't I?' he said. 'But the court will have to talk to us before it's listed for trial again, won't they?'

'Yes. They'll make sure you're free.'

Scott put the phone down and turned from the counter. As he did so he saw that the café sold Ordnance Survey maps. He realised now that this place must be one of the walkers' rests. He took a copy, sat down and started to search it for Upper House.

'Will you be walking, then?' said Mrs Hannay.

'I don't know. I have to find out where I'm going. It's a place called Upper House.' Then he found the Water Board Farm and put his finger on it. 'Here it is.' He ran his other hand south round the long fingers of the lake. It was about twenty-five miles by road from where he was now, and even then the nearest road was some way away from the farm itself, although it looked as though there was a track up to the farmhouse. By car it meant a long drive down and around, but there was one thin line that trailed directly over the hill, due west towards the town where he was. He showed Mrs Hannay the map. 'What's this road?' he said.

'That's a forestry road. Look, you can see where it begins there.' She pointed through the window.

Near the top of the sloping hillside, opposite where Scott had stood with the sheep, a lane petered out and a track cut upwards through the pine forest.

She ran her finger along the map. 'That track goes over the top and then down alongside the lake. There's Water Board at the other end, and the house you want is above, here.' She moved her finger up beyond the farm. Scott could tell by the contouring that it was high in the hills. 'That's Upper House.'

'You know it?'

'Yes,' she said, 'the engineer's house.'

'How best to get there?'

'From where you are now, walk,' she said. 'Even from the other side you can only get there by Land Rover or tractor. 'You'd still have to leave your car and walk, so you might as well leave it here.'

Scott could see now that the house was very isolated.

'The other way to get at it is from the main road.' She put her finger on the road through the pass further north. 'But you'd have to get up the sharp climb here.' There was a broken brown line Scott recognised as a cliff.

Now he thought about it, it was a cliff he already knew. He hadn't realised he was so close.

'But you'd have to walk over the mountain to get down to the farm. It's shorter, but you wouldn't manage it easily.' She looked at his clothes. 'Not dressed like that.'

'I used to climb there,' said Scott. He had his finger on the pass.

'Then you'll know, then,' she said.

'Don't worry. I wouldn't want to do that again,' he said. 'I didn't have a very good time.'

He went to buy a pair of boots. In the same shop he bought a plastic anorak and a rucksack. Then in the spirit of it he bought some thick socks, even considered buying a compass, but stopped himself. Then he found a really large-scale map, and he bought that.

When he got back to the café, he asked the obvious question. 'Is the house on the phone?'

'No,' she said. 'But you can leave messages at the Water Board Farm below. Doris Prytherch will take messages.'

'Do you know everybody about here?' asked Scott.

'Yes,' she said, 'and everybody knows me. I'm Nora.'

She made for the phone and spoke partly in Welsh and partly in English. 'Prytherch took a girl, an American girl, up there already this morning. That'll be who you are looking for, no doubt.'

That was a relief.

'So you won't have an unrewarded walk, then,' she said.

He packed his things into the rucksack. He didn't have much and it hardly weighed on his back at all. He went to the car park, hoping he could somehow hide the car's registration number. He found it had been done already. Mrs Hannay had covered it with a green tarpaulin. 'We don't like to encourage the young men to steal,' she said. 'Not that they need much encouragement. They're a light-fingered lot round here.'

Scott felt ridiculously grateful. 'You don't come from here, then?'

'What, me?' Mrs Hannay chortled as though he had said the most absurd thing in the world. 'No, not me, I come from Mumbles. I'm from the south, none of this hard North Wales thing about me.'

She beamed at Scott, looking up at him. She was hardly taller than five foot.

'Please don't leave anything in the car, except the map, that's OK. These young men aren't going anywhere and they know it. They don't need maps,' she said, handing him the brown envelope and the sentencing papers. Scott pushed them into an outside pocket of the rucksack.

'Now make sure you're properly equipped. There's a chemist, John Evans, down the road. It's a good track all the way to the house but it's a long walk for someone as out of condition as yourself.'

She couldn't have meant what he thought, could she?

'Down the road here, then left into the lane, past Bethesda, past Owen the Cows, up the hill and turn right. You'll see it's marked Forestry Commission. About five hundred yards further on there's a board showing the routes. Your best way is down by the lake. You may even hear the bells, if you're lucky.'

Scott set off, stopping at the chemist. Perhaps she meant salt tablets or Kendal mint cake, but he bought contraceptives.

He walked easily in the morning sun.

The lane dictated his direction into the woods above him. He had clearly misjudged the distances and it was the best part of two hours before he reached the beginning of the track that he had seen so clearly from the café window. The surface changed. Now he was walking on hard earth although it was as level and clear as before.

He was pleased with his boots. He had bought a soft pair, almost climber's boots, like the ones he used to own. They didn't need breaking in, though for hard use day after day they wouldn't be strong enough.

After a few hundred yards the track separated by a board showing directions. He traced the paths and saw that the larger plan confirmed what Mrs Hannay had said. The lakeside path was better; the other path, though shorter, was much more difficult.

He heard a sound behind him and turned but could see no further back than the last bend. There was nothing there. He was completely alone and enclosed by the wood, cut off from the bright fields that he had crossed as completely as if he had closed a door behind him.

From the sign the track took him steadily upwards. It grew cooler. The green and brown of the trees became darker. To his right there was a leather-coloured stream running down between wide banks which narrowed as he climbed higher. As it narrowed, it flowed faster and became silver when it splashed on the rocks. Scott's path turned to cross it just below where a pool had gathered at the foot of a fall.

The sound of the water echoed in the trees. Again from behind he heard a sound, but, looking back, realised it was only the echo of his steps on the wooden boards of the bridge. He stood for a while engrossed in the swirling water below. Where it moved over the rock it gleamed white and clean, but where it gathered at the edges of the bank, overhung by green, it was black. He looked up.

The waterfall was not large, no more than twenty feet high, but the water flew from it in a pulsing torrent. Further up he could see where, at the edge of the old wood, pine trees took over in ordered ranks enclosing the unmarketable, real woodland growing near the stream.

He turned slowly, surveying how the small undisturbed wood gave way to pine on all sides and, now he was high enough, below him as well.

From where he was, he was able to see parts of the track far below as it wound upwards. Suddenly he saw a man appear and then disappear. He watched but the figure did not reappear. He traced that part of the track with his eye and worked out that it was about there that it had run level for a while before branching up towards the climb he was now making.

The man was a good hour's walking behind him, perhaps more. He waited a moment but still the figure did not reappear. Maybe he had turned to the left and branched off. Perhaps a forester, a walker; no, not a forester, he'd be in a four-wheel-drive. Scott wandered on. At least he wasn't a solicitor or a bloody client whose worries he had to deal with.

It was well past eleven. In London he would have been in court half an hour or more probably, waiting for the session to begin. Given the staff situation they rarely started before eleven. What a waste. It was amusing how the baggage of life jiggled around in your mind. Who gave a damn about those things? Efficiency.

He looked up. He had continued walking and was much higher. He had been as indifferent to the spectacle about him as if he had been walking down Fleet Street. Not that Fleet Street was any spectacle, at least not now that the newspapers had all been replaced by people buying and selling money.

The track was going through the pine belt now, and he could see ahead of him more sky as the trees thinned. He must be near the top. With an effort he stopped his internal dialogue. He had carried with him the awful chatter that surrounds everyone in the city – the newspapers, the radio, all the rest of the media clamour. Then he realised he had just changed the subject, not turned it off.

The trees began to thin out and he could see that two hundred yards ahead he would be out of the woods. As he left the comparative darkness of the trees, the horizon widened around him, the closeness drained away, and soon he was able to turn and see for miles around.

Half a mile further on and he stood at the top of the pass. Way below him, stretching into the distance, lay a huge lake – placid, still, perfect. He stood looking at it for a long time. The chatter had stopped.

Charlton had stopped at the Samuel Johnson in Lichfield later on in the same afternoon that Scott had phoned from there. As he had expected, nobody had even seen the man who had come in earlier and used the phone; still less did they know which way he had gone.

He sat outside in his car, undecided. He called his contact number at Telecom. Ted had gone home, but surprisingly the new shift was well briefed.

'I asked for a list of numbers which was programmed in to a telephone to be identified,' he said to the operator. 'The London number is . . .'

He was interrupted. 'Yes, we have it.' They really were well organised.

'There were ten pre-entered numbers. We've got the addresses.'

'Are any of them out-of-London numbers?'

'Yes. Two in Brighton. One to Word Perfect in Berkshire. One to Southend, one to Fowey in Cornwall, subscriber Judith Gunn, and one to Chester.'

Chester. Could Scott be going to Chester?

'No. Wait a moment. The Chester number has not been reprogrammed. He can't have used it since Phoneday, that's four months now.'

Phoneday. What the hell was Phoneday? Charlton didn't bother. He tried an alternative. 'Have there been any other calls on the credit card? Since the one from Lichfield, that is.'

'You've got lucky. We've had one from North Wales about half an hour ago, to ... hang on, here's the number. To London. It lasted seven seconds. That sounds like an answerphone clicked in and he didn't talk. It was made from a street call-box near Llangollen. That's North Wales, isn't it?'

'Great,' said Charlton. 'I need to be contacted the next time the card is used.'

He set off towards Shrewsbury.

He crossed the border into Wales just north of Oswestry and took a road he knew. It was out of the way but the extra hour it would take for him to get to Llangollen would probably mean difficulty in finding a bed. He drove fast, knowing where he was going, slowing down only as he passed the Garth Boys' Home, outcast on the edge of the town.

He went straight to the hotel – more of a pub, really – there would be a bed there. It was much the same, though the brewery had attempted to make it seem more modern. But even they had had the sense not to take away the great wooden bar, the wood divisions and the black settles.

They had a room. He got a glass of beer, a thick sandwich, and he sat in the corner and watched the men at the bar. It had been many years since he had been here but occasionally he thought he saw a face he recognised. He did not count upon being recognised himself. Indeed, had he even thought about it, he would have dismissed it as unlikely.

'You're Charlton, aren't you?' A man slipped into the seat opposite him.

During the whole of the rest of the conversation in this secluded corner neither of the men raised his voice and no one noticed them talking.

'Yes,' said Charlton.

'You'll remember me. I'm Bennet.'

Charlton showed no sign whatever of surprise. He regularly met people of all sorts, both good and evil.

'I remember you,' he said.

'I came back to live here.'

'Why?'

'Because it was my home.'

'Not much of a home.'

Bennet had lived in the world. He had often had no food to eat at all. Once he had nearly been killed where he was sleeping in the street. He had learned from what had happened to him.

He said without rancour, 'If you had it in you to understand what a home is, then you would realise that any home is better than none. This is my home.'

Charlton was not going to be taken in. He knew about this sort of man, but he was surprised by his strength and the confidence of his reply.

'You were a thief.'

'Yes. You employed me as a thief.'

'You were a good one.'

'You, you and the others, made sure of that.'

'You took the money and you lived well.'

'What other choice did I have? To go and lean on the meat rack to be hired out to your friends?'

'I wasn't responsible for that. I had no interest in that.'

'You allowed it to go on.'

'I didn't allow it. It was nothing to do with me.'

'It would have stopped if you had told the truth at the inquiry. If you had ever told the truth.'

Charlton was silent for a moment and then he said, 'I think it was you who dipped that wallet with sixteen thousand pounds in it.'

Bennet said nothing.

'Some people say that there was even more in it than that.'

Again Bennet said nothing.

'You were working that day, and that was the last day we saw you. That means you still owe' – he paused – 'a third, that's five thousand three hundred and some, maybe more.'

'I owe you nothing,' said Bennet. 'You owe me my childhood. You owe me something no one can give me back.'

The whole time Bennet spoke very quietly.

Charlton watched him. What could he want? He had always been wary of him and when he had disappeared he had not been sorry. He stood up and said, 'Would you like a drink?'

'I don't drink,' said Bennet.

Charlton fetched a beer from the bar. 'That's very surprising. When I knew you you were well into skag.'

'Yeah. And who was selling it to me? Another department of the company store.'

He leaned forward. 'You're a policeman, Charlton, otherwise I'd take you apart. But because you're a policeman you've got power.'

Charlton looked back at him with contempt and then he affected surprise.

'I don't understand you. You were paid well.'

'That's because you don't understand what corruption is. It doesn't stop at a bit of licensed crime. Eventually it becomes an end in itself. I was lucky. I got out.'

'And you came here.' Charlton paused and thought, then said, 'It was about then the supply of boys from Garth dried up.'

'Yes.'

There was silence, then again Bennet leaned forward. 'I don't know why you're here or what you want, but if you stay one moment beyond tomorrow morning you'll have an accident.'

'You and who?' said Charlton.

'Me and a lot of the people in this village.'

The next morning Charlton left.

As he pulled out of the square in front of the pub right at the centre of the village the phone in the car rang. He stopped. He was directly outside a shop that filled nearly one side of the square. Section by section the shop supplied nearly everything the village could want – at one end was a newsagent and at the other end it dealt in lawnmowers, machinery and farm goods.

David Bennet, the owner, was helping his staff open the business. He paused for a moment to watch Charlton's car. Charlton was talking on the car phone.

Ted was back on duty. 'The card's been used again. He was calling out of the Walker's Rest Café, proprietress Nora Hannay. He was ringing a number in Essex. This was two minutes ago. Here's the address. It's about two hours from where you are now.'

The moment Charlton walked into Nora Hannay's café and spoke to her, she knew he was lying. 'I'm a friend of a man called Scott. He told me he'd be here, and that if he wasn't that he would have left for . . . He's a medium-build sort of chap, he looks . . .'

Charlton had found that if you didn't finish your sentences then information sometimes came more easily.

'I know who you mean,' said Mrs Hannay.

'Was he here long ago?'

'He left just after breakfast this morning.' Without meaning to, she looked towards the hills through the café window.

'Over the top?' said Charlton.

'Yes.'

'On foot?'

'Yes.'

Charlton had already sensed her unwillingness. He guessed she probably realised what he was. It was not difficult to pick up people's reactions. His life had consisted of getting reluctant responses to questions. He knew when he was not going to get an answer.

'Did he say where he was going?'

'No.' Well, it was an answer, but only just.

Charlton returned to his car and drove down the lane towards the hill. Scott must have a couple of hours' start on him, but if he was walking he'd soon catch him up.

Scott set off down from the top towards the lake. It was easy walking now, and he had been pleased to find at the top that the long walk up hadn't worn him out. The air and the light were opening him up.

The valley spread out below. Off to the right it opened into another valley, and then further in the distance into another, all of the valleys scooped out from the escarpment he had just crossed. The whole area drained into the lake. Birmingham's drinking bowl. He had seen on the map that the lake was dammed but couldn't see the dam from where he was. The lake curled round the hills to his left. The dam must be well out of sight.

The path wound down, veering to the right of the lake, and soon plunged, as it had on the other side of the hill, into pine woods. It dropped further and further down, doubling back on itself to lose height, and again was soon into older, more unkempt woods where broadleaf trees crushed in on each other.

Scott saw a stream begin, tiny at first then gathering strength from rivulets that joined it on either side. It grew and grew until it was the size of the stream he had passed earlier.

He crossed it by a wooden bridge and experienced the same feeling of being followed as he had before. He waited and watched until he saw, as he had before, a figure appear at one of the bends in the track, this time high above him. The follower was catching him up. He pressed on. According to the map he had some miles to go and he had no time to wait. The figure was another walker probably. Anyway, he wanted to be on his own.

Charlton was moving faster, occasionally leaving the path, cutting a bend in order to save time.

As Scott walked he checked the map. There was no doubt, now that he could see the lie of the land, that his best option was to keep to the right of the lake, follow the path along the side and then cross at the dam or below. It was not possible to follow the other side of the lake all the way since the path was barred by a river that tumbled down the side of the hill in a waterfall.

Mrs Hannay had described it accurately. If he went that way he could cross the river at the start of the waterfall or he could climb right to the top and walk along the ridge itself, but that was a two-hour climb. He could do it, but the waterside route would be much quicker and safer. Mrs Hannay hadn't given much for his chances of getting across the waterfall. 'Not at this time of year,' she'd said. 'It's still very full, and cold: the river runs off the big water-catch at the top of the ridge.'

A water-catch, when water gathers on the top of a hill: Scott remembered hearing the expression when he had lived up here.

Now he could see it he realised she was right. The high falls shone and sparkled in the distance, curving out from the rock into the lake below. It was spectacular. He could imagine what a walk across the lip would be like, especially if the weather changed. He looked around and back towards the Irish Sea. It was fine now but he knew from experience that the weather could change up here completely in half an hour. A mist could come in from the sea and it could be driving with rain before you put your lunch away.

He had talked about it with Mrs Hannay and she had reckoned that he might reach the dam by four in the afternoon. From there Upper House was perhaps two hours. He was doing well. He had come out of the pines and had entered a cleared area above the lake. It was about two and any time now he would reach the point where he would turn to his right for the level walk beside the water.

The lake was only forty or fifty feet below and above him to his left there was a great flat rock, surrounded by scrubby trees, overlooking the valley like a Royal Box. That was the place at which to eat Mrs Hannay's packed lunch. He turned off the path, dropped down a large ditch that drained the track, and climbed up to the rock.

He wasn't the first person who had been there and the others had made their presence felt. They went back years. A comment on Prince Charles's investiture was scratched on the rock. Lord! When was that? He had seen some pictures of it the other day and the Queen's clothes had made it seem from another age. There was even a 'Free George Davis' slogan. Who would remember what that was all about?

He settled to the bag of sandwiches and the isotonic drink she had packed. He examined the can. Isotonic stuff goes straight into you apparently, not stopping at the usual places where drink stops. The difference between it and ordinary drink, he concluded, was similar to the difference between prejudices and opinions.

He had started to pack up the can and the waste paper, rather self-consciously putting it all neatly back into his bag, when there was a crash behind him. His first instinct was to stand up, but he didn't. He peered over the lip of the rock. Had he stood up he would immediately have been seen. About forty feet away from him, pushing through the bushes, cutting the corner of one of the sharp bends in the track, was Charlton. Scott dropped his head.

How on earth had he followed him? Was he psychic or something? He looked again over the rock. The detective – God, he was certainly that – was setting off towards the lake.

He sat back. From where he was he could see what Charlton could not yet see, the lakeside path curving out to the right from the bottom of the hill. It would take Charlton five to ten minutes to get there, and when he got there he would only have to walk two hundred yards before he saw what he couldn't now: that there was no one on the path for two miles. He would immediately realise what had happened and he would come back.

Scott had two choices: he could go back up the way he had come or take the other route past the waterfall. He looked up the hill. He didn't want to go back. If he went to his left on the more difficult route he would have the cover of the rock and low growth for about a mile. But then he would have to cross the waterfalls. He looked at them glistening in the distance and gulped. But if he had to, he had to. He crawled to the edge of the rock, feeling utterly absurd, and slipped down the other side.

Above him lay the hillside. He pushed his way through the trees that had gathered around the edge of the rock, over another ditch, a good ten feet deep, taking a minute to get through, then set off upwards. This was a bit more like hard work.

He worked his way up. Occasionally he glanced down but there was no sign that Charlton had seen him. Eventually he made it to the woods that grew back from the stream and again watched. Nothing. He had slipped away unnoticed. Far below him he could see the road on the other side of the lake and thought he could see a figure, but this time walking back. Perhaps he had given up.

Scott turned. Ahead of him lay the pool that gathered at the edge of the waterfall. He looked up. The stream came down from the top in a narrow cleft; there was no way across there. He'd have to go through the pool.

It didn't seem to be very deep but he couldn't be sure. He was not going to wade across without something to hold on to. If he fell he might go straight over the edge. It wasn't flowing very fast since it was brimming at the edge. There must be times when the water going over was a mere trickle and others, when the rain came, when it went over in a rush, but now the rocks at the edge were like teeth, holding most of the water back.

But there were gaps.

Ridiculously he thought of Terry-Thomas, gap-toothed, but the gaps were not going to be a joke. One was a good four feet wide, plenty wide enough to be swept through.

How was he going to do it?

Wade through or step from rock to rock? This wasn't a film and he knew what he wasn't going to do. He wasn't a film star. He took hold of a clump of grass and stepped into the water at the side. It reached up to his calves. So far so good. Tentatively he moved towards the edge of the fall.

He could feel the water tugging at his trousers, but only gently.

He reached the waterfall edge. There was a large rock. It must be this rock that helped form the pool. It had yellow moss on the top. It seemed the water never got this high.

He felt his way out towards the middle. The bed of the pool was rock as well. That figured. If it had been anything else it would have been scoured out by the swirling water. As he thought about this, his feet squelched down, mud oozing over the side of the boot. Well, perhaps not all of it had been scoured out.

The rocks at the edge reached above his knees. He was as safe now as if he had been standing behind a low wall, even though he was up to his thighs in water. But now he was looking over the cliff and it was very clear what would happen if one of the rocks gave way. Why should they? They stood the pressure of the water when it was much higher than this. They didn't feel loose.

As he reached the centre of the fall he could feel the tug of the water increase. At first it was gentle then suddenly it became incredibly strong. If he had not been holding on he might well have been dragged down.

He looked back into the pool and could see that where he had been a moment ago was in effect standing water. This was a torrent, although the movement was below and didn't show on the surface.

He moved back, pulled a piece of turf from the side and threw it into the middle of the pool. For a moment it floated there, not moving, then with increasing speed it shot over the edge. So, not all water that was moving fast churned and broke on the surface. He couldn't walk through that. He'd be swept off his feet instantly.

He was going to have to climb on to the rocks right at the edge and step across. Like Sylvester Stallone. He went back to the first rock and climbed up on to it. His feet streamed with water and his left boot was black with silt. They weren't going to grip very well.

He stood on the rock and hesitated. He needed to take about four steps, then one long step. Another short step right in the middle, one more long step, then he'd be all right. He could throw himself into the water if necessary, as long as he got past the central flow. He'd better do it. Now.

He crossed the rocks as though he were crossing the street. There was a heart-stopping glimpse of whirling water way below him to his right, a moment when his foot seemed to slip, but his forward movement left the slipping step behind, and with a sickening lurch he found himself sitting

light-headed on the grass on the other side.
The mist came down and with a strange hissing noise it began to rain.
He started to think about his life.

King John was not a bad man,
But he had his little ways,
Sometimes no one would speak to him
For days and days and days.

Christ, what had he been doing all these years?
He looked back at where he had come from and he couldn't see the other side of the pool. It was astonishing. The mist had come down hard. He supposed it wasn't mist but cloud. Was there a difference?
He went straight up the hillside.
The effect of the cloud was strange. Though he could not see anything there was light all around him. He got out the map and by holding it right up to his eyes he could just make it out. Suddenly the mist lifted for a moment and he could see which way to go. The sky came down again, obscuring everything as before, but now he was able to carry on.
After a while the ground confirmed his quick glimpse. The hill climbed up to his left and then dropped down to his right. It was odd since sitting where he had been it had seemed to be the other way round.
It became easier. He found a sheep path and began to lose height. It stopped raining, though whether it had been raining or whether he had just been inside a rain cloud wasn't clear. It was still just as wet.
He stopped to look at the map often, worried that he was getting nearer and nearer the cliff above the lake. Occasionally he chose a path that went upwards to regain height, until there came a time when moving to his left didn't seem to make any great difference.
Then the light that seemed to come from inside the mist began to fade. He wasn't able to move faster and he began to worry about spending the night on the hill. The gradual levelling of the ground reassured him. He must be coming down now and he had gone far enough to be reaching at least the second half of the lake.
Then slowly, for no apparent reason at all, the mist dissolved and he found he was walking on the lower slopes of the hill, the still lake bathed in evening sun two hundred yards away. There was no cliff now. He was completely alone. Ahead of him he could see a track winding off to his left.

That must be the way to Upper House.

When he approached the door of the house he was walking automatically. He felt utterly tired out. He also found that he was limping but couldn't make out why. His clothes were soaked.

The evening was ending and the hills around him were darkening, but the danger that he might lose his way had gone, since a light from the house shone down the hill. He had shoved the map into his rucksack long ago.

Now he was going to have to be polite, deal with small talk, and somehow explain his appearance. Was he going to have to tell them the whole story. He formed some words as he walked along and tried to speak them but his voice seemed to be lumpy.

As he got closer he could see that the house was built on a flat rocky area. Perhaps the top of a small hill had been sliced off. It was approached by a path which curled around so that just before he reached the level of the house he was facing back the way he came. He pushed up the path, already feeling better as he neared the end. It must be at least seven or eight o'clock. He had been going for ten hours, though during the last couple of hours moving very slowly. He was very weary. But that was what he had wanted to be, wasn't it?

The path turned and the astonishing view for which the house had been located here opened up to him. The whole of the great lake shimmered below like a polished silver plate let into the bed of a black, black basin.

Up to the right, the hill from where he had come reared up like a dark wave, and at the top he could see a thin silver trickle where the waterfall fell into the lake. To his left the vast dam stood, holding back the water above the deep unflooded valley that stretched way into the distance beneath it.

Far below he could see points of light, presumably the Water Board Farm, and arching over everything the huge sky, streaked with a last few flashes from the dying day. It was all completely still. As far as he could judge he was the only moving creature. He stood there silently.

'I thought you would come.' Catherine's voice came from the door. She stood with the light behind her. 'I knew you would come,' she repeated, speaking to herself.

As he moved into the light her hand went to her mouth in a classic pose of amazement. To Scott she seemed to be moving in slow motion.

'Jesus!' she said. 'What happened to you?'

'I got wet,' he said.

She took him into the house and lifted the rucksack from his shoulders. Even though it was hardly any weight at all he immediately began to feel he was floating.

'Your face,' she said, and touched his forehead. When she took her hand away Scott realised there was blood on it. Where had that happened? Was it when he fell from the jump? 'My God. It was lucky you met no one on the path. They would have run like crazy. You look like something out of a horror movie.'

She led him further into the house, Scott moving tentatively, venturing into someone else's place, every step an apology. She picked it up immediately. 'We're alone,' she said. 'Come on.' She led him up the stairs.

Scott could see her better now as she turned, moving backwards, taking his hands. His mouth worked a bit and he said, 'It's good to see you.'

'You're welcome,' she said. 'As long as you don't say sorry like every other Englishman I've met. In fact, don't say anything.'

They went up the stairs and along a dark passage, stopping at the door of a huge bathroom. In the middle of the room there was a bath. At one end there were two wild taps poised like water chutes, at the other a kind of sentry box built on to it with doors – a shower. On the wall to his left there was a large wash-basin, again with the wild taps and a vast chunk of soap at the end of a brass swan's neck sticking out from the wall.

She stopped him at the door and crouched at his feet, unlacing his boots. She was in almost the same position as when he had last seen her, sending him off to work at the judges' seminar. He saw her head from above as she worked at his feet. This time he touched her hair, which felt warm and rough. She didn't move her head away.

The boots, soaked through, were hard to get off. 'Maybe we'll find a fish in them,' she said, 'like Thoreau's circumstantial evidence.'

He sat down and tried to help, but she pushed him back with a shove in the chest. He nearly fell flat on his back. 'Stay still,' she said. It was inexpressibly pleasant to be treated like a child. She started working the boot up and down, to get it over the heel.

It immediately hurt and he grimaced. She said, 'Have you twisted it?'

'No,' he said, 'I don't think so. Just new boots.'

'Hang on,' she said, and he lay down on his back. She came back and cut the laces. Both boots came off easily then. She got him up – by now he wasn't really trying, feeling a bit fraudulent – and took him into the bathroom. They stood in front of a mirror. Now he could see what she meant.

His sweater was torn from the arm to the waist, and hung on him like a petticoat. His trousers were sodden and there was a long tear in one leg. His left arm was covered in mud and his hand, when he lifted it, was deeply scratched, with black drying blood all down the forearm. But it was his face which looked the worst.

Clearly he had bled from the top of his head. It was that that must have felt so sticky. The blood had run backwards rather than down his face and had matted in his hair. But at both sides of his head and on his jaw there was black dried blood.

He tried to say, 'It's all on the surface.'

'I think you'd better have a bath,' she said. She let fly with the taps and left the room.

Before he got into the bath he got most of the blood off at the basin. He washed his arm and found the scratch that had caused the bleeding. It opened again for a moment but then closed and he turned his attention to his chest. There were red marks beginning to show down his side. All from that one fall, and he had not even noticed it at the time. He must have hit something.

He thought of the waterfall, and there was a flash of experience, not a real memory, which can be contemplated and looked at, but a reliving of the moment, over as quickly as the event itself was over, and just as damaging. It was the kind of memory that was not going to spread and share itself with everything else. But when it came back it was always going to disable him for a moment. He found it had now. He was gripping the sides of the hand-basin.

He remembered another occasion, when he had really fallen; he was able to relive it exactly, the feel of the large round boulder under his frantic hands, the surprisingly thin rope and what he thought was a scream. That memory was stored, complete and still capable of harming him. Here was another piece of junk to add to it. What was it that Catherine had repeated? Yeats. 'The foul rag-and-bone shop of the heart . . .'

'Yeats, you're quoting Yeats,' the American woman lawyer had said.

Heavens, when was that? Only three days ago.

* * *

The door opened.

He thought Catherine had left out of modesty. Not a bit. She'd got something to drink.

He stood at the sink. He was clean now and stripped to the waist. He still had the rags of his trousers on. She came up behind him and undid them and slid his shorts down. 'You're quite well built you know,' she said, and she ran her nails up the outside of his thighs.

The effect was astonishing.

He felt every hair on his body move. He thought of saying something but didn't, just enjoying the feeling. The throbbing of his side and head joined in as she slid her hands round his body.

What a fraud he was! So much for the exhausted man staggering out of the dark.

'Oddly enough, I don't think you're as tired as you look, or rather you're more resilient than you think you are,' she said. He began to dissolve. His head started swimming, the scent of her body got stronger.

'This is the bathroom exercise as taught to the Duchess of Windsor by the Chinese,' she said.

He didn't reply. He couldn't. He reached for her. Her body was pressed right against him.

'No,' she said. 'One of the main points about the Chinese bathroom exercise is that the man does nothing at all until right at the end. But then again, at the end it's all up to him.'

He drank dry martini in the huge bath, a good seven feet long; he could almost swim in it. Where he lay there was a metal contraption. 'A martini holder,' she said. 'After all, it was an American who built this house.'

The drink tasted like iced fire.

'Want to know the recipe?' she said. 'The trick is you put the vermouth and the angostura on the ice, not the gin. Buñuel's recipe – and he told my uncle.'

Scott's feet were tingling. All the various aches were friendly now, reinforcing the pleasure of lying there. He wasn't badly hurt at all, it had just looked dramatic. His voice had come back.

'Whose house is this?'

'It's the family's. My great-uncle built it. It was thrown in with the contract for the dam.'

'He built the dam?'

'His company did. But he owned the company. Here you are.' She fitted an extension to one of the taps, a piece of solid brass that stretched out towards him. 'We call it the piano pedal. You can turn the water on with your toes. If you ask me, an absolute necessity for civilised life.'

'But you're American. What are you doing building dams in Wales?'

'We travel.'

'What happened to you?' she said.

'I fell while crossing the waterfall.'

'Which way did you come?'

'From the west.'

'But the best way is round the other side of the lake then over the dam.'

'I was being chased. I had to go the other way.' It sounded so ridiculous that he submerged himself for a moment.

'By Charlton?'

'Yes.'

'How did he know where you were?'

'God knows.'

He told her the story.

'You walked across the waterfall? You must be mad.'

Delicately, he put some more hot water in the bath with his big toe. 'I was like a gazelle,' he said.

They sat in the kitchen, a large, square, warm room. 'The story is that some of the flagstones came from the church, before it was deconsecrated.'

'You mean gravestones?'

'No one had looked on the other side, but I don't think so, not the right shape.'

'The church was drowned?'

'Yes, and for a long time this house was a symbol of it.'

'I stopped to get some food on the way,' she said. 'But the cherries we had already in the cupboard.' They were eating cherry pie.

'Cherry pie. You made cherry pie. Why?'

'I just wanted to make a pie.'

'But cherry pie. That's a pie you make for welcoming people.'

'Yes.'

'I don't get entitled to cherry pie by just turning up?'

'No,' she said, 'you don't.'

'It's out of *Little Women*.'

'Yes,' she said.

'Where does that fit in with Syracuse University Women's Group rules of interpersonal contact?'

'It doesn't. It comes from an older, more delicate age,' she said. 'I junked all that other stuff.'

'How could Charlton have known where you were going?'

'He must have spoken to Nora Hannay.'

'But how did he get there?'

'The only way I can think is that someone saw the number of the car.'

'But how did he get that?'

'From the man at the Madely Hall car park?'

'No way. I spoke to him while waiting for the cab. He didn't know anything from all-but.'

They had shut the house down and had gone to bed and were lying next to each other as if they'd been married for years.

'I don't think he got this address from Nora Hannay.'

'Why?'

'Because he's a policeman. He wouldn't have left his car.'

'Like people in the desert?'

'That's what they always say. But he wouldn't. He'd have driven round, got to the Water Board Farm then got them to get him down to the lake path.'

'Is this the only house round here?'

'Well, it's not the only one you get to by coming over the top. There are two farms the other side and further up there's Taldir.'

'That's the place in that poem.'

'Yeah. It won't be obvious where you went.'

There was silence for a moment.

'What are you going to do?'

'I'll stay here, if I'm welcome.'

'You're welcome,' she said.

Charlton went back to the café. He was tired, wet and annoyed. Mrs

Hannay gave him the room Scott had used and the music kept him awake till three.

'Most people are not disturbed by it. They come off the hills tired,' Mrs Hannay said. 'Then they sleep the sleep of the just.'

She was leaning on the counter while he ate.

'Well, it kept me awake.'

'Then I shall have to change your room.'

'I doubt if I will be staying. You say you don't know where he went.'

'No.'

'He must have asked you the best way.'

Mrs Hannay didn't know it but if you don't want to say anything you have to say nothing at all. Once a conversation starts you have to say something.

'We talked about it. He bought a map.'

'Do you know the area over there?'

'Yes,' she said.

'Had he been here before?'

'I don't think so.'

'You'll have told him the best way, then?'

'Yes.'

'Which route did you say he should take?' Charlton took a map from the rack.

Once you've started it's even more difficult to stop. She traced the track.

'Where does the track go?'

'Well, it goes anywhere. You can turn off at all these places.'

'Who do you know there?'

Mrs Hannay got a grip of herself. She didn't want to tell this bullying man anything at all.

'Do you know, I don't know any of them over there. There are so many little farms and places in the by-ways. Anyway, me, I'm from Sketty, Mumbles way, down Swansea, and we keep ourselves to ourselves down there.'

Charlton knew he had lost her. And he had lost Scott.

Chapter 22

The large bedroom was the perfect place to lie and watch the clouds go by. There were huge windows on three sides of the room and from where Scott and Catherine lay, on a large bed raised up slightly, they could see to the end of the lake.

'The storm's coming now,' said Catherine.

On the top of the far hill it had started raining.

The rain advanced like an army, filling and spreading sideways to engulf the area as it swept down from the top. First it made the pine trees sway, then, as though they had been covered in gauze, it obscured them. Next it rubbed out the darker line of older trees that followed the stream down the hill.

Before the rain reached the bottom of the slope, advance gusts skittered across the surface of the placid lake, shooting ahead and then turning back.

The rain hit the lake. The surface became black. Scott could even see tiny whitecaps being whipped up at the shore. Then he realised the speed of the storm as it swept over the surface.

'We've got less than a minute,' said Catherine. 'Listen for the bells.'

They lay motionless, Catherine's leg lying across Scott's thigh, her head resting on his shoulder.

Scott could see a single curved front now, a clearly defined line, coming towards them. High above the surface of the lake clouds poured in behind the rain, flooding the valley and scouring along the high sides and cliffs.

It would have been like this the day before when he ran up the gully, clouds sweeping down towards him, and it must have looked as if, absurdly, he was trying to outrun the bubbling clouds.

'Listen for the bells,' Catherine repeated.

245

As the storm moved the clouds raced around the curving hillside. They outstripped the main storm, gathering speed, and eventually burst from the curve into the middle of the lake. Then they seemed to lose their impetus and hung still over the water in the path of the main mass bearing down on it.

'Listen now,' said Catherine, and as the advancing sheet of rain engulfed its lost cloud, the whole valley shuddered with the impact. The surface of the lake seemed to groan, and a vast booming toll hovered in the air, neither starting nor stopping, but shuddering like a bell beginning to sound.

Just when it seemed the peal would ring out, the noise died away, fading into the hills. Scott heard the hissing sound he had heard the day before and the windows shivered. The torrent rushed up the hill and the house was drenched in water.

Catherine pulled the blanket round her and Scott felt the warmth of her body as she pressed into him.

'Why is it good sex isn't tiring?' he asked.

'Again?' she said.

The rain crashed on the windows. He turned her over and slid a pillow down her back. He could feel the flatness of her stomach and her hips, emphasised by the pillow as it offered her body to him.

He traced her mouth, open slightly, just showing the tips of her teeth and then her tongue touching the corner of her lips. He examined her nose, slightly crooked, and felt the downy strands of her hair at the side of her temple. He touched the fine tracery at the nape of her neck, and could feel the hollow at the back of her head.

He ran his fingers over her shoulders and down her arms, feeling the crooked bumps of her elbow. He touched the curving line at her side and could feel her hip swelling out. Then he gripped her and lifted her onto him so hard that it would normally have hurt, but it only intensified the pleasure and they clung together in the magic room over the lake, cut off from time, complete.

'There's a village. It was flooded when the valley was dammed and they say those are the church bells sounding. But of course they're not.'

Catherine was making coffee.

The rain had passed and the day was brightening. Scott sat at a stool. He was eating an egg.

'Proper Welsh butter is very salty,' she said. 'Some people don't like it. They think it's rancid, because of its dark yellow colour.'

She was barefoot, wearing a black silk nightgown that, when she moved, seemed to flow. 'The liquefaction of her clothes.'

Scott said, 'I'm Welsh.'

'How can you be Welsh, with a name like Scott?'

'You don't know my middle names.'

'Well?'

'One of them is Llewelyn.'

'That's Welsh enough for anyone.'

'Yes. I was born in Yorkshire, though.'

'How are you Welsh then?'

'My family is from the Gower.'

'Where's that?'

'It's along from Swansea.'

'What are you doing in London?'

'I'm a displaced person,' he said.

'What do you think has happened to Charlton?'

'Well, with any luck he got bloody wet.' Scott laughed. 'And he didn't get the woman.'

He looked at her sideways to see if she was offended and saw that she was smiling to herself. She was just as pleased at what had happened as he was. 'Anything else?' she said as she gave him the coffee.

'What's all this submissive stuff?'

'I'm not being submissive. I just feel good.' She followed a train of thought. 'Submissive. You're just interpreting it as submissive. Just because you feel you dominated me.'

'I did,' he said. 'I did, and it was real. Not just satisfying myself.'

They sat silently and listened to the wind clearing away the remnants of the rainstorm.

'What do we do if Charlton comes knocking at the door?'

'He won't.'

'Why not?'

'Because he won't find the house. You can't see it from land. It's completely concealed except from the far end of the lake and, even then, it doesn't look like a house but a slate outcrop. The only way you can get here is if you look at the map and decide to come here.'

'Why won't he do that?'

'Because if you look at the map this is one amongst so many isolated buildings that the chances of deciding on this one are almost nil.'

' "The chances are nil." That's what I said about Charlton coming to Wales at all. Anyway,' he remembered suddenly, 'I told the woman at the café that I was coming here. Maybe she told him.'

They were both quiet.

'I don't think she did, though,' said Catherine.

'Why not?'

'Because he's a policeman. He wouldn't have followed you on foot. He would have gone round the lake and got transport up to the house somehow. He'd only have followed on foot if he didn't know where you were going.' It was what she had said before and it seemed to make sense.

'If he saw you he couldn't have got across the falls anyway.'

Scott thought back to that horrifying moment. Again he felt the heave in his stomach. He was sitting in the hissing rain again looking back at the jump.

'No. He didn't get across. I doubt if he even knew I had gone across.' He looked into the distance. 'It must have been then I lost that anorak.'

'Was there anything in it?'

'No,' he said. 'I put everything in the rucksack.' He got up. It was lying, still wet, against the wall. 'Look.' He took out the shoes and the jacket. 'Here are the papers, Richard's envelope, and the papers for the seminar.' He flipped through them. 'By the way, you got me into deep trouble with your ideas on how to sentence the man in the lift.'

'All men are rapists,' she said.

'And you're one of nature's victims,' he said, throwing the papers on a chair.

For the remainder of the day the papers that Cantor had asked be brought to court remained where he had thrown them.

Then they were shifted to the dresser top and from there to a window sill. After that they were picked up with a pile of other stuff – a timetable, an article on egg production, and a receipt for petrol – and moved into the hall.

They were becoming caught up in the steady circular flow that washes stray paper, books, water bills, spare gloves, and scissors around a house, before they reach the bin.

Chapter 23

Ronnie Knox was sitting in his room in the Temple with his feet up. He was reading one of Cardinal Cajetan's commentaries on Aquinas. He had never been too impressed by Cajetan, since it seemed to him that in many ways he had got hold of the wrong end of the stick.

There was a knock on the door and his clerk came in.

This was unusual. Nowadays members of chambers were summoned to the clerk's room by an announcement through the telephone system. The new system had surprised Ronnie when he first heard it. He had not been able, for a moment, to work out where the disembodied voice had come from, and the words 'We need Mr Knox' had, for a long moment, frozen him in his seat. In Ronnie Knox's firmament, disembodied messages didn't normally originate from the clerk's room.

But here was the clerk, on foot, as it were. Something was up.

'Mr Knox, sir. We've got a problem.'

'Yes,' said Ronnie slowly.

He knew what that meant. He was about to be the solution. The only difference then would be that he himself would have a problem and Cajetan would have to take a back seat and, what was more, tonight was lecture night. He had arranged dinner at the Travellers' and there was every chance the Metropolitan would come.

'Mr Scott's not here.'

'Yes,' said Ronnie even more slowly. Scott did solely crime. If this was a late return it was not going to be in the High Court.

'A case of his has come in at short notice.'

Ronnie was right.

'Oh,' he said.

249

His senior clerk pressed on, so Ronnie decided to grasp the nettle. There was no way he was going to get out of this. 'When is it on?'

'Two o'clock tomorrow. Though there'll be no evidence called tomorrow. The jury's going to be sworn and then sent away until the next day. So you've got this evening and the whole of tomorrow to prepare it. We've agreed a conference in the afternoon when the court rises.'

The senior clerk was pleased. Obviously Mr Knox was going to agree to do it, though he never had any real doubts that he would. Mr Knox was what he would call a good friend to chambers.

'Where is it?' For a moment Ronnie had fears of Norwich, which, for him, meant getting up half an hour earlier at five.

'Elephant and Castle.'

'Very civilised,' said Ronnie, 'at least as far as getting there is concerned.' He rather preferred Norwich, which, for him, had a pre-Reformation air, and there was that waitress in the Norfolk Club. He thought about the snooker table. But then again there was that early morning train journey.

'Case of Hector. Judge Scribner.'

'What?' said Ronnie, and he was suddenly on his feet. 'Hector? Scott can't return that case. It's dynamite.'

'He hasn't returned it. They've suddenly brought it on when he can't do it. I told the court on Monday morning that the client wanted him and that Mr Scott was unavailable this week and they agreed. But they've listed it anyway. They didn't want to. I rang and reminded them of our conversation; they knew it wasn't meant to be in but they've had orders, I think.'

The clerk seemed unusually disturbed. Clearly he had really tried.

'So it's in tomorrow and Lawson wants you. You've worked for them before, haven't you?'

'Yes,' said Ronnie, 'I did a right of way case for their nice Mr Pagnamenta once.'

Judge Scribner was in as close as he could be to a good mood. He had not much to do in the morning. He had put two cases over, since by the time the various reports would be ready he would be safe back in his own court. That had left him an hour before lunch with nothing on. He had read *The Times* and then borrowed Betty's *Daily Mail*.

Now he was being asked for half an hour before the court sat and was being reassured that the court would then rise at three. It was scarcely a hard day's work.

He could then take his spaniel for a walk down by the river.

'Yes. Give 'em half an hour but no longer. I'll come in at half past two on the dot.' Betty went out of his room to give the lawyers the message.

Cantor said, 'I'm applying to change the indictment and here is the new case opening for you.'

'It's a bit late to go mucking about with the indictment, isn't it? These defendants have known what they have been charged with for months now, and right at the last moment you want to change it. Hardly fair.'

'I'm entitled to apply to amend it. And you can object.'

'A lot of use that is with Scribner,' said John Plumstead. 'And what's this?' He was reading Cantor's new summary of the way he was going to put his case. 'You've changed your case now. You're not saying the Hectors lived in the flat any more. You can't do that.'

'I can put my case in any way I like,' Cantor said.

'You've changed your case because of the way the evidence came out at the last trial.'

'What do you want me to do? Put the case in a way that I know is not correct?'

Of course, Cantor was right. He could do whatever he wanted. The jury weren't going to be interested in what they would think were technicalities. They would just go on the evidence they heard.

'Oh, and I won't be calling Charlton this time. He's not available.'

'We will have to object,' said Plumstead.

'As you wish,' said Cantor, turning on his heel.

When the court sat, Ronnie tried to stop the case going ahead.

'I first have to ask that the case be adjourned. It is a complicated matter and Mr Scott has had conduct of this matter until now. I don't feel it proper to try to take it over at the last moment.'

'I am sorry, Mr Knox,' Scribner said, 'this case cannot be listed at counsel's convenience. If Mr Scott wishes to do the case he should be here.'

'The list office was told he was not available this week and they agreed the case would not come in.'

'When they did that they did not know the full position. The case goes on. We have accommodated you by not starting it till tomorrow morning. You have ample time.'

It was hopeless.

Now it was Cantor's turn. 'My application is to amend the indictment. Presently the defendants are charged with a conspiracy to manufacture drugs. I wish to alter that to conspiracy to supply drugs.'

Scribner obviously knew this was coming. 'You can have no objection, can you?'

John Plumstead stood up.

'Yes. We do object. We submit it is unfair for the Crown to amend the indictment at this late stage.'

'But Mr Plumstead, the indictment may be altered at any stage – even after conviction – if it causes no unfairness to the defence. How do you say this is unfair?'

Of course, the difficulty was that there was no precise way in which it was unfair.

'And if you wish the jury to know of the change you are at liberty to bring it out, aren't you?'

Again this was true.

Scribner went on, 'At first, on the evidence, the Crown thought your clients were manufacturers. Now upon reappraisal they say they cannot sustain such a charge. How is that unfair?'

Scribner had seen perfectly well how the case had begun to collapse last time; so had everyone. The real unfairness was that the defence were not going to be allowed to do it again. But that didn't count.

'In fact, upon reflection, it is to your advantage, isn't it? Some may think this is a less serious charge.'

There was no arguing with Scribner.

Philip King raised the absence of Charlton and got the same reaction.

'The Crown aren't bound to call him. He was only called last time in response to a request. And, Mr King, the fewer witnesses the Crown is able to call the weaker their case must be, isn't that so?'

Philip pressed his argument.

'You say that the officer contradicted the Crown's case. But what that officer thought or did not think is not evidence, is it? And this time the prosecution case is different, is it not? Perhaps the Crown does not wish to rely upon the mistakes that officer clearly made.'

There was nothing for it. They were stuck. The prosecution knew what the defence was going to be and they were trimming their case to fit.

Cantor had not even been asked to reply to their objections, though he had his reply ready. 'This is not a game,' he would have said.

Ronnie sat down with John Hector. How was he going to explain this? The change in the way the prosecution were putting the case merely confirmed Hector's opinion of the whole affair, and Charlton's absence was the last straw.

'Mr Scott destroyed him,' Hector said, 'so now they're frightened of calling him. You know and I know that they have changed their case, and you know the reason.'

'I do,' said Ronnie.

Ronnie had seen the notes on the way the evidence had come out in the first trial and had been astonished at how far Scott had succeeded in discrediting it. 'But our difficulty is that when we complain the jury will merely think it is all just lawyers arguing.'

Hector looked at his wife, who looked back at him in despair.

'But I've been set up, Mr Knox.'

What could Ronnie say?

'We've had another call on the credit card.'

Charlton had heard nothing from the phone company for four days.

'It's from an address in North Wales. The subscriber is Prytherch, the address is the Water Board Farm. There were two calls. Two London numbers: a barristers' offices and a garage in Welling. The calls were made about twenty minutes ago.'

'Get me on my mobile if anything happens again,' said Charlton. He reckoned he could get to North Wales in about five hours.

Scott and Catherine had walked down to the farm. They needed milk and bread. Mrs Prytherch had a freezer full of bread and lots of fresh milk.

The open hills shone around them. Above, very high up, there was a hawk turning slowly in the air. The whole valley wore a benign air, but Scott remembered it was over this hill that he had seen the storm rush a few days before.

'When you're here, all that stuff spinning around inside your head is unimportant. You have to keep in step with what is about to come over the top of the hill,' she said.

They walked on.

Again Scott was amazed by her capacity to say out loud what he was thinking. He said, 'I was offered a garden once. I was staying in a huge house. A group of people lived in it, a kind of community. I worked in the garden for a while. I left the Bar to do it. It was in the Lake District.'

He remembered the extraordinary view across the sands towards Blackpool and the stillness of the very early morning, locked between the sea on one side and the mountains on the other.

'There was a walled garden. It was amazingly fertile, but it hadn't been properly worked for forty years. It was laid out like a vast wheel, one section priming the next, so the seasons revolved on it like a giant axle. But I realised that if I started it up I would become trapped by it. It would have its own rhythm, much greater or more powerful than any rhythm one could maintain for oneself, and the only thing to do would be to stay in step with it, what you just said. At that time I was frightened. Now, of course, I realise it was a missed opportunity.'

They came to the edge of a rise and slid down the stones on the other side of it. 'I stayed a lawyer.'

The stones rumbled about them. Below them now the hawk swooped to the grass, but then rose again with the effortlessness with which it had fallen.

'A trial lawyer. I took up bullying full time.'

'Did I tell you that?'

'No. I knew it all the time but didn't really notice it, I suppose. Like a footballer doesn't notice being fit. You take it for granted as part of the deal.'

The hawk circled above them.

'I don't say everyone is like that. Probably it's the reason I'm not really good at the job, just fairly good. You remember what Jennings said to me? Being rude is a refuge for the incompetent, something like that, and Cantor said he couldn't understand why I was a lawyer at all. Well, now I think I agree with both of them.'

'I don't remember that at all.'

Scott thought back. 'No. Of course, I'm sorry, it wasn't you there. I was mixing you up with Sally Donne.'

'Well, that's a compliment.'

He looked at her. She was smiling.

'Not very tactful, certainly,' he said. 'Why don't you like her?'

'Because she represents everything that you think is impressive. You let her put you down because you think she is more successful than you. You admire her because she has learned how to play a game. Do you really think she has any understanding of what's going on? You're just impressed – just because she's incisive and thin.'

'What an awful fate.'

'She's a complete invention. Someone painted her by numbers. She painted herself by numbers.'

A farmhouse appeared in the distance, still a couple of miles away. Behind it Scott could see the track that led to the lake.

'That's the way you have to come if you're arriving by car. You've got to leave your car right at the bottom and walk up. That's the way Charlton would have to come.'

'What's over there?' He pointed to another track that cut away from them up the hills. 'Where does that go?'

'That takes you up past Taldir. That's the house the poet, Paul Evans, wrote about. After that the trail goes further north up to the main road. That's the other way out of here, but you'd have to climb down the cliff to get to the road. I couldn't do it.'

They were approaching the farmhouse now.

The grass was springy and short. Sheep cropped right up to the front door so that the great slate doorstep opened straight on to the hill.

'Have they got a telephone I can use?' Scott said.

Dr John, the forensic scientist, was quite satisfied with his performance in the witness box. He didn't make the same mistake twice.

He said, 'The swabs taken from the defendants' hands showed no traces of drug. That means they had not been in the room very long. It also means that they cannot have taken any part in the mixing of the drugs. It is right I should point that out.'

Nor had Cantor made the same mistake. He hadn't spoken of Hector mixing the drugs, no phrases like 'being up to their elbows in it' this time.

'The defendants had clearly only just arrived, ladies and gentlemen,' he had said to the jury, 'their purpose being not to mix the drugs but to sell them. They were to sell the finished product.'

There was nothing for Ronnie Knox to get hold of. The evidence was still the same but the small changes the prosecution had made to the way they put the case made it impossible to deal with.

Mrs Hector watched the case from the public gallery. She could see that the prosecution were relentlessly proving that her husband was a drug dealer. She watched Cantor and the girl sitting next to him. They were clever people, she thought. 'Why are they so stupid? Can't they see it's not true?' It was obvious to her.

The barman of the Potato Patch had been damaging to the Crown case last time. Sally Donne, brought in to assist Cantor, took him through his evidence. She had read the transcript of the previous case and knew what to avoid.

'You say that the man came into your public house looking for someone to buy a Range Rover?'

'Yes.'

'Of course, you don't know that was the true reason he came in, do you?'

Ronnie tried to object. 'The witness is being led. The answer is being suggested by the question.'

But Scribner remarked that it was a perfectly reasonable question and repeated it, though in slightly different words. 'You can't say whether or not this man was just trying to make contact with people willing to act illegally or whether he actually had a car for sale, can you? No? Obviously not. Yes, Miss Donne, carry on, please.'

'I suppose there's lots of buying and selling going on in your pub? All sorts of things?' Sally asked.

'That's a leading question again,' Ronnie objected.

'No it's not. It's just a statement of the obvious. Have you ever been to a public house where it was not so?' said Scribner. 'Really, Mr Knox, we must live in the real world.'

The jury loved it and they loved Sally Donne. She seemed such a perfectly ordinary person; she knew the facts of life.

'Carrots for instance,' she said. 'We know the defendant was selling carrots.'

Hector contemplated twelve to fifteen years in prison. By the end of that time, even with remission, he would be an old man.

'It's already started.'

Ronnie Knox happened to be back in chambers when Scott rang.

'How's it going?'

'Terrible. They've changed the case. They're not calling Charlton. He's not available. It's overwhelming. Yes, the list office agreed that it ought not to come in but it was listed nevertheless, and we couldn't contact you. Scribner refused an adjournment. Frankly, Mr Hector is in despair. No, there's nothing you can do to help. It's too late now.'

Chapter 24

'Mrs Hannay didn't tell Charlton where you had gone,' said Catherine.

'How do you know?'

'She told Mrs Prytherch on the phone. They chat together for hours.'

'So he has no idea where we are.'

'Only somewhere in the valley. Charlie Thomas doesn't know either.'

'Who's Charlie Thomas?'

'The local policeman.'

'How do you know that?'

'Because he asked Mrs Prytherch. And she didn't tell him.'

'Why are they being so quiet?'

'They didn't like Charlton. He was rude to Mrs Hannay.'

'That figures.'

Scott and Catherine were walking back from the Water Board Farm. They had got some bread and a big trout. 'I think I'll bake it,' said Catherine.

After a while Scott said, 'I spoke to Ronnie Knox. He says the trial has begun again.'

'What, without you?' she said.

'Yes. We told them I couldn't do it this week and at first the listing office agreed. But then they put it in. Someone ordered them to.'

'That would be Scribner,' she said.

'Oh no. He wouldn't have that control.'

'Of course he would. He probably did it so that you couldn't be there.'

'No,' Scott said again.

He was upset. The first trial had been stopped entirely because of his behaviour and as a result he had given the prosecution a chance to perfect their case. In effect he had convicted Hector. He thought about Mrs Hector and her faith in him.

'Of course he did. You were the danger.'

'What? Me?'

'Yes. You'd got hold of them by the tail and he wanted to get rid of you.'

'Judges don't behave like that. He doesn't care whether there is a conviction or not. Why should it matter to him?'

'That's bull. He was angry as hell at what you were doing. Anyone with half a brain could see it. What is it about you English that makes you think that your judges are not members of the human race like everyone else?'

Scott said nothing.

'I'll tell you why. Because you're not part of the human race either. Or you weren't. Recently you look like you're thinking of joining.'

'Charlton is not going to give evidence.'

'How can they get out of it?'

'Well, he never was a formal witness. He only gave evidence because I asked that he should and at that stage they could see no reason why he shouldn't. This time around they've thought better of it and they say he is unavailable. You can't force them to call someone unless he's on the original list of witnesses.'

'Where's Charlton, then?'

'Perhaps he's looking for us.'

'You're well out of it,' she said. 'If you ask me the whole thing is corrupt – all the way to the White House.'

They were making their way up the track when they heard a rattling behind them.

A collie bounded past, yelping with joy.

'It's Prytherch,' said Catherine, and she stood off the track and stuck her thumb out.

'Hop on, Katie,' shouted the farmer. He was dressed in an old tweed jacket and flat cap. He smiled at Scott. 'Hold on very tight now. Ding ding,' he said, pulling on an invisible bell rope.

They rattled off up the track, the noise and the shaking of the tractor drowning any chance of conversation. They could only grin at each other over Prytherch's back.

London was a thousand miles away.

The black and white cross collie ran in joyful curves on either side of them and, far above, a buzzard poured its intensity of seeing on the hill.

In the cold, flat courtroom the police officer said, 'Yes, I was present at the arrest of Mr Hector in the flat. Mr Charlton undertook the actual arrest of the absent defendant. I was standing by him and noted what he said. No, I do not know where he is now. I think he is in Spain. I do not know whether Mr Charlton knew him. I was not told. If I was told I have forgotten. I have forgotten whether Mr Charlton told me how the police knew that there were drugs in the flat. I do not know if he knew in advance that there were drugs in the house. I do not know if Mr Charlton was contacted on the phone. I do not know what his telephone number was then. I do not think the number you have read me is the number now. I do not know if it was then. I would have no way of finding out. I cannot help you. If I ever knew I have forgotten now. I did not think it of any importance and have not made a note of it. I do not see the relevance of these questions. You would have to ask Mr Charlton. No, I do not know where he is. No, I do not think he is being called. That is not my decision.'

Ronnie Knox gasped.

It was like cross-examining a 'Speak Your Weight' machine. Wasn't there some play where that happened?

He tried again.

'If Mr Charlton went into the flat knowing that this man was in there . . .'

Scribner interrupted. 'This officer cannot answer that question, Mr Knox. How can he comment upon what someone else was thinking?'

It was hopeless.

Scott sat in the kitchen. Catherine had the fish on the table. 'We need paper to gut it on.'

They looked around. There was nothing.

'Just some paper to stop the blood staining the pine. Any old paper will do.'

'How about the sentencing papers? The things you got me into trouble with.'

'That'll do.'

The papers weren't in the room any longer and they wondered where they were.

261

Then Catherine said, 'I think they're with the other stuff on the floor by the bench seat.'

Scott fetched the bundle and the brown envelope and tore sheets of the case summaries out, spreading them over the old scrubbed table. Drugs. Rape. Handling stolen property. Probation reports.

'Now, you show me how you clean a trout,' he said, 'and I'll tell you if you're doing it right.'

He sat and watched.

As he did so he opened the brown envelope.

'This is Richard's stuff. We have to get it back to him, so we're going to have to remember to take it down to the car.'

But they weren't Richard's papers. They were marked 'Metropolitan Police. Informer file Tredegar. Highly confidential'.

'Good God,' said Scott. 'What's this?'

He swept the other papers aside and began to leaf through the file. Catherine stood beside him with a knife in her hand. There was blood on it.

'It's the informer details. Look. It sets out all the operations he's done. Here's Ramus. Has it got Hector? Hector, where's Hector?'

He was so excited that he couldn't work out the order of the papers for a moment.

'Yes. Here's Hector. Look, it's got everything. The address of the Potato Patch in Rainham. Target lists. There's Hector's name. He was just one of a number of people targeted. It was pure chance that it was him. It could have been anyone on the list. The police didn't give a damn as long as they got a body.'

'I can see. I can see,' said Catherine.

She pulled out a memo, holding it with the tips of her wet fingers. Her hands were itching with the drying water.

'Look,' she said, 'what did I say? It says, "Cantor is instructed to act. He must do this." I told you. The whole thing is all arranged.'

'And they've done it dozens of times,' said Scott. 'Look, there's even a profit calculation. And details of how they're splitting the reward money. It's a business.'

They looked at each other. Catherine was still holding the knife, the innards of the fish drying on her hands. She stepped over to the sink. 'That's why he's after us, of course.'

Scott sat amazed. 'These are the papers that were handed to me at the end of the trial. The messenger was obviously confused by my being the only one there. He assumed I was the prosecuting lawyer, and I assumed they were from your firm. No wonder. No wonder Charlton's after us.'

They sat and read the papers. Scott said, 'The judge can't have seen them. If he had, he couldn't possibly have denied us a sight of them. They acquit Mr Hector instantly. His defence is completely true. These people were running a business getting other people into trouble.'

'What do you mean, the judge didn't see it?' she said. 'Stop being so naïve. They're all in it together.'

'I need to know how far the trial has got,' he said.

Hector was giving evidence.

'Now you say, Mr Hector, that you were going to the flat where you were found with the drugs in order to buy a car. Where was this car?'

'I think it was outside.'

'You travelled all the way to north London to buy a car which you hadn't seen?'

'Well, it was a Range Rover, and there was a Range Rover in the street outside.'

'That's as much as you knew about the car?'

'I was going to look, to see if I wanted to buy it, wasn't I?'

'You know the police found no car?'

'No, I don't. I don't know what they found.'

'Well, don't you think if they had found a car we would have heard about it?'

Ronnie Knox objected and Scribner agreed. 'You can't say that, can you, Mr Cantor? We don't know what was found and what wasn't, do we?'

But then he made it worse. 'Of course, you're entitled to enquire, aren't you, Mr Knox? If anything had been found you could have insisted on its being mentioned.'

'You say you were going there to buy a car. Why then did you tell the police that you had just dropped in?'

'Because the car was moody.'

'Moody?' said Cantor, as though a nasty smell had just appeared.

'Dishonest,' said Mr Hector.

'So you were prepared to lie?'

'Well. Yes.'

'Prepared to lie to the police?'

'Yes.'

'I suggest you were sitting there with a million pounds' worth of drugs in the room. Were you prepared to lie about that?'

'No. Not about that. That was nothing to do with me.'

'You weren't prepared to lie about that?'

'No.'

'But that's much more serious than going to buy a stolen motor car from someone.'

Hector didn't reply.

Cantor asked again. 'Do you agree that this is much more serious than thinking of buying a stolen car?'

'Yes.'

'But you wouldn't have lied about it?'

'No.'

'You're telling us the truth about this million pounds' worth of drugs, even though you were prepared to lie about some car you wanted to buy? Are you sure?'

Ronnie listened in despair. It was like taking candy from a baby.

Catherine said, 'We can get to London before the trial finishes. If we walk down to Prytherch's he'll take us to the other end of the lake, even up the hill, in the Land Rover. We can arrange for the local taxi to meet us at the bottom on the other side. I can ring Mrs Hannay from the farm. She'll fix it. We'll get the car and be on the way to London by eleven o'clock, or earlier.'

They left for the Water Board Farm early the next morning. If they got to Mrs Prytherch's in time, perhaps Scott would be able to get Ronnie on the phone before he left for court.

When they began to breast the rise above Prytherch's farm they saw the tractor jolting towards them.

'There's someone with him,' said Catherine. 'Stop a moment. They won't have seen us yet.'

Scott thought he knew what he was seeing but he wasn't sure until Catherine said 'It's Charlton', then he was certain. In a few moments the tractor would gain enough height for them to be seen clearly and there was nowhere to hide.

'What shall we do?'

'Shall I take the papers?' she said.

'No, he'll search you as well, then he'd have a case against you. I'll have to take them.'

They turned and backed up the hill. There was a shout from below. They had been seen. They started running back up towards the house, but Scott knew that was hopeless, the house was a dead end. To their right lay the track he had asked about the day before. 'Is that the other way out?'

'Yes,' she said.

'Have you been there?'

'Yes.'

'To the cliffs where the climbers go?'

'Yes.'

'Well, you collect the car. Charlton's got nothing against you. You can still persuade Prytherch to take you. If you can, meet me where the road skirts the bottom of the cliff, just below the pass. Do you know it?'

He gave her the car keys and started running, at first down the hill, towards where Charlton was approaching on the tractor, and then up, past the lip of the ridge and straight up the hill, where no tractor could follow him. His rucksack started banging on his back. He tightened it as he ran.

There was another shout. He looked back and saw Charlton pointing and talking to Prytherch. Then he saw the policeman jump from the tractor and come after him.

Well, he wasn't going to be caught. He had a good start and he knew he was fitter. He only had to reach the cliff. He was at home there and he would be safe.

Charlton had gone over the map before coming up and had confirmed with Prytherch that the only other way out was down the cliff face. The way Scott was going was a dead end. He would have to turn back and that was when he would catch him.

He saw Scott reaching the crest of the hill, moving to Charlton's left, which meant he was going higher all the time, further into the dead end. He only had to follow. He stopped looking, put his head down and forced his way upwards.

He followed Scott for an hour and then another. Sometimes they ran, sometimes they walked, always separated by much the same distance. Charlton could see Scott clearly. Occasionally he would lose sight of him as he crested a hill but when he reached the same point he would invariably see him ahead again. All Scott could do was run. There was nowhere to hide.

There was another sharp climb.

Charlton was blowing now but he didn't think he was being left behind. Indeed, he reckoned he was catching up. For a moment, when he got to the top, he couldn't see Scott, then he did. He had changed direction and was moving even further up the hill, then Charlton saw him going down. There was only one way to go there.

When he reached the top Charlton saw that Scott was running down the narrowing curve that led to the cliff. That made it even easier. He came off the top after him, encouraged and moving quickly.

Scott was intending to go down the cliff. Well, let him try. He didn't know what he was letting himself in for.

After running down from the summit of the hill, Scott arrived at the top of the cliff face. He crouched and looked down. The gully wasn't really a climb, more of a scramble. Of course he could do it. You don't forget completely, do you?

He looked up. Behind him he sensed movement. He turned and, nearer than he expected, there was Charlton, moving fast and efficiently, carrying something in his hand. Was it a radio? It looked like a gun. No, that would be absurd.

He was going to have to start. He checked his boots to see if they were tied properly, took hold of the rock at the top and swung out.

At first it was easy and he climbed steadily down.

Above him a great blue sky with small clouds stretched away into the distance. He could just make out the green blue of the Irish Sea far over to the west. He felt again the astonishing peace of the rock, utterly detached. Even Charlton back there seemed like a dream.

Further up the pass he could see the road winding down. There was a car. It was the right shape to be the Mercedes but he couldn't see it clearly. Then it disappeared behind one of the huge boulders that littered the approach to the pass. He tried to slow the whole thing down. If he rushed it, he would fall.

From above him there was the sound of a pebble falling. It bounded down the side and, hitting the outcrop above him, leapt out into space over his head. That must be Charlton reaching the clifftop. He'd better get going again. If the shape of the climb was as he remembered it, this was where he would have to take care. Charlton would never be able to follow him, but for a while he would be exposed and

Charlton might even try to get at him if he could see him.

He leaned out and lowered himself, stretching over till he felt the foothold. He reached over to his left. Now he could see the traverse from which he had fallen all those years ago. He hadn't realised it, but from this side of the Clogwyn rock the traverse connected to the gully he was using. He could see the end of the first pitch where his climbing companion must have sat giving him that damned advice. He'd never seen it before. He'd never got that far.

He was climbing quite easily, so he inspected it. It was a point where his life had reached a dead end and changed direction. He could see a piton where the rope would have been secured. He wondered if there had been one there then. Fixed pitons hadn't figured much when he had been climbing. In fact they were thought to be rather bad form. It couldn't be the same one, that was stupid. It was nearly twenty years ago; it would have been torn away ages ago.

He climbed down steadily.

Now he was at the same level as Clogwyn. The boulder was quite close now, only fifteen feet away, and he could see round it, to where he had been standing when he tried the Clogwyn leap. He was well down from the top but exposed now, and he guessed he could be seen from above. The climbing became more difficult. He found that stretching for the holds was becoming a strain, but he was still feeling clear and steady. His grip was strong.

He tried to lean away from the rock like he'd always been told. He remembered how really good climbers hardly seemed to make contact with the face at all. They had a dancing motion, always on the tips of their toes, almost as if they were running on the rock.

He reached down, was able to make two moves and shifted sharply to his left. Perhaps he had moved out of sight. He looked up but couldn't see.

At that moment a rush of sound rumbled above him. He realised what was happening, but it was too late to do anything about it. A stone hit him on the shoulder and then what seemed like a shower of gravel spattered on to the side of his face. He pulled hard in and tried to flatten himself, but his position meant that his right leg was stretched out and it was difficult to press it in. A rock – it was a rock this time, not just a stone – hit his wrist. He could feel nothing in that hand and, as he looked, he could see that he had relaxed his grip. His hand stayed on the rock but it seemed only to be lying there. He tried to move it. Nothing happened.

A huge shower of stones came down. Luckily they were from a different angle and missed him completely. Then silence. His hand fell from the hold and he hung on the rock face by one arm.

His left foot began to shake. He remembered the feeling and knew that if he allowed it to carry on it would shake him off. He pressed hard on his other foot to relax the pressure and the shaking stopped, but now he was completely unbalanced.

The one advantage was that his right hand had a really good hold. He pulled hard, lifted himself slightly and found he was able to lean on the face of the rock, his chest taking much of the weight. This saved him for the moment. He could rest.

He lifted his left arm to where he could see it. At least it was still attached to him, though it didn't feel like it. He rubbed it on the rock and felt the roughness. Slowly the feeling came back and, with it, pain. But he was going to have to use it. He couldn't climb with one hand, for Christ's sake. He began to feel frightened.

From the road below Catherine looked up at the rock face. Right at the top of the cliff she could see a figure moving backwards and forwards above the gully. She looked carefully.

There seemed to be a figure about a third of the way down. Now it was moving, but as it did so there was a puff of dust from above, and she could make out stones and rocks cascading down the face of the cliff. One of the larger rocks hit the face above the climbing figure and bounded out into space. As it landed on the ground below the cliff she could hear it. It made a rustling noise as it skittered down the scree towards her.

She ran up from the road, all the time getting a better view as she approached the top of the bank. The climbing figure wasn't moving now. It was hanging there. There seemed to be something wrong with its left arm. Was it Scott?

There was no rope. Normally ropes hung like tracery, identifying the climbers. There was no rope. It must be Scott.

Charlton was trying to kill him. 'Oh, don't let him fall,' she said to herself. This time she was being honest about a man.

Perhaps if she was honest that would help him.

'Don't let him fall. Please don't let him fall.'

* * *

Scott hung where he was.

He found he could lean on the rock easily. He was almost relaxed; certainly he was regaining his strength. His left arm hurt less. He tested it with a hold. He was able to support his weight on it. Perhaps he could just rest here till Charlton went away?

He turned his attention to his body.

It was odd. When climbing you could examine how each part was working, quite detached, as though looking at a machine. His right leg. He had a good foothold but he wouldn't be able to keep it secure for any length of time, the pressure was too tight, he was too stretched, he couldn't rest. No. He would be able to lie where he was for a short while but not for long, not for long enough for Charlton to give up and go.

He looked round.

Below him the rock shelved outwards.

He remembered the moves now. They were easy, but as he moved down he would be more and more exposed. As if to prove his point another shower of stones bounded past. They landed exactly where he would have been if he had carried on down. If he was hit there he would have no chance. He'd be wiped off the cliff like a fly off a wall.

He looked up. The same thing. He was lucky that Charlton had let loose the stones at just the moment when he had been protected between the two exposed sections.

He looked to his right It was sheer, there was no way out there. The only way would be to go left. It was off-route but he'd have to try. He pulled himself back upright and felt across to his left. There was a handle and a good one. Now for the foothold. He pulled himself further round the face and realised he was turning a corner into a cleft. There was a ridge. He moved on to it. It was extraordinary – with one small turn he had left the original route completely and was in, for him, unexplored territory.

He was in a chimney.

He looked up. There was no way up. About ten feet above him it was blocked off. But he could go into the chimney and out again, then on to a traverse. He inched along. He reached the traverse. This was easy, he felt much safer. If anything, it was less difficult than the gully itself. He was going up slightly now, one pull and he was able to step up into a wide space. He was able to sit down and look to see where he was.

He was behind Clogwyn.

He had crossed the gap he had looked down on before and was at the pitch where climbers secured the rope after the Clogwyn leap. This was the point he never reached in another life. He could rest.

But not for long.

This time a rock crashed off the ledge where he was sitting. He looked up and saw Charlton above him. He was about to throw another rock. The only way out was around the boulder, the boulder from which he had fallen before.

He looked at it.

Near where he sat was the piton he had seen earlier when climbing down. But he had nothing with him, there was nothing he could use to secure himself. This was crazy. If he hadn't managed the move before, when he was younger and fitter, how could he hope to manage it now?

Another rock crashed on to the ledge. It hit the face just above him and showered him with grit. Charlton was not going to stop. Better not think, just do it.

He stood up and edged round the face of the boulder – at least that put him out of Charlton's view.

He stood there for a moment measuring the next move and then there was an explosion. Something hit the boulder near where he was and whirred off into the distance. It was the ricochet which made him realise what it was. He recognised it from films. Charlton was shooting at him.

It was astonishing.

He had risked using a gun, that was how important those papers were to him. Was he trying to kill him?

Well, he wasn't going to stand there to find out.

He moved a little further round the boulder, picking his way along the ledge. The ledge petered out where it became part of the boulder swelling out of the rock.

He stretched the palms of his hands across the surface of the stone and the feeling of the rock came back to him.

It had never really left him, it was exactly as he remembered it in his dreams. He remembered squeezing the rock between his outstretched arms, holding on by an effort of will, which of course couldn't succeed, and then slowly peeling away from the rock and falling backwards into space. That time he had a rope to hold him and he had bounced in great thirty foot leaps at the end of it. Not now though.

This wasn't the time to replay old memories.

He had to think.

The technique was to get your following foot as far along the ledge as possible, then to reach around to the handhold on the other side of the boulder. Once he'd done that he had to swing out and get on to the traverse on the other side.

Lean out, trust yourself.

Don't cling on too much.

People who cling always fall; people whose lives are one long, frightened clenching of the spirit always fall.

It was the first stretch that was difficult. That was why he had fallen the last time.

He remembered falling. He remembered the scream. How could the voices of the watchers have reached him so quickly? Unless it was he who had screamed.

He had never thought of that before. He had come all the way back here to realise that the screaming voice he had heard over and over in his dreams was his own.

He had reached the end of the ledge now. He was quite steady. His arms felt better and he didn't feel as tired.

It was odd. He felt good. Why should that be?

He remembered that down in the cells in Lewes Crown Court, the old cells under the pavement, where the water used to drop and you could see people's shoes as they walked overhead, he had once said to a client who'd just been convicted, 'I feel bad about this,' and reasonably enough the client had replied, 'Not half as bad as I do.'

He was always one stage away from things. It never happened to him. Well, it was happening now.

He pushed his arm out, committed himself to the move and missed it.

He missed it like he had missed it the first time. He was clinging on to the rock again, trying to squeeze it between his outstretched arms and slowly slipping. This time there was no one to speak to, no one to tell he was falling, and this time there was no rope. This time he was going to be killed.

The blood rushed in his ears and there was a screaming sound. So that was it. It wasn't him screaming.

Catherine had scrambled up the scree and was no more than fifty yards from the cliff when the rock bounced off the ledge where Scott was sitting. It hit the stone at the bottom of the cliff and skittered down past her. Then there was a sharp cracking noise.

She had got too close to see exactly what was happening high above her and had to move back. Scott had stood up and was moving around a great round bulge in the cliff. She couldn't see clearly but it seemed to her that the ledge on which he was standing seemed to stop and then there was only the simple round surface of the boulder. How could he get round that? Then she realised, it was the Clogwyn boulder.

He paused and edged further to the centre of it. Then stopped again. She stood looking upwards with her hand clasping her throat and her mouth, rigid, penitent.

He was adjusting his feet. Then he moved his body and she realised he was going to jump. He was going to jump, for Christ's sake. Jump. 'You can't jump, not there,' she said. Then he did. There was a convulsive movement and like a lizard on a wall he hung on the sheer surface, spreadeagled on the rock, and then he started slipping, sliding slowly off it.

She opened her mouth and screamed.

Her scream echoed around the cliffs and came back to her.

But the slipping stopped. He slid down the face of the rock and stopped. He seemed to be holding on to something with his left hand. Whatever it was it took his whole weight. He was using it to support himself and then suddenly he was away and on to the ledge the other side.

Now he was moving quickly down the sloping ledge.

To Catherine he seemed almost to be dancing – balancing and moving on the tips of his fingers and toes. It was beautiful to watch.

If he had been swinging down a boulevard he couldn't have been more relaxed. He was coming down quickly. She ran up to the base of the cliff and there he was above her. He even jumped the last six feet, landing on his toes, facing her.

'I thought you were going to fall.'

She could barely speak.

'So did I,' he said. 'I nearly did.'

They ran for the car. As they got in, they looked up and Catherine saw a figure on the cliff.

'There's Charlton,' she said. 'He's stuck up there and he's in for a very long walk. It'll take him a good three hours even to get to the road.' Scott pulled the car out and she added, 'Unless he comes down the cliff,' and she turned and looked at him. 'And there's not many that can do that.'

Was that admiration he saw in her eyes? Well, he wasn't going to believe it.

'You didn't tell me you could climb,' she said.

He felt like saying, 'I didn't know myself.'

'You came down Clogwyn without a rope.'

He looked out of the window. He had always been told that it was what you tried to do that mattered, not what you did. But it wasn't true. It wasn't enough. He had tried to do Clogwyn that other time and that hadn't made him feel any better when he failed. He had tried to tell himself that failure didn't matter, it was trying that counted. That didn't work either.

They crossed the ridge and started coming down out of the mountains. He had three hours to get as far away as possible.

'When I saw you go round the Clogwyn boulder I screamed.'

'Yes, that was a bit hairy,' he said, and immediately wished he hadn't said it. He didn't want to turn the experience into some awful cool thing.

'You didn't hear me scream? It looked as though you were falling.'

Scott looked at the road twisting down ahead of them. 'I was falling. I didn't hear you scream because of the noise in my ears.'

She said nothing.

'I made the move round the Clogwyn like I'd been told and there was nothing there to hold on to. I missed the hold. I started sliding down the rock. Then I found that some vandal' – he laughed – 'some vandal had put a fixed piton right in the middle of the boulder, right where I was sliding. I suppose I'm meant to say the route is spoiled now. But it saved my life.'

He turned and looked at her. She was crying.

'What is it?'

'I thought you were going to fall,' she said, 'and I realised how much that mattered to me.'

Chapter 25

They weren't stopped until they had reached the centre of London.

'I think we're being followed,' said Scott.

A beige saloon car slotted in behind them as they went down Park Lane. It hung on round Hyde Park Corner and into Belgrave Square. Scott became suspicious. He went round the square and up to Knightsbridge the back way, past the crescent of incredibly expensive houses.

The car was still there despite the unlikely route he had taken.

'Charlton must have got our number at Mrs Hannay's car park, and he's phoned it on.' He watched the policemen for a while. They were certainly making no attempt at being discreet.

'And they don't mind us knowing we're being followed either,' he said.

He turned left into Sloane Street, past the bookshop, the bank, the interior decorator's shop. 'That's what the inside of a rich Arab's house looks like,' he said, pointing at the gilt and glass in the shop window. Suddenly he found that he felt completely indifferent to what these people were doing. He was different. He felt justified.

They went down past the Danish Embassy and then he said 'Let's stop and see what happens.' But, before he slowed, the beige car pulled past and an arm came out of the window. Scott stopped and got out.

A young police officer in plain clothes said, 'Didn't you see me signalling you to stop?' He was not looking at Scott but bending down to look into the car.

Before Scott could answer, the policeman said to Catherine, 'Get out of the car, please, madam.'

Scott looked back at the police car. Instead of coming too the other policeman was talking into a radio. Scott looked more closely. It wasn't a radio, it was a telephone. Scott guessed he was talking to Charlton.

'We have had a report of a stolen car,' the first police officer said.

'With this number plate?' said Scott. 'Who reported it?' It seemed too obvious a response but he had hit it right. The officer didn't answer him.

'Whose car is this, sir?'

'It isn't mine. It belongs to Richard Pisarski. You'll find him at the Danson Lane Garage in Welling. I can give you his number if you wish.'

'That won't be necessary,' said the policeman, who seemed to have learned his lines from a film, 'but I should like to see in the back of the car, please.'

Scott opened the back of the car. His rucksack was the only thing there.

'I am going to search this car, sir. I am entitled to do so under the powers given by the Police and Criminal Evidence Act.'

'Yes,' said Scott, 'I know that. But what grounds do you have for suspicion?'

'I am not obliged to tell you that,' said the policeman, looking at him for the first time. Scott guessed he was on the verge of saying something about Scott's attitude.

'You have to have reasonable grounds. If you have them, how can it cause you any difficulty to tell me?' Scott repeated.

'I don't have to tell you,' said the officer. Here was the arbitrary indifference that his clients had so often told him about.

'Yes, you do. You have to record your grounds for making the search and give a note.'

'We shall see,' said the policeman.

He picked up Scott's bag and pulled out the shoes and jacket. Other than that the bag was empty. Then he searched the car. He lifted the carpets and then the back seat. He checked under the spare tyre. Nothing. Now there was only Scott and Catherine.

'Do you want to search us?' Scott turned towards Catherine. She opened her bag. The policeman looked at her cotton dress. She clearly wasn't concealing anything. Scott opened his arms and the policeman patted him down.

'Now you have to give your reasons.' Scott was beginning to annoy him.

'I have decided that no search is required.'

'You just made one,' said Scott.

'If I had, I would make out a search record,' said the policeman, 'but since I haven't, I won't.'

There was no point in arguing.

'I'll speak to Charlton, if he wants,' Scott said.

The policeman looked at him and walked back to the car to take the phone. There was a short conversation, then Scott was offered the handset.

'If you want to arrest me, then tell your men to arrest me now,' said Scott.

'Where are you going?' Charlton asked.

'I'm not telling you,' said Scott. 'Unless you want them to take me with them.' He was looking directly at both the young officers. Their behaviour wasn't their fault. This was the way they were trained to deal with people who might at any moment be serious trouble. Good manners weren't relevant. 'But I can tell you this. I've stopped running from you now,' he said.

The phone went dead.

'Well, I challenged him to arrest me,' Scott said, 'and he wouldn't. So now we know. It's personal.'

They drove down to Sloane Square.

'In one way that's more dangerous,' he said as they reached the door of the flat. 'At least the law is a simple plodding thing. But Charlton, he could do anything. I mean, look at this.'

The flat was in chaos.

'Do you want to go back to Forest Hill?' he said.

'When are you going to start behaving properly?'

'What do you mean?'

'Do you want me to say "I want to stay with you", or do you want to send me home?'

Scott looked at her. She was right. He had for a moment forgotten the freedom he had won in the last few hours. He'd forgotten he was free to like himself.

'I want you to stay with me,' he said.

'Great,' she said. 'Now that's fixed, how about a drink?'

'I must ring Ronnie Knox first. You get it.'

He phoned the number but Ronnie was out and he had to make do with an answerphone. He said, 'Don't let them close the evidence, Ronnie, I've got something that will help. I'll see you tomorrow.' The tape was full and he couldn't get any more in.

The warm atmosphere of the flat settled around them as they started to put it back in order, then the evening began to close in.

The phone rang. Catherine answered it. She asked who it was and when she heard the answer Scott saw her face change.

'It's Jennings,' she said. 'He wants to talk to you.'

Scott took the phone.

'I hear you've been away,' said Jennings.

It was difficult to be rude.

'Yes,' Scott said. 'Why are you ringing?'

'I would like to talk to you.'

'Go ahead.'

'No, I would like to meet you.'

'Why?'

'I think we need to talk.'

'Why?'

'Because there are outstanding things to do with the Bar and the courts that we should deal with.' Scott looked around on hearing a tapping noise and he could see Catherine listening in on the bedroom extension. She was nodding her head at him.

'OK,' said Scott. 'Where?'

'At my club.'

'When?'

'In an hour.'

'I am with someone,' said Scott. 'I shan't come alone.'

'Nor shall I,' said Jennings.

'I have it now,' said Gregory. 'I've found a witness who knows Charlton, the lot of them. He's told me the whole story.'

He was talking to Arlot who was listening impassively.

Again Gregory couldn't work out whether or not he was telling Arlot something he already knew. It was odd. Arlot didn't seem to be involved in what he had asked Gregory to do, nor to care greatly one way or the other. Certainly Gregory had never received any real help from him, only the introduction to the man he'd met in Dulwich and the remark about the newspapers – and he had never discussed what it was he was investigating.

It was almost as though Arlot had merely set him on the trail and then waited to see what would happen, as if he was getting someone to do the work for form's sake only.

Gregory found himself becoming cautious. Perhaps just spilling out what he knew wasn't wise. If Arlot was staying buttoned up perhaps he should do the same. He ought not just to spill out what he knew. At that moment he realised it was the same impulse of caution that had prevented him from mentioning Sally Donne. If she was part of the organisation he was working for, why should she be at a meeting of CrackDown? Did Arlot know she was there? Had she told Arlot? He carried on talking.

'They were getting lads coming out of the Boys' Home and taking them to London, and creating an informer network, generating reward money. They were being trained up, a modern version of Fagin's kitchen.'

Two days before this Gregory had finally found Bennet. He'd got the name through the journalist who had written in *Private Eye* and when he had phoned him Bennet had almost bitten his hand off with eagerness. 'David Bennet, yes, that's me.' When Gregory told him what he wanted he said he would come up to London the next day. 'I saw Charlton sniffing round the village this weekend. If he thinks he's going to start the whole thing over again, then he's got another think coming.'

The man was clearly anxious to tell his story.

Gregory stopped. He was becoming more watchful.

Arlot looked at him, gathered that he was not going any further and said, 'Corruption is one thing. But entrapment, trapping people into committing criminal offences, isn't corruption. The courts have said that it is legitimate. Anything the courts say is legitimate they encourage.'

That was what Eddie Morgan had said to Gregory. He had used exactly the same words.

Eddie Morgan lived in Wapping.

His flat overlooked the Thames. He was surrounded by money brokers from the City in a block of dockland flats carved from an old warehouse. In fact he lived in style.

He let Gregory in and showed him through the brightly lit flat and out on to the balcony. Gregory watched the brown river flowing sluggishly past. To his right the sun was setting over Tower Bridge, spreading a green glow over the warehouses and offices. In the distance he could hear the low growl of the evening traffic as the City emptied.

A thick barge full of rubbish wallowed past, its huge weight forcing the oily water apart. It disappeared to the east followed by a crowd of angry seagulls. An early evening party boat chugged past in the opposite direction, heading for Westminster, where it would collect its passengers.

Eddie reappeared carrying a bottle and two long, elegant glasses.

'This New Zealand wine is marvellous,' he said. 'Wait till you taste this. Martinborough Vineyards. Not the stuff you get normally. This is their special one.'

He poured it out and handed Gregory a glass. The wine was cold and sweet on Gregory's tongue. Wherever he went people seemed to be telling him what to drink.

'How did you find me?' Eddie asked.

'David Bennet told me. He said you wouldn't mind.'

'No, that's all right, that's all right. I don't stay in touch with him. I think it would be unfair. He's out of it all. How is he?'

'I only met him once,' Gregory said. 'So I don't really know.'

'He retired,' Eddie said as he settled into his chair, putting his feet on the railing. 'Ooof, do you get that pong? We get it every evening if the wind is in the wrong direction.'

The brewery smell passed over them and then seemed to lift.

'I wonder what happened to the Bristol hum?' said Eddie.

'What was that?'

'In Bristol some years ago people noticed a humming noise. Very quiet, but it was there all the time in the background. It didn't seem to have any source. Some people were going crazy with it.'

Gregory remembered reading about it and he said, 'Yes. I never saw what happened.'

'How do you find out? How would you find out? Go to Bristol and listen?'

'Ring the local paper,' Gregory said. 'They'd know.'

'They would. Yes they would,' Eddie said reflectively. 'I'd like to do that. Maybe the guy who was doing it packed his bags and went away.'

They drank the wine.

Gregory felt completely at home with this man. He had the skill to make you feel immediately he was a friend.

'Who are you?' Eddie asked.

'I'm from Customs. I can show you my warrant if you wish.' He had decided to tell the truth. It would be the only way. 'I've been sent to work with the police to see if we can use their methods at all.'

280

'Time was,' said Eddie, 'when police and Customs wouldn't talk to each other. Perhaps they're still not. Look at the Chrastny case. In that case the wife's barrister even hinted that the police had an interest in allowing him to escape.'

Gregory made a noncommittal noise. Eddie didn't seem to want an answer.

He went on, 'James Morton contacted me but I wouldn't talk to him.'

'Who's James Morton?'

'He writes books on crime. His last one was about supergrasses. He knows everyone. But I wasn't going to talk, it would have been bad for business.'

Gregory chuckled and made a movement as though he was settling back in his chair. 'Bad for business,' he repeated.

He got the tone just right.

Eddie reacted, not defensively, but in the same light way. 'Well, for me it is a business. Though I'm a freelance where the police are salaried.'

Gregory said nothing.

Eddie said, 'I had a drink in the House of Commons with this MP. I knew him in the old days. I said to him – he's an important lawyer – "All right," I said, "they want to privatise law enforcement? You know I've already done it." '

He picked up the bottle and poured Gregory more wine.

Then he looked at him and said directly, 'If the Customs want to employ me then they'll have to agree to my rates. I'm not cheap.'

Gregory suddenly realised why Eddie had agreed to talk to him. He thought he was another customer.

'Oh, we'll agree to the rates,' he said. 'Have you any idea what ordinary investigation work costs nowadays?'

'That's just what I said to this MP. Of course I know what it costs. I can do the same work as twenty policemen, only better, quicker, cheaper, for a fraction of the cost. Surveillance costs, for instance. An ordinary tailing operation – to do it properly needs twelve policemen, six cars, radios, drinks bills, sometimes even parking fines. I can give you the same result for almost nothing.

'And,' he said, gesturing at Gregory, 'you don't have to call me to court to give evidence, not like the surveillance team. The judge will always say that undercover information need not be revealed. I give you all the evidence you need – Chummy caught bang to rights. The courts have said it is legitimate.'

They sat there.

'And if you are really desperate we'll even supply you with the right judge,' Eddie said.

He went on. Gregory realised this must be his sales pitch.

'You want bodies? I'll give you bodies. Go along to Isleworth Crown Court next week. There are two cases coming up, they're both mine. This time I was working for the Nigerians. Both the couriers were from political families. But normally you can find a courier by walking into a bar. They're cheap in Lagos.

'Find someone whose husband has been thrown in jail by the regime there, or someone whose husband is ill, and offer them two thousand. Give them some cocaine – out there the military sell it – then tip off the Customs here. What do the judges here care? They've got a tariff laid down by the Court of Appeal for sentence, and they all compete with each other to push the tariff higher.'

He got up to fetch another bottle.

Gregory realised that if he sat still and said nothing then he would get the whole story. Eddie Morgan needed to talk. He needed to show that the efficiency of what he was doing made it all right, justified it. He needed someone to bless him.

Gregory turned to look into the room behind him. It was glowing with light. Along one wall there was a bookcase stuffed with the glowing jackets of hardback bestsellers, *Honour Among Thieves*, *Dexter Dias* and, next to it, a state-of-the-art fax machine, spotlit, and as beautiful as any sculpture. Beyond that there was a Degas statuette. What was it? The Ballerina, a perfect reproduction. Behind that a wall full of pictures, glowing scenes of hills, sheep, and, in the distance, mountains.

The room was completed at one end by a smoked-glass dining table and eight high-backed chairs. If Eddie was running a business he was obviously doing it very well.

Eddie came back.

He had another bottle, some thin slices of salami and what looked like smoked fillet. Another plate had pieces of cheese on it. He had certainly opened him up. All he had to do now was listen.

'At first I was an amateur. I remember my first bust. A guy sitting on the steps of Piccadilly. He tried to sell me some Mandrax. He didn't know what he started. I got a quid.'

'Why did you get involved?'

282

'Who knows? London. You get here. You're on your own and there's no standards to judge by, and it's exciting. When I went back to the boys' home – I grew up in a boys' home – the ones I'd left behind could see I was a success. They used to come to see me in London. That's how I met Bennet.'

Eddie had stopped trying to sell anything. He had become melancholy.

'You get taken advantage of, you know. Then you realise that's all there is, people taking advantage of each other. It's a marketplace, all right, everything is up for sale in the marketplace.'

He opened the bottle and flipped the cork into the river. They both got up to peer at it as it bobbed downstream.

'I've been thinking about it. What's interesting is how the only real force is economics, not friendship, not love, but economics. The Tories know that. Marx knew that. The only people who don't know it are the dummies stuck in the middle bleating about society – there is no such thing as society, as the lady said.

'Take my business. It's just a business, nothing more. And because it's a business it works in the same way as other businesses, the same rules apply to it. The business appears, the courts sanction it, they say we can't do without honest citizens like me, so I get a foothold. They give it a bit of protection – the very fact I am operating at all is kept secret, absolutely what I want. The company takes a few years to find its proper market, then boom, it takes off.

'Times can change. Recently the rules of disclosure of evidence threatened us again, but the Home Secretary saw the implications and he put the protection back. Now business is going to take off again.

'You see, it's normal, growing and receding, depending on market forces, only in my case it's a very restricted sort of market.'

They stared at the skyline.

'Everything flows from that. What I've got for sale Justice buys. That's why she's got a weighing machine. She's a dealer like everyone else.'

On the other side of the river Greenwich Naval College loomed up in the growing dark, for sale.

'And modern methods. I use modern methods, or at least I apply old methods to new targets. In the old days supergrasses were only used in big cases. And they were used only after the event. The police caught someone and persuaded him to change sides, but me, I go in from the start. I go looking for work. We can target people, people who deserve to be arrested, people who are guilty anyway.

'It's two birds with one stone then. Even working on my own I can keep a district crime squad busy. And I do good, I can help clean up their patch. They just give me the list of names who need sorting out, they know who's guilty.

'Everyone's happy. They justify their budget and the Home Secretary says, "Look how well we're doing." That's why the police don't want the whole business threatened by rules which disclose how they operate.

'I'm using techniques that used to be employed in big unwieldy supergrass cases, only now I'm applying them to small arrests. Modern business methods. It's called down-sizing. I represent the new Britain.'

The river flowed implacably past the balcony down to the sea.

Jennings looked perfectly at home in the club, in the darkness, sunk low in an armchair. Scott could hardly make him out beyond his eyes and teeth. But, settled as they were in low chairs around the large fire, the atmosphere of the club made it seem natural that they should talk so, hardly seeing each other, in conversational, confidential tones.

'I can well understand,' said Jennings, 'that you might find it shocking that such things go on. But they are necessary. The entrapment of criminals is not something done lightly but because the beneficial effects are very great. Obviously criminals are caught, but there is also the wider effect. Mistrust and suspicion are sown in the criminal fraternity.

'If a man is entrapped into buying forged dollars, for instance, then the next person who is offered forged dollars, from whatever source the offer comes, is nervous. He'll have heard stories of the man trapped by informers and he will naturally think, "Is this another set-up?" These are matters for policy decisions. The decisions have been made by those who know and those decisions have been endorsed by the courts.'

Scott felt himself bridle at the idea of accepting something just because a policy decision had been made. But then he had always disliked authority and knew that his judgment was warped that way. That was why he had never been appropriate material for promotion in any organisation. Look how he had behaved towards Scribner.

'Of course, other people become involved in carrying out the policy, even members of the Bar.' Jennings gestured at Sally Donne sitting on a sofa opposite the fire. 'But these are difficult and delicate matters. Sometimes a person's life can be at risk if a name is even breathed. If counsel for the Crown is to know these precious details then we must be sure we know counsel for the Crown.'

He sat up in the light of the fire.

'After all, you yourself had difficulties with a pupil, did you not, Scott?'

Scott saw a smile on Sally Donne's face and for the first time began to dislike her.

'For a while it was thought she was involved in something, until you showed otherwise. That might have hurt you badly.'

Jennings looked pleased with himself at Scott's reaction.

'You show surprise. But of course I have been briefed about you, and quite properly so. That's what information means, trying to understand people's motives.'

Coffee arrived.

The waiter said, 'Madam, gentlemen,' and served it swiftly, with delicate skill.

Scott found his mind wandering again, seduced by the colours and sounds. Is ladies the real plural of madam? How do you say madam to a group? Ladies seemed wrong, slightly vulgar. The kind of thing you call as you leave a pub. 'Good night, sweet ladies' wouldn't be right for Jennings's club.

Scott looked around.

He was surprised they even allowed women in here at all. There certainly weren't any women members. He remembered reading that there was some sort of meeting about that. This was, though the members would no doubt not agree, an establishment club.

The waiter moved around the group. He had brought some brandy as well. Jennings must have ordered it.

'My last club,' said Jennings eventually, when the waiter left, 'filled up with riff-raff. Businessmen with country memberships. People dined their clients when they came to London. It was a relief to move here.'

He swilled the brandy round the balloon glass.

Looking at him, Scott realised that, for all his sophistication, he was still gross. He looked at Sally Donne. She was wearing the most beautiful embroidered waistcoat. She seemed completely relaxed. Scott had noticed that recently she had become very gracious to everyone. When he bumped into her she acknowledged him with a curious inclination of her head, as though she had been elected Queen. Perhaps contact with Jennings had changed her. Jennings had not explained yet why she was there. Maybe she was a witness. Well, Scott hadn't explained what Catherine was doing either.

'You must understand that the information you have is perfectly normal. Why otherwise would it have been kept on file and not destroyed? It can have no value to others and has no wider implications other than for those few people it protects, people who are involved.'

Scott said nothing. He had not admitted having the papers yet. He was listening to Jennings's argument. The man must be at least partly right. If the documents were so dangerous, why were they kept at all?

Jennings said, 'The judge must have seen them. The process means that he has to take the decision as to whether they are revealed or not. That decision's not for us to take. It's his. You must agree with that.'

Again Jennings was right. Scott had had decisions made against him in courts for years. It wasn't for him to disregard them. He would have felt that if he had been sitting as a judge and it had been his decision.

Jennings seemed to sense that he was getting through.

'In court, we live and work in a very artificial atmosphere. We don't have to deal with real life. The problems those papers deal with are the problems of the people who have to go out on the street. After all, the most dangerous animal we barristers ever meet is a rude judge.'

He laughed, and Scott felt his dislike increase. Jennings really was a very nasty piece of work. He pushed the feeling away from him. If he was influenced by feelings he would make the wrong decision.

He glanced at Catherine and could see what she was thinking. The look on her face was terrible.

'I know I can say this. If you decide to help . . . No, that's wrong. If you decide . . .' He paused to locate the right expression. '. . . if you decide to return the papers, if you decide that returning them is the proper course, given their importance, then . . .' He stopped again as if to underline the momentous nature of what he was saying. 'I think I am authorised to say that it would not be held against you. These things are noticed. You may want an appointment someday.'

Scott stared at him. The man was offering him a judgeship, and what was more it was probably an offer within his influence to affect.

Sally Donne laughed as though embarrassed by what had just been said.

'Come on, Butler. Let's put it directly. What you mean is that of course it was a mistake Scott got the papers and no one can blame for him for that, but the proper thing to do is to return them. You don't steal your opponent's brief, do you?'

She turned to Scott and said, 'You would normally use any information you received, but not in this case. It's too important for the whole system. After all, if this kind of thing happens, what trust would there be left amongst barristers?'

'The police would use it,' said Catherine. 'The police, if they got hold of the defendant's instructions to his solicitor, would use it. What's the difference?'

Jennings looked annoyed.

'The difference is that they are the police, and if I remember that case correctly they got hold of those papers in a perfectly lawful search. Here the judge has already said these papers ought not to be used.'

Catherine had broken the spell.

Scott wasn't going to be taken in by this rubbish. He looked at Jennings. 'How do you know that? How do you know he has seen them? What have you got to do with this whole thing anyway? You're not briefed in it. Even we don't know what he was shown.'

Then he remembered what Betty the usher had told him and said, 'Oh yes, I remember now. On the morning the judge refused to let us see the undisclosed material, you were in his room with Charlton and Cantor.'

Jennings looked at him.

He was about to say, How did you know that? – at least that's what it looked like to Scott – but instead he said, 'No I wasn't. What makes you think that?'

Scott knew he was lying.

As they walked down the staircase Catherine said, 'You nearly believed in it, not believed it, but believed in it.' She emphasised the difference. 'He asked you to . . . what's the phrase? – "play the game", didn't he? And for a moment you nearly did, you nearly joined in the game. He said he could make you a judge.'

'There's a story by Somerset Maugham,' said Scott. He stopped on the stairs. 'I can't remember what it's called now. Something about opportunity. About a colonial civil servant and his wife. They're living in some outlandish place and he can't stand the other people there, rugger buggers, jolly good chaps propping up the club bar. But he's different and so is his wife. They live a life of culture. It's well described – books, pictures, music.

'Of course, everybody feels this couple are all hoity-toity and they are resented for thinking they are above everyone. So they live a lonely life. Then one day he, the husband, is called upon to be brave, to go and confront a riot. And he doesn't do it. The expression would be that he funked it.

'But his wife stands by him. The story ends when they're going home. The train eventually pulls in at Victoria Station. And then she leaves him. She's not going to show her feelings out there amongst the people who despised them, but the moment she's back she leaves him. And he never saw it coming, he's still talking about the insufferable people out in the colony and the fun they are going to have in London.

'So.' He stopped, thinking about it. 'It's all very well being full of principle, even honest principle, thinking you know best. But how do you know that you're not just full of shit?'

Standing on the staircase, he said to Catherine, 'How do I know I'm right? How do I know I'm right and that all these people I dislike – the judge, Cantor, Jennings, even Sally – are wrong? The judge said these papers should not be revealed. He's the judge. It's his decision, not mine. Mine is to do my job, not his. Why should I think that I know so much that I can disregard his judgment – even if I do dislike him? How do I know I'm not just a windbag, like the guy in the story?'

'You don't,' she said. 'You just have to live with the possibility. But how about doing what you think is right for a change?'

They carried on down the stairs.

Women were obliged to go down the back stairs of the club and Scott had gone with Catherine rather than with Jennings. They arrived at the bottom to see him waiting for them in the main entrance hall.

He was obviously angry.

He had been angry when they got up to leave. His offer had been refused. The porter was fussing around him, holding out a coat, but Jennings was waving him away. He seemed distracted by something else. Scott saw him glance over his shoulder. He followed his look and through the glass doors he saw Charlton.

The porter held Catherine's coat out. Scott took it and started putting it over her shoulders. It was tangled and an arm needed sorting out. He took his time. 'Charlton's outside,' he said in her ear.

'What shall we do?'

'I don't know. We'll just have to confront him.'

At that moment there was a roar of laughter. A side door to the hall opened and the remnants of a dinner party, the men in dinner jackets, spilled out. 'Jeremy, Butler,' the party greeted them.

Scott looked. They were all members of the Bar.

'Hallo, Gordon, what's this?' he said.

'It's the "Great Indian Restaurant Conflagration" celebration dinner,' Gordon said, emphasising each word by poking his finger into Scott's chest. 'Six weeks at the Bailey, total acquittal. Even the ushers were acquitted.'

Others had gathered now and Scott recognised the faces around him. 'What are you doing here, Jeremy?' one of them called. 'You're not a member here. And who,' he said, striking an eighteenth-century connoisseur's pose at Catherine, 'is this dashed attractive young lady?'

'But Gordon . . .' This time the speaker really had had too much to drink. 'I thought you said that ladies were not allowed in here. Is Butler Jennings kicking over the traces?'

They all gathered around Jennings.

'C'mon, Jennings, are you leading a feminist putsch or something? You'll have the Director of Public Prosecutions in here next.'

'Were you in this case, Jeremy? I can't remember who was and who wasn't now. I remember Nicholas here prosecuted it, and Watters was the judge, but were you in it?'

'What happened to Watters? Where is he now?'

'He went home early.'

'Jeremy wasn't in it, you fool. Where would he have sat? There was no room.'

'I think I've drunk too much. Good wine, Gordon.'

'Tim was in it. He was the one who the witness couldn't see. Don't you remember he had to wave his hands in the air to get the man's attention before he could cross-examine him?'

'That's impressive, isn't it? He must have dominated the court.'

'No, that was Simon. What Tim did was, he forgot which case he was in. That's what he did. He tried to cross-examine someone in another court and nobody noticed for quite a time.'

'Taxi!'

'Someone get a taxi.'

'Well, anyway, here's to arson. My favourite crime. Long may it continue. It's almost impossible to prove.'

'Not as difficult as getting policemen convicted.'

The whole mass tumbled out on to the pavement. Scott could see Charlton being forced back by the crowd.

'Gordon,' he said, 'are you taking a cab?'

'Yes.'

'Well, we're going to get in it with you.'

'You're welcome.'

'Bye, Jennings.'

'See you, Butler.'

'Oh, I feel knackered. I ate too much.'

'Goodbye.'

'Goodbye.'

A cab stopped and Scott and Catherine were in it, ducking low through the door, before Charlton could move. Gordon climbed in and leaned out of the window towards his friends. Again Charlton's view was blocked.

'Bye, Tony. Goodnight, Graham. Good luck in the Court of Appeal tomorrow.'

He leant back and the cab set off, turning left down St Martin's Lane.

'Gordon. Listen. I want you to take Catherine home. She'll tell you where, behind Sloane Square. It's not out of your way. I'm going to get out of the cab as it crosses the lights at Trafalgar Square.'

Gordon looked at him, puzzled. Scott took his keys out and gave them to Catherine. 'I'll phone. Even if I don't, I'll be at court tomorrow morning.'

Gordon watched them with a faintly surprised air, but in the end his impeccable manners survived the situation. 'All right, Jeremy, anything you say.'

Scott opened the dividing window and said to the cabbie, 'Can you keep to the left through Trafalgar Square and let me out just before St Martin's?' The cab stopped just in the right place. Scott had to wait till the handbrake was applied and then he was out.

He crossed the pavement into the passage alongside St Martin's, ran past the market stalls and into the underground entrance.

Here we go again, he thought, and I said I wasn't going to run. He dodged around a late-night *Big Issue* seller, ricocheted off the tiled wall and made his way down towards Charing Cross.

As he ran he tried to work it out. Should he head for the tube or take the turning up to the top again? There was no time for debate. What if he had to wait five minutes for a tube to arrive? What would he do? Jump off the platform and disappear into the tunnel? This wasn't a film.

He took the turning up the stairs back into Charing Cross.

He had no idea whether or not he was being followed. At least there was no one thundering down the passage after him. Well, if no one was coming he could slow up. He stopped running. He was going down the hill towards the arches, turned left and started moving away from the station. He stopped outside Prouds Oriental and Eastern Art.

There was an exquisite staircase, a staircase on wheels such as would be used in a library, but designed also to be a chest of drawers. He looked at it, alert to the sound of any footsteps coming round the corner.

There was nothing. He had got away. He circled round the corner of the shop and stood in the doorway. He could see down directly towards the river. To the left was the British Skin and Bone Society. He'd been there once for a cocktail party.

No one appeared. If he went left he could turn into Lower Robert Street, the tunnel that led down to the Thames.

He needed only a second to cross the road and then he was in the tunnel. Both sides were cobbled and slippery but it was well lit and moments later he was down beneath the buildings.

To the right the road led to the river. To the left there was a dead end partially blocked off from view. He turned and was immediately out of sight.

A car entered the tunnel from the top and appeared at the corner. At his feet there was a bundle. As the car receded the bundle stirred and a head appeared from a blanket. 'Whass the time?'

'About ten,' Scott said.

'In the morning?'

'No, night,' said Scott, sentencing the stirring man to another eight hours of cold on the hard pavement.

'Is this where you live?' he asked stupidly. It was difficult to appreciate the gulf across which he was speaking. The man looked at him, morose with sleep and cold. He didn't reply.

Scott gave him a pound coin and walked away towards the river. Oddly he didn't feel that he had tried to buy absolution; he had just given a pound away. His steps echoed as he walked out of the tunnel.

At the end of the street he saw a police van parked sideways on. There was no way out in that direction. He mustn't get too worked up. It could be a complete coincidence, almost certainly was.

To his right there was an area chained off from the road. In the daytime it would have been the parking space for a couple of directors' cars. The cost of parking their cars would keep the shivering Scotsman in Special Brew with money left over, a house as well maybe. Behind the space he noticed that the fence separating the road from the embankment gardens had been bent downwards. He'd be able to get over that.

The gardens were made up entirely of shadows. Slowly, as his eyes adjusted, the light reflected from the buildings gave him enough to see by. There was a winding path, and on either side of it benches. On each bench there was a bundle, every ten feet a bundle. He had entered a graveyard of sleeping men.

He moved downriver towards the Temple. Sooner or later he was going to have to sort out what he was going to do. One of the benches was empty and he sat down. Behind him there was a wheezing noise and he turned to look. Beneath the bushes on a thick matting of cardboard was another cocoon.

Then, at the far end of the gardens, the police van crept in through the gates, its lights like eyes. As it went past the benches the sleepers were tumbled off on to the ground. From the tight packages men spilled out like stuffing, slowly trying to gather themselves together and hug the warmth back into their bodies. The van moved on, the lights shining mercilessly. They weren't after him.

Scott got up and walked past the white scouring light out into the night towards the Temple.

Chapter 26

Elephant and Castle Crown Court

R v. Achille and Ors

Last day of evidence. Speeches.

Coram: H H J Scribner

Scott spent the night in chambers and walked to the court in the morning. When he got to Elephant and Castle he saw the beige car parked outside. Charlton was talking to the two officers who had stopped him the night before.

Obviously now Jennings's offer had been refused they intended to do something direct, so he wasn't going to be able to use the main entrance.

He went down the lane to the side of the court where the prison vans entered. There was a policeman standing there as well, this time in uniform. Scott guessed he had been put there to stop anybody going in the side way. He carried on round the court. The only entrance that wasn't guarded was the judges' entrance, but he couldn't use that. He might run into Scribner.

Indeed, as he watched, he saw Teflin arrive, neatly dressed in a raincoat. The judge pressed the bell and the big gates were opened for him. Scott retreated back down the road. He was going to have to bide his time. He retreated up the road and sat down on a wall.

* * *

Inside the court the jury were asked to leave the court and Cantor said, 'The defence in this case have continually sought to attack the prosecution witnesses, all of whom are police officers. They have attacked on the basis that they have concealed the truth.

'Your Honour knows this is not the case. I anticipate . . .' Cantor felt good this morning and his language began to betray his self-satisfaction. 'I anticipate that this same attack will not be repeated in defence speeches.'

He gestured towards defence counsel.

'We all know that the name of any informant in this case, if there is one, has been concealed as a result of your direct ruling. Indeed, I have often been forced . . .' Here he allowed himself the joke he had made before. 'I have sometimes sounded like the Prime Minister repeating the formula at Question Time – I have been forced over and over again to interrupt questions in order to protect the integrity of your decision. Now I want the jury told of what happened. Such is the conduct of the defence that they have in effect brought the matter out into the open.'

He sat down.

Ronnie thought, At least this is delaying the end of the evidence. But Scott had better hurry up if he wants to do anything.

Scribner looked pleased.

He said, 'Well, gentlemen, I think that's right, isn't it? I have now heard the defence in this case, for what it's worth, and have decided that the name of the informant would not help the defence. That is why it has not been disclosed. Why should the jury not be told of my decision?'

John Plumstead was the first to answer. 'If the jury is told that, then it would amount to telling them that you think the defence is not true. The jury would be told that you know the truth and that we are wrong about it. I must invite Your Honour to reconsider. To tell the jury what has happened in their absence would be an extraordinary thing to do.'

Scribner acknowledged what he said with a smile and stopped him by saying, 'Mr King, what do you say?'

'Obviously my learned friend is right.'

John Hector sat at the back of the court listening to the exchange. It seemed to have nothing to do with reality. This learned friend stuff. Even defence counsel who were meant to be on his side, did it.

'My learned friend is quite right. The effect, if you were to tell the jury that, would be the same as if you were to say, "I have seen the real facts and the defence are wrong." '

'Mr Knox?' Scribner was obviously going through the motions. He was going to agree with the prosecution.

Ronnie got up to make the argument again. He had been prevented from making his points throughout the trial and he had no reason to think that he was going to do any better this time. 'Your Honour knows that there was evidence given at the last trial that quite clearly demonstrated that the police had been tipped off from this very flat . . .'

Scribner interrupted, 'I know nothing of the sort.'

'Your Honour will remember the cross-examination of Mr Charlton—'

'Cross-examination is just that. It is a series of questions. Cross-examination does not prove anything.'

'Mr Charlton admitted . . .'

'No, he did not,' said the judge. 'I cannot say that. That jury may have decided he admitted something. But they were discharged. I cannot decide anything.'

'There was evidence that a call was made.'

'You had the chance or producing that evidence at this trial.'

'No I did not,' said Ronnie. 'I could not prove the number. That was something the Crown knows about. I cannot prove a police telephone number if it has been changed.'

'You have not proved it. I have seen the papers that you claim would prove your case, Mr Knox, and have decided they do not help you. Yet you continue to say that their production would prove your case. If I do not tell the jury that it was my decision, then the Crown is at a disadvantage, is that not right?'

Hector tried to follow the argument. The judge was saying the Crown were at a disadvantage. How could that be? It was the prosecution who were concealing things.

Scribner carried on. 'The jury should know, shouldn't they, that it is my decision that the police need not answer the question – that I have decided this because the answer would not help you?'

'But in effect you are telling them that the defence has no foundation,' said Ronnie. John Plumstead made clear that he agreed.

'But that is a consequence of your questions, is it not, gentlemen? If you had not pursued the matter before the jury then there would be no need for me to say anything. As it is you have attacked the prosecution in a way that they are unable to answer. How can that be fair?'

Ronnie Knox sat down. The evidence was going to end in a few minutes if Scott did not arrive, and by then it would be too late.

Scott saw the judge's gate open and the porter stood outside for a moment, looking up and down. This was his chance. He jogged across the road. 'Jonesy, Jonesy,' he said. 'Let me in the back way. I want to avoid my client.'

The porter looked at him, at first not recognising him, then he said, 'You look rough, Mr Scott.'

'I've got my stuff upstairs in the robing room. I don't want my client to see me dressed like this.' He took advantage of the porter's remark.

'Been out on the tiles, Mr Scott? C'mon in.'

He let Scott in. 'You can't go in through the courts. Judge Scribner's already sitting. You'll have to go this way round to the front entrance.'

Scott nodded and set off down the passage that would have taken him straight into Charlton's arms, but looking back he noticed that Jonesy wasn't watching and he dodged into the judges' corridor which went behind the courts.

He could hear sounds from Scribner's court and, again checking that no one was watching, he stepped into the lobby and softly opened the door. All that separated him from the court was the thick velvet curtain. It was like standing in the wings of a stage. He heard John Plumstead's voice. It was oddly reassuring. 'I must invite Your Honour to reconsider. To tell the jury what has happened in their absence would be an extraordinary thing to do.'

Then Scribner's voice. 'Mr King what do you say?' Scott recognised the tone of a judge who had made his mind up.

It would have been good to have been able to stand and listen but he had to get on. He came out of the entrance to the courtroom and went up to the library. From the library he would be able to get across to the other side of the building.

The library was quiet as usual, a place straight out of the 1950s – cherrywood and parquet. He crossed to the window and opened it. He was lucky – the internal windows were never locked. He pulled himself out and set off along the metal struts that supported the roof to his left. It was a journey he had made before and it was easy, as long as he was careful with the final swing down to the window. He reached the ledge and pushed on the window. It was locked.

* * *

Mrs Hector sat in the gallery watching what was going on in the court below her. The judge was saying that the defence was not acting fairly. But it was he who was not fair, not allowing her husband's case to be proved. It was too much for her, and she got up. She pushed past the men on her left and went down from the gallery to the hallway. Gregory watched her go.

Mrs Hector had seen this coming.

Her husband had tried to be cheerful that morning when they were preparing to leave for court. He had made nothing of it when she caught him packing a small bag. Toothbrush, toothpaste, some batteries and a radio. She knew immediately what it was. He was not expecting to come home from court that night. They had looked at each other and both of them knew he was going away for a long time.

'Do you think the judge will take your bail away?' she said.

'I think he will. He's the old-fashioned sort. He'll just do it suddenly.'

'Tonight?'

'I wouldn't be surprised.'

In the old days he had had a tin of Old Holborn. The two-ounce tin, worn down to the bare metal, all the enamelling gone. He never used it at home It reminded him of prison. Inside the lid there was a photograph of her, taken when she was much younger, before the children were born. Nothing mattered then. What fun they had had. She looked for the tin in the bag. There it was. She took it and opened it. The photograph was still there.

She looked at him. 'There's nowhere to run to,' he said. 'Nowhere. We're too old now.'

She was on the point of asking what she hadn't asked before. This offence, did you do it? But she didn't need to. Instead she said, 'It's just these people, this prosecutor, this judge – they seem so sure of themselves. So sure of something they know nothing about, something they can't know anything about. It's frightening how sure they are.'

As she went down the gallery stairs she felt quite faint. The smell and dust of the court, the old-book smell, the damp on people's clothes – they had all got into her being. She wanted never to smell such things again. She put her hand to her mouth and stumbled slightly. Betty was at the bottom of the stairs and saw her nearly fall.

'Are you all right?' Betty came over and supported her.

'I just came over a bit funny,' said Mrs Hector.

'I'm not surprised,' said Betty. 'All that arguing. All that fuss. It's enough to make anybody ill. Would you like a glass of water? Or a cup of tea?'

Mrs Hector was grateful. On the opposite side of the lobby was a door marked 'Private'. Betty pushed it open and they went in. They were immediately in the back of the court building. It was as though they had gone through the green baize door in a great house. There was even an old-fashioned dumb waiter in the wall. The area had the feel of servants' quarters. Indeed, when the court was built it was probably just that.

'This is our area,' said Betty. 'No one comes in here.'

She took Mrs Hector down the passage and up a short flight of white pine stairs. They found themselves in a large square room with some old leather chairs. In the corner there was a low sink with a mop in it, a real old-fashioned sluice. There were windows overlooking a white-tiled courtyard. In the middle there was a sad-looking tree. But there were magazines, a table with a teapot and kettle, and, on the wall, pictures of kittens and a calendar of daffodils and timbered houses. It was homely. Mrs Hector saw that there was even some knitting on one of the chairs.

'I'm all right for a while. Tommy's taken over in court and I'm due for a break. Let's have some tea.'

Betty went to her bag and pulled out some Glengettie tea. 'It's not easy to find it any more,' she said, 'but it's the best.'

Mrs Hector felt immediately at home. 'I used to have Glengettie, but you can't get it near us now, the Maid Marian shop closed down. I haven't had Glengettie tea for years now.'

Betty said, 'Now you sit down, dear,' and Mrs Hector sank gratefully into one of the chairs. 'The others use tea bags, you know. But I can't be doing with them at all.' She started warming the pot, holding it over the steaming spout of the kettle.

They looked at each other, surprised that from different sides of the fence they had suddenly come together.

'I'm going to say it,' said Betty, 'though I'm saying it as shouldn't. But I don't think it's right. I think it's all wrong. That Mr Scott should not have been prevented from doing your case. Judge Scribner is not allowing your husband . . .' She stopped. Mrs Hector had started sobbing.

Betty poured water into the teapot. She knew that these things could not be cured. She remembered her Ted and the accident, and the pain, and the look in his eyes as she watched him trying. You just have to bear it.

She sat down and poured out a cup. The room seemed to detach itself from the court. It was a normal part of the world. Mrs Hector took the tea and pulled herself together. She looked at Betty's knitting and admired the pattern. They were quiet together.

When the tapping came, at first they couldn't work out what it was. Betty went to the frosted-glass window and opened it. As she did so Scott appeared. 'Oh thank God it's you, Betty. Let me in,' he said, 'let me in.'

Betty pushed the window up and Scott climbed through.

Mrs Hector watched him in astonishment. 'Just like old times,' Scott said, and he put his arm around Betty's shoulders.

He explained to Mrs Hector, 'I had to sleep in the court once or twice. I had nowhere else and this was the way I used to come in and out.'

Both women stared at him.

'I couldn't come in the main entrance. I went there but Charlton was waiting for me. I wasn't going to risk it.'

They said nothing.

'I'll explain. But I don't have time now. Two things. Did you get a letter from me this morning?' Betty went to her bag and pulled out a large brown envelope. 'Thank God for that,' said Scott as he grasped the package. 'Second. You've got to get Mr Knox out here now. I don't mind how. He has to come now. Immediately. Please, Betty, trust me.'

'I don't know, Mr Scott,' she said.

'Please, Betty. Please.'

She got up and said, 'Well, Mr Scott, if you say so.'

'Are you going to be able to help us?' asked Mrs Hector.

'Do you know, I think I can,' said Scott.

Betty went back to court. The judge was addressing the jury. 'It has been decided, because of the arguments the defence are adopting, that I should tell you that the name of any informer – and the Crown do not accept that there was an informer – has been concealed, on my decision.

'As you will have appreciated, questions were being asked which could have led to the identification of the person who led the police to the flat. Members of the jury, it is my responsibility to decide what can and cannot be pursued. Of course, I could insist on questions being answered. I have not done so here. It is my judgment that no good would come of questions about the identity of the informer. It would not help you in your decision.

So be it. We shall now turn to the closing address for the Crown. Mr Cantor, you may begin.'

Ronnie Knox twisted round in distress and whispered to Catherine, 'Where is he?'

Betty went to where the clerk of the court was sitting as Cantor got to his feet. She whispered to the clerk and the clerk rose and spoke to the judge.

Cantor cleared his throat and started. 'Dirt has been thrown, ladies and gentlemen . . . All sorts of disreputable things have been alleged . . .' The judge interrupted him. 'I am told that Mr Knox is needed urgently outside. My usher assures me it is extremely important.' He looked at Betty, who nodded, blushing a deep red.

She had never done such a thing before and she was amazed at her own courage. 'If my usher says it is so, then obviously it is important. Please go, Mr Knox. We shall wait for you.'

Ronnie got to his feet. He was quite pale.

He left the court with Betty. 'Quiet, Mr Knox,' she said. 'Don't say anything. Come with me.' She led him through the door marked 'Private'.

'What's this?' he said. 'I've never been here. What is it?' He entered the room and stopped, relieved and astonished when he saw Scott.

Scott didn't give him a chance to speak. 'Where are you?' he said. 'How far have you got?'

'Speeches,' said Ronnie.

'Thank God,' said Scott. 'I've got more evidence. Look.'

He pulled out a sheet of paper from the brown envelope.

'It proves the phone call was made to Charlton just before Mr Hector arrived at the flat. And here, this is Charlton's note of it. It's in his handwriting. It's on a printed police action form and it talks about the raid being already arranged and only waiting for the phone call as a signal. The whole thing was arranged between Charlton and Morgan. You've got to call me to give evidence.'

'Where did you get this?'

'If I don't tell you, you can't be accused of being involved. Go back, tell the judge you have more evidence. And then call me. I'll blow the case out of the water.'

Ronnie Knox opened his mouth and then closed it. Sometimes the rules didn't matter.

He went back to the court. 'Your Honour, thank you for the time.' He looked at the clock. It was ten to eleven. 'I am afraid I may have to delay the court a moment longer.'

Scribner bridled.

But Ronnie knew how to use the judge's impatience in his own favour and said, 'Or alternatively I can carry on immediately with no break in time.' He looked up at the clock again, emphasising the time involved. 'I shall take only seconds of the court's time if I begin now.'

Scribner did not have a clue what he was talking about, but his impatience overrode his natural caution. 'Say what you have to say, Mr Knox,' he said.

What Ronnie said shocked him, but once said the jury had heard it and there was nothing to be done but to allow the application.

'I now have available to me evidence which will prove that a phone call was made from the flat to the police arranging the raid that trapped Mr Hector. It proves he was set up. I can call that evidence now.'

'It would have been better if you had had the evidence ready at the right time, Mr Knox.'

'Indeed so, Your Honour. You are always so correct,' Ronnie said unctuously. Now he was enjoying himself. He hadn't slept much the night before and the relief was pouring over him. Moments like these didn't come often. 'Mea culpa. Mea culpa,' he said, lifting his large ringed fingers in a blessing. 'But there we are.'

He paused, dramatically, and then said loudly, 'Call Mr Jeremy Scott, please.'

There was a gasp from where the lawyers sat, and Scribner jolted bolt upright.

Ronnie sat down and the court waited.

Charlton had been expecting an interruption. He had been standing beside the screen at the door when Betty had come into the court and stopped the trial, then he had followed her out.

She went down the passage opposite the court with Knox. Charlton followed and saw them go up the staircase to a side room. He stood at the bottom to the side of the staircase. Knox was only in the room for a moment, then he came out and walked back past Charlton without noticing him.

Charlton stepped into the doorway behind him. It was a lavatory. He closed the door, leaving a crack to see through. The door opposite opened again, and Betty appeared, speaking to Scott. She went down the passage and out into the court corridor. Mrs Hector followed her. Charlton waited and, when Scott came out, he stepped in front of him.

'You bastard,' he said. 'I want those papers.'

'It's too late,' said Scott. 'I'm going into court now. I'm going to give evidence against you.'

'Perhaps you are,' said Charlton, 'but you're not taking anything in with you. I'll have those documents.'

He tore at Scott's jacket. It opened and the policeman's hand went to his inner pocket.

'I haven't got anything with me at all, Mr Charlton,' said Scott. 'That would have been stupid, wouldn't it?'

'Where are they, then?' said Charlton, grabbing him by the shirt front and slamming him against the wall.

'Not on me,' said Scott.

'Then if you haven't got them you can't hurt me, can you? Without the documents it's only your word against mine.'

In the background they both heard the court door open and a voice cry out, 'Jeremy Scott.'

'I can and I'm going to, Charlton.'

Charlton hit Scott full in the face and his head cracked back against the wall. 'Where are they, then?' Charlton said, and he drew his hand back to hit him again.

At that moment the door to the passage opened and Betty stood looking at them.

'Thank you, Betty,' Scott said. 'Now let go of me, Charlton, or do you want the usher to tell the court I am being prevented from coming in?'

Scott's head was aching.

Charlton let go of him. 'All right, you can have him,' he said to Betty. 'I've searched him. He's safe.'

Scott found he could hardly see straight. The blow to his head seemed to be reverberating. Betty led him down the passage and into the court.

The aching added to what was anyway a strange feeling. The chase last night and the lack of sleep was affecting him. He hadn't washed or shaved. He walked past counsel's row where he would normally have sat. He couldn't ever remember being here when he was not in formal robes, wig and gown.

He saw Cantor watching him with a look of contempt. Presumably he had guessed what was coming.

He reached the witness-box steps and found himself leaning on the stair-rail. He became conscious of the scruffiness of his clothing. He had torn his jacket climbing into the court and the blow to his head made him feel awful. He looked up. The back of the court was filling up. The word that something was happening had got round like wildfire.

He had once seen a barrister give evidence in one of the courts out in the country. Was it Brighton or Lewes? The same thing had happened there. The robing room had emptied in a flash. And it had happened at Southampton. Hadn't a judge given evidence there and been disbelieved on his oath by a jury? That court had been like a crowded cinema when he gave evidence. Scott remembered that judge. He was a particularly nasty man and there was great amusement when he was disbelieved.

Now the court was packed. He had never seen it so full.

Most of his cases were heard before a few uninterested onlookers escaping from the cold. But now there was not even standing room. Everyone's attention was on him. So this was how his clients felt. He thought of the occasions when he had stood at the cell door to hear a prison officer refusing clean clothing to a prisoner.

'We can't take it now.'

'But he needs it to give evidence.'

'I can't help that, love.'

'He looks awful. He won't feel right.'

'Those are the rules, dear.'

Sometimes Scott had been instructed formally to apologise for a prisoner's appearance. But now he wasn't going to apologise for anything, not even his appearance. That time was over.

He reached the top of the steps and was astonished by the view the witness box commanded. He had never stood there before. The whole court was reduced to a sea of faces looking up at him. He was set at least five feet higher than everyone else in the court and they were all sitting down.

The faces looked up at him, expectant. To his right someone pushed over a glass and it crashed to the ground. All the faces turned away momentarily at the sound. What had been a white sea looking up at him suddenly became dark, as though a switch had been thrown.

Scott remembered a story he had heard of an accident avoided by a famous racing driver. As the driver approached a corner he noticed that the white screen of faces, normally looking in his direction, was turned away. He immediately braked. Round the corner there was a massive pile-up. The crowd was watching it. Had he not slowed he would have run into it.

Scott noticed that all these memories flashed by in the time it took him to reach out and take the card with the oath. How quick, almost instantaneous, is the mind's running commentary on events.

Betwixt the stirrup and the ground
Mercy I asked, mercy I found.

'I swear to tell the truth, the whole truth and nothing but the truth.' As he finished the oath he brushed away a tickle on his head and was shocked to see his hand come down covered with blood. Betty had already noticed and handed him a tissue. He stood holding the bloody paper to his head, the court watching him, astonished.

'I had an accident, Your Honour,' he said.

He looked down and saw Charlton standing by the door. In the gallery Gregory watched, sitting next to Arlot.

Scribner looked at Scott with dislike on his face.

'Your name?' said Ronnie.

'My name is Jeremy Scott, and I am a lawyer originally instructed in this case.'

'You are aware of the issues in this trial?'

'I am.'

'You are aware of the evidence that a telephone call was made, shortly before the police came, from the flat where Mr Hector was arrested?'

'I am,' said Scott.

For the first time he looked at Hector, who was leaning forward expectantly.

Scribner interrupted. 'I trust Mr Scott is not going to give evidence merely of what others said to him. Even what was said to him in court is hearsay.'

Ronnie Knox said, 'He is aware of that, as Your Honour might well imagine. None of what he will say is hearsay.'

The jury began to lean forward. They had realised a little more slowly than anyone else that something extraordinary was happening.

Scribner said, 'Well, in that case Mr Scott appreciates what he may and what he may not say.'

Ronnie asked, 'The number to which the call from the flat was made was 819 2281. Can you say what that number is?'

'I object,' said Cantor.

Scott did not say anything.

'The witness cannot merely say what he believes to be the case.'

Scott said nothing. He was going to have to be very careful. One false word and Scribner would have the jury out and the opportunity for giving the evidence would be gone.

Ronnie said, 'I am aware of that.'

Cantor sat down.

Arlot leaned over to Gregory and said, 'Cantor isn't up to it, is he?' Gregory looked at him in astonishment. 'Did you know this was going to happen?'

'I had an idea it might,' Arlot said.

Down below, Ronnie Knox said, 'Do you have a document that can help in this respect?'

Charlton looked up sharply. Where was the document? He was sure Scott had taken nothing into court. 'Yes, I do,' said Scott.

'May I see it, please?' said Ronnie.

Scott leaned forward and gestured to Betty, who went to the exhibits table. She picked up the brown envelope from where she had put it on her return to court. Scott pulled out the action note.

'Here is a note of a telephone call received at Mr Charlton's number, 819 2281, that's at the District Crime Squad, ten forty-nine a.m. the morning of the raid. As I remember, the telephone bill for the flat, which will be exhibited, gives exactly the same time.'

'Page forty-one.' Ronnie Knox told the jury where to find it. 'Yes, it is precisely the same.'

'This note is in Detective Inspector Charlton's handwriting.'

'How do you know that?' asked Scribner.

Things were getting tense.

'Because he signed it,' Scott said. 'If you want you can ask him. Look, he's leaving the court now.'

The massed heads turned instantly as Scott pointed. At just that moment Charlton, with his hand on the door, turned and looked back at the court. His face was stark with panic. He opened the door and was gone.

'He's gone now,' said Scott unnecessarily.

'Be quiet,' said Scribner.

The tide of feeling in the court was already turning, and the judge's comment set it racing in Scott's favour.

'Let me see that,' Scribner said.

Betty took the document from Scott and carried it to the judge. He looked at it, made a note and brusquely waved it away. Betty took it back and made her way down the stairs, past the witness box where Scott was standing above her, and across to counsel's benches.

In the time it took her to do this the court was hushed. A drop of blood gathered on Scott's forehead and fell on to the rail of the witness box.

Cantor took the paper and read it.

The silence stretched out.

Cantor turned round and showed the document to Sally Donne. Scott noticed her then for the first time. He was relaxing now and looked along the benches. Behind Ronnie he suddenly saw Catherine. He hadn't seen her before when Ronnie stood up. She looked amazing. She had changed her clothes and was in her French music student outfit, granny spectacles, red hair tied back severely.

He felt better. The energy poured back into him and, when he turned and saw Scribner scowling at him, he smiled.

'What are you laughing at?' said Scribner. It was Scott's first real opportunity.

'I was reflecting how odd it was that this information should have been concealed from the jury, since it confirms absolutely what Mr Hector has been saying all along.'

'Be quiet,' said the judge, but by this time his commands were merely petulant.

Cantor said, looking at Scott, 'This is a privileged document.'

There was silence. Then Scott said, 'Is that a question?'

Cantor changed tack. 'Where did you get it?'

'A police messenger gave it to me.'

'You kept it?'

'Dead right I did,' Scott said. This was becoming fun.

'You should have returned it.'

'Why?'

'Because it's stolen property.'

'No it isn't. It was given to me.'

'By mistake.'

'Who says?'

'I do.'

'Why? Did you know about it?' said Scott.

Cantor was silent. If he admitted he knew about the document he would be admitting that he was part of the cover-up.

Then he said, 'I am here to ask the questions.'

'Go on, then.'

Cantor was desperate. He should have sat down. 'How do we know it isn't a forgery?'

It was the question Scott was waiting for. If Sally had been doing this he wouldn't have been asked that.

'There are two answers to that,' he said, and stopped. He looked at the judge. He wanted clear permission to speak. Then they couldn't complain.

'Go on,' said Scribner.

'First, you could ask Charlton who wrote it. But he's gone now.'

He paused. The tension in the court was as tight as he had ever felt.

'And second, you can look at the rest of the file. I've got it in the envelope here. It's got your name in it, Cantor, and Butler Jennings's, and the judge's.'

In the silence his voice sounded strong.

'You're all in it. All of you.'

Chapter 27

Scott and Catherine came out of the court.

'We can either eat out or at home.'

'What shall we do this afternoon?'

'I thought we might spend it in my place, in bed,' he said.

'That sounds a good idea. Let's not eat too much beforehand,' she said.

They wandered into the small roads behind Borough.

Next to the School for Performing Arts the garden was coming to life. The grass had just been cut for the first time and the cherry trees were in blossom.

As they stepped up to where the old altar used to be, some of the blossom floated down and landed on Catherine's shoulder. Neither of them noticed it.

'Mrs Hector kissed you,' she commented.

'Yes. That occasionally happens,' he said.

'What did Mr Hector say to you?'

'I'd be hearing from him.'

'Normally that would be a little ominous.'

'Not this time. It probably means a bottle of whisky.'

It was warm and they were able to sit on the bench, quite relaxed. 'Haven't you seen the big bottle of whisky I use as a doorstop? I got that from a Lawson's client.'

The wind blew the trees above them but still it wasn't cold. Scott looked out at the red-brick alms houses opposite. He remembered sliding down the rock. It was only the day before.

He shivered.

'I was frightened, you know. I was frightened all the time I was climbing down that rock, and I remembered what the man in the pub had said about that poet . . .'

'Paul Evans.'

'Yes, Paul Evans. He said, "Trust you to die on a mountain, Paul. You never cared for ropes called 'God' or 'politics' or even 'career'." I've been terrified all my life. I've had more ropes holding me up than you could count. But they're all gone now.'

'But nothing's going to happen to your career now. It's Scribner who should be worried. He can't report you now. Not after what happened.'

'No, I didn't mean that my career has gone. I mean the ropes have gone. I don't care any more.'

He put his hand around her shoulder and held her. He didn't need to ask permission any more.

'I'm free now. I'm free to choose you.'

She leaned against him and he could smell the musk in her hair. She looked at his hand on her shoulder and felt the roughness of his skin against her cheek. She was beginning to get used to him.

Gregory and Arlot saw Charlton getting into a car outside the court. Gregory said, 'Look, explain something to me for once. Are we going to arrest him?'

'What for? What would be the point? Now we know where he is and what he's up to, he can't cause any real trouble. It's much better that we know what's going on than we should stop him and then have someone we don't know doing it.'

Arlot waved at a cab.

'Ignorance ain't bliss in this job. Look, you were a barman once . . .' He stopped when he saw the puzzled look on Gregory's face. 'No, sorry, that was Scott, wasn't it? I was getting my background dossiers mixed up. But think about it. If you employ a barman and you know how much he is stealing you're better off than if you don't, especially if he's not taking much. Now we know about Charlton, we know where we are. We know what Scribner and the others are doing. They probably won't do it again, will they? We'll have your report. We'll have Sally Donne's. We'll know where we are. After all, this thing is a business now and we all believe in business.'

'Sally's report?' said Gregory. 'Sally Donne? She is working for you, then? You know I saw her at one of the CrackDown meetings?'

'Oh yes. She's a member. We put her there.'

Gregory thought about it.

'But that means she knew Hector was being set up by Charlton. Yet she took part in the prosecution. How could she do that?'

'Because she knows the facts of life, not like that Scott. After all, they would only set Hector up because they knew he was guilty. Wouldn't they? What would be the point otherwise?'